The Heart of Stone

Cheryl Blaydon

North
Country
Press

The Heart of Stone

ISBN 978-1-943424-00-9
Library of Congress Control Number: 2015940150

North Country Press
Unity, Maine

For Laddie

Acknowledgments

A heartfelt thank you to my early readers…Hilary Bartlett, Lynne Nicoletta, Cynthia Pottle, Jan Van Hasselt and Meridith Watts. You provided your time, patience and input whenever I asked. I couldn't have done it without you.

Special thanks to Patricia Newell, my publisher at North Country Press, for never losing faith in me and the stories I wanted to tell.

Chapter One

Heat pulsed in her veins while just yards away, cool, beckoning waves tumbled toward them, the left-behind foam glittering on pristine sand. Her simple bouquet of white carnations and baby's breath had already begun to droop; the satin ribbon—something blue—bound the stems and bore wet stains from holding so tight. She knew the tropic sun would soon ravage the soft flowers as well as the waiting assemblage.

A damp spot had formed on the bodice of her wedding dress, the place where the silver locket—something old—lay comfortably. The antique piece, an inheritance from a great-grandmother in Maine.

Fidgeting with the thin silver band encircling her wrist—something borrowed—she tried to concentrate on the anticipation seen on Jason's face when she had shown him 'something new' recently purchased for their St. Bart's honeymoon. The enticing silk 'teddy' she would wear beneath a little red dress for dancing; both items already packed for the short air hop to that romantic hotel on the point. But right now, with his conspicuous absence, none of that mattered.

Prudence Stone was ready to get married. Her biological clock had been loudly ticking. The infernal noise of an imaginary timepiece that she envisioned rusting from saltwater exposure. That is before Jason, whose motives were suddenly in question. Still, she kept her eyes peeled toward the path half-expecting to see his best man supporting him after last night's bachelor party and even that would have been better than a no-show. Instead, her mind spun into overdrive as she mentally strung the last months together.

Jason, the perfect boyfriend, had walked through the doors of her bookstore straight into her heart. More importantly, he had understood her appetite for all things island-related and though not well disguised, had used that knowledge to woo her into a relationship. Would bring her with him whenever possible, venturing out in the little boat provided by the marine research laboratory where he put in his hours. She loved that he studied the habitats of sea turtles and other aquatic life or categorized the brown pelican behavior all the while she was trying to predict the human kind. Handsome, well-liked and a kindred travel buff, he truly loved his work. And in time, she loved him. Took quiet pleasure in the simplest things—kissing the small scar on his chin, the tiny welt a reminder of a diving accident; the scent of his skin as they dried off in the sun whenever they'd been able to sneak into little coves hidden by thick tangles of mangrove and the gifts of shells he thought she'd like. The bottom of the boat continually smelled of drying seawater and barnacle encrusted rope and empty buckets that were never out of use, but none of that had mattered…they were happy just being together, or so she'd thought until about an hour ago.

"Where *is* he?"

"Don't worry; he'll be here," Julie said intuiting her friend's growing anxiety. Perspiration had begun to glisten on her forehead and the beginnings of a nervous tic decried that confidence. "And forget what the palm reader said about the locket; I shouldn't have pushed you to see her just before your wedding."

"Too late now," Prudence replied, patting the piece. She hated acknowledging how much the old woman had affected her. Besides, what could a simple locket have to do with what was happening here.

Julie, her business partner and, occasionally bossy, best friend, had this bizarre obsession about that West Indian palm reader. Though Prudence had always poo pooed such nonsense, many of their friends had readings performed, whether palms, tarots or tea leaves. But waiting in this awkward way for her missing groom, those stranger's words—that the story of the locket held an unsettled past—only added a sour note to Julie's apology.

Standing to one side, the disgruntled sandal-wearing Justice of the Peace, dressed head to toe in dark clothing, had broken out in a heavy sweat. The outfit begged sympathy, the stupidity of wearing deeply saturated tones in this heat. The wait continued and he waited for any sign at all from the bride. But all she offered him was her anguish and at last sensing a fortunate breeze, he turned around and faced the sea, grateful to be excused.

Pru's hair, released by the wind, hid her reddening face as she sought Jason's in the crowd. Then she caught the murmurs from the guests milling about restless without a drumbeat and knew in her gut she had been stood up.

"The guests are beginning to question," Julie whispered in her ear. "Do you want me to say anything?"

"I don't care; whatever," Prudence shot back, but noticed that Julie held her by the waist as if to anchor her in place, perhaps fearing she might faint.

"Feel the blessed wind," Prudence said, her voice shredding with heartbreak. She wanted to charge into the ocean, anything to escape her feelings. But as her lacy, full-length dress accepted the stiff breeze, she noticed the tiny seed pearls of sand clinging tenaciously to its hem. *Hope comes in all forms,* she thought trying to brush them away wishing she could do the same with her pain.

She clutched Julie's arm, "Time's run out; he isn't coming."

"I'm going to kill him," Julie professed under her breath. A muttered curse followed, one that Prudence knew had been learned from that same favored seer. Julie's wide green eyes reflected the softer shade of her dress as it moved with the vehemence of her words.

"Not much point to that," Prudence said choking back her tears while trying to keep upright with a dignity she no longer possessed. "How could I have been so blind?"

3

"Well, let's be real, you hated the idea of becoming Mrs. Spronk." Julie scoffed with a foolish attempt at humor, anything to lessen her friend's heartache.

It really was unthinkable to Prudence that she would choose to keep the tongue-twister, Stone-Spronk, as the moniker to be scrawled on every document for the rest of her life. But now she would never even have that point to argue. "Go ahead, Jules, tell everyone the wedding is off, please." She caught Mr. Nelson re-checking his watch and knew he was worried about being late to another affair, a more staid one requiring that somber attire. And they had already been out here nearly ninety minutes.

Thank God Ben didn't have to see this, she thought trying to pull herself together. It was not the type of thing her father would have handled well. Victoria was a whole other matter. Her mother, rest her soul and the torment of all who knew her, might have livened things up with her pre-sips of champagne or if nothing else, managed to turn the attention away from the missing groom. Either way, Prudence had obviously been left at that proverbial altar for all to see, sunburn and sand on her face in place of egg that would have more easily washed off.

How could I have missed the signs? Prudence chastised. *Julie said he was too smooth but I wouldn't listen.* Perhaps love was indeed blind, it certainly had endless tomes written about it, many with sad heroines swallowing tears or pills or booze. Was anything worth all that?

She had always felt like some repressed student of anthropology and maybe if she stayed out here long enough, she could find that free-spirited girl again, the one not joined at the hip with a man like Jason. The one who had innocently fallen into romance-sweetened interludes, the type waiting to be relished in locations that whispered in one's ear about longings and desires and moonlit cruises. All of which could have been inspired by any island in the archipelago of the Caribbean Sea. Admittedly, those relationships fizzled quickly because the crazy nomads still reveling in the sands of their youth, were always seeking and constantly moving. Entanglements to be tasted only, never savored; a learning curve for all the women hurt and left behind. And like most just past twenty and beginning to spread her wings in a new place, Prudence had taken her turn. Now nearing thirty, a more mature version of that girl had been left waiting on another tropic strand, possibly no better off than when she'd started.

Disappointed by that image, she stood in place, a sad statue knowing Julie would handle the rest…the glaring questions and pitied looks. From her position Prudence glimpsed the last of the stragglers moving off the beach and knowing Julie would be worried, she tossed her bouquet carelessly into the sea. Then, picking up the hem of her dress, she turned and walked slowly through the warm compressions in the sand…the left-behind footprints of all those who had witnessed her shame.

Birds chittered away, dipping in and out of the hanging flower pots, ignoring Pru's broom and the feral cat creeping around the wall. *It's been two months,* she calculated as she swept the seating area with a weariness that still hugged her shoulders even though the old routines had surprisingly fallen back into place. Nothing had changed. Yellow Bird Books, probably the brightest store on St. Thomas, still glowed with a tropical flare and the avian patterned cushions continued to complement the hibiscus yellow paint on the long porch where customers congregated.

Catching sight of the mailman, Prudence ducked inside, knowing he would leave the packet of mail on the metal porch table nearest the door. She had been reluctant to talk about her circumstances and particularly to the sweet postal carrier who innocently wanted to know what she hadn't had the heart to tell him. After the failed wedding, she had gone solo to St. Bart's, a need to get out of the public eye as well as the righteous act of 'sticking it' to Jason as occupancy would cancel out any chance of a refund.

Once the postman was far enough away, she picked up the bundle and spotted a personally addressed manila envelope. The word FORWARD was heavily stamped and smeared in three places. Unlike the previously sent locket, Byron Thayer, Esq., the Maine attorney, had mistakenly mailed this envelope to a different zip code. Though only off by one number, it had been enough to send it traveling through the chain of islands. The unexpected arrival of the locket had coincided with her big day and was perfect for her dress and while the dress had been tossed out with the trash, the locket was in a drawer out of harm's way. And now it appeared that Hannah had something else to give her.

She skimmed the very lengthy letter included with a formal copy of Great-grandmother's will. It was shocking in its intent. Yet she found it was difficult to feign terrible sadness over the loss of a woman she'd only heard about through eavesdropping. Her mother had not been kind about Ben's New England relatives and Victoria, after too many martinis had made it clear that she wouldn't have '*those* white trash in *her* house'.

Prudence tried to digest the letter when certain words stuck in her throat like dry bread...*fly to Maine!* After what she'd just been through! On top of the lousy bastard walking out on her; she'd nearly been killed when leaving St. Bart's, the small *Cessna* subjected to wind turbulence at the ill-prepared hands of a maverick pilot showing off. It made her want to vomit just thinking about it.

The attorney's letter was implicit, however; in accordance with the instructions of Hannah's will, Prudence was to formally take possession of the property in some obscure little spot on the northeastern seaboard. From certain indications, she was expected to stay which did not sit well at all and she intended to nip that in the bud when she got there.

By the time Julie arrived for work, Prudence had done all the chores and was seething with unanswerable questions. She had worked herself into a state over the necessity of leaving; all the whys and how she'd find the money and length of time she would have to stay in Maine and what owning that property would actually entail. In her mind, it could just as easily have been sold off and the proceeds banked for her; she was the only relative left in line to inherit. Prudence certainly had no desire to go back and forth at will or whim, not that she wanted to leave St. Thomas at all.

Thankfully, Julie was a genius with figures and thanks to Ben, Prudence had initially been able to use monies from her mother's life insurance to help purchase the crusty old building that now sparkled from their care and creativity. But there wasn't enough money left for what might lay ahead.

By the time Prudence was scheduled to leave for Maine, Julie had spent countless hours pulling apart the finer aspects of their joint venture with the intention of buying out Pru's half. It was important to keep the business running smoothly and still provide a dependable monthly stipend while in Maine. After many days on the phone to bankers, sheets of calculations and late night discussions, they had at least a small plan in play. But at the last minute, Prudence nearly dug in her heels. This was home, where she belonged…her paradise, even without the previously hoped-for groom.

Chapter Two

Stale cabin air, fearful murmured soliloquies (some of them hers), shrieking toddlers bored of sitting still and fussy babies whose ears obviously hurt from the air pressure. Prudence had endured complaints from passengers expecting more than was ever offered, snarling over their peanuts and smaller seats, a fault of new row configurations or their increasingly larger bodies, she couldn't be sure. But there had been a time when the seats were cheaper and a stewardess pleasantly proffered meal choices, wine or liquor and no one paid for water, times her father had enjoyed telling of when he would visit. Trips when he'd met the occasional movie star combining work and holiday on one of the tropical islands or some cleric going on retreat. Today there is a 'flight attendant' and he is very disagreeable, as if it is Pru's fault that she is high-strung and requires calming each time they hit air pockets, ones that cause her to reach for a little paper bag, the one she had complained was missing from the seat pouch in front of her even though she thankfully hadn't had to use it.

Before her father died and her childhood home in Massachusetts emptied, she had made one or two trips back to the states to see Ben and at least had the anticipation of returning to one Caribbean island or another, wherever she happened to reside at the time. The calico and bandanna-colored brightness wrapping the places she relished, breathtaking and simultaneously flirtatious against an azure sky. But this was not one of those times; she was going in the wrong direction and there was no turning back, at least not yet.

Exasperation swept over her again *well, this is just grand...a house in Maine!* She'd re-read the document many times since first taking it out of its embossed maroon cover; the pages of quality vellum clearly spelling out in black and white the indisputable inheritance...**To my great-granddaughter,**

Prudence Stone, I bequeath all my jewelry and my beloved Thatcher Lane cottage in the village of Oyster Cove, Maine. It was now a dog-eared statement of times to come she thought as she placed it face down on the tray table.

Ben came to the forefront of all her thoughts these days, his untimely death the cause and effect of this latest situation. *Sole heir,* repeated so often it had become like a mantra. Whether out of frustration or habit, she rubbed the smooth case around her neck, having forgiven the dark-eyed West Indian seer without once considering doing the same for Jason. Besides, it seemed only right to wear the important piece from the relative who had just bequeathed her estate. The rest of the jewelry referred to in the will was but a few pair of earrings and a thin gold band presumably a wedding ring. In reality, the continual touching and stroking as though a talisman also had quite a lot to do with being on an airplane again, a touchy subject since the St. Bart's trip. The one week vacation meant to forget the failed wedding and stitch up the threads of 'torn asunder' before even tying the knot, had instead left her equilibrium somewhere over the nearly missed mountaintop, the precious getaway then squandered in fear. And in the aftermath of receiving the will, she had re-wound the old seer's words and what they had intimated and they too accompanied her on this trip to Maine.

Looking directly into the sun, Prudence squinted at the pillowed clouds, the shock of white as far as the eye could see. They would soon be descending through its darker center, the silence-thickened layers and she would hold her breath she was certain until they re-entered the blue-sky June day that the captain had just assured them of. *Maybe I should have worn the pearls for luck after all,* she mused. She had planned to wear them for her wedding and then the locket arrived in advance of the will with its small intrigue and seemed more appropriate for a less sophisticated ceremony in the sand. When he'd given her the pearls, a proud father's graduation gift, Ben had absently rolled the lustrous strand between his fingers, a 'tell'—like her handling of the locket—that he was worrying about her future. She had seen him hold his rosary in a similar manner, the little black and silver beads that he used when things were bad with her mother.

As she put the Oyster Cove document back into the well-used tote with one last glance-through, Prudence tried to imagine what Ben would make of it all…this new fear of flying and that she was to become a homeowner at last. Of the two, this part was the most difficult since it meant having to leave behind a truly fabulous island lifestyle. She held close the lasting image of him as he'd been while she was growing up, articulating lessons in his den surrounded by the mismatched variety of collected globes that he loved using to pinpoint the object of interest. She might even have believed in the usage of beads purported to assist prayers because he favored topics like religion, referring at times to those who offered them up in hot desert locales where strands similar to those found in most any Catholic household, were used in different languages and to a differently named god. As if prayers had done him any good. And he'd tried them all but nothing could save her mother from the alcohol that consumed her, that in the end she'd taken to adding pills until one day she'd simply overdosed on it all. The loss of Ben was a different matter. But even with the obvious love and sentimentality, she had just added a tinge of resentment to the memories because of what his death had left her to deal with, the fact that she knew little if anything about the long-widowed Hannah Ellison. And that she was more than apprehensive about moving to such an alien landscape.

So instead of the pearls, she'd changed her mind at the last minute. A fluke really since while dressing she had suddenly conjured the memory that they were borne of mollusks and those were without a backbone and did she really need to start out in a new place with that idea in her head. She was already on tenterhooks about the entire affair.

Are you listening Ben? Unlike her father, she had trouble believing in the concept of heaven. And though she was well past the need for paternal guidance, she could still use the champion in her corner even with some of the blame landing on him. So much information about her lineage had gone astray, especially the ties to Hannah, but this did little to assuage her present fear or allay her qualms that she just might be inheriting an albatross that wouldn't hang quite so nicely around her neck.

She realized this entire affair might have been a moot point from the beginning because of the difficulty in finding those who transited so often through the many Caribbean portals. But instead she was scheduled for tomorrow morning's meeting with Mr. Thayer in the township of Stonycroft—purportedly not far from Oyster Cove—certainly not a place of her heart's doing. And did she have the temerity to ask about the archaic seeming statement in his letter? In fact, it might have been plucked from one of Ben's tomes on religion or ancient history, the ones still in storage.

'Mrs. Ellison was found in her chintz reading chair; a book of poems by Millay on the floor where it had fallen from her already stiffening fingers as she transitioned to another place.' Prudence had never heard of anyone 'transitioning' and she'd certainly seen enough death in her young lifetime.

There was a sudden shudder as the plane began its drop through the clouds. From memory alone and as though yesterday, her heart raced as it had inside the falling *Cessna.* Flying and the sense of exploration had once been as natural as breathing, but no longer. It is also hard to swallow what has nearly been eclipsed by her present fear…the regrets because of what she had mistakenly taken for granted. It had been an enormous undertaking for the young business partners, but the results had paid off. And now she was leaving behind her dearest friend along with their trendy, island-themed bookstore and the joy of being with like-minded people in a place filled with color and light and easy rhythms. Not to be forgotten were the many miles racked up traveling between islands—before the near miss—ones that she probably wouldn't be seeing again anytime soon.

Those who knew her well were aware of how much she adored the de rigueur of island life; those raucous tribes of greeters with hoisted rum punches, great bonhomie and adventuresome appetites always fed by the nurturing warmth of sunshine. They stood their ground at many an airport, waiting with an aura of *Carnival* to welcome the traveling minions, the ones who without fanfare were emptied from the planes along with their jumbled, tossed-about luggage. Depending on the style of 'island hoppers' (from four seats to forty), those passengers no matter how weary, always bore a startled expression immediately followed by awe as they witnessed 'paradise' for the first time…just as she had done so many years earlier.

She rationalized that this new phobia was ludicrous, especially after experiencing so much while testing her mettle like all young women of her ilk. Gathering places destined just for them or so it had seemed…the many jaunts related to the slow-paced activities adapted to the heat-seared tarmacs boiling under unrelenting infrared rays.

Binging and pinging brought her back to the present, sounds alerting her to the overhead instructions and before the snippy attendant would ask, she replaced the tray table, brought her seatback into an upright position and pressed her head against the stiff blue fabric attempting to hold at bay the state of anxious discomfort. Feeling a change in pressure, she swallowed hard and her ears popped and she twisted the silver chain with a reflexive grip. Suddenly the ground beneath the fuselage was rushing up to meet the fast approaching tires, then landed with a surprising bump and thud and another bump before settling down on the runway. *Safe,* she exhaled gratefully, allowing the locket to resume its proper place just above her cleavage.

I should at least try for Ben's sake, after all this is the land of his ancestors...and mine. Prudence had no trouble remembering Victoria's attitude as she thought of those long buried souls, the scathing remarks she had been noted for. The trouble with her mother's attitude, Prudence eventually realized, was her inability to equate her opinions of others with the unflattering term 'lush' that became associated with her reputation. It had been somewhere in her pre-teens that Prudence had her first inkling that she had most likely been named by Ben because she had been expected to make intelligent and wise— prudent—decisions. And while she appreciated his trust in her, the burden was a lot to carry around during her early school years in Massachusetts. It was also one of the reasons she was still smarting from the wedding fiasco.

While she waited for the cabin door to open, she picked out the bustling activity; touchdown had set in motion the motorized baggage carts and those trained to maneuver the large jet into its assigned gate position. This only re-emphasized the vast differences in the familiar, but less busy locales that she had happily called home. Everything was bigger and faster than the legions of airports she'd traveled through and before she could count them up, her seatmate stirred. *Finally! How can anyone sleep through landing?* She marveled as he yawned and stretched his cramped long legs and patted his mussed hair. "My kids are waiting for me behind that tinted window," he offered as if she would sense how commonplace that was.

"I'm not so used to the jets anymore; do they enjoy seeing them come in?" Prudence asked, with what friendliness she could muster for someone who'd not spoken, but snored for most of the time.

"I travel a lot, so both my kids are used to it by now, but the youngest one always said the planes looked like the porpoises she'd seen at *Sea World* because of their big round noses. Cute, right?"

"Yes," she smiled with what Julie would call her plastic face. "What do you do?" she asked, as it seemed only polite. "New England branch manager for the phone company," he said before the volume went up a notch and the announcements drowned him out and she was free to do what time demanded. To distract from thoughts of crashing, she had also performed some breathing techniques and in the time allowed before descent and the tires hit terra firma, the only ploy left in her little arsenal—her make-up pouch. The only reason she even had it with her was to please Julie, who had indicated it might be nice to subscribe to a more polished look for this debut in northern New England. Prudence had packed the touching wedding gift, an almost too-dainty brocade case that would always remind her of the honeymoon that never happened.

But no matter how beautiful the little bag was Prudence had developed a slight distaste for its contents since she rarely wore more than lipstick and a tan. Or perhaps it was the man who'd walked out on her that created the distasteful residue that had become all mixed up with the gift. But even if only a tool, she'd put it to good use and had carefully dabbed the necessary colors from their highly unusual cloisonné containers, striving not to overdo. The effect had surprised and pleased her as the effort not only enhanced her facial contours, but also decried the last thirteen years blitzed by the unrelenting tropic sun.

She snapped the petite case closed one last time having assured herself that the lively coral lipstick was intact since she had a habit of chewing her pencil. This time rather pronouncedly while making some notes for tomorrow's meeting with Mr. Thayer. She struggled in the confined space to stand which only left her stooped from the waist and straightened the body-hugging jersey dress, the one picked specifically to show off her five-foot-six frame and emphasize the recently introduced no-carb diet. Stuffing her face with sweets had been just another side effect of being jilted.

15

Having grown up in the north, she remembered that it would likely still be cool in this part of the country and had brought a color-coordinated double-knit jacket just in case. She adjusted it around her shoulders, touched the locket for good luck and hoped that her put-together appearance would exude far more confidence than she actually felt. Meanwhile, a minor crescendo was building all around as people were jostling for place and tugging things from the overheads; it was time. Prudence responded to the noisy cues and tilting her chin in defiance of all that made her nervous, got up and followed the many tired and disheveled groaners off the plane and into the unknown past belonging to Hannah Ellison.

At the end of the moveable bridge, that unaccustomed link between plane and terminal (in place of a rolling stairway that greeted the Caribbean passengers), amidst a small throng of people and in bold, black lettering, '**WELCOME TO MAINE HAL**' waved slowly side to side. Exiting passengers were craning their necks for the important party who merited the attention-getting sign, perhaps hoping to have something to report about later and Prudence, both inquisitive and just plain nosy, did the same although not particularly for the same reason. It had long ago become a game—to identify the many bland, vanilla masks that managed to express boredom rather than interest, always eliciting one of Ben's old 'saws' as he liked to call them.

They'd been particularly close, and with what she was about to face head on she would need all the help she could get from his handed-down statements; ones she could access on occasion to strengthen her resolve. But as always, times like this could quickly bring to mind the way he'd looked the last time they'd been together, not as the robust hero of her childhood, though still handsome, but a tired, thinner imitation of his former self. Victoria's death though a number of years prior, had taken away more than his appetite and had left him with graying hair that had gone beyond the gracefully etched temples yet still

16

accentuated the maple syrup shade. That and the newly framed bifocals gave him what she considered a debonair appearance making Prudence wonder at the time whether or not he had been soured by such a dysfunctional marriage or might one day find a good woman to really appreciate him. She had been counting on the latter; that is until the fatal car accident.

But it was his favorite phrase referencing the various and sundry and unsmiling travelers who daily bled into similar terminals; ones that he knew more about than Prudence...*more than likely there's not a ribbon of thought among them about the shear portability of one's existence*...that had never failed to amuse her. She had always debated that while he found it annoying that a mass of humanity might be under-whelmed by new experiences, more than likely it would be her particular vagabond nature they'd find lacking. Even though his neglect with regard to facts pertaining to Hannah Ellison has placed her in such an unimaginable situation, Prudence would always remain grateful that he'd instilled her with such curiosity. And she was going to need to shore herself up with words like those if she was to honor what had come to her through his untimely death.

At least there isn't a long line, she realized as she dragged her heavy bag nearly bursting at the seams from the carousel toward the Hertz rental counter, the buzz from all the communal voices still humming a minor tune. And though not particularly tired, it would be easier to savor the new location in the quiet confines of a smooth running car. This would be an especially nice treat after the beat-up, gear-grinding noises of the ancient foreign jalopy she had left behind, the one pockmarked with holes that threatened to drop the battery onto the road whenever she hit a bump.

With the map by her side and her eyes on the unfamiliar road, she could only glimpse at the tall trees that slipped by under the previously predicted vivid blue sky, but as the tires droned methodically emitting a steady rhythm on more even pavement than she was accustomed to, she finally began to unwind and take in what nature had provided. The 'land of the pine trees', as stated by her curious island cohort because both in friendship or dealing with business, Ms. Julie Myers checked out everything. But Prudence still doubted she'd ever grasp or even really care, about the many species ubiquitous to the region. Evergreen forests...firs and spruce, yellow or white pine, whatever had been the Christmas tree of choice throughout her childhood.

Her eyes were tiring and the roadside becoming a blur of dark green and yet, like the small openings between the masses, a new angst was creeping into her subconscious. But this newest concern had nothing to do with the earlier dread and more with self-confidence for she was embarking on a journey that for the first time felt like hostile territory and all because of the missing pieces. A horn beeped once, twice and the third time made her realize from the raised finger, that she was driving below the required limit and in the passing lane to boot. She'd been off in her own little world again.

With a burst of acceleration, she was reminded of the many other things that had been required to move in haste because of that fateful letter. They had weathered much in order to acclimate to different ways of doing things and always on 'island time' and had created what they believed would be a lifelong bond. And Prudence knew that she could always count on her best friend for good advice, but also the occasional 'kick in the ass' if necessary. She knew that when she called later to bring Julie up to speed, she should probably couch a lot of her anxiety since Julie knew full well about Pru's tendency to overdramatize, even when she had legitimate reason. Julie had proven to be the best type of friend, lighthearted and never dull and after they'd found the very old building in disrepair and in need of a reputable facelift, had helped turn it into something to be proud of. By the time Prudence received the providential documents from Maine, it had become a popular gathering place for children and artists and the community at large. They'd

18

created ambiance in every area of the store...arranging things from bestsellers to handmade floor cloths as well as a special children's corner. Though Prudence had never found the right globe to spark the kids' interests, she had found an old copper samovar to increase adult curiosity. Their hard work had paid off and everything within those walls that Prudence looked upon as she said her goodbyes, had been and would remain a piece of her heart. It would gleam and continue to appeal even without her presence. For anyone viewing the building for the first time, it appears delectably secluded within the lush, omnipresent greenery and raised as though on a dais at the far end of a popular courtyard restaurant. The business now boasts a place to relax and enjoy the conviviality of like-minded readers or lose oneself in an author's words just as they had intended. It had been a bittersweet farewell and not without its second thoughts.

Most importantly, it had been Julie, the elder by only four years, who could not only handle unexpected situations at the store with great aplomb, but had also held Prudence together when Jason had failed her. To the torment of her sensitive soul, she would always remember that day and Julie's incantations, some sort of spell that was supposed to be correct for the circumstance. There had been no voodoo doll handy, she'd said. None of it mattered of course, because he'd never come and she'd never found out why. He hadn't left an obvious trail and she had refused to expend the energy it would have taken to find him. Prudence had vowed that very day never to place herself in such a vulnerable position again while Julie had tried to convince her that one day it would be a distant memory to laugh about. Had insisted on reminding her of those earlier years when it was enough just to revel in their freedom; the high-jinx played out with the men in their pasts, the ones who cheated and lied and added their names to the garland of heartbreak as easily as stringing a Christmas tree. They had both had their share of youthful dalliances and had recovered easily enough and had experienced much among the locals. When they weren't playing at life, they were learning. The old women in particular, loved sharing the deeply moving tales of spirits or shape-shifters. And ghosts even. Stories about heroes and slaves, lore that would last forever. Through Pru's sadness, Julie kept reminding her how much they'd learned from these wise, tenderhearted people. Anything to dull the pain in her friend's heart, help her believe in her island existence as before, be whole again. But then the news had arrived from Maine.

Logically Prudence realized much of what she had experienced were lessons meant to be learned; she certainly wouldn't be the first woman to be trod upon or lose her heart to a scoundrel or even her virginity when least expecting to. But whatever it was, perhaps in the end, Jason had turned out to be exactly the type of man Ben had tried to warn her about; the one who could talk a woman into anything, con her out of her self-esteem as he became the decision maker and her loyalties as he weaned her from her friends, all except for Julie. And then, just as in the movies but without a star's flare, he had simply upped and 'taken a powder', leaving her with no plausible explanation and a lot of tears. Though she would never know for sure, he had obviously tired of her when she no longer proved a challenge.

Of course it was her best friend and confidant and when necessary, kind-hearted mother earth, who had been there for her from the moment he'd walked out, had stepped in to pick up the emotional shards that gathered like dust motes around Pru's constantly weeping frame. And when the heartbreak had become too raw to witness, pointedly announced, "Enough…this continual sadness is clinging with all the grace of a wet slip!" Prudence had wanted to have the statement engraved for posterity to remind her of her vulnerability, but as Julie clearly emphasized, Pru's undying gratitude was quite enough.

Logic aside, Prudence had little doubt now as the highway spun out before her, that she hadn't completed the five notable stages of grief. Stuck at anger, whatever number that was, had caused a protective shell to form around her heart, thus enforcing thoughts of celibacy. *That might prove handy while mired in some backwater of Maine,* she thought and a loud honk brought her out of her reverie. Shaking her head as if that could dislodge the cobwebs of wasted remorse and getting her bearings, she checked the directions and carefully made the turn-off from Route 1.

Main Street in Stonycroft; certainly a place with more brick and stone than tropical style and appeal until she spotted the water off in the distance to her right. Flawlessly spread out and inherently attached to the unexpected inheritance was a differently hued palette. A place with the required visual appeal; a key that had always opened the doors to her travel destinations and one which must play a role in this latest dilemma if she had any hope of enjoying it here. *Water, the penultimate seducer.*

She drove slowly searching for the hotel sign as she passed a large harbor. It was dotted with fishing boats of all sizes and a couple of big schooner rigs, but fewer of the recreational sailboats that bobbed gracefully at anchor not far from her island apartment; the colorful hulls in red, white or blue, a testament to their windswept freedom.

The large marina with its tall pilings appeared a hub of activity; folks gathered in clusters at one end of the long pier, burly men lugging crates and carrying what looked to be their fishing gear, unfamiliar and yet entirely reminiscent. The sound of engines coupled with the smell of diesel that drifted through the car window could have easily been from all of the dive boats and cruise ships that filled the main harbor back on the island. It brought her up short and as if she wasn't already concerned enough, fresh doubts about her home away from home began to wedge their way into her psyche before she could do anything about it. At that moment, the Salter Inn which had been chosen at the lawyer's direction, came into view with its distinct location just outside the quaint downtown business district on the glistening shoreline of Penobscot Bay. It was a segment of water that on her map ran the coastline to the Atlantic Ocean and alluringly wrapped a few of the smaller islands. Her tired eyes and stiff, achy body welcomed the unexpected and rather grand scene before her. Everything was coming into its springtime essence, a winsome green so unlike the arid blades which were the aftermath of a recent drought, a view she'd left only that morning. In front of her was a kaleidoscope of color: frilly blue irises, vibrant orange poppies and deep hued azaleas, the pictorial stuff of travel brochures and she instantly tossed aside a few of her pre-conceived notions about this cold, hard coast, much of what she had allowed her nervousness to dictate.

Her mind whirled as she took it all in *this is really amazing!* No sooner had she acknowledged that than a strong blast of cold northern wind blew across her face, a light slap just to let her know it was Maine and not quite summer. It was chilling and disrupted the blonde-highlighted fringe of her newly coiffed hair—something else to help signify change—throwing all the well-trimmed strands into chaos as she hefted her bag from the trunk all the while straining for the view beyond. She couldn't check in fast enough and simply dropped her luggage inside her room and after skimming a few brochures from the lobby rack, rushed back outside unable to give up the scent off the ocean even for a moment.

The stiff breeze again swiped at her hair and hemline but this time carried with it a very familiar noise…the luffing sails of a passing boat just coming about. She squinted and without binoculars could barely make out the three occupants dressed in matching colored jackets…perhaps testing new equipment or trying out a different crew for an upcoming event. The captain, his windbreaker billowing out like a very small sail, steadily maneuvered her—an awfully pretty racing machine—into position. Then she heard the assisting putt-putt of the engine and smiled at the remembered activity, the many hours spent doing the exact same thing years ago when crewing on a luxury sailboat. She might not be able to see their faces, but she could hear them quite clearly. Sound echoes loudly over water and she knew from past experience they would be completely unaware their voices had reached her, revealing much of their private conversation as it crossed the expanse. She averted her eyes against the eavesdropping, embarrassed that she'd heard so much, but not before they'd turned the boat into the sunlight which now bounced off all the chrome, and changed the direction of their comic outburst.

As it waned, the sun began to dab the bay as though spattered paint, creating a patterned glare like little broken mirrors. She shielded her eyes from its intensity as it began to capture the top of a smallish white tower turning it a soft yellow which inadvertently exposed it like a candle on a dense green cake. She glanced at the little pamphlet indicating it to be a moderately sized landmark, one of at least three nearby. There were photos of one tucked into a hillside, one on a large rocky surface and one with a jetty as the way to reach it and bring in supplies.

Even without Julie's input, Prudence had been aware that the local architecture differed greatly from those structures she'd just left behind, so patrician really, many styles that would take time to get used to: gambrel, cape, federal, revival, saltbox or even farmhouses dating so many years back that she'd never keep them all straight. That curious research about Maine had created a long list of things for Prudence to learn about. *Lighthouses will be the first on my list as soon as I'm settled,* she sighed, watching the light playing on the water and hard granite surfaces.

She stayed that way until hunger beckoned, finally seeking warmth from the hotel's rustic interior and congenial staff in order to savor it all with a glass of wine in front of a brick-faced fireplace before dinner. By then she was huddled in her too light jacket and glad for the crackling logs. *Will it be enough,* she wondered, this being smitten by the brand new? Would it even be a semblance of what was needed to sustain her in the coming weeks?

It had been a huge day and staring at her reflection, it crossed her mind that many such questions might stand in her way. She had also eaten a far too heavy boiled dinner, leaving her unsettled and with nothing left but the rehashing—a post-mortem on an extraordinary trip. The hours in the air, the quiet but road-weary miles and then playing the enthusiastic tourist for a little while and because of the meager airline fare, the meal that had left her feeling out of sorts and slightly punchy. On top of that, she had called Julie to assure her that all was well and the flight thankfully uneventful. She had quite naturally been more curious about the area, had wanted to know everything in detail and kept Prudence on the phone much longer than expected with the million and one questions and now every one of those moments was registered in the bathroom mirror as Prudence grudgingly labored to remove the unfamiliar makeup, disliking the wipes that smelled like cheap perfume.

There was only one thing she was sure of that could soothe her into a good night's sleep and settle the crazy emotions running amuck in her brain, and that would be the sound of lapping water. The room was pleasant enough with its beige walls and waterfowl print drapes with a coordinating green and beige spread. Certainly not what she'd expected but then she had no reference point to measure it against. But it did have a nice small deck space, though as she walked to the sliders, she knew she'd hardly get a chance to use it. She pulled at the drapery panels and slid the glass door a few inches so that she could hear that wonderful reminder of home just as one of the small waves buffeted the shoreline. *A perfect end to an exhausting day!*

It happened around any body of water, this lure that engulfed her like a comforting shawl, but would this make up for the left behind and the soon to be, all because of the imponderable will? With that looming question mark now as obvious as the flash from one of the closer lighthouses, she opened the drapes the full extent of the doorway. The only thing visible in that dark backdrop were what looked like bumps on the horizon; obviously nearby islands as seen on the map earlier in the day. It was difficult in the dimness to know their actual size but before it mattered, they had faded into the starry night sky.

Her senses had been blunted; each one assaulted by the day's events and as the strong light continued to glance the walls in predictable intervals, it brought more into focus than the simple hotel furnishings. It managed to point out how much she was leaving behind and that weighed more heavily than the indigestible dinner. She wasn't religious at least not like Ben, but at that moment Prudence began to pray that she would be able to make the right decisions on behalf of all that she held dear. She would either take care of business in a hurry or stay on because of him and get to know what Hannah was all about, at least for a little while.

She stood there trance-like with the beige velour bed blanket wrapped around the flimsy nightshirt, her favorite that she refused to leave behind. She stared at the empty darkness beyond using whatever of his words she could remember and then the unthinkable…*Hannah's locket is so warm and yet strangely comforting.* She responded as though a switch had been turned on her bare skin, the delicate patch just above the little hollow of her cleavage as if she had been sitting in the sun for a long time. Hannah's cherished locket felt as though it had awakened from a cold metallic sleep, a first since receiving it.

It had not only taken her by surprise when it arrived on St. Thomas, but had instantly seemed rare with its tattered velvet cord which she had changed to a loop-patterned silver chain for safety's sake and to be able to wear on her wedding day. To her surprise, the jeweler had been able with his delicate tools to open it revealing a tiny sepia photo inside. But the few times she'd worn it, pieces of clothing had cushioned its metal shell. What on earth could Hannah have had in mind gifting it to her? Or was her imagination at play again, making high drama from nothing, a trait that had become nearly synonymous with her name. Since childhood with her nose always in a book, Ben had warned her of melodrama, a habit she'd obviously not kicked. And yet, no matter the mental acrobatics, the locket remained warm, and that wasn't her imagination.

What had the lawyer's letter said...that Hannah never took it off? Maybe now she wouldn't either. Overtired and only half believing the sensation was due to total exhaustion, the type that hovered in wait to drop her for the night, she closed the door but left the drapes apart. She touched the memento gently just to be sure, her bookish imaginings already beckoning...*the locket is home again...* before laying her fatigued body onto the large bed. Then drawn like Alice to the rabbit hole she slipped dreamily into a bewitching space between reality and great-grandmother Hannah's world just as the darkness closed in all around her.

Chapter Three

It's all wrong, Prudence thought as she awoke in the strange place. There was a recognizable ague of homesickness attacking her body, a perturbing condition for which there was no medication. Gauze-filtered sunlight and birdsong had been replaced by the unfamiliar scent of fabrics and mixed fibers housed in a closed room. She composed herself and wrapping the spread around her, cracked open the door just enough to freshen the space since the wind was blowing. Damp morning air crept in and brought varied and conflicting noises to her well-tuned ear.

Such mangled dreams, she remembered. Heavy traffic moving across a strange landscape and garbled sounds coming from her throat had woken her at least twice. Each time forcing her to check on the locket. Even with its surprising warmth, she'd had a strong desire to keep it on during the night. Perhaps she'd wear it always, she'd thought, as if she had been told that was the right thing to do. It wasn't very difficult —to sleep with it on—she always slept on her back. She was known for her death-like pose, hands folded across her chest in blissful, quiet slumber. It was one thing that had truly bothered Jason. Their first time together, he'd thought she had expired and had leaned in to feel her pulse only to be pushed back by the nasty glare of her eyes because he had startled her awake.

Now she realized that it had been one thing he'd had no control over. Had she been wiser, she might have recognized that well-hidden misogynous trait, his absolute need for control.

This morning was a different matter; the king-size bed—thanks to Mr. Thayer's business connections—had been tossed about as though a party had taken place in the wee hours, and the pendant was back to normal though hardly what she would call cold. She'd obviously been very restless; the self-doubts and uncertainties had roamed quite freely and mingled with all the guests at her imaginary dinner party. Ben had been there, wearing a yachtsman's cap of all things, and Victoria too, although she couldn't be certain it was her face behind the black witch's veil. It was a terrible thing to feel such latent animosity toward the woman who had given her birth. Perhaps one day she'll only remember the kinder moments of her childhood, times when they at least appeared to be a happy family. She has already learned that hatred or a lack of forgiveness will only make her sick and she has the beginning stage of an ulcer to prove it.

Prudence struggled with her attire for the morning meeting with Mr. Thayer and in the end, settled on an outfit in linen. Wrinkles appeared as if by magic and by the time she entered the dining room with its view of the sea, she felt a mess. Then an empty longing hit her head on. Though not an unattractive sight, it was not *her* view. She had to force herself to eat and shamelessly danced her fork around the extraordinarily generous breakfast fare, feigning interest before pushing the large platter away to the dismay of the wait staff. *They don't want to know about the tiny, sugar-nabbing birds who are turning up on my St. Thomas balcony while I sit here all alone.* The big square table with its lack of spilled sugar caused another wave of homesickness. The little crystals would have been their sweet share of her coffee ritual. *The staff are polite enough, but obviously preoccupied,* she admitted. But the proffered bland and watered down coffee denied her a decent caffeine high and this would leave her cranky on top of everything else.

Prudence was running late. She was also unable to comprehend the previous night's crazy fantasizing; after all she was no longer the child crouching among Ben's things. It had been foolish not to shut out the magnified beam from the lighthouse. That and the ensuing dreams of Wonderland had cost her much needed sleep and she was paying for it now. Walking to her rental car, she realized the next few hours might be difficult. The attorney would be waiting to impart all that his professional expertise had been hired to render based upon the pending formalities. Not knowing whatever might be required after that simply unnerved her.

Byron Thayer took in the lithe and somewhat bewildering creature seated before him, the relative of his deceased client fortunate in his mind to inherit such a solid property. He noted that she had worn the pendant Hannah had wanted her to have and that she touched it often as though reassuring herself of its presence. To his dismay she had also arrived late, appearing a little disoriented and from the puffiness around her eyes, he presumed a lack of sleep as well. He had been striving for the right tone ever since she'd sat down, never comfortable with a careless heed to punctuality and wasn't at all certain that he had succeeded.

Accordingly, he had tried to give the young lady a bit of slack; she had never been here and perhaps had had a restless night in a strange new place, though he'd made certain her accommodations would be adequate. She was of medium height, attractive and in her fresh-faced way, quite healthy looking he had to admit, though a bit on the jittery side. But she was more importantly the great-granddaughter of a woman he had revered for many years. Could still remember the strong feelings he'd felt the first time they'd met, how lovely she'd seemed even in her early forties, and how kind knowing he was the new attorney in town. While taking Hannah through the pertinent legal paces required at that time, he'd developed feelings, more than a crush, even with their seventeen-year age difference, something that had prevented him from ever settling for someone else and something he had carefully kept to himself. Not even his indomitable secretary, fortunately on vacation at the moment or she might after this meeting, suspect that it had been Hannah who'd introduced him to poetry and music, things that his life had never before included and things that now enriched his daily existence.

To this day, while working late, he left the apartment door open so that he could hear the strains of his favorite operas as they drifted down to his office, the sound greatly enhanced by the stairwell. He would miss her presence in his life even though neither had ever spoken of love in any real way. She had inquired if he was married or had a girlfriend, all innocent patter to pass the time, but he couldn't possibly have told her his true feelings. Perhaps today things would have been different, but not back then, never.

Walking into his office, Prudence Stone instantly became a strong reminder of all that had passed, his unfulfilled dreams because he had sensed there was someone else in Hannah's heart and would never have embarrassed himself by prying. And now as he tried to concentrate on his duty with most of the paperwork completed, he felt it time to tell the still baffled young woman a little more about her great-grandmother, at least what he was privy to. Studying her face as she scanned the room, the more he saw the resemblance to Hannah. Without anticipating such a thing, he was struck by the way that made him feel toward her, almost a need to protect and that shocked him. So much had been locked up inside his heart, he hadn't expected the past to beckon so strongly. And once he had done everything he could to enlighten her, he had only to make one last visit to the old house. The thought rather distressed him and he hoped the rest of the day would go well, for everyone's sake.

Though out of sorts, Prudence couldn't help herself and with a natural perspicacity, had carefully scanned her surroundings. She had immediately noticed the telltale evidence of a recent facelift both outside and in. Left behind scaffolding like a blundered sculpture spotted while parking the rental, and the assaulting odor of latex paint noted as soon as she'd opened the office door. The smell lingered on walls the color of peeled onions, proof enough of recent changes. A darker value—more green in the tint—highlighted tin ceiling medallions that ringed three gleaming stained glass pendants hung strategically over the attorney's desk by lengths of black, powder-coated chains, both prominent and pristine in their newness. There was a deep red, expensive-looking wool runner, an Aubusson, if she remembered correctly from her childhood home; one her mother had coveted until Ben had in a time of turmoil, surprised her with it. So perhaps this one had been picked out by a wife as well. Still, none of it appealed. Pru's tastes had long ago swung over to the bright, airy pastel colors and cottons of the tropics.

The new furniture was unmistakable too; still had that untouched look about it. She thought it an odd selection for a New England law firm, had expected period pieces gleaming from lemon wax and even a little stuffy looking. But it was austere enough, perhaps a bit too orderly even, the décor obviously meant to impart an air of stability, a solidness that was possibly the hallmark of his life.

"This stairway is really special," she said, jumping up unexpectedly while exclaiming over the beautiful carved newel post, trying to get her bearings and lose a little of her sudden shyness.

"I always hope clients will enjoy that bit of history in an old building like this," he said following her lead. "While mine is topped by this interesting finial, there are many styles out there; a simple square cap or patterned wood blocks and round billiard ball sized orbs that were often meant to cover little hollowed out spaces believed to be used as hiding places for important papers such as a deed to a house. Not uncommon at all," he continued, obviously happy that she'd broken the ice in such an innocuous way. "I'm sorry to say that is not the case with this one."

As he moved back behind his desk, she wondered if that had been a 'tease' regarding the inherited house by the sea and for the first time since receiving the news, felt a spark of excitement instead of the persistent dread of what lay ahead.

For some reason, Thayer felt the need to take refuge behind his classic 'partners' desk, the only piece that wasn't newly purchased; couldn't remember the last time he'd felt this uncomfortable without knowing exactly why, though he suspected it had to do with the resemblance to Hannah. Even as she'd aged, Prudence Stone's great-grandmother had retained her beauty although gently coiffed in the wrinkles of time. And because he knew what to expect from those clients closer to his own age, this likeness had managed to unsettle him. Fortunately, he felt no compunction to retire just yet; he could still put in a good day's work when he had to.

He watched her once again coolly appraising him and the décor in a way that said she wasn't overly impressed (except for the staircase), was anxious to have things done with. He wasn't much taken with it all either, though he never would have said so. The unusual settee—a 'settle'—was altogether too uncomfortable which had somehow escaped him in the showroom, but as his secretary had pointed out, he'd hardly ever be sitting on it anyway. She had helped him with the color scheme as well. As he watched Prudence taking it all in, he realized the accent colors had probably been chosen from his wardrobe preferences over the years because the familiar brownish-red was everywhere one looked: furniture fabric, leather journal, desktop accessories and what little wall art he'd allowed, and even the vest he'd chosen for today's meeting.

Prudence and Thayer locked eyes. Was it showing, she wondered…the uncertainty of such a premature inheritance legally binding her to a house in Maine, a location approximately fifteen hundred air miles away from her adopted place on the planet? Was it possible it would cause a reaction similar to that which had instilled such a new fear of flying and had threatened to undo her aqua-blue, tropical existence; the almost paralyzing type that had nearly prevented this meeting?

She had never been good with feeling out of control over her environment; even her free-spirited roaming had been well thought out. As if reading her discomfort, he rose and simultaneously removed his jacket and hung it precisely over the back of the handsome oak chair, a movement that automatically shed the dutiful professional arrogance of a gray, three-piece suit. *He must be in his seventies,* she guessed already feeling more at ease by that singular gesture. While it may have been the heavy weave competing with the warmth of the room, losing that one piece of somber attire had unexpectedly made him more approachable and then something else. It had also exposed the straining buttons of his broadcloth maroon vest…the portly uncle…a breath of fresh air innocuously seeped through the walls of solemnity. *Saved again, pulled from the maudlin brink.* She winced at the thought of her mental high drama, the type she could easily create when unsure of herself.

He cleared his throat quite loudly and she shifted her weight in her already wrinkled linen slacks, questioning her wardrobe choice for the second time this morning. For some reason, she primly folded her hands, perhaps the conscientious act of the errant third-grader she once was.

"Are you all right, my dear?" He asked as he poured her a glass of water.

"I guess." She replied. "It's just that it's a little overwhelming. I really had no idea of any of this prior to your letter. My father never indicated that I might one day be in line for such largesse," she emphasized, accepting the glass without mentioning that no matter what this generosity entailed…with or without a proleptic view…that life would be inherently altered. She didn't say that she could nearly hear the sound of her future in a place she would never have chosen. Or how the imagined bile of pent up anxiety following on the heels of his letter had continued to stick in her throat and still threatened to choke her. *Drink the water and be done with it!* She silently chastised, sensing drama gone awry again. The mere idea of being uprooted from a place that had made her inordinately happy was the culprit, the start of this mental discourse. Because that is exactly what happened…she'd left St. Thomas behind without an end date, and apparently for **the way life should be,** a phrase noted somewhere in a Maine vacation guide, reinforced by roadway signs and one she so far doubted.

Thayer, however, appeared to be in his element, espousing the facts with vocal chords well suited for a courtroom as he presented her with a typed compilation of names and dates that pertained to Hannah as well as extended members of both the Ellison and Stone clans. There were many now deceased players involved, but for the moment, she was particularly interested in Hannah's sister, Elizabeth as well as Mr. Ellison, the man Hannah had married, the one who used both first and middle names as though hyphenated—James Prescott. Naturally on the list were her paternal grandparents, Amanda and Jeremy Stone. Thayer already knew that Prudence was unfortunately the untimely orphan of Benjamin and Victoria, but now she had new branches to add to the family tree.

"Your great-grandmother Hannah and her older sister were raised on the family farm located on the outskirts of the town of Bingham near the Kennebec River. Their mother had died a few years after Hannah's birth, leaving the elder daughter, Elisabeth in charge. She then married one Jared Clark and her father lived with them on the farm until his death some years later. From what Hannah told me, I presume it was the typically hard life of families living off the land back in the late 1800's when Elisabeth was born and prior to that even.

He continued without breaking stride. "When of age, Hannah married Mr. Ellison; the year was 1926. Sadly, he didn't turn out to be exactly whom or what she'd been led to believe. Apparently, he was what is known as a con man, even did a short stint in prison before he died.

"There were many complications in the years to come…they had a child, Amanda, and they all moved down here to the coast where supposedly they had a lovely home waiting, purchased by James Prescott, that turned out to be rather derelict and that after he died, saddled Hannah with a monumental problem. She had little money and needed to send her daughter back to live with her sister until she could square everything with his debtors and the house itself.

"Unfortunately, as Hannah relayed to me, once back in her mother's care Amanda grew into a most unreasonable young woman and at around eighteen took up with Jeremy, eventually running away to Massachusetts with him. This as you can imagine distressed Hannah to no end and hurt even more when Amanda denied her the grandmotherly privileges that she so longed for. She rarely saw your father and it just about broke her heart," he stated sympathetically as he remembered Hannah's face in the telling.

"I'm guessing from your expression that you had little knowledge of these events; perhaps even Benjamin hadn't known of Mr. Ellison's shady past or simply chose to withhold that fact from you until a more appropriate time."

Prudence could feel the moisture building and blinked the sensation away; these things had after all happened many years before. "I don't have a real sense of her," she said trying to make a point she wasn't even sure of. "My guess is they kept conversations like that for when I was out of range when I was little and then of course, I went away to school and my mother had died and we'd had more important things to talk about and subsequently I left the mainland," she blurted without stopping for breath, knowing full well she couldn't bring herself to tell this perfect stranger the desperate things a drunken Victoria had said in the heat of an argument. "Knowing Ben, I don't think he would have been comfortable telling me about their behavior; that wouldn't have been his way," she continued, additional proof in these proffered statements as to why he had become such a great father.

"I do have one small memento that is still packed away, a rather primitive portrait of Hannah that Ben painted when he was a much younger man. He fell in love with watercolors somewhere along the way and while not very talented at it, he said that painting soothed him. It had hung in his library, a reminder of times lost I suppose." It was also the one room her mother rarely visited. "Now that you've given me more of the details, I have to say I feel kind of cheated, sort of a stranger to my own lineage. It sure would have been easier if Dad and I had at least visited once before any of this," Prudence said, broadly aiming her arm toward the providential paperwork.

She could tell from his facial expression that he was sympathetic to her situation even without those missing pieces to her childhood. Thayer perhaps possessed a self-restraint she was unused to, but he was trying to be kind and she thought, someone to rely on. Even the 'Esquire' seemed more suitable now that she'd spent some time with him.

"In the months before her death, Mrs. Ellison made a few additional changes to her existing will, adding the locket by leaving it with me for safekeeping. I can only imagine she sensed her time on this earth was coming to an end, because I don't think she would have relinquished it otherwise as I'd never seen her without it.

"And at the same time she literally implored me to produce her great-granddaughter…which was no easy task I might add. She was most insistent that when she died, you should take over the property on Thatcher Lane," he said without accusation. Then he tapped two fingers on the small missive in front of him, "she would have most definitely wanted me to read this piece to you."

The favored sonnet must have held some importance if he insisted on reading it aloud, but instead of a pretty stanza, it was strewn with thoughts of death and dying and ebbing tides and disappearing into the sea. Prudence, never once suspecting what their meaning implied, knew a little of maritime lore and could only presume Hannah liked that particular one because of her age and life near the water, the place she was about to take over.

Did we carry any of her work, she wondered of the author, nostalgia already a new friend, especially since the lonely breakfast hour. She hadn't been gone from work but a few days and already felt the St. Thomas bookstore slipping away from her. And since she'd always been a bit lackluster about poetry, this particular sonnet sounded morose even to her untrained ear. But *dear* Byron was definitely getting into the spirit of this one with a natural flowing cadence, removing the last vestige of 'stodgy' from his unique bearing, warming the eminent messenger considerably.

The self-doubts remained, however, for she was still very alone and unlike Mr. Thayer, way out of her element. "This should have been my father's inheritance," Prudence stated with all the weight of universal law falling on her slim shoulders, and the knowledge that Ben would have expected her to handle it and be grateful…he had taught her well.

She breathed deeply to center herself, an easy trick learned once upon a time in a yoga class back when that was all it took to relax. And as though a preordained response, a broad angle of light began streaming through the triple-hung windows that were fitted with antiquated wavy glass panes, the type she had until then only read about. The radiant infusion, a strong dose of early summer sun, had managed to soften both the situation and the stranger before her. It also seemed to remove the last of the awkwardness between them, perhaps a sign.

Thayer replaced the bookmark, closed Hannah's book and grabbed his jacket before coming around to the front of the desk.

"Maybe you'll stay then and get to know her for both of you," Thayer stated with great feeling as he put his arms through the suit jacket. He would need to change to his summer-weight soon; the days were growing warmer.

"I presume you're ready to see your great-grandmother's cottage?" He'd exposed enough of what Hannah had confided to him …it was time for practicalities.

"I am a little anxious," she replied, stifling an inappropriate yawn from lack of sleep, hours interrupted by visions of fairytale characters and the very unpleasant one that reminded Prudence of her mother. Apparently this inheritance had managed to conjure subsurface memories, things long buried as part of her 'survival' mode, just one more layer of that protective shell she'd become so comfortable living in.

"My condolences again for your losses, Miss Stone," he voiced with sincerity as he walked her to the doorway with a troubling gait, the result of recurring bouts of arthritis. "What I hope you will understand from these documents is that although you've never before been to Maine, your roots go deep in our soil. And I promise my office will do everything possible to help you."

In that one moment as he held the door for her, Prudence thought she felt her great-grandmother's trust in him—the essence unveiled of the man he'd been before age had provided a new mask and that would simply have to suffice.

Chapter Four

The faded tree-shaped air freshener, a relic well past its time, did nothing to allay her qualms about whether the tired old sedan would make it to their destination or whether she'd succumb to one of her allergy attacks from what was left of the odd scent. Prudence kept her eyes glued to the scenery as if that would alleviate the smell, at once zeroing in on the neat farms and noble old houses. There were also huge lots, well-tended fields and those not so well kept, but with massive logs obviously waiting to be hauled, split or sawn according to plan. Suddenly Thayer took a hard left and they were within range of the water, one broad band of deep blue punctuated by small whitecaps that unfurled and furled repeatedly like ribbons on a spindle. The ultramarine color only interrupted by the plentiful trees and what he called rock cairns, built up and mossed over, and then they passed a lighthouse, smaller by far than the others that had already insinuated themselves into her mind. This one, according to its wet paint sign indicating the spruced-up condition, only added to the breathtaking beauty of the widespread scenery. The air suddenly smelled of drying seaweed—low tide—which dispelled the sickly sweet scent of the cardboard tree, something she had tried to rid by opening the window. She was totally unprepared for the rest; hadn't seen photographs in any family album which would have detailed the insouciant framework of Oyster Cove. It was utterly peaceful and to the naked eye nearly asleep with a carefree arrogance defying change. She had periodically glanced at the little regional map resting on her lap again cursing the stupidity of wearing linen, following along as he'd driven the many bends and turns on what looked like a long, knobby-fingered peninsula with the village planted at its end. She had never imagined any of it. Not even the lawyer's lengthy letter or the time spent in his office had so much as hinted that Hannah's house at 18

Thatcher Lane would rather defiantly straddle layers of ledge as though it had grown through it. Or that the laid-back neighborhood was such a dizzying composition and, yes in places, a funky mix of materials and design. Houses set along the water's edge in an off-the-beaten hamlet nestled in the hands of time, a place she would soon come to know.

"This is stunning!" Prudence declared of the cottage, an understatement in itself, since it was far bigger than expected, looking to be three stories though the height could be deceiving. There was a lovely covered area that he had called a veranda, which faced a seemingly active waterfront, though not as bustling as the one in Stonycroft. In the islands the word deck would have sufficed, but his choice managed to make it seem even more important than she'd let herself believe.

"That it is, Miss Stone, but as I already mentioned, it will require a bit of work to bring it back up to par. The roof seems fine enough, at least for now, but the clapboards will need scraping and painting and also some of those scallop-shaped shingles along the uppermost portion above the wood, have begun to warp. I believe the chimney is intact although you may want to bring in a mason to be sure; have him check for cracks in the mortar and moisture or discoloration and the lining as well; make sure it's all sealed. I haven't really assessed the interior the way a realtor would either so I'm not certain how you'll feel about the inside. I also hope all of this expenditure won't cause you too much difficulty, but I'm afraid Mrs. Ellison's estate was nearly bare except for property; not much extra except to pay for taxes and legal fees."

Prudence accepted that no matter what he'd already told her, she hadn't completely understood about this gift. And though not suspecting any misappropriation of funds from the elder woman's account, she would need to be mindful of how often she called upon him for assistance. Hourly consulting fees were not budgeted into her proceeds from Julie and she was reluctant to tap into the funds from her father's life insurance too often in case of an emergency.

"Also, I thought it might be practical to introduce yourself to both Aurora Durn and Jean Bond. I became so sidetracked with the other matters that I neglected to mention them back in my office. They were not only Hannah's neighbors but also her close friends for a great many years and I had recently heard through my secretary that Aurora might be moving soon. They were part of the trio that included your great-grandmother…the 'widows of Thatcher Lane'…Hannah loved to say as if they were a dance troop or something. A sisterhood she called it, especially needed in those difficult early years."

"Thank you; that's very nice of you." *Don't know what I'll say to them,* she thought trying to picture friends of a woman she had no clue about, never once imagining their importance to her newly acquired residence.

No matter her very first impressions, Byron Thayer had proved to be a courtly man through and through and after crossing the threshold in front of her, he placed a very old and weighty key in her palm and closed her fingers around it…a surprising fatherly gesture. The key felt comforting, a little like the locket but without a sense of heat emanating from it, but it felt like it belonged in her hand. Before she could comment, her gaze fell upon an iron pot, soot-black like the stove it sat on. "What on earth is that for?" she asked.

"We use them here in the winter mostly; helps to humidify the air or can be filled with spices like cinnamon and cloves for a festive holiday scent, something your great-grandmother used to do actually. But there's plenty of moisture here with the sea blasting in."

The teapot shaped container rested on the back of the wood burning stove that protruded from the fireplace surround and sat on a small slab of slate in what he called the 'parlor'. First impressions weren't always the best; the inside was definitely not 'stunning', at least not to her island-oriented taste and her

41

mind flew into decorating mode before she could take control of it.

"I'm not so sure about that stove, maybe I could remove it..." she paused, hoping she hadn't sounded ungrateful.

"Whatever you think, Miss Stone, it is your house now," he politely replied, the ancient stove no longer his purview. There had been many a day he'd been required to tinker with it when Hannah couldn't manage and he'd been happy to help. The house hadn't changed much since he'd begun his business relationship with her even though he had, something he noted without rebuke each time he looked in the mirror these days for it no longer seemed to matter. She had on one occasion paid him the compliment of looking dapper when he'd shown up in a new suit. Back then he also had more hair and was quite a bit trimmer than he is now, the fault of a bachelor's bad eating habits. Hannah couldn't have known what her remark had done for his ego, but he had used many excuses over the years for dropping off anything of legal importance if he were to be in the vicinity or even a book on his secretary's behalf since she too relished good books. He enjoyed being here and she'd always made him feel welcome, pulling out the tea fixings as if he were a special guest.

How well did he really know great-grandmother Ellison, Prudence wondered, sensing perhaps a sudden change in his bearing?

"I'll just wait here if you don't mind?" he offered from the foot of the stairs as he continued to take in the familiar front room.

See what the rest looks like before you judge, she admonished before speaking up. "It definitely has a homey quality and really a lot bigger than anything I'd expected," she said as she walked into the very old-fashioned parlor, her new 'living room'. She saw nothing of distinction that would give away the years of refurbishing that Thayer had talked about; the distasteful conditions Hannah had taken on after James Prescott.

42

No leftover signs of family activities, no dents from moving furniture about. Everything appeared well-ordered for the singular life that was Hannah's these many years, though the rugs were a bit on the shabby side...*but then it's only the first floor.*

The room needed brightening in a bad way. That meant either removing the wallpaper or simply painting over it, although the woodwork was marvelous...*like one of the schooners docked in St. John or maybe it was Tortola...no matter, it's wonderful!* As her eyes followed the trim, she spotted a photograph set in a dark green frame specked with gold flecks leaned into the wall to keep it from falling from the narrow shelf. The gentleman in the picture had dark hair and mustache and a starched collar so stiff it appeared to be holding his head up.

"Am I correct, Mr. Thayer, that this would be Hannah and her family?" she asked, already recognizing her father's face in the pretty woman's although she was unable to match Ben's syrup-colored hair to the black and white image.

"Yes, that's one probably taken near the Bingham property belonging to her sister, Elisabeth. That's where they'd met and lived for a couple of years, I believe. Most of what I know of him is what I learned through Hannah at the time I became her attorney and I suppose, confidant...at least in some things.

"Hannah and Amanda had become accustomed to being on their own what with all his wheeling and dealing I guess you young people would call it. Fortunately, Hannah inherited this house even with his legal difficulties, but once she came of age, there were some bitter fights about that too. Mind you, I don't gossip, but her daughter was a spiteful young woman from everything Hannah implied; thought she was owed much. Not unlike children from any generation I suspect, given what I've been told by friends who have them."

"From what you've told me Great-grandmother was still relatively young when her husband died and yet she never remarried?"

"We only talked about that once, as I recall. You see, we were sitting out there, drinking tea—she was very fond of tea," he said, pointing toward the curtained French door that led to the veranda. "But I'll never forget the way she looked when I inquired of her future. She had been staring seaward and fondling that silver pendant, a little like you do as a matter of fact, and when she turned to me shaking her head, her eyes were so utterly sad that I never asked again. That might be just the thing to discuss with one of the ladies," he said, happy to be off the hook before he gave away too much about himself. That had been the exact moment he'd made up his mind never to fess up to his devotion to her; wouldn't have been able to bear the hurt she would have to cause him by telling him the truth. She had always looked upon him as a professional whom she'd grown fond of, nothing more. Knowing Hannah's character, she more than likely would have felt it necessary to find another attorney as well and he would have been worse off or so he'd felt at that time. Looking back, it might have been the best medicine for a troubled heart as it may have caused him to seek another, more appropriate relationship and the years since might not have been so lonely.

She picked up a hint of melancholy in his voice, sensing he'd shared that private moment at some personal cost and again wondered about his feelings for Hannah. Prudence studied the faces more closely now, particularly James Prescott's.

It's not his picture in the locket after all! A sense of relief came over her but now she was inspired; she would have to find the man that Hannah had held to her heart no matter what else happened…it was only right and that thought surprised her. After all, she hadn't even wanted to be here. "I see," she said, pretending as he spoke of Hannah that he hadn't put a small chink in his professional façade. Prudence turned without reply and wandered into the kitchen suddenly anxious to open windows and bring in the sea air. She had no intention of calling further attention to the locket although she hadn't realized till

44

now how often she'd managed to do just that. But she was almost certain Mr. Thayer had thought it merely a nice piece of jewelry without actually scrutinizing it before mailing it, especially since it wasn't easily opened. He honestly didn't seem the type to mull over a woman's locket either unless of course, it had come from him. And she didn't think there was much chance of that.

Since he was waiting, she quickly pored over the assortment of utensils and noted the aging equipment and cursorily poked through the forest green cupboards that stood out harshly on the soft-toned eggshell walls. She surveyed it all hurriedly, recognizing there was a lot to be done: change that dark heavily peeling paint, something that had probably gotten ahead of Hannah over the years; empty the cluttered pantry shelved with items that may or may not have been there a long time, not that she would take the chance and perhaps utilizing a closet-like space that was already plumbed, turning it into a stylish little powder room, especially if she intended to sell which was still in question. But if she wanted to build a nest-egg, she'd have to bring it up to date to get the biggest bang for her buck. And last but not least, she would give the wood floors throughout a good buffing as well. "I know I'm going to love the views once I get all these windows cleaned," she stated with as much positive inflection as she could muster as she retraced her steps.

"That will be ongoing, I'm afraid, what with the salt spray."

It was a daunting list and one not to be taken lightly. If nothing else, she understood hard work, an ethic engrained in her since childhood and since she was here, she would try to make the best of it…she hoped!

As she joined him, he gripped the varnished banister—which to her dismay, had no post adornment of any sort to indicate a hiding place—and hauled his uneven weight up the creaking treads to the second floor. Then, always the gentleman, he stood back while she entered the first bedroom. Prudence would have immediately known it was Hannah's. *Now this is something to rave about!* It was done up in a pale-patterned, ivory-toned wallpaper that she actually liked and housed a large sleigh-bed covered with a thick, creamy down comforter that reminded her of buttermilk. With the nights still cool, this type of cover would keep her warm and maybe even safeguard her sleep from the strange imaginings of her new surroundings.

Placed strategically in front of the window was a richly stained bentwood rocker with cane seat and back and worn curved arms where perhaps Hannah's had rested while knitting or crocheting or even reading, small telltale signs of habit. "I haven't seen one of these since I left home," she said as he stood silently by. The chair seemed situated in order to enhance the sounds of the sea or to wait for something or someone, a lonely appearance nonetheless. But a modernistic decorative touch had been created by a single curtain panel pulled back with a pretty rosebud tack that allowed the viewer just enough light and air to infiltrate at all times. In keeping with the color scheme, a deep pink chenille throw appeared to have been flung over one of the arms and had nearly slipped to the floor. It practically invited her to pick it up and she instinctively placed it around her shoulders. It was as comforting as the key; it too belonged there. *There is something going on in this house,* she contemplated as she wandered about the tidied room *and it's definitely not ghosts* she scolded since she didn't believe in them. She folded the soft wrap and placed it back on the chair without questioning Mr. Thayer.

The adjoining bathroom was almost as interesting as the bedroom. An ancient claw-foot tub that should have been prominent, now played second fiddle to what must have been a more recently installed geriatric shower enclosure opposite, complete with seat and grip bars, after all great-grandmother was ninety-three. The room seemed to be a repository for a cache of outdated appointments: a small assortment of mercury glass containers that were being used to hold personal grooming tools; a slightly tarnished brush and mirror and a small mirrored tray trimmed in silver. It was all of a bygone era and still looked

46

romantic to Prudence because of the sun from the little window that sprinkled light over them. These were definitely not items to be discarded for they provided the first small pathway into Hannah's tastes, objects at least to bring substance to the woman Prudence had never met.

Mr. Thayer looking a little more uncomfortable in Hannah's personal quarters, stood by as she moved to the second bedroom accompanied by the sound of creaking from the darkly painted floorboards.

"Do you think this will be a problem?" she asked, emphasizing her footsteps as she moved to the next room hoping she had not disturbed anything that may have been quietly sleeping in a place of ownership. She immediately pictured mice or bats perhaps in the rafters she couldn't see.

"I don't think it's something to worry about, really; mine do the same thing. Unless you feel something actually loose, of course. These boards contract and expand with the weather; think of it as just another part of old-house upkeep."

Expecting this next room to be similar to Hannah's, it was charmingly all dressed in pale yellow paint with simple white floorboards and trim. "What a pretty room!" She emphasized without need of reply as she took in the white furniture, some of it very old wicker. Considering the main floor and the heavier looking pieces throughout, it was so far the gayest part of the house. To Prudence it spoke of the daydreams of a young girl...*Amanda's room, maybe, during better times.* There was a smaller three-piece bathroom between it and a third room devoid of bedroom furniture, possibly a sewing room. Or it may have simply been a room without an actual purpose, as though the owner had run out of funds or the heart to fix it up. It was hard to tell.

"Where do these stairs lead?"

"I think it's simply a storage closet of some sort, but I never had any reason to go up there until Hannah passed and then found out the door was locked...Hannah wasn't into locking her doors and I always knew where she kept the original front door key, the one I gave to you. The two other doors downstairs from the remodeling, are the only ones she had keys made for at my insistence I must add, since times are changing, but she never used them.

"She'd say things like *'who'd want my old stuff'*. You must understand your great-grandmother could be pretty stubborn and of course, nothing ever did happen," he offered. "But that lock up there is also meant for the old-fashioned type key. There was nothing else in the safe deposit box other than papers relating to the house, which of course, I shall turn over to you."

"Well, I guess that's something I can deal with later on and thank you by the way, for having someone clean up here after Hannah died." Prudence replied, grateful not to have to pull out bucket and mop on her first night.

"You're welcome. My secretary handled this as well. She thought it would make it easier on you to have a properly refreshed bedroom and bath to enable you to move right in. Good old Mrs. Lawton has been with me for more than fifteen years and always knows just who to call in these kinds of situations. But she only asked them to do your basic broom-clean downstairs, presuming there would be many other things you'd prefer to handle yourself with regard to your own tastes and so on."

"That was enough, really," Prudence replied, recalling Thayer's original letter and copy of the certificate stating a worn-out heart had caused Hannah's death and the wonderfully efficient secretary had also at his behest, handled the mortuary, cremation and disposition of Hannah's ashes, leaving her with none of the morbid doings that she'd already had her fill of. "I'll be sure to catch Mrs. Lawton when she returns from vacation and thank her personally, but the first thing I have to do is put in some food and organize the kitchen so I can have a place to work from."

Indicating with a wave of hand that also managed to control the misplaced hairs on his thinning pate, "As to the shopping, that shouldn't be any problem for you; there's a village market with most everything and plenty of fresh seafood available down at the town wharf, all within a do-able walking distance. A big box store and grocery are out on Route 1, which you'll see on our way back to my office to pick up your rental and by then you should be familiar enough with the way to get what you need on your own," he finalized.

She had been taking clues from his behavior all day and thought she understood what Hannah felt when dealing with this unusual man…a sense of duty that extended even to her…more than she could have asked for in the circumstance.

The tasks multiplied in her head as she drove slowly back to the Cove, concerned she would get lost even with good directions. She was totally exhausted; overwhelmed to be correct and opening the front door alone felt as though she'd entered another universe. *What am I doing here, of all places?* She contemplated as she unwrapped the few groceries to get her off the ground and running. Tonight's big dinner would, however, only be a turkey sandwich; there wasn't an ounce of energy in her weary body for figuring out anything more complex than that. And the kitchen needed so much help that in her present state she couldn't begin to formulate a plan. Instead, she unpacked a heavier sweater leaving the rest for later and pulled the covers off the deck chairs, happy to see Hannah had chosen them for comfort.

Yesterday's wind had already turned soft and as she busied herself building a large sandwich to take outside, she turned on the old cream-colored radio tucked into the counter wall. Twisting the dial until she'd found an 'easy listening' station, she noted the missing lilt in the announcers' voices, words without the accustomed accents and a fresh pang of homesickness bottomed out in her empty stomach. *I can do this,* she affirmed picking up her plate and walking outside but keeping the door to the deck open so the music would follow.

She didn't know how long she'd nodded off, but the air had a different tang and an odd sound seemed to be coming from the middle of nowhere. The sky had such a strange appearance, thickly massed and dull white but tinged with the earlier sunlight and beginning to consume the nearby stretches of water visible from Hannah's deck, the 'out to sea' vista the lawyer had highlighted. Shaking herself from the rumpled slump she'd become without intention, crumbs flew everywhere; she'd dozed off with half the sandwich lying unopposed on her lap. It had turned stale from the damp all around her. *That's incoming fog*, she realized, moving back inside with the somnolence of a body craving sleep in a room that had made her welcome. Practically undressing on the way, the only thought in her head was sinking into that big bed. *I feel like I could sleep for a week.*

The wind which apparently hadn't abated for long startled her awake; scared up the old bones of the house creaking and wheezing with the effort. She'd been having fitful dreams, but this time they were minus Alice and rabbit hole. Instead it was the woman in the photo mouthing words she couldn't hear, a look of sadness on her pretty face. She must have fallen back to sleep because by the time first light entered the bedroom, Prudence felt less a stranger there than she could have anticipated the day before.

Prudence soon found that home ownership meant visits to the town office, two banks and a few more trips to Mr. Thayer's office. With so much to do, there was little time for conversations with her best friend. But whenever possible, the growing attachment to the locket and the often thought of 'presence' in the house were what took center stage. Prudence assured Julie that it was no more than a sensation but that Great-grandmother must have had an 'agenda' in bequeathing her the house, because as far as Prudence was concerned, her soul still lingered. At least that's the way Ben used to talk when someone died before 'matters' were settled, whatever that meant. Julie really loved all things supernatural, otherworldly and just plain weird so whatever conclusions Prudence offered would peak her interest. That's how they'd ended up at the West Indian woman's lair in the first place because Julie had wanted a 'reading' done as soon as the locket arrived and had urged a very reluctant Prudence to partake.

"Maybe you just need to find out whose face it is that Hannah chose for the locket; that might make everything much clearer," Julie suggested. "Let me go back to Analese and talk with her."

"I'd actually forgotten her name, but go for it if it makes you happy. Tell her there might be a spirit in the house—please no ghosts hovering—just an unsettled soul and see what she thinks," Prudence said, chuckling as she put down the phone. These calls always occurred later in the evening by which time she would be overly tired and in her susceptibility, her dreams would be invaded by long ago island lore bordering on similar topics…the ghost of a woman roaming a cane field all night searching for the baby that she'd birthed there (now that was a story) or the ghosts watching from the 'spirit' trees. How could she not have disturbing dreams!

Besides catering to Julie's supernatural proclivities, Prudence needed to find a second-hand car; the rental would become highly prohibitive very soon. And while she was sensing a bit of male patronization, she tried to point out the Mainers' frugality running through her veins which often had little or no effect and the task went on. Her feminist mentality would rise to the surface and then she would think of Ben and 'deal' with the situation in a way he would have expected. Even now, she would forget he was actually gone and have the receiver in her hand before realizing and her loss would kick in all over again.

Early into the third week according to the angry red marks on the kitchen calendar and having lost a lot of her patience and good will, she had inadvertently wandered down a disarmingly pretty dirt road and been lured toward a playfully dappled stretch of wildflowers. She had picked some to take home, admired them as a whole and then when about to leave, spotted something bright red and too big to be a flower. Drawn by that bold paper tag, she found a faded and squat little car deep within the blooming rainbow thickness and all but swallowed by the growth. *Look at this old heap,* she thought, remembering how she had first learned to drive a stick shift. Had she not noticed the uncharacteristic color on the side window peeking through all the other dainty pale ones, the car may have remained that way until its white body was disguised by winter snow.

And not only had the makeshift tag been stuck on by duct tape, there was more of it patching the upholstery and even the door handles and dashboard. *This must be an omen of some kind; there's probably a roll of it in every island household...maybe here too.* Feeling more confident, she called the childishly scrawled phone number and happily, the owner would practically give the car away just to get it hauled off the property...before his rambunctious kids turned it into a playhouse.

Living in the islands had taught her resourcefulness among other things and she had done well with similar 'clunkers', nothing fancy just functional and subjected to the same emblematic saltwater spray as noted here. And though having to bear up under the stern gaze (at least at first) of the frizzy-haired auto mechanic down at the corner Gulf station thinking her to be just another annoying 'outlander' no matter her ties to Maine, he proved to be really good at his job. The little car, its original pearl white body badly dimmed by age and freckled with rust and now minus most of the tape, actually ran quite well with his help, if not his verbosity.

'Ayuh', was all he would answer without further elaboration to just about any question. She finally realized it was just his way and she honestly believed he was beginning to soften, even told her to call him Zack once he'd begun to attack the rattling in what she said sounded to her like a lawn mower engine. He was definitely smitten with the tiny VW Beetle, even made a few house calls taking it for a spin—'just need to make sure it's runnin' good' is all he'd say as though his reputation depended on it. Of course, Julie had to put it into Pru's head that his devotion to the car might also have something to do with being smitten with her. After that Prudence couldn't look at him without blushing. But now because of his care she more easily explored the environs of Oyster Cove hoping to dispel the remoteness and isolation from all that she loved. And the pampered little vehicle sat pompously in the tire paths of previous autos, displaying its newly elevated status. It had become a most appropriate appendage as it blended especially well with the house under an umbrella of a settling fog. Just as Prudence was also falling prey to the nature of this frequent coastal phenomenon.

Solace by the sea…the unexpected mantra upon waking each morning. The days have tumbled conspiratorially into weeks and all of them have drawn her in closer to this house on the ledge and have suddenly overshadowed many of her original concerns. She is no longer surrounded by shadow images of fronds swaying in a balmy breeze that once rustled filmy cotton curtains, but by the antiquated and fading paper on walls groaning against the wind and often engulfed by a thick gray mist. Even the weather has become a fascination to someone used to seasons that never changed more noticeably than the minor drop in temperature during the Christmas winds or high humidity before an impending hurricane. Every day brought an element of surprise and even the weathermen seemed hard pressed to get it right. Prudence has acclimated to a degree with so much to be accomplished, and while she had learned a lot of 'do it yourself' skills with the plenitude of jobs prior to the bookstore, especially with regard to boats and woodworking, she hadn't really been prepared for this. Initially, there'd been a plugged water line and then a leaking pipe; a couple of rotting deck boards and soon after that, the replacement of an old commode. And then as if by magic or perhaps just from the doing and planning and breathtaking vistas, the actuality of ownership has taken hold and Hannah's house and its surrounds a source of unanticipated joy. The cottage, even with all its warts and flaws, righteously belongs in this stoic and unpretentious location, one as idyllic and filled with antediluvian ways as her own idealistic nature could have ever hoped for. And surprisingly when many of those initial concerns and at least a lot of the homesickness had finally subsided, she understood that no prediction however stated in the fateful letter from Mr. Thayer could have foretold any of it.

The Cove itself is remarkably blessed with many natural gifts, some that are actually portrayed through a few small, minor works of art that had been left to her, ones on the walls for so long that if she removes them, the wallpaper beneath will look brand new. Hannah's selection were mostly watercolors, perhaps something that may have even influenced a very young Ben Stone.

Prudence astutely recognized how the entire area justly pays homage to many of the famous paintings of Maine by artists like Bricker, Kent or Homer. Names she had only a passing knowledge of and that only because of the books Julie had chosen for their artist clientele. But many of those works depicting the sea were already coming to life right outside her windows, far from the prominent gallery walls and gussied up by the dictates of nature's orchestra—iambic pentameters of water and rock uniting. The ocean, each day a panoply of colors: steel-edged greens, obsidian-tinted grays, or melancholy shades of cobalt and often emboldened with storm surges; all of it somehow matching or contradicting her changing moods as if it could hear each one in her breathing. They are emotional swings and always momentary and mostly due to the concerns about staying in this new territory away from all that had once been unhampered by domestic occurrences. And just when she has thoughts of giving up, familiar tropical scents of briny spray will permeate the air and seep through the pores of the house. That tang that floats in like downy matter is far stronger here in Maine and yet it often feels like a visit from an old friend, a needed cure-all for whatever might ail her and most days that is simply the need for answers.

Chapter Five

The charm and eccentricities of Hannah's cottage—a strange mix of Victorian and God knows what—have made her laugh and cry and at times nearly brought Prudence to her knees. The commemorative treasure (like a smooth stone left in sunlight), the one with the man's photo inside, is continually around her neck just as it was Hannah's, the quest for his identity never far from Pru's thoughts. And as per Mr. Thayer's suggestion, Prudence at last found time to call on one of Hannah's dearest friends, the very endearing ninety-year-old Aurora Durn.

No taller than five-one and once unwrapped from her immediate bafflement, the tiny woman looking up at her had stated with some certainty that Prudence bore a great similarity to her late relative. But that wasn't until Aurora figured out that the young woman on her doorstep wasn't there to repair the television. It obviously hadn't been a good morning for Aurora; the set was on the blink and she'd opened the door with a hopeful expression only to be disappointed and then like a child, delighted. Dressed in a forties style print cotton jumper loosely slipped over a white short-sleeved tee shirt that exposed thin arms that to Pru's surprise, easily reached out to hug. From that day on Aurora's appearance remained that of an angelic tree-top ornament with fluffy gray hair held by sparkling bobbles—girlish barrettes—attempting without success to hold at bay the unruly curls framing her innocent face.

It soon became obvious that the diminutive widow had difficulty staying on topic and would just as easily fade in and out of conversations sometimes to their mutual frustration, but that mattered less than the fact she'd been Hannah's best friend for many years. However improbable, Prudence intuited that she would soon become one of hers.

She quickly discovered that Aurora preferred Monday mornings for these visits, something she chose to establish right away. She didn't want to be interrupted during afternoon programming, one of the small habits of the very old according to Aurora's niece, Kitty, whose curly hair was the only recognizable family trait. She had mentioned this soon as they'd met and that other mornings were occupied with a few home-help aides and drop-in visits to evaluate Aurora's stability. She was engaged in moving her aunt to the top of the list at a county facility that specialized in the various stages of the aging mind with different help at each juncture. There were small apartments and assisted living spaces and then should the mental acuity change for the worse, housing to keep the residents safe from harm with a full-time staff to attend to their needs. Prudence had been made aware that thoughts of Aurora being on her own very much longer had become a constant worry and the wait had already gone on too long.

Certain mornings the little widow could be very talkative, something Prudence had already surmised would only happen in her own good time no matter how much she prodded. And to her dismay, so far Aurora hadn't divulged the one thing she craved...knowledge of the locket's history. But it was obvious that Aurora missed Hannah a great deal, and sometimes when she wasn't quite as lucid as one hoped, she even mistook Prudence for her old friend. It was touchingly sad and yet no matter their conversation or the immediacy Prudence was seeking, whatever was gleaned from them, was given from a true friend's perspective. And considering Aurora's age and condition, all of it was a blessing. Today appeared to be one of those times and Prudence was savoring every word. *The widow Durn has been keeping secrets too,* she thought nearly holding her breath for more on this, her fourth visit.

"Hannah married that man after he sold her a bill of goods about what their future would be like; all rosy and wonderful don't you know, filling her head with images of the big house near the water. What he hadn't told her was that the house was falling apart and they were already up to the seawalls in debt,"

58

she said putting down a little two-cup pot of tea with a heavy hand as if for emphasis. "Hannah had to work at the Post Office to make ends meet," Aurora continued, a little of her disdain creating a certainty Prudence hadn't expected.

"What happened to little Amanda?" she asked wondering if Aurora could put that in context. "Great-gran's attorney hinted there might have been some trouble between them," she said choosing words that might open a new door so she wouldn't have to wait for another doled-out crumb even though she truly looked forward to the visits.

"Don't know if I should be the one to tell personal things, but I guess you can't ask anybody else now can you?"

It was always surprising to her that Aurora could be so feisty when least expected, could turn a look on you that meant business and yet down deep, she was so very loving. *Must be an age thing, or maybe a 'Maine' thing...God, one more THING to learn!* "Well, I did go see Mrs. Bond," Prudence reminded knowing Aurora hardly seemed fond of talking about her. "But truth be told, she was a little 'stiff' I guess you'd say, when I introduced myself and when she noticed Hannah's locket, she nearly slammed the door in my face," Prudence added hoping to elicit sympathy but also some answers. The 'other' widow had been downright rude.

"Yep, that would do it," Aurora answered, taking on a strange expression. "She can't bear to see it; just brings her back to a very unpleasant time in her life, all thanks to our Hannah," she offered with a wink that transformed her manners from vinegar to honey all at once. Switching fast enough to cause whiplash, she picked up the loose thread. "Amanda came back to the Cove as soon as Hannah got things squared with the house, around age twelve I think and it was a rough few years for your Great-gran, that's for sure," Aurora said leaving Mrs. Bond in the dust.

"She was an unruly child; had her mother's looks, but her father's deplorable temperament. I remember that word like it was yesterday, 'deplorable' is what our Hannah said when she talked about 'James Prescott'. How she hated the way he bragged and made himself so important.

"Poor woman really tried, but the girl was too willful. It was actually better for everyone when Amanda ran away to get married and I don't say that lightly," she assured her while removing the teacups, shooing Prudence out kindly...the 'session' was over.

For all her smallness, Aurora was one tough cookie, Prudence acknowledged, thankful to be on her good side. But even if this was Ben's mother being spoken of, she would continue to pursue the answers to the numerous questions in her mental queue waiting their turn with Aurora; it's just how it was. And then she realized the old gal was talking to herself and closed the door gently as she left.

Walking down the lane toward home...a difficult reference for Prudence to use. She hoped time would make the difference. *Still easier to call it Hannah's,* she mused as always after a stint with Aurora. It appeared that she might be doomed to wonder about the way the locket had come into her possession. It was something that Hannah might have given her years before, a gift to lay claim to another generation, even entice Prudence to visit. *If only I could get Aurora to open up.* But Hannah obviously had not been ready to part with it until absolutely necessary for any reason which seemed to agree with Thayer's assessment. Prudence was certain that its meaning was more than an ornamental one coveted by a woman's desire to adorn herself. If the gift had only been the earrings or even a brooch, it might not have caused so much consternation. But between the mysterious photo and the way the metal had grabbed her complete attention that first night at the Salter Inn, she couldn't help herself...it was almost all she did think about, at least when she wasn't knee deep in some household project. Admittedly, she was becoming awfully attached to the place and Oyster Cove and every so often caught herself questioning whether she really wanted to put it up for sale.

However, as she often hoped, perhaps on a clear day—an incongruous thought with regard to Aurora's present state of mind—she would be able to fill in the missing links. But then again, would what's behind that locked door house the answers? Short of finding the key, she might have to wait an awfully long time if it is all left to Hannah's best friend and she wondered whether that might be part of the grand scheme of things. *The more time I'm here, the harder to leave.*

She looked up, feeling the damp before she actually saw the wet mist beginning to weave through the spaces between the houses. It was a sight she was becoming used to but it still fascinated her. At the moment, it was draping the edges of gutters and shakes daintily, like a filmy mantilla on a foreign bride. She knew within moments, it will have consumed the entire lane and blocked out the view of the waterfront and embosomed all of Oyster Cove.

Then the wind picked up speed and the mist blew through and swallowed the trees, dimming her cottage with its ethereal net, easily transporting her to an imagined time when it was Hannah's world. Then she heard the responding call of the foghorn in the distance and was again strangely soothed by its presence. *What was it like Great-gran?* Those melancholy strains, the now familiar muffled bellow that interrupts sleep along with the groan and rumble of hardworking engines? *Did you also have the momentary intrusion on the verge of the last edges of a dream, comforting sounds of motors…hardworking fishermen borne along on cresting waves?* Prudence listened to the repetitive haunting sound, touching the locket just in case even though it hadn't 'spoken' to her in that demanding way since the very first night on Maine soil.

It's such a bleating forlorn note; going to be like pea soup out there today, she thought watching as it became dense and weighty…navigating would be a rough slog for anyone in these conditions, even walking in it was full of surprises. She had come to understand a few of the difficulties when she'd first met some of the lobstermen. She often stopped to watch them loading their traps and lollipop-colored buoys down at the wharf and they sometimes seemed flattered by her inquisitiveness, though they didn't say much. But she'd overheard an exchange one morning that gave her a small window into their world, a harrowing story of engine trouble in the thick of things and the difficulties of being found without being easily seen and knowing they would definitely need those bright markers today.

All those names, she reflects quizzically...*The Maggie and Alice; Maggie Too; The Martha B; Mary's Choice, even the Hanna*...the women rule! But having previously been so indoctrinated to the swooshing of sails (boats with names like *Wind Song, Whistler* or *Breezy*) tacking for home on a turquoise and emerald sea, she is surprisingly consoled by all the chugging, cranking, clattering noises that are part of each day. These sounds often bleed through the partially open window during the first groggy, not-quite-awake edges of dawn set in this northern terrain and offer a close-to-shore din as well as the likely sight of orange and yellow slicker-clad silhouettes poking determinedly through the wall of gray.

It has all ensnared her as naturally as the sea creatures were caught in their lair: the sensuous, lifting fog that selfishly relinquishes the broad stretches of granite; the long gentle rollers that rise and glide forward in greeting, washing it briefly before falling back like the sounds of a soft prayer in the outdoor temple...a quiet kiss goodbye. These are the moments of grace she has been gifted. In each case, she has found one more thing to gush over while lighting a romantic and fortifying fire in the now open hearth after the soul-searching removal of the untidy stove (silently asking for Hannah's forgiveness beforehand). And because the first days of good weather as witnessed in the attorney's office were an introduction and not a testimony of certainty, there have been many such fires to take the damp away and dream. She has done her best to make the house feel like her own and yet there is something so very comforting when she sits in this room as though the woman she never knew might be watching over her. And she is intent on making friends with her.

"You should see the gulls here, Jules; they're huge, not like our squawky terns at all. They're like a mass of origami creatures trailing the fishing boats, noisily hovering over the day's catch; they're everywhere," Prudence exclaimed from her place in front of the fire, having just filled her in on the visit with Aurora over a glass of red wine.

"Prudence, you always surprise me," Julie said from her office where she'd been working late. She'd been getting updates every week like clockwork but she was usually home sipping along with Prudence. It was their way of having cocktail hour together.

"Then let me surprise you with more. I'm certain there is a connection between this locket and Great-gran's living here alone all these years. She could have moved from Thatcher Lane like Aurora is about to. Mr. Thayer would certainly have assisted her in any change. I feel it in my bones…unless that's just the damp air I'm not used to," she quipped.

"Does this mean you're no longer head-over-teakettle in love with the place?" Julie asked.

"Doesn't that sound like something these old gals would say? I know I was reluctant to come, but with each visit with my great-gran's friend, I feel a little closer to her and this place and I LOVE the fog!

"Everything is completely different but it's just as beautiful. Remember how impressed we were with those giant boulders that formed the caves on Virgin Gorda? Well, out my back door, I can find ones that look like flinty old broads with surf-stained skirts watching over the coastline. Wait till you see this place, Jules, you absolutely have to come," she raved again. "My imagination has run wild; the place is just the opposite of all the soft edges I think of when missing the islands. I don't know how to explain it, other than it feels very protective."

"God, Pru, I hope you're writing all of this down. Next thing you know, I'm going to have to carry a book of musings by Prudence Stone!"

"You're a real hoot, but let's face it, it really speaks to me...maybe just because of my ancestors, I don't know."

"Yes, Prudence, and you're just as wacky as you ever were and I miss you lots...now, goodnight."

Prudence sputtered a failed 'raspberry' into the receiver and hung up as Julie was choking on her drink with laughter. *That'll teach her,* she laughed and then remembered about the shell she'd found the day before. She always told Julie about the finds from her mini field trips. When tired of scraping paint or laying new cupboard paper and not wanting to give up one of Hannah's exercise habits...the walks that in the years before their bones became too brittle for sure-footedness and those widowed friends covered every inch of shoreline...Prudence has begun duplicating the same route. She uses this unfettered time away from the house to clear her head and put the days into perspective. There was so much that could and did go wrong in an old property, one she is now responsible for, and that tromping about was the best way she knew to deal with it. She had quite unwittingly discovered a larger than usual depression—a free-form tide pool—one of many along the ledges that can offer up the pretty collectibles with each new wave. She can be easily spotted roaming along with an old bucket, determined to find the unexpected. Maybe even a little something special she can give to darling Aurora for instigating the whole thing.

From those little outings, Prudence had acquired a dazzling sea glass collection that now has pride of place in the tiny powder room just off the kitchen, the room that finally came to fruition through hours and days of hard work and a little creativity. Add to that the newly collected round-bottomed shell—a wonderful container for frequently gathered oddments of colored glass—and it is simply perfection on the square decoupage tray. This prize from a neighborhood yard sale just last weekend. These gatherings seem to be a popular pastime in the village and a great way to meet new people. For now, however, the bright display sits upon what was once merely a stool that she has painted a deep charcoal and even without provenance, the old piece of furniture stands out handsomely against the textured white wallpaper with its embossed Victorian pattern.

During her search for the unusual, hoping to put her stamp on the house, she'd come across a charmingly and somewhat swanky fixture for the now patched and repainted ceiling. And like a child, she flips the light switch on and off to watch the way the small metal circles with their hanging crystal 'tears' appear to shimmer like the fringe of a flapper's dress. The contrived décor reminds her of a tiny ballroom—all black, white and gray—a tuxedo with glitter that may have been brushed from a partner's ball gown. It matters not that the rings are slightly off-center, something that probably happened when stuffed into someone's storage box for too long; only that it makes her smile.

The plain wood-trimmed window faces seaward and doesn't need softening by a distracting curtain. It had been cracked open throughout the redecorating, not only to let the paint fumes escape, but to also let in all of the noises associated with the waterfront. Not at all surprising, it was the heavy-breasted herring gulls mewling and screeching and vying for food and creating minor dramatic vignettes that had occasionally stopped her paintbrush in mid-air. Had made her pause from whatever she was doing because of the sounds which might have been a group of disagreeable shrews on an outing instead of simply noisy birds. She is helpless in their presence and can only laugh out loud at their scene-stealing antics. They are a hand wave away, harping for leftovers or cannily riding atop foamy crests.

They soar over treetops and perch on rooftops or harbor pilings like sentinels awaiting the fleet.

Much against Aurora's advice knowing as she did what could happen, Prudence has blundered into an unlikely adoption by putting out that first piece of bread for the already overfed, very regal, bright-eyed repeat offender who taps at the kitchen window each and every morning, setting herself upon a deck rail as though her due. She looks at Prudence through her beady eye tilting her head just so, as telling as anything...the Cove is obviously a sanctuary for them both.

Pru's calls to Julie are filled with it all and when tired of hearing about seagulls and salt air, Julie stops her mid-sentence as only a good friend can, in order to talk about whomever she might be dating at the moment. It is never a live-in, however, her attitude against that sharpened when she saw what happened to her best friend because of the despicable Mr. Spronk. Or they might even spend an entire hour discussing food because of the many differences and Pru's lack of knowledge when it comes to the northern white fish, leaving them no better off than when they'd started.

In the meantime she is adjusting, working her way slowly through the emotional demons and only faltering when she sees a couple wandering the shore hand in hand and thoughts of Jason invade her protected space. This hardened spit of land is slowly becoming a place where she can create, if only in her mind, the closeness of the woman who possessed the fortitude to live in this manner. Through it all...the sorting, cleaning, rummaging and getting-to-know the structure, she has begun to sense some organic formula tethering her future to this same spot. And while Julie pretends to understand, it is apparent to both of them that Oyster Cove is winning this newest battle for Pru's heart.

There is still much to be done, of course; small repairs doled out to whomever is available in a location that caters to the seasonal people and the short time in which to perform them. She has already learned that a day blessed by good weather for

66

perhaps bass fishing, would take precedence over a leaky pipe in need of repair. And if her needs were bunched up with the rest of those of the neighborhood, their prayed-for rainy days could cause a difficult chain reaction with everyone vying for top spot and nothing at all getting done. But she has recently been out 'scouting' for the right contractor to hire since the rest of the repairs are too big for the usual cottage handyman. She will need to dip into savings but her new acquaintance at the bank must walk her through the means to do that.

Prudence, always a list-maker, has made many and filled them with a multitude of mundane tasks yet to be accomplished inside this secretive-seeming place, a house that surely must hold answers it has so far refused to give up. She keeps the questions compartmentalized, as she must in order to proceed. Otherwise she would accomplish nothing at all because the need to know what took place here years ago would be all consuming. *You've become like a dog with a bone, niggling and scratching.* Of course, there might not have been any of these musings had the door not been locked or had she found the key, but that has made the situation much more tantalizing for her fertile mind.

Prudence has no illusions about belonging either; not the way she felt comfortable in the islands, at least not yet. And there are many residents of Thatcher Lane and the entire village for that matter that still do not know her other than to extend a cordial greeting. But she's grateful for those who are reaching out and making her feel at home, except of course Mrs. Bond, the one person who might make a difference. But this inclusion is something she has begun to crave *when* she allows herself to think about it.

She also now recognizes her newly emerging personality for what it is, one in which she is less bewildered and no longer so adrift. And this is not just because of the usual culprits like time-consuming and interesting projects or those acquaintances with different mores or even because of the blossoming friendship with Aurora. It is in the things she still keeps to herself…the

67

imagined whispers…*gentle susurrations*…heard in the waves that nuzzle the shore as in hushed conversations between friends. They beg discovery and she is resigned to follow through, convinced by her own imaginings that it is all innately tied to the cherished locket and the comforting warmth she waits to feel again.

Chapter Six

Lawns of lush, velvety green, and all painstakingly manicured, act as buffers between the notable houses spread the length of Barnabus Road. This dead end street located two long blocks away from the water on the high side of the Cove is where Herman Jenkins could often be found making his mark. He'd been tackling an extensive rehab project on a particularly large house on the corner lot when he'd first spied the young woman taking it all in. He believed he knew everyone up and down these streets, having done work for most all of them over the years, so at first he presumed she may have been a renter or houseguest in one of the tinier dwellings on the shore. They got a lot of visitors down here during the summer and his attention should have been on the worm-eaten railing, a difficult replication because of the way it had been set upon the wrap-around veranda instead of an ogling newcomer with the persistent presence. The rail had originally been decorated with a highly intricate trim line and each time he'd take a break out of frustration, scratching his head in dismay, he would catch her watching.

Even from a distance this eager stranger looked to be familiarizing herself with the neighborhood streets, taking note of the small blue and white signs that pointed the direction to little galleries and stores throughout the village. She smelled the flowers or simply gazed wide-eyed at the grander homes, those he'd been proud to work on. He then began to notice that she was passing by most every day and obviously had found something fascinating in what he was doing. She'd hang back well out of the way as he attacked the old deck boards with the thud of his heavy hammer, the 'thwack' reverberating across the fronting expanse of unadulterated green.

This one was a stately house, the type he loved best and part of the remaining few of its kind set away from the water's edge that still possessed a 'widow's walk'. He hadn't wanted to stare, was far too busy anyway; but from where he'd stood, she always appeared mesmerized by it in the dreamy way she peered upward. He could almost feel the 'sigh' from a distance. So he might not have been surprised had he been able to read her thoughts.

Prudence had truly been awestruck from the moment she'd seen what had been taking place not far from Great-gran's house, by the dignity of the tired old structure being remodeled and what her imagination could project from it. Actually, she had been wishing—not once realizing he'd caught her watching—that she'd been allotted one of those stylish platforms remembered from some architectural volume in Ben's vast library years before. Stirred by many of her favorite books, something that wasn't obvious to a watchful eye, she had been concocting her own story...*she is there on that special perch and wearing the pretty straw hat to protect against the heat, its flowing yellow ribbon streaming out on the wind. It would have been a gift from the man she would be waiting for, the sails of his ship appearing on the horizon toward home as she shields her eyes against the sun's glare*...the rest is yet to come.

The Cove had spontaneously ignited her highly active imagination, especially after so many years having submitted to the lure of West Indian folklore and it was not difficult to pretend a life that would take place within that landmark building. After all, she had been a bookseller as well as a diligent reader. But as she studied the way that the muscled craftsman handled and stroked the clean unpainted wood every time he positioned a length in place, she knew it was more than that. She was certain that he would be the right one to hire; he would be kind to her old cottage too and kindness seemed the appropriate emotion for a left-behind house that was to become a home once again.

"You seem mighty curious young lady, anything I can help you with?" Herman asked, at last breaking the comfortable silence.

70

"I'm Prudence Stone," she said extending a hand. "I just took over the old Ellison house on Thatcher Lane and I've gone about as far as I can on my own. There's quite a bit that needs doing yet, mostly on the outside now. Any chance you would be able to fit me into your schedule."

"I know the place well. You must be the great-granddaughter from away…can't keep any secrets around here, not with young Zack workin' on your car an' all; it's a small town. I was real sorry to hear about Hannah; she was a mighty fine woman," he offered gently. "If it's okay, I can come take a look after I finish up today and give you some idea what I think."

His kind words made an impression on her as well as the fact that he even had a passing relationship with her great-grandmother, and he showed up as promised. After checking over the structure, assessing from top to bottom, he wrote up an estimate and said he could begin in about a week. But even after that, Prudence refused to give up her earlier vigil and between chores, walked over to watch him as he lovingly transformed the decaying veranda spanning the front of the tall, graceful house turning it into something more like a fanciful apron on a well-endowed matron. For some obscure reason this made her decide that along with sprucing up the cottage, she would rename it since everyone including her, called it Hannah's house or the old Ellison place…neither very imaginative really. She chose 'Gull House', fitting on many levels…her enjoyment over the ever-present harpies that continually flew overhead and in particular the tapping adoptee, and also just to be different because that was her way. But whatever the reason, Prudence knew that she and Herman would make a good team.

He proved that to her when somewhere in the middle of the listed projects, he unexpectedly christened the cottage by making a small wooden name board and posted it prominently next to the front door of #18. Having been born and raised only a few miles from the Cove, he had bothered to understand her new predilection for the thieving, loveable birds especially in a

71

place where one couldn't get away from them even if they tried. Herman recognized spunk when he saw it too, being similarly independent and thought he remembered some of the stories of her great-grandmother and the other widows. But ever since he'd started working for her, he had felt that something else was gnawing at this ambitious young woman, a new partner in crime so to speak, especially when it came to the unpredictable. Not that he would dare ask. Whatever it was, he told himself, his wife Beth would sort it out for him. She had taken an instant liking to her and as was so like Beth, had taken her into their kitchen as well and Beth definitely had a way of getting to the bottom of things.

Prudence never once minded that Herman's approach to problem solving was different because their ideas meshed so well. This bold, plainspoken man possessed a many-faceted personality. He was congenial and confident in his trade, but was also exacting and sometimes even downright jovial. She'd found out once she got to know him and like many Mainers, he was not given to lavish conversations and particularly when he was working. Often clad in his paint-spattered, plaid-shirted ruggedness, he had a habit of talking to himself, obviously preferring the dependability of his own dialog and she would find herself unavoidably eavesdropping. And no matter the words…hushed or expletive-hurled, the gnawed pencil was as handy and ever present tucked behind an ear or between parsed lips as the unruly shock of gray speckled hair flopping over one eye was bothersome to his efforts.

She had quickly learned that Herman, with all his expertise with old New England cottages, had even broader ideas than she and with their comfortable collaboration, the plainer version of the house gave way without a struggle, at least that's how easy he made it look. In the weeks he'd been at work, it had also become sparingly embellished with a bit of gingerbread fretwork here and unexpected spots of color there and now the insertion

72

of a piece of stained glass with a bright bird motif she'd found at one of those frequent Saturday yard sales.

"This fits in much better than I'd thought," Herman said as he secured the glass into an oddball window in the upper portion of the house visible to the street.

"Well, back home, Julie and I were considered 'trendsetters'! You should have seen the color of the reading porch; but to be fair we used a multi-colored parrotfish design for the bookshop," she called up as he peered down from the ladder.

When he finished with that project, he walked along the decking thinking how she still referred to the island as home and gently kicked the long box laying there in wait.

"You know that Beth is going to want one just like this, don't you...and you're making more work for me?" Herman asked light-heartedly as he unwrapped the long cardboard container exposing a large bamboo matchstick shade for the veranda.

"Don't complain now; you know it will give her a lot of pleasure to spend a few more hours outdoors without the sun beating down on her fair skin."

His wife had more than likely bent Pru's ear about the longevity or lack of, regarding the seasons, so this newly purchased item came without surprise...actually nothing involving his wife surprised him anymore. She was a 'pistol' he often told his buddies. Beth came from a long line of Mainers, hailing back to the 1600's and though no longer a young woman, she had maintained the same qualities that had made Herman fall in love. She was a little grayer and thicker in the waist now, but so was he and importantly, they still shared the bed in the same way, spooned together in solidarity.

Prudence had come to understand that both Herman and Beth felt as she did about the house, that it was something to revere in a place that honored the past. And through their friendship, she had started gaining a new confidence that perhaps the unique changes to the marvelous old building might actually turn into a sort of bellwether, the type for future generations, especially if she were lucky enough one day to spawn any. Of course, they loved the idea of her finding a good man and raising a family here in the Cove; couldn't think of anything more apropos. Prudence, shocked by the notion of that happening, couldn't tell them that after Jason, she'd pretty much tucked those thoughts away.

But no matter what eventually occurred, she now recognized that she must be prepared to annoy the widow Bond, presently the only nemesis in this entire community equation because it had been made perfectly clear that she already had. She and Herman had apparently gone too far for the old lady's tastes and that coupled with some unexplained animosity, placed Prudence on *the* list, the one with all the other non-conformists. Unfortunately, Mr. Thayer had been unable to offer her fair warning about that one.

Soon after being welcomed into the home of the widow Durn, Prudence had done what the old folks called the neighborly thing and 'gone-a'-callin' at the home of eighty-seven-year-old Jean. The woman's appearance had shocked her; she resembled an unmade bed from head to toe. Of course Aurora hadn't been told this tidbit in case it would seem rude. And it wasn't just Jean's oddly mixed clothing hanging loosely on an average frame (though that wasn't obvious either); it was more importantly the permanent scowl on thin, lined lips and bags—satchels if one wanted to be cruel—residing beneath her dark irises that when glaring at Prudence, were the color of contempt. She had totally rebuffed Pru's effort to acquaint herself.

The widow Bond had almost winced in pain at the mention of Hannah's name and left Prudence standing awkwardly on the whiskered doormat without an invitation in. Intuition told her that there was much more to Jean's rudeness, especially given what Thayer had said about a sisterhood, but was damned if she could understand. Aurora was no help either not in her present state or maybe she couldn't figure out how to explain it away, so Prudence was now left with the agitation of not knowing.

Immediately after that failed first visit, she had gone back to the cottage miffed and red-faced only to find Herman waiting for his check. He'd just completed another small job and though she could tell he was curious, she was far too embarrassed to mention what had happened. Why bother hanging out the dirty laundry before you know how it became soiled in the first place? He had even asked her if she was going to stay when the house was finished almost as if he had picked up on her internal dialog.

He and Beth, who could be a mix of exuberance and sass, had not only befriended her in myriad little ways, but also jointly championed her relationship to the Cove in general. They made it clear they wanted her to remain no matter what when the work was finished, had played on her heartstrings about it being so natural in the way she fit with Hannah's house. Prudence had heard all the stories about the difficulties of new people fitting in, but apparently since Hannah had wanted her here, that seemed good enough for them. And Beth, in particular, loved the idea of a new generation of Mainer residing there instead of more 'people from away' who had no ties at all, as she was unafraid to say. This really hadn't surprised Prudence since living on an island where a similar voice could be heard amongst the locals. But for Beth it was the people who made waves by showing up at the town meetings and raising their 'high and mighty' opinions as Beth would so often reiterate. Herman couldn't be bothered attending since he rarely stayed up late and those could turn into hours of chatter with no end result. The last one, he'd told Prudence, had Beth railing against the newcomer who wanted to put in road signs for 'duck crossings' of all things, especially since the critters often changed routes and who would be moving the signs by the way? Had nearly tossed him out of his recliner where he'd dozed while she was out he'd said. Prudence knew they had the best of relationships and that he loved Beth's involvement so long as he didn't have to partake.

Prudence had come to understand her as well...just another quirky, and more often than not, loveable denizens of Oyster Cove.

Beth, when not lecturing about 'the way life should be' to anyone who might ask, actually thought she was being subtle when appealing to Pru's familial duties though Prudence took it to be a result of their being childless. Not that she minded being the recipient of the best chowder she'd ever eaten, or Beth's insistence on teaching her the efforts involved in cooking, properly disassembling and enjoying the succulent 'lobstah' that she so favored. Prudence had specific pieces of clothing to wear when invited for dinner at the Jenkins house because the lasting smell of the messy liquid that she always managed to spill and spurt everywhere, never seemed to come out, even after repeated washings.

It was while in their quaint-looking kitchen with its farmhouse sink and French plaid curtains that often reeked of the carcasses, that Prudence became indoctrinated to the true righteousness of Mrs. Jenkins, especially when it came to local politics and who was the best person to get a job done. Beth had even cajoled her into attending a couple of the meetings in Herman's stead, but she had known instantly, that no matter how much she enjoyed Beth's company, a town hall meeting was not her bailiwick. Her newfound love for the Cove and her familial ties didn't merit that much fist pumping and indignation; she had bigger issues to deal with at home.

Once again Prudence ended up in Beth's kitchen at her bidding though Herman used her as an errand girl at the same time. It seemed uncanny when either of them could tell she needed a break from the house. And Beth would be waiting with a pitcher of homemade lemonade. But today, she also had lunch waiting and the 'cute' set of tools splayed out at the table. They still looked as though they were meant to perform surgery and maybe they were if you considered how the sweet white meat inside the hard-to-open shell needed to be gathered. "We don't use those to eat the island version; you know, the beautifully broiled, butter-topped langouste I've told you about?" Prudence teased, rather embarrassed by her clumsiness. "These instruments of torture are not required," she'd said as Beth was forced to take over once again.

It hadn't taken her long to figure out that her new allies ate the homely crustaceans in various forms four out of five nights and more than likely enjoyed their Saturday night 'date' wherever the mood took them. Prudence knew for a fact that on his way home from work, Herman, who loved a good steak, would empty his few traps permitted by the town for personal use and that Beth would quickly concoct their meals from his haul. But Prudence had a sneaky suspicion that while he might miss his beef; Beth, given her druthers, would dine on lobster every single day of the week.

Often on her way home with the lingering scent of lobster still on her hands, Prudence considered that she'd found something special with this middle-aged couple who'd gone above and beyond being just neighborly. Beth would bring over dinners she'd frozen in small containers to be defrosted when needed and Herman attacked even the smallest projects without complaint and yet he was the enigma, a rare breed. Maybe that was only because other than her father, she was unused to men who remained committed to both work and home, traits that none of her boyfriends had possessed.

It was a thought that stayed with her as she waited for his arrival this morning while she was setting out a line of interesting containers on the deck (she still had trouble with 'veranda'). It was amazing given the size of his hands and the nature of his work, that he was so comfortable handling delicate nursery buds and she'd tried not to laugh the first time she watched him. He looked so funny and yet sweet when she'd caught him gentling the baby plants from their tiny plastic pots, speaking softly as he put them into the designated urns. She knew they made an odd team, but they worked well together and this made her feel part of something larger.

"Hold on little lady, don't you go lifting those big ceramic jugs by yourself...I'll be right up to help you," Herman called from the truck. He'd caught her struggling them into place because she'd been daydreaming and hadn't heard the relic that he drove and the rattling that usually preceded his appearance.

It wasn't long before the porch became a veritable potted garden with the addition of recently acquired flea market gems, something she hadn't been able to achieve at her apartment on St. Thomas with its miniscule balcony. She'd had to pay a premium for that ocean view but it had been well worth it and now that she had such a new vista to enjoy, she had ceased to miss it quite so much.

"Okay, let's go find a spot for the perennials," he said as soon as he'd finished lugging the heavy stuff into place.

He's already taken it for granted that I'm staying, Prudence surmised as she followed his heavy-booted footsteps.

"This is the perfect spot for planting peonies next spring," he pointed out. "Wind won't be so bad over here by the side for border plants I also have in mind. Beth will be bringing them by soon; you'll see.

At that moment something, perhaps a flashing image of her mother's peonies in a back garden (grown before Victoria had totally succumbed to her demons), told her she needed to see that happen...to witness the small green orbs split open to reveal a cloud of silky-soft petals that ultimately form perfect velveteen bundles. The ethereal pinks and pearly white varieties would unquestionably emit a sacred, heady perfume and in her mind were already cut and arranged and prettily exhibited on the table in the entryway, their fragrance scoring the brine scent with a sweeter one harder to define.

"I'm so glad you didn't let me toss out the wobbly 'pie crust' table," she said when he'd outlined the plot for the intended blossoms. His efforts had paid off and the refinished and very vintage mahogany piece was a beauty to behold, a place for these future flowers.

"Told you, never throw away good wood," he'd responded with a sternness that was all show. "And by the way, don't tell old man Whitley I'm almost finished with our projects," he said pointing his chin toward the house next door. "I promised I'd help your friend Kate next," he said referring to Pru's pretty new pal. He was getting old, but he wasn't dead! Could still spot a lovely woman from a distance.

Pru's next door neighbor had recently cornered her with compliments about all that she and Herman had accomplished in so short a time, but Herman wasn't having any of it; thought it was because the cagey old man needed his leaking roof patched and he wasn't in the mood to take that on. All Prudence knew was that Leonard Whitley's most urgent need seemed to be finding a retired and amiable 'companion' who would travel south with him after he closed up his summer cottage. Not all of the buildings were adapted as four-season homes, which only reinforced her own good fortune.

Herman, who'd said out of earshot of his wife that he had found her new friend Kate 'refreshing'. Naturally, Prudence understood that was compared to the meddling Whitley. She had never found him meddlesome, but definitely interesting. And their friendship notwithstanding, in this relatively small neighborhood, a place that lends itself to a modicum of inclusion into the lives of those around her, it was necessary to give a little regarding the oddities of others if she intended to stay. To Beth's dismay, however, she still hasn't confirmed that she will remain. Prudence can't admit that she changes her tune almost daily. On one hand, she is falling hard for Oyster Cove and on the other, the emptiness sometimes catches her off guard and she is ready to flee back to St. Thomas where a haven of familiarity awaits. She has been offered opportunities to meet up with other nearby residents at the end of particularly tiring days and those occasions help diminish the 'newcomer' status. She embraces the ones who've reached out, especially Kate Newcomb. *So glad I made it to the last potluck,* she thought. Julie had been pestering her about getting out more and meeting some new men. She'd tried to alleviate her best friend's concerns but so far she'd only met the married ones; that is until Michael Newcomb had suggested one or two of his bachelor friends. Her heart had still not caught up to her logical thoughts, so she had declined his intentions but it did a world of good for Julie. Now as she waited for Kate to swing by, all she could think of was 'her' islands and how much they'd meant.

She had become inspired by living in small communities much like this one and had cherished that faraway spit of sun-drenched sand. She was hoping to feel a similar connection here too, albeit in a different manner because that was before the locket and there hadn't ever been a mysteriously missing key at stake. She couldn't help but notice and then miss some of the more obvious differences...bosomy, cherubic women hanging out laundry in their bare feet or walking down their lanes with baskets on their heads; marketplaces teeming with dark-skinned vendors and the sound of music always pouring from someone's open windows or boom-box. It was of course a more out-of-doors existence and whether music or food, much of it was always in your face and sometimes messy and sometimes loud but almost always great fun.

Most of the quiet and solitude one yearns for when thinking of a tranquil island life and getting away from it all, is not in actuality what they find. As far as she was concerned, that is more about what happens when the sun goes down and everything seems softened with the afterglow of heat and sunburn and drinks too strong for the novice imbiber. It is all consumed and enjoyed to the sound of gentling water as it laps against the sand at last cooling without the blistering rays and the day's activities. These are the inner yearnings fulfilled without the visitors realizing they had them. The rest is just 'local color' in its boldest, brightest and sometimes smelliest best: festive parades with steel drums and Mocko Jumbies; neighbors squawking at runaway chickens or their daughter's lazy no-good boyfriend, as well as loudly hawked fish sold dockside in the middle of a sweltering day.

When Prudence left Massachusetts, she had craved something apart from the well-touted splendor of warm sultry islands advertised in travel magazines, and found what she'd wanted when she stepped onto that very first island so many years ago as if she'd been born to it. She had felt at one with the universe...it was 'home'. Without even knowing it in terms she could readily point to, she had needed the connection that eventually came with those different from her and all that she had grown up with. She finally came to realize that Ben had surreptitiously encouraged that exploration because of his worldly optimism, perhaps seeing himself without actually saying so.

Yet with her obvious New England bloodline, she is now trying to re-examine her needs and re-imagine a life without those whose soft warmth exuded seemingly unhampered by obvious custom or behavior and many times simply less clothing. Islanders were often a mishmash of various nationalities fathered over the decades by different countries. Therefore, new formats had evolved through those years and nooks were carved wherever one felt comfortable being.

Here, Prudence sensed more rigidity toward behavior and privacy; hadn't ever just dropped in on a neighbor without calling first, unless of course she'd noticed them outside where it wouldn't seem rude. These new people, ones she was still trying to read, were in some cases provincial, taciturn and maybe even a little buttoned-up. Or in other cases, they might share more information in a half hour than one ever needed to know. If they liked you, it seemed they felt you worthy of knowing what their child was doing during mid-term vacation and with whom; what their specialist had told them about their inner workings or what their husband said the night before while

81

zipping up a dress for an unexpected evening out. They might let you know that what you were purchasing was way overpriced and where you could do better, or how to cook a particular type of fish because they thought you wouldn't possibly know it by yourself. Prudence had experienced that one early on and found out later that the woman really did know her stuff when it came to fresh cod.

But they were a unique breed here as well and eventually, she hoped to learn what they all knew, what Hannah must have known…that they couldn't get along without each other. If only she could hang in there and give it a chance.

Somehow in the midst of it all, Prudence managed to find time for Aurora, even though there hadn't been a lot of it to spare or the energy left for socializing in the hours after completing the custodial work that the house demanded. But still, the tiny woman thrived on these intermittent visits and appeared to love their little game, the one they had unconsciously created. Prudence didn't really know how to play this one well because only Aurora knew the main characters and how they would move around the monopoly board of Thatcher Lane but she kept trying anyway.

"He was a very close friend of Hannah's, Prudence, very close," was all she'd said about the mysterious man in the locket before changing the subject to her laundry detergent dilemma the last time they'd spoken. At times like that Prudence would have given anything to be able to ask Jean. Instead she simply rolled her eyes in frustration while waiting for Aurora to channel something new. Being able to talk to Jean about Hannah was a mere pipedream; she couldn't break the ice queen's façade. Something just didn't gel. All Prudence had to go on was that Hannah had been widowed, had a rebellious daughter and a close, 'very close friend', whose name was Timothy…not much at all.

So as with all opportune happenings, she'd been at the potluck with Kate and Michael, one where they'd sought each other out when talk of kids and birthday parties and kindergarten events starting taking over the conversations. Summertime brought in a younger assortment of families and that led to topics that neither Kate nor Pru had an interest in.

Kate was around Pru's age and very like Julie though not in appearance since Kate was ginger-haired with tawny eyes and far taller than either Julie or Prudence. But they'd quickly become friends, sharing neighborhood news over coffee or a glass of wine in the late afternoons if she was out walking the dog. Michael was nice enough too, but always preoccupied with technology and formats, nothing that Prudence could understand.

It seemed inevitable that soon after that fateful meeting Kate began dropping by Gull House regularly, stopping to assess the progress, complimenting Herman who never once tired of the admiration. Had him eating out of her hand with that English accent of hers, needing him to handle a small project before they went away.

As Prudence got to know her, she found they shared a great many things; not only their similar age but also travel experiences and life views in general which came as a great relief in the aftermath of the Bond dilemma. Since that time and since she'd had to give up her job because of their impending move, the very outspoken Kate stopped by more often. But the quick morning chats were what kept Prudence going. It had become the one constant that Kate seemed determined to carry out, saying it was good for both of them, these little morning reprieves from the self-imposed schedules and the episodes with Jean Bond.

But Mike Newcomb had accepted a bonus-filled job offer out of the country and within a short few days, Prudence would no longer be able to rely on Kate's comforting banter and presence in general. The Newcomb's lived only three doors away from Jean, so Kate was really the only one Prudence felt comfortable commiserating with regarding the woman's intolerable personality. Kate's problems with Jean did not stem from the animosity toward Hannah and the now ever-present great-granddaughter; they were purely due to Jean's average smugness about things that shouldn't have concerned her.

Unlike Aurora, whose demeanor was gentle and kind, Jean's persona was always stiff and unapproachable; her appearance as witnessed that very first time, a melting pot of fashion. She had none of the other woman's soft roundness, the type that always made Prudence want to hug her. Instead, Jean, shapeless in choices long out of stock even at the little bargain stores up and down the coast, possessed a demeanor that repelled a warm hug in a heartbeat.

The clothing matter wouldn't have been necessarily bad because there was Yankee frugality to be considered, but it was because she mixed and matched and overlaid items that didn't fit together and this morning was no different.

Damn, there she is, Prudence frowned, scrunching down to avoid being seen. She could hear the fishing boats running the shoreline to check traps and was grateful for their shared rituals as they groaned by with the occasional wave from one of the burly men. While offering a spectacular view, her choice spot allowed her to be seen by the men and women that worked the area waters, ones who'd started to recognize her throughout the village, a small thing but another step toward feeling at home here. It also had inadvertently given Prudence a sidelong view of Jean's front door…not something noted when moving in.

But before setting out to wait for Kate, and a small part of her morning ritual, Prudence always makes one stop to genuflect before the insistent Herman's miniature geraniums, checking for tiny intruders and plucking troublesome weeds. The array of small spreading flowers that are Beth's favorites had been their house-warming gift and yet the baby rose look-alikes always managed to evoke a memory of a past lover which then reminds her what she is still missing. Perhaps that was their intent knowing that there is no one special in her life and wanting there to be one, no matter how subtle she's been in her reluctance. But the bare truth is that while she is too young to be without, she isn't ready to brazen it out and fall in love again.

The wind was picking up and as she waits for Kate, it seems as if all the self-appointed schedules have left her wanting and a little empty. Once Kate leaves, it will be more difficult to confront this fact once again. She's kept a stiff upper lip, as Kate would say, through everything; missing home and Julie and her work, but most of what she'd set out to do with the house has nearly been accomplished and if necessary it could go on the market at this stage. She's never been so indecisive.

Wrapping the old remnant from Hannah's closet around her shoulders, her nostrils once again fill with the powdery scent languishing on the deep pink boucle cardigan. She pulled it tighter. *If only you could tell me what I need to do.*

She's rarely been outside in the early mornings without the sweater as she hasn't fully adjusted to the daily climate changes, never knowing whether it will be hot one minute or foggy and damp the next. The sky was forever changing and some days, huge thick 'banks' of bright white stretched across the water like a bottom-up window shade leaving an amazing color blue exposed at the top. Or the fog might whimsically cling to and gently caress everything it embodied, a little like it had done every other day this week.

She too has had to pay a few visits to the local thrift shop for their crewneck sweaters and even a couple of flannel shirts she'd found in their men's section offered at a bargain price. Living waterside in this locale feels much different from being coddled by the mellow breezes that are pushed by the Caribbean trades in that other. Around here on most days her neighbors saw her with getups that made her look a bit like Herman's clone, work shirts with rolled sleeves in varying degrees of plaid, the only ones that fit. But unlike his, these top her island-made shorts— the colorfully printed scenes showing off trim, tanned legs. Beth has dared him to wear his knee-length shorts when it's really hot, but he won't budge, says the girls would be chasing him down the street.

I can never get enough of this she reaffirmed, running her hand over the slab of striated granite, loving the feel as though a living, breathing thing. It represents perhaps the most innocent part of the overall picture of this new life in Maine and the best place to start her day. She has always been drawn to and by the sea and has witnessed many types of stone in the process. These slabs integral to Oyster Cove, have been assaulted by high tidal waves for so long they have taken on a life of their own. Many have been stepped and flattened and smoothed to a fine finish akin to the harbor seals who take respite upon them, while others ward her off with their jagged-edged jack-o-lantern teeth.

More importantly, however, it is out here atop these magnificent formations that she has confessed the depth of her fears and concerns and called upon Great-gran to give her the strength and will to stay. And more than once, gratitude has left her lips because of the rewarding trappings of this rich environment that Hannah has left in her care. It is here that she also asks the questions, the why's and how's of her ancestor's life and who, important still, is the man in the locket? What was his place in her life after all? And while Aurora's short versions have helped slightly, in actuality they have added to the confusion. Apparently Tim or Timothy as Aurora preferred, had actually been in Hannah's employ. That seemed odd considering that his face had been snugged inside the delicately etched portrait case for all these years. All of this did nothing but create more nagging questions, which she in turn would mentally shunt off to the place behind the locked door as though they were the used toys of a grown child. In her current state, anything that couldn't be resolved belonged there, lost for the time being along with that necessary key.

Now where's she gone? Prudence had suddenly misplaced the unattractive widow who had momentarily moved out of range, but then found her once again when she saw the moving colors. Today, the widow Bond was dressed in the inevitable, though not yet as dramatic as it would become when she took off what Pru's mother might have called a housedress. The floral 'dressing gown' as Kate would name it, was topped with a too short pink cardigan and worn with multi-striped socks in varying hues of red and pink that were stuffed into 'fisherman' sandals. Jean had apparently stopped to water her plants. From Pru's vantage point, her neighbor's posture meant she was perturbed over something across the road from her house and when she looked in Pru's direction, Prudence quickly turned her head, pretending to be minding her own business. In actuality, Jean would not be able to tell one way or the other because even though the youngest of the three widows, her eyesight wasn't at all good.

Prudence surreptitiously scrutinized her as she trundled with the gait of someone with bad legs and swollen ankles or possibly only uncomfortable shoes as she headed for the rolled up *Portland Press Herald* in the little box at the edge of her lawn. But even if she mustered up real sympathy for whatever the elder woman's condition, something she automatically did regarding anyone's infirmities, Prudence still felt the old crone was just plain mean.

Just then a blond jogger in a nylon running costume sprinted past Pru's perch, momentarily taking her mind off Jean. The wholesome twenty-something girl had been running past the cottage for a couple of weeks now, reminding Prudence of her own exuberance for anything aerobic at that age. Not that she was ancient, but she no longer adhered to the rigid routines she had in her early twenties and preferred more strength training these days.

As usual, a long ponytail was held securely by the strap of a ball-cap—today a bright blue one—and bounced rapidly in time with the jogger's steps. She was always moving too fast for conversation and Prudence had become curious about her route, not believing she lived in the village.

"Good morning," Prudence called out, happy to have a pleasant diversion and automatically wondering whether the young woman had ever suffered the early pangs of love gone sour as she had at a similar age. Since the split-up with Jason, she mentally flits back and forth, her frayed edges creating new insecurities. If only he'd broken up with her *before* the wedding! She could have handled that, but she's obviously been unable to get past being jilted so openly and even that disgusted her. *What happened to the old Prudence; the one with grit?*

"Morning," pony-tailed gal tossed back with a half wave and smiling broadly, but definitely on a mission, perhaps a required number of miles. Today would not be the day to ask, she realized as the girl held up her pedometer and picked up her speed.

Checking her own watch as the runner's backside disappeared from view *and here come the 'boys'...right on time.* They too were dressed for a mission once their walk ended (Herman had called them 'golf nuts') and were heading her way. Since neither of the two had ever spoken to her, she was left to imagine their ages and circumstance. She surmised mid-fifties as they strode toward her, overdoing their beefy arm pumps...showing off she thought. Her first recollection of them was just after she'd arrived and perhaps she thought their personalities would thaw with mid-summer's sun. Instead, she'd sensed an obstinacy about them that irritated her to no end, stayed with her like a sliver just beneath the skin—irksome. Never having been the brunt of neighborhood clannishness, Prudence had tried even harder to be friendly, but most often any greetings simply hit the air and fell flat on the pavement without benefit of response other than a nod. Looking back on the past weeks, she realized neither had ever bothered to inquire of Hannah either or if she were a summer resident like them. Herman said they had been coming back for quite a few years, and yet she had never seen them at the little social gatherings she'd attended.

Lord knows after meeting the more congenial types with whom she knew daily life would remain pleasant, she'd expected little more from them. Perhaps, she thought, the two cronies are simply as disagreeable as that ornery woman or better yet, as Pru's mother had said to her as a young child— anyone that grumpy in the morning is probably just constipated! *Wait till Kate hears that one!*

Herman had once caught her stewing over their disregard and having learned a little more from Beth, agreed that it was their friendship with the hard-shelled widow Bond and her negative feelings toward Prudence taking up residence at Hannah's that was at the crux of it. He tended to 'hear' things when he worked around the neighborhood or even down at the pier oddly enough. Small towns were all the same, a little gossip went a very long way. What she had learned was that the men lived in a narrow, two-story cottage at the end of the Lane that had come together under Jean's guidance, whereas Prudence had gone about everything on her own, except for Herman of course, but when it came to the small flamboyant touches and particularly paint, she had been adamant about her choices. Not only colors for the doors and deck, but then she'd added the new name for the cottage that had been beautifully scripted on a signboard painted the identical color. While others weren't exactly jumping on the same bandwagon, four more cottage owners had put creative names alongside their house numbers as well. Since Mrs. Bond apparently felt, being *the* longest remaining resident (obviously discounting Aurora) on Thatcher Lane that it was *her* neighborhood to oversee. Therefore, she was constantly in a state of agitation.

Seems Prudence had unexpectedly started a small trend without permission and though none was required, she had to agree that she might have crossed some imaginary line. But she continued to justify the need to feel that closeness with the tropics and there'd only been one hue available in the tiers of sampler sheets that would give her that much needed alliance in

89

a new domain, something with a hint of Caribbean thrown in for good measure.

"Are you sure you want this paint?" the hardware store owner had declared when she put the little strip of cardboard on the counter for him to mix. "Ain't you livin' out at the old Ellison place? Don't seem quite the right shade, if you ask me."

News of this particular purchase had spread quickly to a few other regular Oyster Cove customers and Prudence supposed given his reaction, it would seem a cockamamie idea for this little colony. The original gem-like shade that mimicked some of the better diving holes near St. Thomas had been mixed judiciously she'd thought, but it had still managed to raise the ire of the relentless and highly opinionated neighborhood watchdogs.

As she relived this small stupid drama, the only thing that kept extreme aggravation at bay was the fact that Kate would turn up right on their heels. Sadly there wouldn't be many such mornings left and because of their imminent departure, she would ask for her help today; she'd run out of options. Besides which, Kate's high energy was highly contagious and as always she'd readily counter all the negativity that the widow Bond imposed, the ones that occasionally spread like shock waves across the length and breadth of Thatcher Lane.

Time for a second cup; she should be here any minute. Dragging Kate toward her destination would be the very large and always messily un-groomed Whipple. The queerly named animal, eager as ever for his morning treats, would soon plow through the neighbor's lilies to get to whatever surprise Prudence had in store for him. They had developed a mutually satisfying doggy love affair and he would show this by spreading copious amounts of drool everywhere.

Kate's lineage, though *terribly* English, was offset by her irreverent sense of humor and one that had endeared her to Prudence from the start. She too had been mesmerized as she'd watched Herman at work on Gull House just as Prudence had done when meeting him.

Unfortunately, her newest compatriot in the war of individuality was about to be uprooted by her husband's fateful transfer to Mumbai, which had at last been solidified by contracts and plane tickets, no turning back now. And because Kate also felt a deep affinity for the Cove, she'd explained tearfully one recent evening over drinks at their place, that it was a necessary move, another rung on his personal ladder to success, something that had come about because of the development of some high-tech, trouble-shooting software.

Prudence enjoyed being at Kate's on the few occasions when it worked within the Newcomb's busy schedule. The house was far smaller than Hannah's cottage and because of that, kept minimalist and a little modern for the Lane, on the inside anyway. Not even a few fine English antiques that Prudence had hoped to find. But Kate's concerns had been stated with great pride as well as a tinge of irony for while Michael was to be ensconced in a prestigious job sorting out problems within the communication systems for various hotels and government offices, Kate's role had been reduced to the 'wife of'. Not her personal cup of tea as she had candidly stated to Prudence at a point when he'd left the room. And, while not putting an end to their budding friendship, it would definitely rack up huge long distance phone charges for them both.

Kate's pronouncements about Jean, the type tossed out during yesterday's visit, would ring in Pru's ears long after Kate had left the country—"Anyone would think she'd been designated the First Lady of Oyster Cove the way she talks...I told Phil this, and I told Phil that...the way she went on and on...who cares whether Phil planted 'rhodies', lilies or left the wild beach roses?"

Kate really can get a little carried away, Prudence mused, knowing that was one of the reasons she loved their friendship. When she got all riled up, her posh accent came across loud and clear as though she were standing on the legendary soap box in London's Hyde Park. But Kate was absolutely right, there were no rules, though listening to one of Jean's weary diatribes, anyone would think the neighborhood to be in deep peril and about to suffer the demise of orderly conduct if the exteriors didn't conform. Prudence was sophisticated enough to know there would always be this sort in any community although in the islands it would more than likely be over whose goat chewed all the plants with no one fessing up.

As she waited Prudence pondered the changes that have occurred in the time since her arrival in early June. More kids skating and biking; adults running or groups walking along the Lane, more out of state plates (many from her home state)…a summer colony in full bloom. It was heartwarming even with the irascible woman and her two sycophants in play. Thoughts of what will happen next also squeezed in like little inchworms measuring the future, moving one direction and then the other. *Kate had some great suggestions about opening another bookstore, but winter! Come on!*

The idea of staying had its appeal and she so wanted to learn the truth about Hannah's life, at least as much as possible. She loved the house, loved the neighborhood even with Jean, and Oyster Cove in general. Couldn't get enough of the ocean and in time wanted to explore more of the lighthouses. And she had found great comfort in her relationship with Aurora, perhaps because she no longer had any immediate family. Which reminded her of the last visit, striving hard as always to untangle a very old web picturing Jean as the spider, and all she'd gotten in response was, "She was lovely once, but had some terrible disappointments and now she's very bitter," Aurora had offered. "Happened not long after we'd become a 'triple threat' as my Charlie liked to say." This had made her blush like a girl murmuring that he had loved to tease. But at least Prudence understood how Jean had been widowed; that her husband, Everett, had gone out fishing one day and had never come back.

The tragedy had apparently led to Jean taking up smoking which then made perfect sense about those little pinched lines around her mouth. They weren't just pure distaste after all. But importantly, some of the 'trouble' had to do with Timothy. "It makes me uncomfortable talking about that," Aurora had said with an exaggerated finality, once again slamming the book on the past and making Prudence more frustrated than when they'd met.

"Halloo," Kate trilled in her lovely alto, shaking Prudence from the slush of old-age dilemmas. She looked particularly smart this morning dressed in slender black cotton slacks, Italian loafers and more than likely because of the predicted heat, a very lightweight black, scoop-necked tee exposing a heavy gold choker. Whipple tugged at the lead, forcing her to hurry. Prudence saw him trample across the small plot of flowers as he always did no matter how often he was reprimanded; but couldn't wait to snuggle his big furry head, a consolation after thoughts of Jean.

"Have you seen her?" Kate asked with an exasperated expression as Prudence jumped up to claim the dog. "She's in another wardrobe jumble; if she weren't so mean, I'd offer to take her shopping, I know she can afford it."

Mrs. Bond has re-emerged in another strangely concocted outfit, having at least removed the dressing gown. But her thinning dyed hair had been tightly wound into a dark bun, very spinster-like and terribly prim even for her. She actually seemed to be heading their way and as they watched, Prudence had all she could do to remember that she and Hannah had once been best friends.

"I did," Prudence responded, taking her eyes from the latest version of her unhappy opponent for another wet smooch from Whipple, "when she first ducked out for the morning paper, not a particularly pleasant sight either. But then neither am I, in my rag-tag work clothes."

"That's not the same thing; you're not trying for a fashion statement and I don't imagine any of us would notice those wardrobe misdemeanors if she were a nicer person. But I truly don't understand what her problem is; she was in another snit and again tried to involve me, something about the Fortnum's drainage ditch. Wouldn't you think she'd have something more important to do than get her knickers in a twist over the neighbors' woes?" Kate spewed, throwing up her hands. "Come to think of it, I actually thought I smelled brandy on her breath— you know that cheap coffee-flavored one they sell over at the market…you don't suppose she's taken to drinking in the morning?"

"God, I hope not; but I guess that would account for some of her insufferable behavior. I've never mentioned it before, but when I first tried to introduce myself, she was downright rude. I felt so small standing there on her doorstep while she glared at me and then her eyes caught my locket and her skin took on the color of candle wax. But I don't want to waste our breath—sans alcohol—on her this morning because I need a favor."

"You can't just leave me hanging like that," Kate said, eyeing the locket.

"I tried making light of it asking if perhaps she remembered that it was Hannah's and how pleased I was to have it but she only 'hmphed' or is it 'harumphed', I can never remember. Then if you can imagine she simply turned on her heel and left me standing at the door," Prudence said, remembering her embarrassment.

"A 'humph', huh?" Kate teased, trying to make the sound that accidentally came out as a snort. "Sorry, couldn't contain myself. But I have to say I'm glad you have Aurora. I never really got to know her and I'm really sorry about that especially since she's sort of losing it now. I suppose when we moved here, we immediately floated toward a different crowd at least until I couldn't bear the tight-ass yacht club types any longer. And of course, now there won't be time. But I think it's grand that

94

you've been able to feel closer to Hannah because of her," Kate said warmly.

"I didn't know you ever hung with that crowd; you've never mentioned it," she said not at all startled by Kate's outspokenness. "But that doesn't matter now. It's poor Aurora I'll continue to worry about, especially on days her brain seems like it's mired in cotton wool."

"It might be the beginning stages of dementia," Kate said, particularly if she's losing touch with reality."

"She knows that as far as Jean's concerned, I'm now a constant reminder of Hannah and all the problems. However, she won't tell me what those were either, so my best guess is they have quite a lot to do with a man named Tim. She has this quaint way of saying things to me, dropping just the right hint while forgetting where they lead, saying that I should look for him. Well, hello, that's exactly what I've been hoping to do!

"For some reason Kate, and aside from a legitimate deficiency, I think that adorable woman is stringing me along, enjoying some small private game. I also think she's really lonely without her old pals and because I'm connected to that past, is stretching out the story in order to keep me around. I don't think she understands that I would visit her no matter what; I just love her.

"But she actually found a few photos of the 'girls' taken on this very deck," Prudence said leading Kate around the side and through the kitchen. "They were maybe thirty-ish, all smiles and waving at the camera, even Jean…maybe it was before her husband died, I don't know. Her curly hair was longer, worn down and dark, but given her age back then, probably not dyed. Maybe I just have trouble looking for the better side of her now, but god Kate, they were all really pretty with lovely figures, Jean too, believe it or not…surprisingly curvy and dressed 'normally'. Aurora looked just as delightful, except her hair wasn't gray, but she had that same softness about her. And Hannah, what can I say; I thought she looked beautiful, but then

95

I'm prejudiced because she reminded me so of Ben, same smile and all.

"And just when I think I'm making progress with Aurora, she's 'gone' again and I know it's because you're leaving that I'm even more anxious…I want to resolve this matter of Timothy! I'm convinced whatever is in the attic will shed some light, but this whole issue is beginning to drive me crazy; I've looked everywhere I can think of. *And* I was kind of hoping you wouldn't mind giving me a hand while I look for that damn key one more time."

"Oh, I'd love to! Where do we begin?" Kate said as if searching for a missing key happened every day. "I bet I never told you the story about my grandmother's house in Surrey. You'll love this…there was a back closet officially off limits to the children and one day, finally getting up my nerve, I disobeyed only to find a skeleton tucked in behind some old winter coats. I nearly wet myself and in the end, it turned out to be the one my grandfather had displayed as a teaching tool during his medical practice!"

"I doubt that's what we'll find up there IF we ever locate that key, but perhaps you'd like to pay a visit to the powder room first," Prudence said, ducking a mock blow from her friend. "But all kidding aside, I just want to be able to get to the bottom of this locked door and definitely want to find out about the face in the locket. And I confess I've—don't laugh—sensed something ever since I moved in, that for lack of a better word I choose to call a spirit, but it really has more to do with what I recall reading about an unsettled soul. I haven't said much about that because without a key to that locked room, it's become a moot point. Mr. Thayer gave me the ones he had and so far my singular rummaging has gotten me nowhere."

"I'm not laughing; I never would. Admit it, it's actually rather exciting. Certainly not what I expected to be doing this morning, but we can make quick work of it. You know it's probably right in front of you and you've just been too busy or too anxious to notice it."

"I almost feel guilty asking you; you're obviously dressed to go somewhere; love the necklace by the way."

"Me too; an anniversary gift from Michael. Guess he's feeling a little guilty about dragging me off again. I have some time before I have to meet him for lunch…another pacifier on his part. I'm sure he's trying to make it up to me since I had to give up my job at the bank and after becoming a loan officer as well."

"Well, I for one wish he weren't dragging you off. But you're still here and though I know you don't generally eat breakfast, I have blueberry muffins as a way of saying thanks. I found an old recipe in the pantry and you, my dear, are my first 'guinea-pig'. And if you don't want any, you can always bring them home to him or share them with Whipple…he never complains," Prudence said, looking out at Whipple snuggled down like a dark mound of soil ready for planting. She was a little embarrassed by her omission since Kate was obviously taking the notion of spirits quite in stride. Bless the English!

"In that case, I'll make an exception. Any chance you've more of that rich brew you're so fond of? I'm overdone with tea this morning."

"Coming right up, along with my experiment. I've never been known for my baking and I'm still not used to this oven. As soon as I get another check from Julie, that's the next acquisition. And I have to admit, Kate, it seems so silly to hinge my bets on that attic room, but it's become an obsession because I don't have access to it."

"My grandmother had this saying—'it's hidden right in front of your face dear'. But they also were guilty of stuffing all manner of things into kitchen drawers they had lined with old wallpaper. But maybe it's somewhere right before your nose that you aren't seeing. Or it might even be taped to the bottom of a music, or jewelry box, someplace Hannah wouldn't have forgotten. I hope it hasn't been thrown out with the trash or something. But I can see where it would make it harder to ignore the room, it being locked that way, almost like your great-grandmother had something to hide, something buried among her things. Not that I'm insinuating anything sinister, mind you. Who knows, she might even have one of those marvelous thick books with an empty center around here somewhere...don't give me that funny look."

"I'm going to ignore the inference, but I think you've been watching too many mystery movies. Did people really use those book props as hiding places?"

"Sherlock Holmes' assistant at your service," Kate responded jauntily, taking the only available apron just in case. "Maybe we'll both be surprised."

After a couple of hours of bending, reaching, prying into and under, nothing turned up except a small and very rusty awl generally used for punching out leather; long-faded and crumbling Polaroid snaps of the house and grounds, and a few skeletal remains of last summer's bugs. She obviously hadn't cleaned as thoroughly as she'd thought.

But Kate was right, none of this made sense because according to Mr. Thayer, Hannah never locked her doors. And she was old and probably wouldn't be trudging up that second set of stairs so why not just leave it unlocked in the first place, lest she misplace that key, something that might come with age. Her brain was on overdrive at all the permutations she could create with that one train of thought. She took a deep, calming breath; it would as Kate said, be lying in plain sight (she hoped). It was as far as Prudence was concerned, more than a bout of drama, it could turn into the Achilles heel she hadn't counted on.

She walked Kate out, fetching Whipple from his spot in the shade, a sense of disappointment hovering between them. She was going to miss her new friend and that shaggy mutt who was about to be temporarily adopted by Michael's brother. Prudence had the oddest sense of abandonment. "Who on earth will help hold back the tide of Jean's wrath and turn it into comedy?" she asked nearing tears.

"Well, I won't have anyone to share my exciting trips with either, or be able to tease you into finding a new man because we both know Michael's all prepared to set you up with one of his single friends," Kate responded, knowing Prudence was not about to give in. "And you had better let me know if one comes along…or else."

"Not to worry, no one will. But should I happen to be wrong, you will be informed," Prudence replied knowing Kate was trying to jolly her out of the mood since tears were welling up in her eyes also.

"The neighborhood won't be the same without you around my friend; won't be any class left at all," Prudence said to stop the tears.

"I'm going to miss you too," Kate replied. "And I really wanted to meet Julie."

"She's been dragging her feet over a visit, seems that little business of ours on St. Thomas is doing very well right now which will help keep those checks coming to me regularly."

Fighting back the familiar feelings of vulnerability without quite knowing why, Prudence said, "But you have to promise to write often and we'll alternate our long distance calls to save money. And thank you by the way for prompting me to get better acquainted with some of the local business owners and the necessary people at your bank. It'll be helpful if and when I'm ready to set up another store again," Prudence offered pragmatically hoping to keep Kate from breaking down and ruining her makeup. *What would Michael think?* And just that thought made Prudence feel that sense of loss again, how her world had switched from a future to a past here in Maine. Jason's exit remains a thorn, but at her loneliest, the days and nights she wishes he had come back she mentally transforms him into a better man. God forbid, Julie ever heard her say that, but loneliness does strange things to the heart and mind. It was a stupid illness for which there was no medical relief and she thought of Hannah, wishing with all her heart she hadn't suffered from such a condition and yet the inferences from Aurora were beginning to lead there. Inexplicably, she has become very protective of her relative. *It's your fault Hannah; I sense you want me to know what happened.*

She walked back to the kitchen to put the rest of the muffins in the trash...they really were awful even if Kate hadn't complained. But Kate had been right about making contacts and she was happy she'd followed up on the important connections her friend had offered. The idea of a bookstore in this new location had at least taken seed if nothing else and from past experience, she knew enough to make those contacts; ones that might be useful and ease her into the business community if needed.

With the key still lost and her friend about to leave and the house at a point where she could pursue different avenues, Prudence continued some of her established routines as a way of performing more networking. There were daily walks to the post office and then the little general store for the day's take on village news—gossip—and a brief stop at the dock for whatever was fresh-caught. On many of those days, she would share a coffee with the woman at the counter of the lobster pound who also tended bar on weekends at a popular pub called the Lone Dory that catered to the boisterous fishermen and a place where she'd often in her busy schedule gotten take-out fish dinners.

Shirley, an out-spoken 'down-home' gal with back-combed bleach-blond hair, was a wealth of information about the local goings on. She was also the bearer of many a salty story she willingly dispensed at any given time. Unfortunately, she was also focused on her desire to fix Prudence up with a cousin Marty as opposed to Tom, if she were so inclined. "I really think Marty's the one for you," she'd said often as she proffered the picture of the muscular lobsterman with curly brown hair and boyish smile. Prudence had declined politely but not because he wasn't good looking. It just seemed odd that Shirley was almost pimping him out which of course made no sense whatsoever since he looked like he could have any woman he desired.

On other days when the larder was full and she didn't feel like rearranging simple furnishings...the *parlor* still had the ambiance of the elderly...she would spend her spare time at the library on the Square. The old white-pillared structure, like the heart of any small town, bears the musty scent of assorted research books stuffed into many of its corners while the more prominent furnishings gleam and give off a light citrus fragrance mixed in with the smell of fresh coffee always on hand for the staff.

Permanence in a previously unknown Maine village had never been on her radar. And yet as the days have gone by tainted with what she now believed was Hannah's soft brushstroke, the one that by summoning her here, will give Great-gran resting peace, Prudence is reluctant to turn her back. Who knows, she might even find answers of her own before her heart becomes enshrined in past bitterness. And so the library has become the quiet place to ponder it all; the past and the future. It is also a place to meet other readers involved in book clubs and scour the real estate sections listed in the vast supply of dailies and weeklies for available properties, should she take the plunge. A new, very slim determination is fueling the hunt for the perfect property within budget as each day she comes closer to staying put.

And like a karmic response, Vivian Sanford showed up. She had walked in preceded by the aroma of freshly baked croissants and pastries on a large tray, a zaftig woman who regularly distributed them to the rotating library volunteers. She was bigger than life itself in an Irish sort of way right down to the smattering of freckles spattering her cheeks. One of the volunteers had been manning the desk and insisted on sharing the wealth of sugary, caloric-laden goodies with Prudence, which in turn produced an introduction to Vivian.

The library had been quieter than usual that morning and other than the dark-eyed Lizzie bending over the counter occasionally with a not very well disguised cupping of an ear, the two women had a private opportunity to get better acquainted.

It was obvious to Prudence during that very first hour that Vivian possessed her same passion for reading and when Lizzie was completely out of earshot helping someone find a particular book, a buxom Vivian had leaned in unselfconsciously. "I am looking for another 'gig' at the moment; getting a little tired of feeding the masses," she'd whispered. Prudence knew right then and there it would be fun to work together; just being in her presence would make her relax and laugh more and without Kate, she would need that. She intuitively sensed that Vivian, while very different from Julie, would also make a great business partner.

Vivian, never to be called 'Viv', was probably in her early forties though it was hard to be certain. She had sparkling blue eyes and glossy red hair and not only a similar thirst for books, but she *knew people*, she'd said, ones who could point them in the right direction. She would, therefore, take it upon herself to do the actual physical search for lease properties freeing up Pru's time for the rest of the interior remodeling, at least while she still had a bit of money coming in from St. Thomas.

They now regularly spent Wednesday mornings in the heavily-trafficked deli rearranging their imaginary schemes to suit their personalities, seated as always with spread-out tear sheets all over the vinyl-covered tabletops. Most times it meant staying right through the breakfast crowd as it flowed into the luncheon group. And like today, they were causing the newly-hired waitress some distress over whether to evict them for the next round of customers or chance getting fired for not watching the time.

"Did you catch her expression," Prudence asked just as they'd finished sorting through financial uncertainties and her unfamiliarity regarding doing business on the Maine coast in general.

"I sure did, but that's her problem. We've been good customers and it's not like people are lined up waiting for us to move. She's just nervous and let's face it she's not making much on tips from us with the little that we order," Vivian said holding up her large mug of coffee and a biscuit. "Maybe we should put a little more on the table today."

Prudence reluctantly put more coins down next to Vivian's; she'd only had coffee this time. "I'm sure it's not the end of the world if we don't find exactly what we're looking for but, considering how compatible we think we are, we have nearly opposite ideas about the interior. I would still like to find a place that looks a little rustic, something warm and inviting. Maybe even a brick wall we could use as a backdrop for a nice wing chair or two. My feeling is that we make the space cozy enough that our customers would feel more like sample reading during the long winter days ahead; you know get a real sense of the book they might purchase?"

"You're right that we're not quite on the same page and don't take this wrong, but I'm a little tired of that ambiance...it seems that's all we have around here, even in my own home for crying out loud. I think maybe people would enjoy someplace brightly lit and plant-friendly. We could still cozy it up and if you wouldn't mind, maybe even a cat in residence. I wouldn't really care where it sat. They are just such comforting creatures to have around," Vivian said hopefully. "You know, they're supposed to help lower blood pressure; pets in general that is."

"I hadn't heard that, but I'm not exactly sure how that would work, having one in the store all the time."

"Well, at least think on it. It's not like it's a priority since we haven't even found the space," Vivian responded as they gathered up their things, waving at the now surly-faced waitress as they headed out the door.

Most Saturday mornings dressed in her short shorts and crop-top—leftovers from another time and probably more than a few exercise classes—Prudence could be found predictably dragging and pushing the old Hoover. The ancient upright lived in the back closet and was really only used for the foyer and front room; the only places with sizeable rugs. And on this particular day, she had a lot more on her mind than dirt. She and Kate had done what they could to find the missing key and Vivian's latest request for a cat had for some reason begun to plague her, sort of stuck like a broken record each time she thought of their future store. She didn't want to hurt Vivian's feelings, but she really didn't like cats all that much; they often made her sneeze and she never felt she could trust them, not like a dog anyway.

She definitely didn't like vacuuming either, which had just caused her to yank at the cord. Then out of the corner of her eye, she saw the table wobble. *Whoops, should have been paying attention.* The looping coil had bunched at the base while she'd been musing. The last thing she needed was to tip the frilly 'pie crust' that Herman had so nicely mended. *He'd have a fit if I break this,* she thought getting on her knees to free the cord.

Wonder if the cleaning people accidentally pushed this rug over the heat grate. The metal edge was all that could be seen peeking out where the smaller oriental ended in the foyer. Why hadn't she ever bothered to pull the rug back? *Just like Kate said, lost in plain sight.* There before her eyes was the curlicue head of a long slender key. The rest was hanging through one of the holes in the ornamental grate, saved from going further down because of that lovely curl. She grabbed it delicately but firmly with her fingertips and only when she had it solidly in her hand, did she breathe properly. Then she left the Hoover where it stood on the unfinished rug and went into the kitchen and quickly poured a glass of water.

Butterflies of excitement or maybe just nerves clashed with the baffling question of how the key had gotten into the grate in the first place and before she knew it, she had stopped moving.

Why aren't you racing up the stairs; this is what you wanted. She exchanged the water for a bottle of beer even though she hardly ever drank it. *It's nearly noon,* she thought looking at the clock, trying to imagine the cleaning service in the house after Hannah died. That was perhaps the only possible explanation as to why the key was on the floor. Would they have even noticed it on the table, or could it have been dropped into that grate by accident while they were cleaning, or maybe dropped there a really long time ago by Hannah who would have simply forgotten it? Not that any of that mattered now but again, she was hesitating.

You've got the key, now go on and open that room...it's what you've been waiting for. Suddenly spooked by the idea of going in alone, she wanted to call Kate. *She can't spare time for any nonsense; she's knee deep in packing boxes.* Then, feeling the need of an ally even though she wasn't sure why, she tried the store on St. Thomas, but the line was continually busy. She kept stalling and realized how much she'd made of this so-called 'spirit'. Holding onto the old black rotary phone, she thought about the stupid, harbored fear all for naught to coin a phrase from Kate. The new Prudence, becoming confident in her inherited house by the sea, wouldn't have held off so long over a missing key if it hadn't been so real to her, would have had Herman remove the damn door from its hinges if necessary! How much has been fostered by the widow Durn and her convoluted hints?

Now embarrassed and feeling more so with each stalled moment and after only a few sips, she left the bottle on the floor next to the stairwell. Then holding the key with the tenacity of a miner about to pan for gold, she climbed the remaining steps all the while recalling Kate's chiding. *There is nothing to be afraid of, you ninny...it's just an old room closed for a long time.* Prudence looked at her hand, expecting it to be shaking but it wasn't and she placed the slim key in the brass keyhole. It clicked softly *oh my god, it's the right one* and she turned the knob. She expected her fingers to tingle and maybe even burn at the contact; she'd worked up quite a case, but the doorknob was fine and then the heat of a long-closed room slapped her in the face. *Whoa!* Drab was an understatement and from the look and feel of it, had probably been that way without concern by a woman who knew what was up here. So far nothing swooped down to attack or ran at her feet as she'd anticipated. She didn't immediately see any signs of 'droppings' so maybe it wouldn't be so bad after all.

Prudence fanned the door back and forth to dispel the staleness and musty odors. It was a dull bit of square footage and without decoration of any kind—only knotty pine walls and dark slatted floorboards that hadn't been painted in a long time. A standard wooden peg rack, probably from the same store where she'd bought her deck paint, was nailed to the wall behind the door which she noticed while swinging the door for air and might not have paid attention to except for the coat—an old yellow oil slicker, a curiosity only in that it hung by a shoulder in a careless way hinting that someone might have left it in a hurry.

On the floor beneath the jacket was a stack of old books dusty enough to write her name on their covers. A few of those were by poets she was now familiar with and as comforting as it was to see that Hannah also had a special bent towards reading, it was way too hot to deal with them right now. To the left of center…startling in itself…a painted cabinet, nearly the same shade that had caused a little current of trouble between neighbors. *Great-grandmother Ellison, you are full of surprises!* The storage unit was placed awkwardly against the sloping ceiling on that side of the room and was evenly divided by a single door and four drawers and because of its depth and position would have to be moved in order to open its door…and all the while the heat began to cloy like stale breath.

Naturally it was heavy and her first attempt, a feeble one according to the ear-jolting screech yielded after trying and after a corner of the raised base gouged a nasty slice into one of the dusty floorboards. She stared at the virginal piece of exposed wood looking generally out of place in all that dust and wondered what in hell she'd gotten herself into—*lots of cleaning apparently.* How foolish to believe she had only to open the attic door and all the answers would be immediately spelled out in black and white…not even close.

But in this dismal room or maybe because of it, there was also a sense of despair that seemed to hang innocuously in the air. Perhaps it was just her own disappointment, but she had expended so much energy worrying about it and she still didn't know what she was looking for. To what purpose had she been lured to this northern outpost? Was it something that went beyond the obvious? Did she have Hannah's well-known pluck and could she continue regardless of her intuition whether or not she was comfortable doing so? There must be more to all of this inheritance than a house on a ledge or even a pretty piece of jewelry, no matter how lovely they are. *And there is no logical reason to be frightened of any of it either,* she thought staring at the unwieldy piece of furniture. It wasn't huge, although cumbersome and not as elegantly tall or put together as a European armoire. And whatever nice wood it may have been cut from was all but disguised by the layers of that familiar sea green paint, only a half shade deeper than Pru's choice.

The cabinet was big enough for items stored between seasons although probably not old enough to have carried the hopes and dreams and triumphs of her earliest ancestors from distant landscapes. *Or it may only house their torments.* The crazies were getting to her, thoughts inside her head from lack of air probably as it was getting harder and harder to concentrate. She needed to find another source besides the doorway and followed a little trail of light across the back wall where, sure enough, there was a window…very small, rectangular, and unfortunately, stuck tight from too much paint. Then the back of her hand caught in what a clever spider had made difficult to pull free since it was now the home of the tenacious eight-legged creature whose tightly woven net made her jump. *Don't be such a Nelly; it's a natural place for webs and mites.*

As she turned from the window, her eyes again fell upon the dangling jacket, only this time its angle annoying her to the point of needing to straighten it before she could continue. Grabbing it by the slipping sleeve she was suddenly quite positive that it had belonged to the man in question…how or why it was here in this room was only conjecture, but she was convinced it was Tim's. Like the key and Hannah's old wrap that Prudence still kept on the rocker, it was comforting to the touch, a feeling she didn't want to let go of. None of this made any sense at all.

She moved back to the cabinet and pushed harder than she thought possible and thankfully, it budged this time, at least enough to open the door and she was pleasantly surprised. Besides a few outdated dresses—one perhaps for church and the others for work—a cotton dressing gown and some little girl things—there was a pretty woolen coat, but with sad signs of mold at its hem. And, a smart-looking narrow leather case peeked from an upper shelf above the clothing. Hurriedly pulling it from its hiding place, she pried the tiny fastener with her fingernail and as suspected, inside was a pair of gloves, medium length and kidskin in near new condition; ones that could have been worn on special occasions with that velvet trimmed coat and matching woolen hat that she'd nearly overlooked.

It was too hard to resist what the gloves would look like on her own hands. She pulled first one, then the other onto her tapered fingers. They fit perfectly! The soft, dove gray material had managed to retain a light fragrance; not the powdery one on the old sweater, but a delicate balance of floral, something perhaps of a bygone era. She could almost hear Kate's voice— *if it weren't so bloody hot*—and might even have kept them on, but her arms had already begun to glisten.

Somewhere along the line, Hannah had acquired what looked to be items of quality, things out of context with her hardship years, leaving Prudence with another set of questions. Then again, they may have been given to her by the arrogant James Prescott or purchased with her hard won savings or maybe even obtained through a small sale of some of his belongings. None of that really mattered so long as they might eventually lead her to a better understanding of her great-grandmother.

She removed the gloves and placed them tenderly into the box like fragile birds fallen from a soft nest and reached for a wrapped muslin sheet squirreled into that same top shelf. It was neatly folded and heavier than expected...*wonder if this is what women used to wear in winter.* The shiny amber quilted petticoat within seemed far more outdated than anything Hannah might have worn so perhaps it belonged to her sister, Elisabeth. Guessing by its weft, it would only have been practical for cold weather, she held it to her flushed face anyway, the softness a temptation, but of course, that only exacerbated the temperature. *Maybe it belonged to Hannah's mother.*

Her legs were stiff and it was just too hot; no amount of fanning would help. She'd have to call Herman to come in and either open the window or put in a new one and a light fixture too. It would mean spending more money, but it was definitely necessary in order to clean this fusty smelling place out. Her skin was getting that crawly sensation as if the dormant species had already been awakened by what little air had come in through the open door.

Just one more thing to check, she thought rising off the floor and pushing away the sticky strands of hair. Holding her breath, she reached into the back of the closet. A tapestry valise had been tucked behind the moldy coat next to a hat box...*what would Ben call this...a portmanteau?* Instead of some wonderful surprise, it was simply stuffed with books; even some slim volumes of poetry, naturally! *This is better,* she thought spying a singular photo amongst the little pile. *But the Dalton family, Hannah's, had been farm people.* This was a woman dressed in a long, ruffled-bodice dress and dainty hat, appearing quite natural standing beside the shore. She even had a pair of binoculars in her hand that were directed seaward, somewhere beyond where she stood.

Suddenly the room was just too much; claustrophobia was winning. She felt faint from the intolerable heat and immediately pulled out one of the two cardboard boxes that were identified as **photographs** and **papers.** Both shabby and tied with old cotton string in the crisscross way of a present. She put the loose picture from the valise in her pocket for safekeeping, deciding on the photo box to take downstairs. It was closest to disintegration and because it would probably be the best chance to find the missing Timothy.

She was headed out when it struck her to grab the slicker too and with a combination of light-headedness and relief she left the room, leaving the troublesome door unlocked and wide open, the way it would remain at least until winter and carried the box down a flight to her bedroom.

Instead of spreading the photos willy-nilly on the bed, she laid the jacket down like a picnic blanket so they could all be scooped up easily when she was ready. Handling them in this condition wouldn't be a good idea because many were stuck solid from that stifling space above. How strange, all that fear for nothing. The room itself was ordinary, stuffy and basically harmless. No ghosts as Julie would like to believe; nothing bad had happened, maybe it was going to be fine after all. She wanted to celebrate with someone and immediately called Kate from the bedroom phone with the good news.

"Much ado about nothing," Kate responded, egging Prudence on as she packed her third storage box today. "Time to let it all percolate if you ask me; take some of those dresses out and see if you can wear any of them…I hear 'vintage' is back in fashion," Kate exclaimed, happy for her friend's good fortune.

"Really, Kate, they just look old, but I have to let the room air out completely or I'll be sneezing for a month," Prudence replied. She was thrilled at the fact that she had something fun to think of instead of the doom and gloom she had already foisted upon her overactive imagination because of a locked room. Kate would stop by tomorrow to have a look for herself. She had little time left before their departure, so Prudence needed to find something really good to show her; something hopefully to do with Tim.

She wandered back downstairs, still laughing at Kate's adaptation of every situation. It was going to be difficult losing her to that foreign land. She snatched a piece of cheese from the fridge along with the left-behind beer, remembering she had put the key in her pocket. *Have to find a secure little place for it or at least an obvious key chain so it won't get lost again.* The door was no longer a barrier; she could afford to savor the moment with a little salt air to cleanse her lungs; her allergies were about to kick in.

She touched her fingers to the locket, comforted by its presence as always and palmed the photo from her pocket. Then she nestled into the oversized rattan deck chair to rehearse, once again grateful her great-grandmother had chosen it for comfort. She would have a whopping good tale for Julie tonight, would blow it out of proportion until she could no longer lie and then tell her how silly all those misguided qualms had been. She would describe the whole thing from beginning to end and Julie would laugh and make Prudence laugh at the 'drama queen' reactions, ones that her closest friends were quite aware of, and all would be well.

She had been trying for weeks to cajole Julie into a visit, spending a lot of telephone time extolling with deeply contrived descriptions and over-exaggerations in order to point out the attributes that she'd discovered, anything to make her come to Maine. She'd made up scenarios to entice... the way the afternoon light hits the trees or the dazzle of blue sky that differs from the soft-brushed Cerulean of the Caribbean; the areas of higgledy-piggledy buildings juxtaposed with the historical ones;

the wildly beautiful Monhegan Island as seen through a lavender haze off in the distance from Pru's 'back yard'.

Soon after meeting, Kate had lured her away from her chores by convincing her she had to see what a truly unique combination of headlands, craggy rock beds and cathedral woods made up the island which is only about four-and-a-half square miles. And because of its many trails Prudence purchased an extravagant pair of hiking boots, but at least now she blends well with the throngs of backpacking visitors who are dropped off daily by chunky boats, no longer a stranger to the Maine coast.

And according to Aurora, Prudence is more like Hannah than she could have guessed; their mutual love of nature and the lure of the lighthouses. They are everywhere, a backdrop for all the professional and amateur photographers, ones who file off the packet or hike throughout Maine to see them. There are books about them in the attending museum stores and about the 'wickies'—those tenders of the lights before mechanization took over. Prudence has filled the haphazard shelving in the cottage with her own collection of photos vying for limited space. This new interest began innocently enough upon her arrival, but it has now grown exponentially and she has memorized colors, patterns and shapes, the indicators known as 'daymarks' that set them all apart and identify them to those who navigate these waters. Oddly enough, she too had felt the need for careful navigation, in life as well as this house where even the walls kept secrets. She has already begun to feel that Hannah may have brought her here, not just incidentally where these landmarks dominate, but intentionally as an offering, a legacy of the Maine that was dearest to her.

The sky is changing again; it's suddenly much cooler. The late August light that was capable of remarkable coloring. According to Beth, it had been a cooler than usual summer, not that Prudence would really know what that meant, but rather than sit and contemplate as she might have at another time, she was impatient to go back to the bedroom.

Setting the half-empty beer on the edge of the sink in exchange for water, she grabbed a bakery roll to quell her sudden hunger...the earlier tidbit of cheese already forgotten. As she tried to keep from gulping the bread, she paused to take in the successful kitchen remodel. It showed off the light to its fullest, just as she had hoped. And it confirmed what she'd suspected when repainting...that she wouldn't mind the winter after all. The sun would provide passive solar heating for this part of the house and the space would always be cheerful. And with that feeling of self-satisfaction, she took the stairs two at a time, racing toward the missing link in Hannah's story.

As she walked into the bedroom, the yellow fabric looked like a sunflower bordering the photos that were a dark heap where she had dumped them. An old, summer weight coverlet found in the bedside chest was underneath the jacket. Prudence knew that her great-grandmother had made the spread's delicate handwork edging as Aurora had said the ladies would sit in her living room once a month and stitch while catching up over tea and this was one of the more satisfactory results.

A beautiful light, the same golden tones washing across the downstairs walls had infiltrated here too and now suffused the wallpaper with its gilt edged glow. She loved this room and the peace it exuded. The slight swoosh of the ocean outside provided a seductive sound that like always, lured her to the partially open window. But the photos beckoned and as she turned to put her glass on the table, she also caught sight of the ray that had fallen right over one tight little clump of stuck-together pictures.

Even carefully prying them apart, she created a small tear in two of the five, but not enough to obscure the scenes, the pretty but ordinary seascapes. She began to lay them out side by side and her breath caught. The other three photos startled her; one was of Hannah alone, a demure smile on her face as she looked up at the photographer. She was dressed in the casual trousers of the late 30's. *She's standing in front of the village lighthouse!* The next one is a little larger...Hannah leaning against a lovely old peapod. It had been hand-tinted and the boat depicted in a pretty shade of green. She was smiling broadly, sure of herself in that moment in time and holding the pendant away from her blouse as if showing it off. The third is of a tall, broad-shouldered man. He was holding his cap toward the boat with pride, his wide grin suitable for a man in love, because Prudence wants to believe he is. *Obviously he is posing for Hannah; the backgrounds are identical.* This picture was identified on the back with a flourished pen, a woman's writing. Taking the locket from around her neck, Prudence placed it on the bed next to the man's face. They were one in the same...Timothy Parker.

It took no longer than a new breath for Prudence to affirm that she would never stop searching until she had the whole story of the man who would have given great-grandmother Hannah something so obviously chosen out of love.

Chapter Seven

Holding the select pictures on her lap, Prudence waited what seemed a long time for the phone on the other end to be picked up. "I'm sitting here in Hannah's chair…the chintz cabbage roses still compete with the wallpaper."

"Is that why you called me, to discuss the chair?" Julie asked across the crackling line.

"No, but I thought it was a nice lead-in since I finally found pictures of Hannah and Tim."

"That's fantastic; what are they like?"

"They look fabulous and to me it's obvious how they felt about each other, and these photos were taken at *my* lighthouse. I have spent hours in this chair trying to figure out what could possibly have happened after he left, but I have to tell you, the not knowing is killing me. It's like a riddle…how could he have so easily disappeared from Hannah's life…where had he gone?"

"You've always said that spot had some kind of power over you and I believe in what the West Indian 'seer' told us."

"She said a lot of things, but since I use it as some kind of refuge, why wouldn't they have done the same. For me, it's a place besides the shoreline, to get away from my day-to-day worries; you know—what's going to happen when the summer people have gone and winter sets in; what's it going to be like rattling around in this old house alone, so it's no wonder I think of that spot as a bit sacrosanct.

"You know, sometimes it even makes me think of Jason and the what-could-have-been syndrome," Prudence blurted before she could stop herself.

"Don't go there again Pru; the man nearly destroyed your self-esteem; he isn't worth more of your time and energy on such thoughts."

"Thanks, but I have actually been able to get past most of that. On the whole my life is really good, except of course, I miss you and my other island friends. I don't rail at him so much anymore though," Prudence said without actually mentioning what she thinks when she remembers that 'past life'…that it would have been wonderful to share this unexpected harmony found in a place that differs so from their tropical one, even though the water still draws like a magnet and the people are equally unique. She had really loved him but she is also reminded of the widow Bond and knows in her heart that hate can eat the soul. She has seen proof of this with her own eyes when looking into Jean's and no one should grow old carrying such a burden.

"Okay, so what else happens there?"

"You have to promise not to laugh; because if you even chuckle, I'll hang up, I promise!"

"I'm listening."

"Well, logically, it doesn't make sense, but then when I go out there I'm usually at the end of my rope and way overtired…I even bring the little cooler with some nibbles and a split of wine so that I can unwind."

"The one I gave you as a going away present; that's sweet."

"Yep, the very same but the rest is a little harder to explain."

"Well they obviously spent time out by *your* lighthouse and now you have proof. Does that help?" Julie asked. "See, I didn't laugh."

"But your voice sounds different; do you actually believe this stuff I'm telling you or are you just humoring me?"

"Why do you think I practically dragged you to see Analese?"

"I wish she could help me but even she can't solve my dilemmas long distance; no one is that good. As I said, it's a good place to think and watch the sun go down—which by the way, if you would just visit, you'd see for yourself—it's peaceful.

"I digress. The tower is ordinary and wears a pretty typical metal ball-topped bonnet like a funny hat if you let your

116

imagination run loose. AND, it's not because of the wine, if that's what you're thinking, but it's so easy there to think that his disappearance has something to do with the ocean and my head gets filled with all the musings and sometimes I actually nod off and dream of that.

"Anyway, we are having the most gorgeous sunsets these days. The trees become tinged in deep orange that bleeds across the sky with patches of blue peeking through...again, you really have to see this for yourself...please. So here we are, the scene is set, the colors have managed to soften and silhouette the tower and then it's mesmerizing and just plain surreal. I'm sure it's just the light and I get a little carried away sometimes—did I hear a snicker? Jules, I dream—at least I think it's a dream—of a woman and she's searching for someone and when I'm awake, I'm so sad. Then like an idiot, I'm scanning the horizon too and then the sky is dark and we're alone with nothing but the whispering sounds of surf cuddling the shore."

"Oh brother, you do have a case for Analese; what an image, and no, I wasn't snickering, actually sniffling; I think I'm coming down with a cold. But remember, she had alluded to unfinished business that last time you saw her. And now I'm going to dream strange dreams tonight no matter."

"I sure have enough of those...enjoy! And thanks for not laughing and please try to work out your schedule...I miss you and have the guest room ready and waiting."

"You got it...I'll do my best...night."

The next day Kate came by for a quick coffee. Prudence produced the photos and told her pretty much the same things she had said to Julie. Kate took it all in the same way she had the notion of spirits which at least meant that Prudence didn't have to explain herself to such a great extent.

"First of all, have you realized how much you look like her? Except the hair of course, but really; it's impossible to think otherwise," Kate said, holding the photo up next to Pru's face. "As to your grand imagination, you know my feelings about spirits, not so far off the mark from that woman Julie was talking about. So for my sake, please take notes or something when you go out there. Then you can fill me in when we talk long distance.

"By the way, as my farewell gift to you, Michael has told me that we may be able to return next summer if all goes well in India," Kate said. "And as an aside, Tim was definitely worth discovering. He's a pretty great looking guy."

"I think so too. Hannah had good taste. I've wavered so much about staying here, especially at first when things didn't go the way I wanted, but I think I've finally made the decision to stay in Maine. I have this crazy need to make things right for Hannah and I don't even know what went wrong, but it's the only logical thing I can do to justify receiving this locket, not to mention the house. And something clicked the moment I saw that photo of them so undeniably happy. Now I need to find out the rest."

"From what you've said, their relationship wasn't at all easy. I think you have your work cut out for you and knowing what I do, I'm sure you'll persevere."

"I kind of feel it's my duty to see it through even though the whole bookstore venture is unsettled. I probably could just as easily go back to St. Thomas, but my instincts tell me that they would have been married unless something bad happened," Prudence said, walking Kate to the door. "And with your great news, I guess I'm here for the duration!"

"I wish I could visit longer, but we're leaving for the airport soon. Think good thoughts, keep in touch often, and hope that all goes well on the other side of the globe…I already miss the Cove," Kate said air-kissing Pru's cheek as she'd always done.

But for all of Pru's instincts, she wasn't aware that she too was preparing herself for romance. A younger Hannah—whom she admittedly resembles—and Timothy had already set the wheels in motion.

With the opening of the attic, everything else in her world had suddenly become brighter and clearer and the crisp, fresh air, a harbinger of fall wafted through the rooms forcing out the last clinging scent of old age. Prudence had already picked the warm white shade that would replace the very stale wallpaper and just the right weight of white fabric for the frayed old chair and eventually the sofa. When completed, it would be a nice reminder of the tropics, cool in the summer and heightened with strong jewel tones in the form of accent pillows and throws for winter. From that very first night in the house, she had liked the way Hannah's chair molded to her body, making her aware how quality purchases can stand the test of time. If all goes well and if she does persevere as Kate indicated, perhaps Hannah's favorite chair would be something to pass down one day, if and it's a big IF, she might actually meet someone to take that next step with.

Aurora should have been the first person to see the photos, but she hadn't been doing very well lately; had begun wandering the Lane apparently looking for her late husband. Fortunately, she never got far since the nosiness of neighbors protected her from that and for the first time, Prudence was grateful for those with that annoying habit. Also, Kitty had finally managed to sign her up for a nice, comfortable room with private bath in an assisted living facility and would probably move her in by the first of October. So it was now or never; a chance to make her memories come to life again, or so Prudence hoped.

Grabbing the last of the little stash of chocolates that she'd always kept handy, Prudence tucked the photos into her bag and walked down the Lane to #25. And just as she was about to pull the doorknocker, it occurred to her that it was Thursday, not the required Monday. *Oh boy—hope this doesn't throw her for a loop.*

Beth opened it right away. "Well, look who's here, Aurora," she called into the next room. "It's your lovely pal, Prudence," she said, winking and tightening her sweater against the sea air.

"I'm just leaving; brought her one of my lobster casseroles," Beth said softly. "I'm worried she's not eating regularly and I know how she likes lobster…don't we all?"

"Beth, you leave me speechless. Hasn't that been pointed out to me ever since I moved into this enclave better known as seafood heaven?" Prudence quipped with the audacity of an easy friendship.

"She's having a good day today; so you go on in and find out what you need to. I'll keep my fingers crossed for you."

Beth had been told about their conversations either by Kitty or perhaps even Aurora on one of these similarly good days. Prudence would have eventually drawn the entire picture for Beth, as they also were becoming good friends, but this made her feel better about being here on the wrong day of the week. She heard Aurora call her name and hugged the other woman goodbye.

To her relief, she received an additional welcoming hug and then saw the 'o' form on Aurora's lips as she spotted the small, square gold wrappings…Godiva could always excite her. Prudence waited until she had scooped up one of the little chocolates, testing it like a child would when they aren't sure of what's inside. Then as she watched, pure glee indicated Aurora had picked wisely—even though they were all alike. Then Prudence placed her bag on the floor beside the sofa and began to hand her one photo at a time.

Aurora looked at them steadily but without words and Prudence hoped her mind was categorizing the time and place. Suddenly recognition informed her movements; the curve of her lips, the slight tilt of her head in a thoughtful gesture and she was there…once again young. Obviously pleased with herself, Aurora patted the spot beside her and then when Prudence was comfortable, began to speak as if she too had been set free of the attic room. "These must have been from around '38 or '39 when Timothy and his good friend, Godfrey, came to the Cove in search of work," she began. "Not that I can remember where they'd come from, but they were both into carpentry and fishing like most men in these parts, especially back then," Aurora stated, drawing upon the photos to propel her. "I know Hannah was working at the Post Office then; she'd put a little 'help wanted' card on the bulletin board near the front window...that's the way we did it in those days.

"She kept telling me the house was way too big to manage and she finally had a bit of income to where she could hire somebody to help with repairs. Well, don't you know not long after, in walks strapping Timothy just as she was about to shut down the counter! She told me in secret, 'nearly knocked my socks off, he was so good lookin'," Aurora winked, supposedly imitating Hannah and getting into an unexpected rhythm.

"And he was...real hardy too, with a nice head of hair besides, kind of light brown except when it looked bleached from being on the water too long. And you can't see it in these photos, but his eyes were a special kind of blue, like that piece of Wedgwood over on the shelf by the kitchen...'smoldering', Hannah used to say.

She stopped for a moment seeing the expression on Pru's face. "Yes, we would say things like that to each other, like all young women, girls really if truth be told, we were so naïve about men at times, not like girls today. And we had our dreams too. I watch the television and see how young people these days forget that about their grandparents.

Then she moved on in that haphazard way she had. "With Jean being widowed so young; her man was a fisherman...terrible thing it was, losing him that way," Aurora said, shaking her head, pausing a little too long without comment. *Where's she gone this time?* Prudence wondered, waiting without interruption so Aurora wouldn't lose the thread. But then Aurora looked up and proudly stated, "Jean and Hannah always seemed to rely on my guidance, probably because my marriage was solid and they were both having their troubles."

121

The time line was getting all scrambled again, but it didn't matter, Aurora was talking. "They sometimes asked my advice about love too and always wanted my recipes. We got very close," she said, closing her eyes momentarily. "Where was I? Oh yes, Timothy. Well, didn't he and Hannah hit it off? He was a good talker; said he knew how to do the work at the cottage, accepted the amount she could afford to pay and put in a solid workday. Hannah always said he was very reliable, always at the house when she came home. She took in laundry in the afternoons. Mind you, Amanda was still with Elisabeth, so they had the house to themselves if you know what I mean."

Aurora's reluctance to reveal personal details had suddenly dissipated and whole sentences poured forth, released by some invisible valve. *So much for naivety!*

"Jean worried a lot back then; she was alone and times were very different, not like you over there all by yourself and happy as can be," Aurora said while Prudence sat stock still thinking she must be putting on a great front if people think everything is hunky-dory (another of Aurora's endless phrases). "And one day Jean set her cap on Timothy, disregarding Godfrey altogether and he was looking for a wife by the bye.

"She knew Tim would be working at Hannah's house during the morning and she made up little picnic lunches for him, delivering the basket by noontime. Hannah never came home before one so you know what she must have been thinking.

"Hannah wasn't the type to have ended a friendship over a man either, but Jean eventually forced it to happen. She knew he was interested in your Great-gran…she was a looker back then… and it drove Jean a little crazy. She was lonely, and young Timothy had become her target. I like to think I helped them some back then and of course, I became widowed too so we helped each other," Aurora offered, veering slightly backward.

"When we visited, Jean was always sympathetic to Hannah's troubles, but I think later it ate away at her that she'd passed over a really nice man while chasing after Timothy. Godfrey had taken up with the minister's daughter, Amy. He might not have been as handsome as Timothy with his strong nose and he was awfully lanky, but he had a big heart. And they built themselves a nice little place in Trescott Mills…I found out when he came to my husband's funeral. And by the time my dear Charlie died, Jean had become as withered as an old prune. Did I tell you, he fell off the roof in '62? It was a pretty stupid thing to do, trying to hang Christmas lights after the first snow. Like ice that roof was, slick as a pick-pocket's hand," she emphasized, leaving no room for doubt and then she childishly popped another candy, savoring it with her eyes closed in satisfaction.

There was no way to find out exactly how or when or where their trysts had taken place or obviously what had actually transpired since Aurora's vivid tale had completely zapped her energy. She had put her head back to rest on an afghan that covered the damask upholstery, a faint smile lingering, maybe remembering. Prudence figured she'd gone to that place back in time with her 'dear Charlie', but for the first time since meeting the widows Prudence clearly understood why Jean, so openly spurned, had harbored all that animosity these many years. She apparently had never found anyone else and might not even admit that she had spoiled her own chance to do so. Her bitterness had spread like angry roots fighting against the death of the host tree and taken a solid hold and now when Aurora moved away, she would be losing the only other person who understood her. Prudence couldn't excuse Jean's bad behavior, but found she sympathized with all of the feelings surrounding lost love; something she herself had experienced firsthand when jilted.

In a flash of movement, Aurora's eyes blinked open wide and as if pulled by a distant force sat upright to indicate she'd remembered something else. "By the time little twelve-year old Amanda came back to live on Thatcher Lane, her mommy and Mr. Parker—such a solid name Timothy Parker—could only see each other while she was in school. They would take walks out near our little lighthouse, you know, the one they painted this spring…Kitty drove me by to watch the sailboats.

"Where was I? Oh right…depending on the season, Hannah said they would sit out on the bank and I suppose, talk of love or matters of the heart, as I like to say. That little girl sensed something was up; canny little thing she was and very jealous of her mother's attention having been deprived of it all those years. I know Hannah wanted to marry him, but she couldn't bear to ruffle the small peace she had achieved with Amanda, always feeling guilty about sending her off to her sister's when times were bad.

"It might be hard for you young people to understand, but Hannah told me she'd had no choice but to push him away, always praying he would come back when the time was right. She wrote long letters to him over in Stonycroft where he'd finally found work on a lobster boat as a stern-man. He even built himself one of those 'peapods'; that's it, that's the one," she said tapping the photograph as if she hadn't already seen it. "And this lovely necklace," Aurora said as she poked a pink fingernail—most likely painted by Beth—at the pendant around Pru's neck. "It was his mother's. He gave it to Hannah for her thirty-fifth birthday. She rushed over here right after he left to show me…odd how I can remember that day like it was yesterday and I don't remember where I put my slippers this morning.

"Oh, Hannah was in love all right," she said wistfully, settling back into the sofa, her energy once again flagging. "She wanted him close to her heart, but he's gone now, like all the rest of them," Aurora said.

Do I dare? "Aurora, do you know what happened to Timothy?"

"Why he died, Prudence, didn't I tell you?"

"Yes, dear you did. I just thought it would be nice to learn when that happened or even how."

"Goodness gracious, I don't really know. I thought it was when Charlie passed, but then I thought it was when Hannah got sick," Aurora said. "Oh dear, I can tell you didn't know Hannah had been very sick," she emphasized when seeing Pru's blank expression. "It was a long time ago, but she near died from grief I think. You can, you know. That's how I felt when my Charlie fell; terrible thing that was, him lying there in the snow like that."

Prudence wouldn't get any more from her today; Aurora was beginning to get things all mixed together. But the 'near dying from grief' might be a clue. Maybe Timothy ended the relationship; perhaps he fell in love with someone else. If only there was an easy way to find out. At least now the aged look of the locket and the original velvet cord made perfect sense, it having come from Timothy's mother. *The photo of the woman with the binoculars...maybe Tim's mother?*

Prudence had kept Aurora talking for as long as she could justify but she also had come to know when rest was called for. The photographs and placing the lovers' story where it belonged in time had to be enough for one day. She left Aurora with her TV on and her thoughts of Charlie still fresh and strolled home slowly, replaying those words, reassured if nothing else, that Hannah had found for however long, a bona fide love, a relationship to soothe away the terrible years with the difficult James Prescott. Now she had a starting point from which to reach for the rest of the story, but not before she paid heed to the more practical side of her life.

She had given over many hours in her quest but it was important that she took the business end of things more seriously if she truly meant to stay. She needed to have additional monies coming in and soon and she'd been smart about her partner. And because she hadn't as yet given Vivian any of the finer details with reference to Hannah and the visits with Aurora and her other concerns about staying in Maine, their new relationship hadn't taken any sharp turns or been sullied in any way by things unable to be explained. And while Vivian was a character to be sure, she was also very pragmatic, a good balance for Pru's idealism. And what could she have given her anyway; so far it was nothing more than a mini-series of events that surrounded her Thatcher Lane home and her place in it.

Vivian, as promised, had been diligent in her search for an ideal location, but each time she'd found one that seemed right, it always managed to fall short of their wish list. The idea that the weather was so unpredictable, that winter might arrive sooner rather than later although not yet the end of September, made Prudence more anxious only because it would bring another set of problems along with the snow…something she hadn't dealt with in many years. It would be so nice to ignore everything and just curl up with the memorabilia and sift through her great-grandmother's life without care, but that wasn't practical or beneficial to anything other than the dreamer living within her head.

Instead, as soon as she opened the cottage door, she bee-lined for the parlor to collect the rest of the photographs and straighten up the room. It too was, even in its old-fashioned way, a welcoming space. The few good pieces of furniture sat side-by-side with things that looked like hand-me-downs or yard sale items, things that must have appealed to Hannah over the years. The woodwork would never go out of style and Prudence had made certain to keep it dusted and polished no matter what else she hadn't time for. One of these days, she'd find the right pieces to exchange, but for now it was comforting to have the endurance of Hannah's life placed before her in this one room. And as she looked around it occurred to her that she had been using her great-grandmother's generosity to fill the gap in her motherless life. She could do right by Hannah in a way she'd never been able to with someone with Victoria's problems.

She laid the kindling and brought in a few logs for an evening fire. *Have to call Herman about more wood soon,* she contemplated. *These are moments to treasure, cozy and alone,* the sound of the ocean hitting the rocks and the hum of harbor activity that was usually preceded by the noisy gulls. Aurora was right after all; her solo existence had a natural rhythm to it and still paralleled to a degree with island life. Although lumbering engine noises had been heard only sporadically on the side of St. Thomas where she had lived, the harbor at Charlotte Amalie was a completely different story…a beehive of activity…both leisure and business oriented. And the Oyster Cove village wharf could be likened to the marketplaces of the past if she looked at it with that eye toward community. So perhaps she had in actuality found the counterpart, at least a semblance of it, to the life she'd worried over giving up.

"You won't believe it, a wonderful space just opened up," Vivian shouted into the phone later that evening. It was a very serendipitous call. "It has hardwood floors, good windows and plain walls that we can do whatever we want with, plus easy access to the main street. It doesn't have a brick wall and it is a bit boxy but the landlord will let us do whatever we need to in order to warm it up and make it special. And since he won't let us put in a stove that I know you would have liked—something about his insurance issues—I'm thinking soft colors and perhaps an indoor water feature of some kind and definitely lots of plants. For some reason, he'd hoped someone would open a modish little art gallery, but didn't seem to mind the idea of a bookstore instead. What do you think? Want to take a look?"

"Absolutely, and it couldn't come at a better time," she replied picking up on Vivian's enthusiasm. "Go ahead and make the appointment. We'll ride up together so we can compare notes on the way back."

She had to laugh at the scene the next day as they drove toward Stonycroft. Instead of taking Vivian's practical car, they were crammed in the small VW, squished like fish in a can against the many items they just might need. It appeared they were prepared for everything except cooking a meal. Even the small two-step ladder lay awkwardly and out of place on the back seat. They were dressed to work and had set their hopes on this property, willing it to be right. The storefront lay just on the outskirts and Vivian, eyes peeled for the real estate sign, pointed for Prudence to turn into the small lot. Most of the businesses in the area appeared to suffer the same lack of parking but were thriving in spite of it. There was a small dance studio opposite, a corner café and a row of storefront shops typical of the area: knitting supplies; a ladies' clothing store; a bar/restaurant and a nearby gas station-convenience store. But it was also very visible to passersby. And the rent was just right.

"That's the owner's car over there," she said, pointing to a Ford Ranger.

They grabbed their bags loaded with the necessary tape measures, pencils and pads and Vivian had thoughtfully brought her camera. She had even borrowed a measuring wheel that she'd wedged between their seats and held onto for the entire ride so it wouldn't hit Prudence in the head. Nothing was to be left to chance.

The structure wasn't particularly impressive; nothing at all like the one on St. Thomas, but what mattered was the interior and how well they advertised it when the time came. Vivian was swinging the bags and practically bouncing ahead, her confidence evident with every movement. Prudence, on the other hand was hauling the ladder and an old portable radio to keep things lively while they worked, trusting that Vivian's perkiness meant that this was indeed a good choice. Prudence tried to match some of her new partner's exuberance, but the outside underwhelmed. Comparisons made no sense either. She would have to make concessions if she were really serious about this project, or it wouldn't work.

"There he is," Vivian whispered as they walked through the door.

Prudence, paying immediate attention to the feel of the empty room and the way the door opened into a vast space of hardwood flooring, hadn't seen who Vivian was talking about. He'd been standing with his back to them in front of a table, rather contemplatively if the way the material of his partially lit shirt was an indication. It puckered with the strain of muscle against an extended arm that disappeared into the darkness as though he were holding a weight. Hearing the door, he turned out of the shadow away from the more obvious papers and the hand that he'd just run through his longish hair—espresso was all she could think of—stopped mid-air as he walked into full light.

Pru's chest constricted as he strode toward them; his jeans and torso-hugging, blue chambray shirt making a lasting impression.

"Hi Vivian," he said with a warm smile. "Nick Pelletier," he said, turning slightly, extending his hand to Prudence.

"Prudence Stone," she replied, accepting the hand as a blush crept upward from her neck. *Vivian just has to do all the talking!*

"I was just going over the building blueprints in case you find that you need to add any partitions; that is, if you decide it's right for you," he said, handing Vivian the key. "Take your time, do whatever you need to and lock up when you're finished. I have a couple more appointments, so you can call me with your decision. Looking straight at Prudence, "Vivian has all the pertinent data regarding the lease and both my phone numbers if you need me.

"I think the idea of a bookstore would revitalize this little neighborhood, so I'm hoping the space suits your tastes. Nice to finally meet you, Prudence," he said, flashing a wide grin back at them as he exited the building.

"What did that mean; what have you been saying to him?"

"Nothing, really…just that my partner was very creative, interesting, and single," she responded, caring little about Pru's embarrassment. "And it just so happens, so is he."

"You really are a piece of work, my friend. The customers won't stand a chance with you here."

129

"So what did you think of our Mr. Pelletier," Vivian queried. "Pretty handsome, right?"

"I guess so, but that isn't why we're here. Let's get to work measuring, okay? Enough about him."

"Since your face is so red, he must have made an impression; don't be so touchy. Who knows what might happen?"

"What might happen is that maybe this is a perfect space; we'll sign the papers and send him his monthly checks, nothing more."

"Ouch," Vivian said, knowing she should mind her own business, but down deep, she felt Prudence would definitely be hearing from that gorgeous hunk of manhood. And she had enough experience to know.

Nicholas Pelletier sat in his car with the keys still in his hand, reluctant to start the engine. He wanted to go back inside, but something told him that might seem foolhardy. After all, Vivian really hadn't said much about the lovely Miss Stone, but he still didn't think she was the type to just melt at his supposed charms, at least the ones other women had 'accused' him of. He was a stubborn man and this one might be a challenge and he liked challenges too and even if he thought there might be some chemistry there, he sensed he'd have to work for her attention.

Prudence, unknown to either Vivian or Nick, had been watching him from the window, pretending to be taking a measurement. It was crazy, she knew, but for a moment, there had been that little 'flip', the surprise feeling inside the pit of the stomach that says look out, pay attention. *Doesn't really matter; you're not ready yet and anything remotely threatening to derail the new plans, can't be a good thing.* Prudence also knew better than to set her hopes on someone else's imagination, especially Vivian's. She always espoused the lack of a need for a man, though she apparently dated quite a few, so why did it matter if Prudence had one or not.

Content within their own thoughts, they spent the entire afternoon and the next morning going through their ideas and walking the footsteps to outline their needs, calling Mr. Pelletier only once for confirmation. At the end of that time and as giddy as schoolgirls, they knew it was perfect. The measurements worked out just right for the overall look of a not-too-citified type of bookstore and yet not too country either. Vivian, as it turned out, was a natural at the business of putting plans into place, fueling the adrenalin for everyone who came within range of her flame-like hair, even their landlord. According to her, Nick had become very impressed with their expectations and perceived layout.

Prudence on the other hand, happily deferred to her for anything that meant dealing directly with the man, wishing to relinquish only her signature and monies when required, still not mentioning the way she felt whenever his name came up. Even Julie had now entered the equation, agreeing to become part of the scheme too and would finally be able to visit Oyster Cove. Prudence had enlisted her help; thought this essential, not only to assist with the pertinent contacts and offer suggestions to the novice Vivian, but at last see for herself the magic of her friend's new world…and maybe that little lighthouse conjured from Pru's crazy notions.

The women wouldn't exactly be duplicating the St. Thomas property, that wouldn't do, but hopefully the end product might create a reading environment that will appeal to at least the majority if not everyone who would drop by…at the moment, that was the ultimate goal. Julie's help and personality and organizational drive would also temper Vivian's overzealous nature and yet provide her with a good foundation. The extra perk to all of this was being able to write off her trip to Maine as a business expense, something Prudence hadn't even thought of.

Chapter Eight

As though the gods had staged the calendar, Julie Myers arrived on a day that virtually exploded with as many variations of russet and gold as nature could provide. The plane came in for a smooth landing as Prudence watched from behind the tinted terminal windows. Her presence on this side of the gate brought back a lot of memories of that first day in Maine as though yesterday. The air was cool, the sky a clear blue and the ground which had just begun to soften when Pru first set foot on Maine soil, was now beginning to harden underfoot. Julie rushed toward her grinning from ear to ear; her hair was longer and she now had a far deeper tan and was even lovelier than Prudence remembered. She looked more sophisticated in her travel garb, almost as though she had developed another layer of confidence after Prudence had left.

"You look fabulous Jules; what's different?"

"Nothing really; I'm just happy and I've been taking a new exercise class, the one with Jeffrey at the hotel gym…you remember him?"

"Sure, but it seems there's something else. Oh well, maybe it's just your hair. It really suits you."

"Thanks, you look great too by the way; although I don't think I've ever seen you this thin. You must really be working hard on this cottage of yours."

"You'll see, but I'm eating like a horse…especially lobster. Wait till you meet Beth," Prudence said having already regaled her with the many idiosyncrasies of all the new people in her life.

"I'm so excited to finally be here," Julie added giddily, pointing at everything like a little girl.

They talked non-stop as always, picking up right where they'd left off like all good friends. And for the entire length of the trip to Oyster Cove Julie kept up a running stream of questions and comments in between all the 'oohs' and 'ahs' at each turn in the road. Prudence had already decided to give her the Chamber of Commerce version first and they fell back into their familiar give and take as the car wound through the little towns, slowing where necessary for pedestrians taking their own sweet time at the crosswalks. Prudence shifted the miraculously smooth-running gears without complaint even for those stragglers not caring whether or not traffic was backing up. The easy glide of the 'stick' never failed to remind her of the still doting mechanic and his 'way' with the ugly bug (Vivian's crass reference).

As they drove through one village with impressive period buildings noted by the plaques on the doors, Julie spotted the big sign announcing that it was the 'prettiest in Maine'.

"I can assure you that Oyster Cove will give them a run for their money," Prudence said proudly. "It's already quieting down around here though; not unlike what happens in the islands when the snowbirds leave. But at least the traffic along Route 1 has begun to normalize from the summer crush; seems everyone appreciates that."

"What's going on over there?" Julie asked, pointing to a long line of people standing in wait at a smallish shed selling lobster rolls.

"Along this little strip during the busy season, food seems to be a major contender for everybody's attention...look around...lots of pretty historic architecture and very tall and highly visible church spires. When I drive from the opposite direction, they surround the town landscape as though they are pointing everyone toward heaven instead of gluttony."

"Perhaps," Julie tossed out with her usual charming candor since between the two, she is the one who still regularly attends. "They are just beckoning those seeking a higher power instead of a lobster roll."

"You have yet to taste one," she scolded jokingly. She had really missed their comfortable bantering as much as she'd missed her best friend's presence.

It was a day meant to impress, especially the color-soaked backdrop that glittered freshly under the canopy of fall, the remembered leaves collected and pressed into scrap books during Pru's youth. "I had a nice conversation with Thayer's secretary, Mrs. Lawton, and she suggested we might carry books about the Native Americans and their place in local history, especially the ones important to this region. I've been hoping to find out more about the Abenacki and Penobscot tribes at first and something I don't have enough knowledge of is Maine's importance during the Civil War," Prudence said while Julie stared out the window. "This could be similar to what you did with the West Indian history section and something fun to research."

"That would be a terrific idea, Pru; I just wish I had more time to explore all of the places you pointed out on the map; it is so beautiful here!"

There was so much to show Julie, but Prudence had to condense the menu, offering only small tastes of the whole, in order to do any of it justice. Unfortunately, Julie had only been able to allot a week away from the Island, all that she could afford given her own workload, even though it wasn't nearly enough time to explore everything. So the best that Prudence could hope for was to whet Julie's appetite so she would want to return.

Much of their time for Julie's first visit would necessarily be taken up with impending retail matters for the store located on the outskirts of Stonycroft within the town line of Trescott Mills. But it would also establish her as the helpful 'go to' person for Vivian as well. This after all, was the primary reason for Julie's time away from St. Thomas and Yellow Bird Books. Although Prudence felt certain once they toured all the areas that had been delineated as important Maine sights that Julie would be besotted with it all, especially the fresh new seascape. She would, Prudence knew, fall absolutely in love with the many classic revivals highlighted by Doric, Ionic or Corinthian columns that would line the route to the newly leased footage, just as she had. They had always been very simpatico in their tastes.

Right now, however, Julie appeared content in the moment and marveled openly at everything old or odd alongside the brand new and all the in-between, which broadly hailed the Mainer's independent spirit. "Eye candy for the discerning; your people must have been fascinating."

"My people...God, it sounds like I have a whole tribe of my own. But I have to admit, I do have a new sense of pride over all of this," Prudence said with a broad stroke at the passing landscape. "But I'm all there is, I'm afraid...no large band of people to gather together around the campfire or in front of my fireplace. Just me and my long gone ancestors rattling their bones seductively, enticing me to stay," Prudence said at last pulling up to the cottage. "Welcome to my humble abode."

"All I can say is WOW."

"Yes, I thought you'd be impressed. I wasn't of course, just nearly fainted when old Mr. Thayer stopped in this same spot back in June. Who would have thought I'd own something like this?"

"I'm so happy for you Pru; you deserve it, really," Julie said with endearment. "But I'm sorry about that," she said, pointing to her luggage that had been crammed into the little car. "I just couldn't figure out what to bring for this time of year...and I don't think you did this justice on the phone; the cottage and surrounds are way more," Julie remarked as they wheeled her luggage inside.

Prudence immediately rushed her through the house to show off the extent of her remodeling which was mostly the kitchen and powder room and a splash of fresh paint here and there, simultaneously explaining a few of the future plans. Then she practically dragged her back outside before it would be too dark to see what she had spent hours raving about and then, just enough time for a quick glass of wine on the deck before dinner. Lastly, Prudence unveiled the photographs of Hannah and Tim, reiterating what she'd already told her about the lighthouses and in particular this one.

"You promise you'll take me to see this?" Julie asked pointing at the village monument, the one of Pru's many imaginings. "I'm so glad to be here and share this with you and I'm exhausted, really. That new employee just isn't cutting it. She looks me right in the eye and tells me she understands what I'm saying and nods yes to all her instructions and then does what she wants. She's making more work for me instead of less and she took my car on an errand for the store and somehow managed to bang up the fender. I have had it with such a 'dipstick' and after a drink I'll fess up to her real name because you know the family and will be surprised by how dumb she is."

Prudence recognized Julie's version of saber rattling, which made her feel more than a little guilty because their St. Thomas business had run like clockwork during their partnership.

"I know what you need my friend; we're going to have dinner at the Lone Dory just up the road, where you'll have 'proper' Maine fare and even though most of the seasonal people are gone, the locals are still hanging out and they are worth seeing. Actually, the place reminds me of Topsider, the way it was when you and I first moved to St. Thomas…full of real characters."

"Sounds like fun for my first night. But if we're walking, I'm going to change into something warmer, the air will do me good."

"I'm about to convince you once and for all that the local lobsters can pass muster against the spiny langouste we're used to. My new reputation depends on it!"

"Your Maine roots are showing again my friend, but I have to admit, they look good on you."

Since she'd already spent a few long distance coins explaining that the Dory was where the very cunning Shirley worked, Prudence hoped Julie's first night on Thatcher Lane would be as amusing as she had touted over the phone. "Beware, Shirley will jump at the chance to 'pimp' those men out the moment she lays eyes on you."

The restaurant was still somewhat quiet, but the bar area resonated with the hearty laughter of the workingmen and a few women happy to be swapping stories as usual. This really was small town at its best and about as 'real' as anyplace could be. Shirley spotted Prudence and waved them to a free high-top table opposite the bar where she could keep an eye on them.

"What a great looking bar," Julie said looking over at the layered reflection from the bottles lined behind the gleaming finish. "That reminds me of the one on St. Thomas, the one outside the hotel that was destroyed by a hurricane quite a few years back."

"I remember, but this one is actually cut from a large dory, one that the fishermen would take off the bigger schooners in order to fish with nets and harpoons."

Suddenly Shirley appeared with their bibs and tools and already knowing that Prudence enjoyed wine had brought two glasses of their only chardonnay.

"These are on the house," she said, taking in Pru's earlier description of her Island friend's sleek hair and green 'cat's eyes'. "This must be Julie," she said extending her hand, sizing her up as though she was a tailor instead of a barkeep and waitress for the night.

"Shirley, I've already mentioned on the way over that you have a couple of good looking cousins, but unfortunately, she's spoken for; you understand," Prudence said noticing that Shirley's hand was reaching into her pocket for the telltale photos.

"Well, sure, but I still think they're worth taking a look at. I'll just leave 'em here while I put in your order. I took it for granted you'd want her to try our best dinner."

"Thanks Shirley and thanks for the wine. We appreciate it," Julie said, finally unwinding, thankful Prudence had ended up in a place so similar to the island hangouts—colder outside, yes, but quirky and without pretense.

"What did I tell you?" Prudence grinned; Shirley hadn't disappointed. "The house wine is also predictable, but one can't be too picky when it's free," Prudence said, raising her glass in toast.

"These guys are not bad looking my friend; are you sure you want to remain celibate forever?" Julie asked, simultaneously checking out the animated faces in the far corner.

"Okay Jules, I know you're still concerned about me, but I'm doing fine, really. I just haven't felt ready to go through all of what dating entails. I will tell you, however, before Vivian does, that our landlord, Nick Pelletier, is a very handsome bachelor. She has this notion that he and I might just like each other…if I would only do something to encourage it."

"Well, that sounds promising. Are you going to encourage it?"

"I haven't given it any more thought. For the time being I just want to get the place up and running," Prudence said, realizing how deceitful she was being. She still couldn't bring herself to admit she had been jolted by his presence. Maybe he would come to the store while they were all there and Julie could size him up for herself. She trusted her opinion over anyone else's.

"I get it; you are not going to join the ranks of women who now believe that you can ask a man out first?"

"Are you kidding; with my track record?"

"Not every man is going to do what Jason did; you have to believe that Pru."

Just then Shirley brought their lobsters and Julie handed her back the photos. "They're really cute, Shirley, but like Prudence said, I'm spoken for. Don't give up; there's bound to be someone nice out there for each of them."

"What do you suppose she's hiding?" Julie asked as she picked up the 'crusher'. "There must be something wrong with them if she hasn't had any takers yet!"

They worked their way through the hard-shelled lobster, splashing the liquid and some of the butter onto themselves. These lobsters were a real challenge and although Prudence had really taken to them, she still found it difficult to eat them without making a huge mess.

"Good thing we're walking back; I'm bursting...they're really rich and I always use too much butter," Julie said. "Great atmosphere too, maybe we can do it again before I leave, my treat?" she asked, knowing there would be debate about that. "I still can't help wonder why two strapping men need help landing a date," she said, hiccupping and laughing at the same time.

"Beats me and speaking of men, Jules, you've been skirting the issue all night. What's going on?"

"I was going to tell you at the right time, but since you've asked, I've met someone. His name is Coop...well actually Cooper Smith and don't you laugh."

"Coopersmith—now why would I laugh?"

"I knew you would do that; you can be such a kid sometimes! But honestly, I really miss having you around especially since this man walked into my life. Prudence, I think he could be *the* one, really. And I was going to tell you right away but I wanted to do that in person...not over the phone...and then you were so excited to show me around and tell me about everything you've been doing; the timing was just off."

"Wow, I seemed to have missed a step since I moved up here," Prudence said. "How did you two meet?"

"It was shortly after you left and I'd been working late and decided to stop at Surfside for dinner. I was simply going in for a take-out meal and was sitting at the bar talking with Ronnie, the bartender. Coop came over from where he'd been sitting and struck up a conversation. I presumed he was just flirting, but I didn't mind, so we just talked and talked and I stayed there with my dinner-to-go."

"And?" Prudence asked.

"And, the next thing I knew he was dropping into the store late in the afternoon before closing and would sit with a coffee until the last customer left and then we'd talk...and talk...and talk. He's very interesting, well-traveled and Black."

"First of all, I can't believe you kept all of this from me during all our late nights on the phone. Did you really think any of this would upset me? The Island has always had its abundance of really nice, available Black men in case you've suddenly gone brain dead," Prudence said with surprise.

"I know that. It's just that I've avoided that particular romantic pitfall ever since moving there. The voice of my parents is always in my head. When I moved to what they imagine as the steamy jungles of some small third-world country instead of the 'sub-tropical' variations of utopia you and I have sought, they made a point of bringing up the problems that inter-racial couples could encounter. And I know they were only trying to be helpful because they really are very liberal. But I'm still their little girl and whatever their intentions, the concerns stuck with me and I guess I've been sort of frightened away from forming that type of relationship, because of them and what they implied."

"Jules, we've overcome red tape and bureaucratic obstacles for years; the world has just survived the Y2K threat; I think you can handle your family."

"I'm from a small town in Nebraska, remember? And my family didn't visit the islands the way your dad did...and they are a little overprotective!"

"Okay, so tell me more about him."

"Coop was on St. Thomas looking for a way to expand his floral business in the islands and he's tired of the New Jersey winters. He also does a lot of traveling and has intimated he would love to have me join him on his next trip."

"Oh, I get it...you think your folks are going to judge him based on the fact that he's a florist, not that he's Black?"

"You're terrible. He's an importer on the large-scale European market you ninny, not a vase filler at 1-800-Bouquets!"

"Then I don't see the problem," Prudence replied supportively.

"There really isn't one. It's all me and my provincial qualms and he is thankfully unaware of this."

"Jules, follow your heart. It's pretty obvious if you look around that there are not a lot of people of color and I miss the diversity and yet, for many of our island friends, it would be a difficult adjustment not only to be in this colder climate, but to leave their homeland."

"I know; some of their family roots are as deep as the old banyan trees. And I don't want to leave the ones I've put down, not yet anyway. Coop wouldn't change any of that; he loves the place even though he wasn't born there. And his world is multi-faceted with regard to travel and climate."

"See, you're already sorting it out."

"Well, you've always managed to make me see the other side of things. Boy, I really needed this visit," Julie said hugging her old friend. Prudence the romantic always made these things sound easier than first thought. Of course, Prudence the broken hearted still hadn't crossed over that scary threshold since that miserable sod, Jason Spronk, had left her. And Jules, noting the flicker of interest when mentioning Nick Pelletier, wished with all her heart that someone wonderful would come into Pru's life as well.

"I think I just may be falling in love with Cooper and if that's the case, I'll just have to find a way to make it work," Julie agreed, at last saying goodnight somewhere in the middle of the wee hours.

"Why did we stay up so late?" Julie asked Sunday morning as she was being shepherded outside, a miniature cloud of steam hovering over the coffee as she warmed her fingers around the mug.

"We covered a lot of ground and admit it, it was fun to sit out and watch the stars, even if it was a little cold," Prudence answered.

"A little cold? Have you forgotten where I've just come from?"

"Don't be such a wimp; I got used to it," Prudence said, making Julie laugh as she practically dragged her toward her favorite ledge, something Prudence had continued to rave about even after all these months.

"Well I do appreciate the loan of your jacket, but remember we've only had four hours sleep so I'm not sure how well I'll navigate."

The morning was heavy with dew and Prudence embraced her dear friend who for the moment had stopped whining. She was looking up toward the heavens, awe written across her face as she suddenly shouted—"Looorrd have mercy!"

"You sound like my old West Indian neighbor, I'd almost forgotten…the perfect exclamation for this particular spot," Prudence said with pride.

"This water, the ledges, this place, makes me want to praise something, anything," Julie said hugging Prudence back, finally understanding why she had called it her temple.

After their suitably homemade prayer offerings from the mighty rock of their mock church, there was nothing left on the morning agenda other than meeting up with Vivian. Prudence had to loan Julie her one and only black wool blazer to go with the slacks she'd brought and as always, she looked terrific in anything she put on. The only dot of color to her now entirely black ensemble was an apple green sweater with a cowl neckline. Some women just had the magic touch. Prudence had no choice with a guest that looked so great; this was not the time for the casual every-day wear and besides, the cooler weather sort of merited something special.

She took a quick look in the foyer mirror, liking what she saw. "Great jacket Pru," Julie exclaimed over the short rust-colored suede Prudence had recently bought on sale. She'd paired it with medium-weight brown slacks, a simple sweater and added a scarf for the occasion and felt as they headed out the door for the aging VW, they at least exuded the requisite professional air. She silently pondered if any of her primping had anything to do with the off chance that Nick would see their cars and drop in.

"If I'm not mistaken, while we were admiring my backyard view, Vivian would more than likely have consumed a nice mimosa or bloody Mary as part of her Sunday morning offering," Prudence said on the highway, raising her voice slightly over the sound the engine...*wonder what Zack will find this time?* "I can just picture her...feet up on the pouf in front of the fire and the Sunday paper spread everywhere around her silk pajamas.

"She told me from the get-go that she liked the finer things in life, even if she lived among the small critters on the farm. Said she'd spent too many years answering to a tightfisted husband and now would spend what she pleased!" Prudence stated as they pulled in beside Vivian's car.

"It's so great to finally meet you, Julie," Vivian said brightly as Prudence brought her into the newly rented premises. As expected, Vivian was dressed for fall in a toned down striped wool poncho over black slacks and black shoes with heels just high enough to say 'smart' and still be comfortable. And it came as no surprise to Prudence that these two women shared a natural ease with strangers, complementing each other and getting acquainted in that chatty manner that women comfortable in their own skin can do. They had already left Prudence standing to one side as they walked purposefully around the space which Nick had said could be divided and which at the moment was not very warm. It was one of those days when it was colder on the inside than out.

"This is where I think we should have our little reading area, what do you think?" Vivian asked Julie as she walked her through the small opening pacing off the section that she was determined to 'sell' Prudence on.

"That could work nicely," Julie replied, checking the expression on Pru's face. Seeing no resistance, she went on to explain, "Maybe you can consider placing a nice accent rug here as well and maybe some kind of cart or low table with an electric kettle and tea fixings...something easy for the customer to prepare themselves...rather than a messy coffee pot. You could always put a Mr. Coffee for your personal use in the back room, out of the way."

"Wow, that sounds perfect," Vivian said excitedly. "I hadn't thought of putting a rug here."

"Great idea Jules; we can't duplicate what I loved about the St. Thomas store, but this really could work," Prudence added.

Prudence relaxed as she saw the vibe happening as though they'd all been working together for many years which of course made all the other discussions fall into place; the projections and plans for the future if all goes well. They carried on for the better part of an hour... as much as could be tolerated without the heat on.

"Time for lunch in Stonycroft my friends," Prudence said herding them out the door. "I'd like Julie to see just how quaint it is before it gets too cold again."

The air still had a good nip to it, but she knew that for a little while today, the remnants of summer's sun would linger long enough to tolerate being at the sidewalk eatery. That is, if they ate fast...Julie was (politely) whimpering about the temperature again.

They chose a table without an umbrella so they could enjoy the scenery and absorb the warmth and as they waited for their orders, a couple of teens drove by honking loudly to gain the attention of the pretty young waitress about to serve them.

"Oh the good old days," Vivian piped up, waving back at the flirtatious young men.

Prudence caught the flash of red with chrome trim, reminding her as well of those teenage days and proms and noted that the waitress' face had begun to color from so much attention. Smiling at the memories, she followed her usual instincts and began to watch the little street vignettes taking place all around them, leaving her friends' voices to float away. She had always been pulled toward human interaction and many of this month's tourists, the 'leaf peepers', would provide that type of raw material.

Some of the pedestrians were busily snapping their cameras at scenes composed just so for those who would later view them while others, mostly couples with branded, overstuffed shopping bags strolling hand-in-hand, were poking in and out of art galleries and jewelry stores. Then, as if she'd been reading a novel, she zeroed in on an extremely good-looking man dressed professionally as he hurriedly strode out of a nearby restaurant and down the street. She presumed he was heading back to an office of some sort and watched as he slowed for a moment to assess his image in a storefront window. As he straightened his tie and stroked his hair from his forehead, Prudence went into a zone all her own. She was certain he would now glance quickly over his shoulder before ducking into the nearest doorway as if on his way to a tryst with a lover important enough to risk such a public agenda. This, of course, was what the character of the book she'd just finished would do. If only she could remember the title!

"Don't mind me," Prudence replied hearing the tail end of Julie's remark. "I was lost in my own little world again."

"It's nice to see that some things don't change," Julie quipped back, pushing aside the extra large portion of heavily spiced apple pie, the one that Prudence hadn't taken notice of because of her daydreaming.

After lunch, they drove toward the Salter Inn location to make a very brief 'pilgrimage' to the lighthouse on the bay. Prudence was anxious to showcase one of the main points of interest, allowing Julie to see for herself where she had started on this new journey.

"Breathtaking," Julie exclaimed, fresh out of exclamatory words but beginning to shiver once again.

"Prudence seems to have developed quite a penchant for these towers," Vivian explained to Julie. "I guess I've just become immune but it's nice to see it through fresh eyes. I probably should have guests more often myself; at least it would give me a chance to enjoy what's in my own backyard so I stop taking things like this for granted," Vivian explained.

"Okay ladies, you have indulged me long enough," Prudence injected after noticing nearly another hour had passed. "I can see Julie is about done in with the cold. Didn't you say something about martinis, Vivian?" Prudence asked.

"Onward ladies," Vivian said, linking arms with her new friends. "This requires team spirit."

In Julie's honor, Vivian had decided to expand the classic versions and concocted a batch of chocolate martinis as they gathered around the large wood countertop in her comfortable country kitchen.

"While I was enjoying my morning coffee, I thought, why not fix my favorite hors d'oeuvres to go with our drinks," Vivian said as she took what looked like little 'logs' wrapped in wax paper from the refrigerator. "I want you to know that I slaved over these babies too!"

The ingredients were written on an index card still out on the counter: Parmesan cheese, flour and a good extra virgin olive oil infused with garlic that had been stewed at a low heat and then discarded. "All that's left now is to slice them into nice uniform circles and bake them," Vivian said as she began the process, checking the card for oven temperature.

As they talked and drank, a fantastic aroma began filling up the kitchen. Prudence knew that Vivian used only the finest ingredients in anything she prepared; loved quality oils, succulent fruits, fancy cheeses from around the globe. She even traveled to Portland when necessary to obtain them as well as the full-bodied wines she preferred. She had honed her tastes as soon as she had the freedom to do so without the constraints of financial censorship from a difficult husband.

They were making so much noise they nearly missed the bell on the timer. Vivian set the piping hot baking sheet on the counter, spanking the greedy fingers that reached for the first extremely hot sample. "These have definitely got to be on the menu for our opening party," Prudence said as she savored the first of the little golden 'coins'.

As they nibbled, unable to stop at just one, Vivian extolled on the attributes of her home on behalf of the guest of honor. The property, shared with a barnyard full of chickens and ducks and even a couple of middle-aged geese, was the stuff of storybooks, spanning out past the kitchen window to a rambling hill beyond. The house itself was a great vintage cape that Vivian obviously enjoyed expounding on—the history of previous dwellers and provenance of particular pieces of furniture and it had all been recently updated with paint and a small section roofed with a ribbed metal. This high quality roofing was just becoming very popular in the area and Vivian's was the loveliest shade of eggplant, something Prudence didn't think she'd have had the nerve to do, especially with Mrs. Bond around!

Vivian pulled out diaries and a few photograph albums, one's Prudence had already seen but still enjoyed and the type of information that warmed Julie's heart. They were the proof that Vivian would be wonderful at her newest career. Her last important job before baking had soothed her need to keep busy, had been as a long-time manager of an up-and-coming furniture store positioned beautifully on Route 1, South, enabling it to cater to year round foot traffic as well as having plenty of parking on the premises. That is until she could no longer stand the continual re-arranging and 'plumping' required of all those pillows and the constant dusting of fragile bric-a-brac.

Vivian's home, set on beautiful acreage and exuding plenty of warmth and hospitality, was the ideal spot to celebrate their wished-for good fortune. And as Prudence had already explained to Julie, Vivian had been divorced quite a while, having decided long ago that marriage was not to her liking…animals, however, were a different story. They were much easier to understand and care for and she had proved it by introducing her guests to Cicero and Tulip, two really overfed Siamese cats. Something about their eyes made Prudence a tad squeamish; they looked as though they could devour her.

"Before I have another martini, let me go over a couple of these wholesaler lists," Julie said, placing her glass aside. "We have Baker & Taylor and Ingram," she said handing out sheets for their perusal. "Vivian, you'll want to go over the intricacies of discounts, shipment handling and current titles," she added. "Right now there are popular best sellers by John Grisham, Patricia Cornwell, Danielle Steel, Nicholas Sparks and quite a few more that I think you will want to carry. Here's the list of titles you can both examine for your first order. Then, of course, you'll want to find some known Maine authors or at least books about Maine to round this out."

Fortunately Vivian was already quite savvy regarding computerized equipment that would be needed to run the shop efficiently. Doing business on an island when she and Jules had first started out hadn't required the depth of electronic data processing that would be needed here, plus more often than not, electronic equipment was decimated by the yearly hurricanes, leaving them without power for many days and sometimes weeks. But happily Vivian excelled in being able to bring their new store up to date electronically. And she had at last talked Prudence into acquiring a cell phone, something even Julie didn't like, and which Prudence still disliked and therefore, seldom used. But the part that Prudence most enjoyed was the creative layout of the floor plan and bringing it all alive.

Suggestions flowed easily and by the time they'd finished their coffee and said their goodnights, they had every space earmarked and had agreed to hire Herman to make a few custom shelves. But oddly, though Vivian had managed to find a nice used chair temporarily stored in her guestroom, there was no more mention of cats.

"I think maybe she noticed my reaction to the Siamese," Prudence said to Julie on the way home. "She never once said anything about having one in the store; something she's been talking about for quite a while." *Might as well be talking to the wall,* Prudence thought. Jules, bundled up like a swaddled baby, had quickly fallen asleep to the sotto voce sound of Pru's words.

Monday morning came far too quickly for Pru's pounding head. Brilliant light poured through the kitchen window setting the room ablaze with its warmth and fracturing her eyeballs with the glare. She could hear the water running through the old pipes as Julie took her shower. Prudence had let her sleep in wishing she had done the same—her thumping head proof of the previous night's pleasures. Strong coffee and a substantial breakfast were required before taking her friend up top to the now rather pristine attic room to see what all the fuss had been about. Prudence had saved it for last.

"So this is what you've been harping about all this time?" Julie asked, entering the room with her third cup of the morning. They had already consumed copious amounts of Pru's favorite espresso strength coffee along with thick slices of bacon with eggs and toast, everything necessary to sop up the previous night's indulgences.

"Well, I realize it no longer looks as ominous as I probably made it sound, but it had its moments."

"No," she remarked, "but it could easily have been a room like those that the 'rusticators' yearned for in the early 1800's. Only then it would have probably been bigger, better furnished and included the entire house," said a slightly wrung-out Jules trying to come to terms with the pounding at her temples. "Was there anything else of significance up here besides the photos of Timothy and Hannah?" Julie asked.

"Well, the cabinet naturally," Prudence replied. "Notice the similarity to the color of my doors?" She added thinking her friend's tone of voice had gone beyond the disagreeable of a hangover.

"As to the color, you are surrounded by the sea after all, so I don't think it all that unusual," Julie said with even less feeling.

"You've gotten awfully matter of fact all of a sudden, but maybe you're right." Prudence said. "My imagination has really been working overtime since I came here and I guess I may have overdone it, but look at the way the photo of Tim turned up, no matter how odd it sounds. But after all, you're the one who introduced me to all that fortune-telling nonsense."

"I don't understand it any more than you do; I just happen to like having tarot cards read for me. Who knows, maybe you were just born with a sixth sense," Julie said more sharply than necessary. Her head was killing her.

"Does this have anything to do with the fact that I'm stuck here in Maine or at least want to be for a while longer than I thought because that acerbic tone doesn't really suit you."

"God, I'm sorry, Pru, all of that camaraderie and conviviality yesterday got the best of me, brought everything home to roost so to speak. I have to say I got a little green with envy at you and Vivian starting up a new store; reminded me of all the fun we had back then and it hasn't been a lot of fun without you lately. I miss my best friend and I'm behaving badly. Forgive me?"

"You know I do, but do you think you could help me go through these papers; truthfully, I waited for your arrival specifically to do so…the box is chocked full. And since you're the one who chronicled the West Indian material so easily, I thought you might actually enjoy this, maybe after we've exhausted your local tour," Prudence said, removing it from the top of the cabinet and carrying it back downstairs.

"And after a few aspirin," Julie added, holding onto the banister. "Sorry I'm so grumpy, but you know I realized when I woke up that everything here has this huge hold on you now and though I'm glad for you on many levels, I wish you were coming home soon...the place just isn't the same without you."

Bingo! Prudence had been right; that was not Julie's personality speaking. "I know, and you don't have to apologize; I understand. I wish this were you and I starting all over again too; even the hard work was a lot of fun."

"Maybe we could just hang around here for a couple of days, relax, take in the lesser-known sights, so to speak, catch up with a few of your other friends...I'd like that."

Prudence was happy that the tide had turned so quickly, but then Julie had always been that way...never held a grudge...maybe with the exception of Jason...and she snapped right out of her little mood as soon as she'd heard herself sounding so jealous and whiney.

After a little 'hair of the dog' to jump start the rest of the day, they spent a few moments with the neighbor Whitley, who couldn't have been more charming if Julie had been a wealthy divorcee of a certain age. Prudence had never seen that side of him and wondered what else he might have up his baggy sweater sleeve.

For Tuesday and Wednesday's tours, Prudence decided they would drive to some of the remarkable gardens; both the perfectly cultivated English style and those free-formed and stepped with small stone walls and round-about pathways and places to sit and look seaward.

"So these are the pretty streets you've told me so much about?" Julie asked.

152

"And that's the house that Herman had been repairing which as you can see, besides my house, it's a great example of the beautiful work he does. But my requirements were nothing compared to what was needed on this one...see the widow's walk at the top."

"Another wow from me. How romantic, just like you said. Something like that just might be a good reason to move north."

"You think?"

The next day was off to Beth's house, even though Herman was working outside the village and would miss their visit. "It took my Herman years to finish this," Beth said motioning them through the rooms. "He was always in-demand and unavailable and so our home was always on the back burner of the money-making ones.

"He'll be disappointed that he missed you girls, but this gives me a better chance to talk about the islands with two independent-minded women. A man just gets in the way of that kind of conversation," Beth said testing the waters with a slight wink, hoping Julie would enjoy her own independent streak.

"But first, tell me you're not planning on going back there are you, Prudence?"

"What makes you think that?"

"Well, this young lady is your best friend and it wouldn't be unusual to feel really homesick after this visit and quite frankly, I—we—don't want to lose you to that mysterious pull of the Caribbean...I've read those travel magazines you know." She and Herman had really taken to the child, as they thought of her.

Prudence looked at Julie guiltily because of their earlier conversation. Beth had no way of knowing the nerve she'd touched. Prudence didn't quite know how to respond.

"I won't lie, Beth; since Jules' been here I do realize how much I miss St. Thomas and our store and particularly the day to day relationship and admittedly, I'm not looking forward to the cold weather, but I'm in no position to move right now." She could hardly tell her all the reasons; it would sound foolish.

"Mrs. Jenkins, I would love it if Prudence came home today, but she's doing what she has to and I'm rooting for her success here. Maybe we can both talk you into a second honeymoon on St. Thomas so that I can show you around and you can see for yourself why we love it so much."

"Call me Beth, please, and won't Herman be surprised when I suggest that?"

"Then it's a deal…when you're ready, I'll be waiting," Julie said graciously.

"We're not right on the water like our Prudence here with that wonderful built up ledge," she said to Julie as she ushered them outside realizing she'd done enough to overstep her bounds. "My husband has to have a place for his tools, his toys and 'my' lobster traps. Most of those plots around Pru's house just aren't spread out enough for him and me either. I like having this rambling garden and growing my own vegetables," Beth said walking them around the grounds that showcased a small, shingled shed covered on one side with pot buoys.

"And you don't have to put up with cranky neighbors either," Prudence said, winking at Beth.

"I know dear, you've been an unsuspecting innocent with regards to 'the widows'. But I have faith in you; you'll get by. You've come from good Maine stock and don't you forget it."

Prudence had saved the small village lighthouse for last. To differentiate from so many, she'd been referring to it as the 'mini light' when she and Julie talked on the phone.

"So this is where you see the 'lady of the night'?" Julie injected.

"Oh, that's not fair, she's supposed to be lonely or searching or something; not readying for work on a dingy street corner."

"I'm sorry, I couldn't help myself. I think we drank too much."

"I know we did and fortunately, that's a rare occurrence," Prudence said as they got back in the car. "I don't know what I thought you'd feel or see, but in any case now you have and

154

you'll just have to wait for the next episode to happen," she said looking back over her shoulder just in case.

"This is very spontaneous, but let's drop in on Aurora," Prudence suggested as they parked the car back at the house. "We can walk over and I think she'd like to meet you; that is if she's in a good mental place today." She'd already brought Julie up to date on the dementia concerns and that Aurora wouldn't be living on the Lane much longer.

"You must be the girl from the Island," Aurora said, causing Prudence to do a double take. The old gal had retained that kernel of information from a previous visit.

Then Aurora ran her soft hands along Julie's tanned cheeks. "You're as pretty as a picture."

"Thank you, Aurora; so are you," Julie replied, quickly warming to her.

Aurora showed Julie the photos of Charlie straight away and then she took them into the kitchen where things were rather helter-skelter…she'd been searching for a cake plate for Kitty without any luck. They took a pass on Aurora's offer of tea, mainly because with this big a distraction there wouldn't be much else on her mind. But it was long enough for Julie to realize how much this darling lady had come to mean to her friend.

"It's easy to see the connection; my guess is Hannah was probably very like her, loving and sweet and important to Aurora as well," Julie said. Exiting the house, they took a left instead of a right.

Months earlier, Prudence had filled an entire phone call with her thoughts about the infamous widow Bond and how along with inheriting the house, she had also been stuck with Jean's animosity. As they walked a bit further, Prudence casually lifted her chin in the direction of Jean's house, not wanting to point for if she did, Jean would just as surely catch her.

"I told you that woman has antennae," Prudence said as Jean started out her door.

Jean must have realized how that looked and began busying herself with some sort of chore. The best they could do was imitate her attitude and walk along pretending she wasn't there.

"She could definitely use a little 'makeover,'" Julie said, remembering the comic descriptions that had come to life in the late night phone calls.

"I knew you had to see to believe," Prudence replied. "But as much as it makes me laugh, it also bothers me to have to feel that way toward her. I truly wish I could have made friends, for Hannah's sake at least."

"My guess is that if you find some of the answers you're looking for, you might be able to do that. There must be a good reason she behaves this way toward you…well not good because it's not nice…but you know, something she thinks legitimate. And it might take longer than you'd like," Julie said, hooking her arm through Pru's as they walked back home, happy to be on the same wavelength again.

"What are we going to do about dinner?" Julie asked.

"Perfect night for the Dory," Pru replied, happy not to have to figure out what to cook. "A good fried fish dinner is a great way to absorb any residual alcohol." Neither were used to martinis.

"Let's take a look at these while we wait; it's still a little early," Prudence said sliding a carton toward Julie.

A box of papers and the rest of the photos had been set aside for the right time and this was a good a time as any. She spread them out on what had become quite the conversation piece that Herman had created from an old door.

"This is unbelievable!" Julie exclaimed all over again about the handcrafted table he'd built and put in front of the large window he'd fashioned from two smaller ones. "And I love this window seat," she said taking in the entire kitchen which now gleamed with polished wood and creamy colored walls and appliances that had been shined for the occasion. Prudence had exchanged Hannah's dark green cupboards for a lighter, fern-green paint and had found a pretty botanical print fabric for the seating area that complemented.

"I wish you could stay longer or come back for Christmas, Jules," Prudence stated as Julie continued to admire everything, running her hands over Herman's handiwork and tucking into the inviting space by the window.

"Me too, but my family would be devastated if I neglected one more Christmas with them."

Prudence poured some sparkling water as they thumbed through some of the pictures. She could tell Julie liked the old black and whites, enjoyed the timelessness they created. Stopping mid-pile, she suddenly handed one over, "Did you see this one; could it be anything significant?"

"I'm not sure, let me take a closer look," Prudence said. It was an unfamiliar and rather ugly barn, which she obviously hadn't noticed since she'd paid so much attention to photos strictly of the village and those seaside-related ones, anything that might lead to Tim.

"Not that side, turn it over, there's writing on the back!"

She did as instructed, immediately chastised for such negligence to detail. But sure enough, printed right where Julie said was the poignant word, *Home* along with the initial *E.*

"I don't know…maybe it means something; Great-grand's attorney did say that Hannah and her sister, Elisabeth, were raised on a farm. Wouldn't it be great if this was the one?"

"Well, my friend, what say we take a nice long drive in your very compact car and go find out? You said you haven't made plans for my last couple of days and it would give me a chance to see some of inland Maine and perhaps help you out at the same time."

"I feel like I've been running you ragged, but if you really want to do this, I'll call the lawyer for directions before we go out for dinner. I know very little about that part of the state but I do know the ride will be pretty this time of year and thank you;

I probably wouldn't get around to going there on my own for quite a while."

"My pleasure," Julie replied, back to her old self once again.

Bright and early Friday morning and with multiple colored highlighters for marking the brand new copy of *DeLorme's Gazetteer*, they set off like a couple of Girl Scouts for the 'interior', and the Kennebec River. It only looked like a vertical slice of blue on the map page, when in actuality it cut a large swath through the state. By mid-morning quite a few of those pristine pages had become dog-eared and/or messily spotted from handling. They'd stopped for coffee and donuts along the way and a sugary residue would remain as a reminder if the map book was ever again put to use. Their inability to find the right roads, which had naturally taken them far a-field of their destination created random detours. This ineptitude was made perfectly clear when the VW pulled into 'Cowshit Corner', a place that couldn't have enjoyed too much notoriety.

"Holy mother of God," Julie exclaimed over the sign. "What wonderful looking cows," she blurted scanning the area for the reason for the name. "Boy, no one back home in Nebraska will believe this one, not even the farm neighbors. It will certainly revive Christmas dinner!"

After many U-turns and lots of coffee interrupted only by rounds of eye-watering laughter, they finally happened upon— because by then, it could only have been accidental—the right stretch of highway connecting to the farm road. Which would have been obvious if either could have read those maps properly in the first place and would have been as Thayer had said…somewhere between D4 and E5. The road had obviously not been maintained in a very long time because it was strewn with potholes and overgrown borders the entire length, but at the very end stood what was left of the very same barn as in the photograph. Though badly deteriorated since the picture had been taken and diminished from its prime by harsh conditions, there was no mistaking it as well as its obvious abandonment. It was so sad looking, with its sagging exterior just lying in wait for the wolf to 'huff and puff' it away. The fields beyond it were fallow and weedy. But as in the photo, a large glass-free, mullioned window stood out beneath a slanting roofline. Only now a lone survivor of the changing weather, a spray of wildflowers had carelessly attached itself to the sill covering part of the hole with what seemed a bittersweet commentary.

They had to wade through the high straw-like grass toward the main house, neither of them wearing proper walking shoes…a couple of island 'bumpkins' they would say later…slipping and sliding in the toe-tangling mess. But unlike the barn, the main building had held onto some of its original charm and appeared relatively intact and with the flanking chestnut trees, could have at one time been a depiction for a New England Christmas card. Prudence knew what would come next. Jules, the history buff would sift through her computer-like brain and define the style of the house.

"What a large piazza," she said. "And look at the biggest of those rocks over there; probably would have bordered a meandering path from the garden to the road and more than likely quarried near here; bet we could find out with a little research," Julie continued as predicted. But then she smiled and pointed to the ceiling of the overhang. "There are two theories for that color blue…one is that it creates the illusion of daylight—mimics the sky. And the other from the south that I particularly like, where it is referred to as *haint* blue and though the same shade, was thought to ward off evil spirits."

"Well, you know where I stand on that theory given our years in the West Indies, right?"

"I agree, *haint* to ward off evil spirits; remind me to tell Analese when I get back to St. Thomas."

"I'm positive a swing must have hung there at one time; see those rusted hooks?" Prudence asked, pointing upward. "It's so quiet here. Imagine the way it might have been, creaking against a soft summer breeze when all the chores are finished and the children are tucked away in their beds."

"There you go again, waxing poetic; Maine is having an effect on you, but I could use some of that back home. My new clerk sometimes behaves as though she is one floor shy of the top, if you know what I mean. Forces me to be serious about everything."

Prudence had already picked up on small changes in Julie's personality, the shorter fuse especially. But most of it was the stress of trying to manage with incompetence, not an easy thing for someone so bright and normally easygoing. She felt another stab of guilt for leaving St. Thomas even if they both understood there hadn't been any choice at the time. She hoped to make it up to her with this little daytrip and whatever history was buried in the boxes back at the house and because that's all she had left to offer.

"Let's go inside;" Prudence said. Julie was entitled to her very own historical diversion from thoughts of work.

They peeked through the grimy windows and spotting a huge fireplace, Prudence tried the loose-jointed doorknob, which was unlocked. "Definitely consider it abandoned," she stated and saw Jules' eyes light up at the prospect of physically entering someone's past.

"Do we dare?" Julie asked.

"I don't see why not; if there was anything valuable inside, it wouldn't be left open like this and it is after all, sort of mine. By the looks of the road and everything else, I doubt if we'll be caught for trespassing."

"I think this is called a 'keeping room'," Julie explained, entering the front room.

"And this is the largest hearth I've ever seen; think of the fun one could have in here," Prudence exclaimed.

"Well, if nothing else, it would keep the house well heated, at least down here," Julie said, hugging her jacket closer and wandering off to the room beyond suddenly walking with new purpose.

The plan had worked, Prudence thought, as she ambled toward the kitchen that had at one time been painted an odd khaki-color, so like one of the historical shades she'd seen replicated for new-builds when she was looking for the cottage paint. Here too there was a wood stove but unlike the one in Hannah's house, this version was very large and probably the primary cook stove. She walked back in search of her friend, who had already managed to disappear. *Happily wandering around and probably taking notes,* she presumed. Then she saw a thin cone of sunlight that had begun to play along a dreary gray wall. That paint color was indistinguishable because of the years and layers of accumulated dirt and neglect. She could only guess what might be underneath the grime emanated by such a large fireplace.

But transfixed by that angle of brightness was the room's only piece of furniture, a lone ladder-back chair minus its middle slat but with its cane seat still intact. And as though by design, the light had captured a beautiful and delicately intricate web spiraling its frame. The ray, like a baptism of nature, pointed out the uncanny resemblance to a Native American dream catcher...*perhaps they had borrowed this spiritual pattern from the unsuspecting insects.*

"I think we can forget about going upstairs," Julie declared. "It's too eerie even for me and there just isn't enough light. Who knows, I might fall through a hole in the floor up there."

Just then Julie's shoe hit a hollow sounding note. She took a step forward, two back then sideways covering the entire area around it. Then she knelt down and used her knuckles.

"Pru, come here, quick!"

Prudence knelt beside her and tapped where Julie had. "I don't see why, but the sound is definitely different and I'm certainly no expert on old houses. Maybe it's just a loose board or cracked underneath from lack of heat. I don't have anything to pry it open with; not even sure what would work," she said as she noticed Jules rummaging the little 'catch all' bag she'd previously stashed in her luggage.

"This might work," Julie said, handing over a professional-looking nail file.

Prudence knelt beside her and dug the sharp point into a seam almost bending the file, but the board wiggled slightly. She then managed to insert it a little further under the edge while Julie used her pen to brace the wood and they continued that way until it began to free up.

"It seems to be the shallow end of a 'crawl' space," Prudence exclaimed as she reached into the hollowed out spot beneath the boards, her eyes glued to the small tin box.

She lifted the dusty container from its hiding place; it was unlocked, obviously in such an innocuous spot, not requiring a key. With tentative fingers, she opened it, praying a spider or some other creature wouldn't jump out and saw a small packet of letters bound by a grosgrain ribbon. Julie beat her to the punch and plucked them from the box as Prudence sat down cross-legged onto the floor as though they were about to begin a yoga session. She slid the letters out since the knot was loose and noticed that two of them were addressed to Elisabeth Clark.

"This is Hannah's sister!" She exclaimed, unfolding the first and holding it up to the minimal light.

Dear Sister,

I miss you and your wise counsel but am so fortunate to have the friendship of two wonderful women who live nearby and know a lot about Thatcher Lane. They have taken me into their fold, particularly dear Aurora Durn. I wish you could meet, as I know you would have so much in common. She also works with fine lace and is teaching me the awkward ways of a crochet hook. And she is a wonderful cook, but unfortunately I do not have time to plan meals for myself because of things that already consume my hours. I worry so about your situation and hope you have not been too troubled by having Amanda stay with you. I miss her every day, but this is no place for a child, not yet. As you know, James Prescott left me with little and when I begged you to keep my daughter for a while, it was not an easy choice. I feel that I have to keep reiterating this fact so that you don't think I'm just selfish. This house is in much worse shape than I could have imagined. The roof leaks, many of the windows require sealing against the elements--storms that pound the coast that I never knew could be so loud. And I've found a hole where the sill of the clapboard meets the earth and though I've tried to plug it up, I still hear scratching in the walls at night. And that keeps me awake and exhausted in the morning. On top of that my finances are strained beyond their meager limits. Again, I apologize for complaining because I know you too have your problems, but it helps me to reinforce to both of us why Amanda has been put into your care.

Please know how much I appreciate what you are doing, especially since you have your own family to consider and I continue to worry about Jared's disposition during all of this time. But on top of the money earned from taking in laundry, I've also acquired a job at our small local Post Office. Therefore, I will try and send additional stipends for my daughter's care as soon as possible. Please know I do not wish to burden you longer than necessary and I will come for her once the house is safe enough.

Bless you,
Hannah
April 1935

"My God, Pru; how awful that must have been for both mother and child. Did you know about that?"

163

"Only the bits and pieces I've learned from Aurora."

"Read the other one," Julie said, now really intrigued.

Dear Elisabeth,

It won't be long now and I am grateful for your patience. I've made a wonderful friend; his name is Timothy Parker. He arrived in the Cove just as I was losing hope regarding the house and feeling at my most vulnerable and we have become somewhat close. I can almost hear your words of caution and I promise I am paying heed seeking only honesty and compassion, all things lacking in my late husband. And Mr. Parker has kindly offered to drive us to the farm next week so that I can at last have Amanda home with me.

My gratitude to you also extends to your understanding of my child's tenacity and high-spirited nature. You have at least been able to encourage her to write to me and though her letters are short and childishly to the point, at least she is finally communicating. I pray over the situation every day knowing it hasn't been easy for her either and hope one day she will come to see it was done out of love for her and her well-being. Perhaps we shouldn't get her hopes up, but if all goes as planned, we will arrive to pick her up on the fourteenth.

Your loving sister, Hannah
March 1939

"This seems an odd place to store away keepsakes," Julie said.

"Maybe it was one spot her husband didn't know about; don't forget it was her family farm before she married, so she would have known every inch of it. More than likely it would have been covered by some type of rug anyway and perhaps she squirreled away household money to send to Hannah," Prudence offered.

"Strange there weren't more letters like that in between those years, but maybe they didn't seem significant enough to keep," Julie said. "But there is one more, without an envelope; it fell on the floor beside you."

Prudence read what appeared to be a very strange letter from Elisabeth.

October 19, 1920

Dearest little Hannah, I awoke this morning with such a pain in my chest, I thought I was dying. I am not ill, not really but heartsick with dread of spending the rest of my life ankle deep in the chores of this land with a man I do not love nor see how I ever will. I so wish I had not run into Doc Wilson at the store yesterday; it has only made my discontent worse knowing what I had to give up. Naturally, I love my son, but now that I am with child again, I am consumed with all that is lost to me forever. I know this won't make sense to you until one day you are of an age where decisions regarding your future are placed before you.

In my case, father always said it was foolishness for me to help Doc in his clinic, even though the man praised me highly, always encouraging me to take up nursing. But instead father betrothed me to Everett; a calculating, cold-hearted man who thinks of nothing except acquiring land in hopes it will give him prestige. Father picked his protégé well since this was always our mother's complaint about him.

Thankfully, my sweet and precious sister, you are too young now to know what any of this means, but it is my fervent wish that when you are old enough to understand, you will have left this Godforsaken place to make your own way in a larger world. That you will accomplish the things I never had an opportunity to do. This farm consumes everyone and saps the joy from the day. Perhaps if I had a different nature, I would not find it so difficult, but I had found my calling and now all that is left is bitterness. This letter is for your eyes only and I shall put it away for safekeeping until I can one day remove it from its hiding place without fear of reprisal. Until then, I shall pray for us both.

Your loving sister, Elisabeth

"How tragic," Julie said.

"Yes, but you can see why she'd want to hide these from her husband. Think how desperate Elisabeth must have felt to be writing this to her ten-year-old sister. From what I can gather through Mr. Thayer's documents, James Prescott Ellison would have been responsible for taking Hannah away from the farm as her sister had wished, but sis couldn't have foretold what difficulties that presented to her younger charge. Their mother, Olivia, had died when Hannah was around three I think, so poor Elisabeth had been saddled with responsibilities all her young life. No wonder she'd been looking for an escape from the farm.

"And what's this?" she asked picking up a tiny drawstring pouch nestled into the corner of the tin. The inside of the box was nearly as dark as the earth beneath and with the excitement over the letters it had gone unnoticed. "This is really pretty," she sighed as she emptied a small cameo brooch into her palm and then up to the fast-disappearing light.

"It's beautiful, Pru," Julie said, fingering the gold filigree surrounding the carving.

"And I hate to say 'finders-keepers', but we can't leave these things here to be swallowed up by time. I'm taking the tin and its contents back with me and let Mr. Thayer know about the brooch, but I don't believe there's anyone to claim it. Elisabeth's children are dead; my father's parents are gone, so legally I believe it's my duty to rescue them from obscurity along with Hannah's belongings."

Feeling slightly giddy and rather self-satisfied, Prudence replaced the board over the empty hole leaving it just the way it had been found. Certainly, there would be no one to come looking at this juncture in time. "We've done enough exploring for one day; let's head home," Prudence said, happy to have a few mementos and one more window opened onto the world of her great-grandmother.

On their drive back to the Cove, they accidentally found the old cemetery near Bingham, Elisabeth's final resting place. Considering their navigational inability, it was a feat for which they were not only surprised, but also grateful since they would be able to pay their respects. But this little stopover was unsettling too because of the many gravestones so old and precariously leaning, like dominos about to fall. Elisabeth's was no different…slim and pockmarked by time, its top edges rounded and hugged by a small cape of fuzzy moss, though her name was still legible enough to touch in greeting or commemoration of a sad-sounding life. The hidden-away letters that wouldn't easily be wiped from memory had formed a picture of questionable years and hard times that both were more than happy to leave behind on the dirty floor of the empty house.

There was no sign of Jared's grave or either of the children's at least in the near vicinity, something she would have to sort out later after Julie had gone and maybe not even until the new business was up and running. Prudence knew it would be ridiculously easy for her to befriend even those long-departed, to make them whole again at least in her mind's eye; she was her father's daughter after all. She was also too much of a delver and a reader and an observer of humanity and it would happen by itself if she weren't careful and now was not the time. She needed to resolve Hannah's mystery first.

The ride back to Oyster Cove was many miles less than their mistaken routes to the farm. It was also remarkably quiet with each deep in thought about a place rich in history and each for different reasons. Once back home, Prudence readied the kindling and small logs, something she knew Julie missed in their tropical locale. She too had originally come from a place with changing seasons before landing on a sun-drenched jewel, much like Prudence.

It was a lovely ending to a heartfelt day; a small fire burning in the grate, Beth's gifted homemade oyster chowder and the gentling melancholy which had stayed with them long after they'd left the farm. It lingered in the quaint living room as they warmed their limbs by the fire and having eaten seconds of the rich soup when Prudence decided it was time to check out the box. "Do you think you can handle a little paperwork after all this?" she asked Julie.

"I think it's a great time, especially now that you have more tangible proof for your mysterious puzzle...see I've brought good luck," Julie said a little sleepily. The exuded heat had mellowed both their moods.

Prudence always thought, out of naivety if nothing else, that the box would contain forms concerning household accounts, perhaps things related to James Prescott's disgraceful financial troubles or even school records for Amanda. Small stacks of paper began to grow on the floor as they categorized the material. Most of what had been saved were clippings cut or torn from various newspapers. The more recent ones having to do with festivals and holiday doings in the Cove. A few household slips were randomly mixed with the articles and those were for things purchased when the house was being repaired.

"Look, dress patterns," Julie yelped unexpectedly. They were neatly folded and of no use to someone as clumsy with a needle and thread as Prudence, but the clippings were definitely worth reading.

"Please let me take the patterns back with me," Julie begged. "I'd like to compare them with clothing in a great book on the 19th century and I promise they'll be guarded with my life. And as soon as I'm finished, I'll mail them right back," she stated.

"I doubt whether they'll require that much looking after; but of course, you can take them. And don't rush, I won't be sewing up a dress any time soon."

Julie felt the last vestige of melancholy lifting, happy to regain the lightness of being that came with their friendship. She and Prudence were more than just business partners. They were the sisters that neither had. Playfulness had reasserted itself and revived her tired-out, overworked mind. She had needed this break away from a difficult patch of time, the hiring and letting go of assistants who never match up to Pru's ethics and drive. Holding one of the patterns up to her body, content to be here, Julie twirled around and caught a glimpse of Prudence touching each item with care. She noted that as she did this, Prudence also fingered the locket. Apparently, she never took off. It was a poignant image in a rare moment and one she would carry back on the plane with her because her visit was nearly over.

While Jules was dancing around the room, antics never to be seen on a runway model, Prudence probed carefully and scanned the headlines and banners from local newspapers and those in other parts of the state, compiling them far more thoughtfully than she had the photographs. This paper might disintegrate if she weren't cautious and now that she'd been to the 'homestead', every item needed respect.

"Look, Jules, look what I've found!" From a corner of a yellowed sheet of newsprint torn slightly at the top, she spied part of a name. Because of the tear, she couldn't make out which paper, but it obviously had something to do with the Kennebec Valley.

Julie had stopped dancing and was leaning over Pru's shoulder while she gently freed the fragile paper from the unsorted pile, staring, mouth agape when she realized what it was. She read the small subtitle: **Trapper Recalls Life as Log Driver,** under which a grizzly, weather-beaten face stared back at them.

"It says this is Wiley Clark! He's Elisabeth's son, Hannah's nephew and he was a champion log driver!"

Julie stopped and peered over Pru's shoulder, the importance of anything related to the woman in the old farmhouse immediately taking precedence over old dress patterns. Even though the date was missing from the torn edge of the newsprint, it was still intact. Then, with barely concealed pride, her friend pressed it as though touching a bruise and smoothed away the creases making Julie feel as though she were witnessing a rare gift.

Julie had known Ben from his days visiting in the islands before all the tragedy and it made sense that Prudence needed more than most might ever understand of such familial connectivity. As Prudence began to read the unusual bio regarding her great-uncle and his unlikely career, Julie listened to that soft-spoken voice, the one that used to read at the children's story hour and was grateful for the second time that day to have been a witness.

The article showcasing Wiley's prowess as a driver, was filled with odd phrases and the exchange between himself and the reporter dialoged the use of 'cant dogs' versus 'peaveys'. And at this point Julie began taking notes because it was confusing and she'd always been a collector of trivial minutiae.

"I can see that you'll start bringing books on Maine history into the St. Thomas store now that we've piqued your interest," Prudence exclaimed, noting for Julie's sake, that Wiley seemed to favor the 'dog', the one used for 'pulling'. They made no more sense than 'birling' that was apparently different from 'driving'.

Much of the article was focused on Wiley's time spent as a lumberjack that apparently had intrigued the reporter, and how the men were required to maneuver wide carpets of logs downriver, all the while leaping from one to another constantly trying to prevent jams at the dangerous bends along the route. As she continued reading, Prudence doubted whether the previously mentioned tools would have made such a treacherous job one bit easier; but it was also difficult to imagine him out on the icy water, spinning rapidly, reversing quickly, or doing whatever it was that would have made him stand out among his peers. It was even harder to fathom any of the men—outfitted as they would have been, in woolen shirts and high-topped caulked boots—performing any part of such a frightening job and regretted not having tangible evidence of it left behind at the farm. It would have been especially grand if a small bit of memorabilia had been found in Hannah's attic besides just books and clothing.

Wiley's tale played out for the reader on three columns of the tea-colored paper and stated that he'd been born on a farm, but that he also considered himself a river man. The newsy piece placed him in his late forties and the following braggadocio indicated he'd honed his youthful skills at hunting and trapping to an award-winning level about as easily as he'd taken to driving: 'Four beaver, nine bear, nine coons and, of course, only one deer'. These answers given to the inquiring reporter about a season's kill, had obviously taken into measure Maine's deer-hunting quota.

By all accounts, at least in what she was able to glean from the newspaper, her great-uncle Wiley was small, alert and very quick and had learned the ways of the river by the time he was fifteen. "Nothing like all those Paul Bunyan caricatures in the children's books," Pru said, handing over the first and largest segment of the two-page interview.

"It says here he 'rode with the best of them' and when asked if it was some feat to do this, Wiley reportedly shook his head, 'not to a boy brought up on the Kennebec'. Wow, this is wonderful stuff," Julie said, recapping what Pru had just read. "He was pretty amazing, don't you think?"

"I do and captivating to say the least," she replied, closing her eyes as she remembered the map showing the length and breadth of the Kennebec stated here to be one of the 'highways' for floating logs to the fast emerging sawmills and shipyards in the days of the earliest colonists.

Prudence began reading the second part to the story, the difficulties that would ensue along with the fear of certain death if the men were caught between or falling under the long logs herded downriver no matter how much bravado expressed to the reporter. And she surmised that bravery might also have been balanced with great camaraderie created by the very nature of imminent peril each time they took to the water. But it was Wiley's mouth-watering descriptions regarding the food during the gatherings at the end of their workday that pulled it together, giving it that human touch.

"Listen to this…'baked beans, brown bread and the best danged biscuits I ever tasted, as good and probably better than ever came out of a stove oven'…that's Wiley's spiel about the camp food," Prudence read.

"Imagine how ravenous that type of work would make them; certainly the sort of rib-sticking food that would have been devoured with the gusto of a starving man," Julie emphasized. "And what a wonderful storyteller your great-uncle was! Too bad we couldn't have enlisted him for a book-signing event."

"Right…Hannah's nephew was certainly adept at setting a scene. I liked the descriptions about living in the large tents set up along the riverbanks long before the shacks had been built, but I especially loved his bits about the food. It's all so much easier to picture through his words. And with his gift of gab, it was probably an environment very suited to the spinning of many a tall tale."

The journalist, Prudence noted, had pressed for more that day and Wiley had responded with what might have been a tacit pride, that he 'picked up logs on Moosehead Lake, drove the East Branch and the Dead River or West Branch and the Main

River from The Forks all the way to Five Mile Island.' Apparently, anything that got away from there would have been lost out to sea.

Prudence laid the fragile paper aside, closed her eyes and lifted her nostrils to the imaginary aroma; the smell of biscuits rising in an iron pan over an open fire, hoping to redeem that singular moment of Wiley's pleasure. But all she got back was the furl of smoke from the burning logs and she sneezed heartily.

At the very bottom of the nearly empty container was an unexpected death certificate for a four-year-old Olive Clark, Wiley's sister and a smaller newspaper clipping regarding Jared, husband of Elisabeth. It stated that he'd died of complications from a hunting accident. It wasn't much to go on and there was no further mention of Wiley's latter years leading Prudence to presume that he probably moved away and was buried elsewhere. At least this bit of information confirmed the lack of markers at the cemetery. There would be time to search historical records for the missing pieces, but at least she had a framework with which to begin when she was ready.

"This has been a terrific experience," Julie declared as she refolded the patterns, putting some of the other things into an orderly manner. I wish I could stay and help with your research, but I know I'll be back…Oyster Cove can be addictive!

"That's what happened to me, Jules and you will always be welcome. And if it works out, Cooper will be too."

There were many dreams wandering freely in the two upstairs bedrooms on that particular night. Julie had been parading around in 19th century garb while standing watch at the lighthouse she'd recently become acquainted with. Prudence on the other hand, found herself in a thick grove of pines, walking and walking with no specific destination in mind but with a small clearing made up of nothing more than light at the end. It would all be gone by morning, but not their memories of a wonderful week spent together on the Maine coast.

Chapter Nine

The story of Wiley Clark's youth, his time spent venturing through the Maine woods and 'driving' the swift rivers, had given Prudence another and somewhat truer sense of the long-buried ancestral past and touched the surface of Hannah's upbringing on that same farm outside of Bingham. Neither she nor Elisabeth would have had it easy there and it pained Prudence to re-read those letters found under the floorboards. The barren rooms hadn't done much to make their imagined childhood any friendlier or more comforting either and she felt it important that all the precious documents have a meaningful spot to commemorate them. A wonderful idea, propagated within Julie's fertile mind, caused Prudence to visit a frame shop to see if resorting to mounting them under glass would do the trick. Before readying to leave for St. Thomas, Julie had remarked that Prudence, because of the lost key, had inadvertently made the room more consequential than merely an attic.

Another project...but still, wouldn't it be wonderful to ouse the mementos and turn that room into more than just a orage unit, perhaps a studio/library/office of her own. Maybe e would even take painting lessons like Ben had; perhaps from of those 'plein air' types who flourished up and down the line. In her own neighborhood, they had been sprouting up ooms rising through the foggy atmosphere. All d them near the cottage, whole groups of them ner instructors and hauling enough gear mules.

r works created with the vibrant e wowed her. The painters often could be of use on safari and spent g the rocks and uneven surfaces and ing the light at least when it finally breaks through the mist. A lot of energy expended in order to complete a small painting. But the more she thinks of all that effort and Ben's struggles with watercolors, the more she's grateful for her love of books. That aside, it seems only right that framed pieces of her family ties would do well in their familiar surroundings...or was she still imagining that the spirits really watched.

Although the week with Julie had passed far too quickly, it had ended on a particularly high note with a final lobster fest in Beth and Herman's big yard followed by a long walk along Hannah's beloved shoreline. As she waved goodbye to Oyster Cove, Julie, dressed once again in her smart-looking travel attire, also had tears in her eyes.

"I'm thinking that we've unlocked much more than a room with Hannah's key," Julie said, trying to keep her voice light.

"As always, you're very astute and I wish you were staying longer," Prudence replied, pulling into the airport parking.

"I'll be back," Julie swore hugging her fiercely as she saw the dampness on Pru's face.

Prudence couldn't look back; she was consumed with the repeated sequence of parting and almost wished she hadn't committed to staying with such conviction the last time Beth had cornered her. She hated feeling this way especially since she thought she had come to terms with her conflicted duality, the two sides of everything that drove her near crazy some days, the balancing act of a Libran personality.

If she returned to St. Thomas, she'd never know what happened to Hannah, plus she'd constantly be reminded of Jason. If she stayed, she would miss everything that previousl informed her identity; the one she'd been happiest with bef being so badly hurt, but she also might miss the chance Nick, at least if what Vivian expressed were true, that he at her with eyes of longing. *Obviously, you haven't be about your expectations Prudence Stone!*

She threw her hands in the air and got into the little 'bug' and drove north, her face still wet from where they'd 'bussed' cheeks, trying not to create anymore melodrama than she could handle for one day.

Vivian might still be there, she thought as she accelerated the tiny car toward the store, moving rapidly through the penumbra of light that would soon blacken as quickly as snapping off a lamp. That was the only thing Prudence truly disliked, hated in fact, the way daylight was stolen at this time of year, made worse when the clocks changed. Her ambitious new partner had planned to photograph the exterior for future ads and she was hoping to catch her before she left for home, maybe even grab a bite to eat. She needed a way to wind down and Vivian was the perfect anecdote to the small lingering wistfulness of airport goodbyes.

But as she turned the corner onto Doyle Street, instead of just the black Blazer, another was parked as well. She immediately hit the break and clutch causing a hiccup from the little VW as she gripped the wheel and turned the car back toward Oyster Cove. It was the Ford Ranger, Nick's car.

By the time she reached her front door, she could hear the ringing from inside. She always forgot the new cell phone making it impossible for the few who knew the number to reach her.

"I know I said I'd try to catch you, Vivian, but I saw Nick's car and something made me hightail it out of there. And yes, it was a childish thing to do, but hey, nobody said I was perfect."

She let Vivian go on ranting for a few more minutes until it registered that Nick had also witnessed her fleeing. Apparently he had just exited the building unaware that she might arrive. Vivian had conscientiously kept it from him because of the last outburst caused by her meddling and had been trying to call her ever since. Prudence, having said sorry but not wanting any 'bad blood' between them, called her again that evening repeating her apologies. She hated confrontation almost as much as Mrs. Bond thrived on it.

It had been a most unsettling night with hours of fretting, ashamed of her behavior and worse. Nick, someone she had hoped not to become involved with, was now causing her to behave badly. She was sipping her morning coffee when the phone rang, jolting the stale doldrums of embattled sleep.

"Prudence, I have Aurora settled in her new space, and she's been asking for you." Kitty said. "Can you come up for a visit on Friday?"

"Absolutely," she told Kitty. "As long as you're certain the change in weekdays won't cause a problem; I really am anxious to see her. How do you think she's managing away from the Lane?"

"She's doing all right and I don't think it will be a problem, especially since she mentioned she'd like you to bring Timothy by for tea," Kitty said. "But if remembering the past makes her happy, that's all I care about, even if she loses reality occasionally."

Prudence chuckled, but said no more, keeping her hopes to herself. She so wanted to continue their last conversation but at least, she thought, by the end of the week there would be something new to amuse the older woman with; maybe even clarify for her the framework of the new business. Although even as she thought it, she wasn't quite sure the word 'clear' should be used in conjunction with anything to do with Aurora these days…*bless her heart.*

The week passed quickly as they bustled about taking care of loose ends so they could nail down an opening date. Vivian had taken the necessary pictures for advertising purposes and Prudence had spoken with someone from the local radio station that played classical music, a chance to pick up a broader range of readers. Just about everything was in place. She hadn't lost her knack for organizing and list making either and the cottage was dotted with sticky-notes and the new corkboard contained multi-colored pins categorized for the many tasks. Still Prudence had to force herself to blot Nick from her mind, which in a way created its own drama, very like trying not to think about the missing key. It had always been in the background.

Each of the fall days now seemed prettier than the one before and none as beautiful as the drive northward on Friday. Arriving at the residential facility, she was instantly impressed with the manicured grounds and unpainted fencing left to fade like driftwood which led to the beautiful buildings that made up the large complex. The sky held the promise of the unexpected Indian summer, something else gleaned from Beth's storehouse of Maine weather factoids and as soon as she pulled into the visitor's space Prudence removed the already too-warm jacket. The wool blend sweater would be more than enough for the short walk across a pedestrian bridge to the unit.

Aurora's apartment was one of five within the wing nestled on the near side of the main building. Her door had been garnished with an autumn themed plaque and was surprisingly opened before Pru's finger lifted the small brass knocker a third time, a good sign that meant she'd been expected. Aurora was dressed in a pair of worn, dark green corduroy slacks and what looked to be a new sweater. Tilting her head just so, she greeted her with a big expectant grin, probably thinking about a hidden piece of Godiva, Prudence realized and hugged her as if she were a cozy doll. Her embrace told her that Aurora was a little thinner than usual. Her curly gray hair smelled of the fruity perfume of a fresh shampoo and was twining around her face with the ever-present two barrettes doing their best to hold it at bay as always. "I am so happy to see you; it's been too long Aurora."

"Do you like my apartment?" she asked in a childlike and unsure voice as if this nod of approval would mean everything. *This is a downsized version of her living room on the Lane, minus the striped wallpaper.* "Of course I do; it's really pretty and suits you perfectly," Prudence stated taking in the furniture. Aurora's favorite pieces had been brought up from the Cove: the embossed salmon-colored divan trimmed with darkly stained mahogany arms and legs; the Queen Anne dining table without its extra leaf and with only four of the eight chairs that existed in the larger room of the Thatcher Lane house and last but not least, a pretty 'pie crust' table similar to Hannah's but larger and with the disk propped vertically in order to fit within a corner near the window.

"This is a good size kitchenette, Aurora, certainly adequate since you have the large dining hall downstairs." Prudence had passed the cheery communal space on her way up that Kitty had said catered to the healthy nutrition of its elderly residents.

"Come see my bedroom, Prudence," Aurora said, taking her out of the kitchen as though cooking or lack of was a foregone conclusion. It was your typical, adequately appointed sleeping quarter painted a soft powder blue with a hardwood floor covered with one of the smaller of Aurora's fine carpets just under the bed where it wouldn't cause her to trip. There was an easily-accessible and wheelchair-friendly bathroom with safe, non-skid flooring as expected.

Aurora looked happy enough, Prudence thought, at least cared for by a conscientious staff from what Kitty had said. The apartment wasn't terribly large in comparison to her house on the Lane, but she was showing Prudence through it with small flourishes as though it were. Then as any good hostess would, led her guest back into the sitting room and the comfy sofa just as she had for those visits to the house on Thatcher Lane. As Prudence sat facing Hannah's old friend, she couldn't help but imagine her great-grandmother in a similar place; it made her long for the lost opportunity of getting to know her with the days still stretched out ahead as some of Aurora's still were. While she had come to love Aurora, Hannah was her blood and it would have meant the world.

Aurora, as always was nattering on about all the memorabilia, the items that had accompanied her to the 'home' and totally failed to notice the tiny shadow of sadness that came over Prudence. It was understandable, just as the fact that Aurora had already forgotten about the tray she'd placed on the low table while she'd been waiting for her visitor. Prudence knew what to do; there was no point feeling sorry for something she couldn't change and began to pour the now highly steeped tea from the brightly polished silver server. Then instead of the expected candy, she placed a biscuit onto Aurora's plate from the pack she'd brought. The cookies were a compressed, currant-filled rectangle, not too sweet and surprisingly available this far away from St. Thomas where Prudence had first discovered them. And they appealed to the elder woman's taste for dried fruit.

"I'm so glad with winter coming, that you have so many large windows in here. You'll have wonderful bright light all season long."

"That's what Kitty said, but I'm worried that it will fade the fabric," Aurora said with a little frown as she patted the cushion.

"I'm sure she'll help you figure that out; you'll see; it will be fine," Prudence replied as she took in the familiar pictures on a nearby wall, ones plucked from the Oyster Cove house and arranged creatively within the limited space. There was only an entry wall and one large living room wall without windows that could have been used for this purpose and centered on the larger of the two was a wedding photo of Aurora and 'dear Charlie'. Circled around it was a graduation photo of Kitty; one with Kitty and her husband Dan posing with their wedding party, a sepia-toned picture of Aurora's parents and one of Charlie's brother Jim.

Like Jean, she was childless, but there were many smaller frames standing like little gardens of posies where they'd been grouped on the various accent tables scattered throughout the room. These photos depicted extended family members and those friends who'd shared past holiday parties held over the years at the Cove. Prudence instantly recognized the one of the 'girls' that Aurora had previously shown her, among them. The faces surrounded her with love and warmth, just the right medicine for this new time in her life.

Prudence felt very at ease; loved how well the windows illuminated the spacious rooms, "Are you adjusting well to your new home?" she queried.

"I guess it's all right. I still get a little confused when I wake up in the morning and forget where I am. At my age it's not easy to change, but I'm nearer to Kitty and her husband. They pop in more often than they did when I was on the Lane. And I've already made a new friend. His name is...oh my, now I can't remember," she said wrinkling her brow.

"That's okay, I'm sure it'll come to you," Prudence placated. "So tell me, how's the food here?"

"The fish sticks are delicious, but I can't say the same for the finnan haddie. I might just have to go in and talk with the cook about it if it doesn't improve soon. They serve it every Friday night. Karl...that's my friend's name...he comes over from his apartment and escorts me to the dining room. I always tell Charlie not to worry because he'll always be the love of my life," she said looking up at her late husband's photo. "How's your love life Prudence?" Aurora asked frankly, abruptly changing the subject as always.

"Gosh, I don't know, about the same I guess. I've been busy, you know, setting up the leased property and all," she replied, already feeling the telltale blush coming on. "I brought pictures by the way. Remember I told you about my friend Vivian and that we're opening a bookshop? And Herman is installing shelves and I'm painting the walls," she yammered on, hoping to take Aurora's mind off her pitiful–sounding social life. "I've already told Kitty to bring you for our opening party, hopefully in a few weeks."

Prudence pulled out the store photographs and Aurora seemed duly impressed, all the while chatting about other residents and what they ate for dinner and what she had trouble with since the call buttons and thermostat controls confused her.

And she hadn't been able to find her favorite sweater, which is why she had Kitty buy the one she now wore. Then the topic moved to the coarse linens and TV reception, changing directions mid-stream in her very familiar way until like a wind-up toy, Aurora stopped, her face slackening as it always did when she vanished somewhere within. Prudence understood; she'd been there a little over an hour. Disappointment welled up, a feeling of hopes dashed; she hadn't even gotten to the topic of the homestead and the found letters. She had so wanted to tell her about their 'exhumation' from the artificial hiding place and how they had subsequently found the cemetery. Wanted to be able to ask her if she knew any more about Great-gran's family, but Aurora wouldn't be hearing any of that today.

By the time she left the premises, she was convinced Kitty had made the best decision about her aunt's welfare and that alone lifted her spirits. And since she was already in the vicinity of the store, she decided to pop in and check the paint color she had finally found the time to apply. It was always good to see walls in different light just to make sure and especially before anything was built into them. Selecting the shade was one aspect she'd insisted on having control over. After the fiasco over the cottage door colors and the animosity garnered from it, she didn't want people to think she was a bit 'daft' as Aurora liked to say, so she'd picked a soft terra cotta for the wall behind the desk/reception area. Vivian had agreed that it would be a beautiful backdrop for the teacher's desk that she had acquired in a wonderful second-hand shop further north on one of her 'get out of Dodge' junkets.

Prudence unlocked the deadbolt, flipping on the switch as she entered. The room was instantly awash in a soft dusky tone which to her meant that it would entice shoppers to browse longer on those cold winter days, ones that worried her most. She walked over to another wall that would remain its original color—nearly the same shade as seen in the attorney's office—and ran her hands over a piece of the new shelving resting vertically against it, pleased at Herman's efficiency as always, knowing the ones he made would enhance the free-standing catalog models. And these particular shelves would hold the latest bestsellers propped in such a way that readers would feel compelled to open them and read the flyleaf. She heard a click coming from the front door.

"Vivian; is that you?"

"You look terrific in that light," Nicholas Pelletier said from across the room, aware he had startled her. "Sorry to barge in like this, but I saw your car as I was passing and thought it would be nice to see how the place was shaping up."

"We're getting there;" she offered, spooked by her new feelings. "You startled me; I thought you were Vivian," she said shakily because he looked terrific. His dark hair was longer than she remembered and she tried not to stare at the place where it crept over his collar which caused her fingers to flex by her side. They itched to smooth it back and she blushed again.

He moved in closer, tempering his steps in accordance with her tone, fearful of scaring away someone as skittish as a young colt...easily spooked and anxious to bolt. "Jenkins has a real talent with wood," he stated nonchalantly, hoping to put her at ease.

Her heart began beating a little faster, pure adrenaline brought on by the nearness to his body. She couldn't quite get a grip on her emotions; didn't at all like the way she suddenly felt so exposed, like a gawky kid waiting for a first kiss. She started to back away, hoping to leave without a fuss.

"Wait, Prudence, don't go. I didn't mean to interrupt you or chase you away."

She stopped, touched by the sincerity in his plea and looked straight at him, ignoring the heat on her high cheekbones. She inhaled his scent and lowered her eyes, afraid he would see the way she had taken in the details of his appearance. He wore his clothes with a casual elegance and today the pale blue crewneck sweater with a white turtleneck jersey underneath emphasized his rugged complexion still tanned from summer activities. Vivian had said he sailed a lot.

"Have you ever been to Italy?" he asked, having already summed her up in two words ...beautifully intriguing.

What an odd question, she thought, shaking her head no. "This color reminds me so much of the areas of Tuscany I visited right after college and you look so perfect in this light, but I'm sorry if I made you uncomfortable."

"Was it as beautiful as I've heard?" she asked, still wondering where this was going.

"More so. But it's the kind of place you really have to see in person," he replied, already picturing them walking through the vineyards together. "Do you think we might settle for a glass of Italian wine someplace nearby and I can tell you all about it?"

She stood there for what seemed to Nick like an eternity, looking trapped and a little helpless, neither of which he understood.

She was certain he would never guess the many avenues her mind had traversed in that tiny spate of time. "Maybe we could meet next Friday at the Dory, say around six?" Prudence finally replied. "Although I can't guarantee they'll have any wine that might resemble what you experienced in Italy."

"I can handle that; I was just hoping that you wouldn't turn me down."

"I have to leave now, lots to do at home. I'll see you there on Friday, okay?" she offered as the only explanation, practically racing for the door. It seemed he always caused her to behave differently.

"Okay, but I don't mind picking you up."

"That's all right, I can walk."

Opening the car door with those words echoing in her brain, she was aware how inadequate her response had been. She could blame it on the months of not dating or even the stubbornness with which she was choosing to live her life now but down deep, she was just plain scared. He appeared on the surface like the ideal man, if there were such a thing. He was good looking to say the least, but more importantly, he seemed grounded and in control of his future at least from what Vivian had injected recently. He had his feet planted solidly and isn't that the type of man most women looked for in a serious relationship. Her only problem is that she can't figure if she wants or can even handle one at this point. It was more than being out of practice, which is all that Jules would say and of course, forget Vivian. She practically put out the welcome mat with his name on it.

By the time Prudence arrived back at Oyster Cove, she had re-run the chance encounter with Nick a hundred times over. What had she been thinking? Theirs was a business arrangement and she wasn't looking for a personal entanglement. But then, it was only a date, one date, not a marriage proposal. God, the way her mind worked. She was dramatic to the end, dredging up the bad feelings from the past and tangling them up with the 'what-ifs' and then stretching it all out to the nth degree, resolving nothing!

She had missed lunch and decided on the last of the lobster, choosing to make this batch into a salad. Beth made certain that there was always plenty of it in Pru's fridge. Prudence pulled out the ingredients, pouring some leftover coffee into a glass with ice as she prepared her meal, picking at the lobster meat as she worked. Then she brought everything to the window seat where she could enjoy the view, silently thanking Herman for about the millionth time for all his wonderful ideas.

She still liked the heft of what was becoming outdated in telephones and disliking the feel and awkwardness of cells, had installed a wall model in this location. She placed the handset against her shoulder and dialed Julie and as she nibbled and sipped, told her about Nick.

"Well it's about time you got back in the running," Julie said.

She could practically hear the wheels cranking, could feel the smile over the wire. "Don't get so excited; it's only one date and it's a week away."

"I don't care if it's a month away; at least it's a start. You've been in mourning long enough and old Spronk wasn't worth that much of your time."

"Okay, I get it; get over myself, right? I'll give you the postmortem on Saturday. By the way, thanks for the updated list of authors. I'll let you know the opening date; sure wish you could be here."

"Me too, but it will be great, you'll see. Just pour on that charm of yours and pretend you're with your old friends on St. Thomas."

"How's it going with Coop by the way?" Prudence asked almost as an afterthought.

"He's away again on business, in Holland this time and returning next month and plans to stay through Thanksgiving. He's never had a Caribbean-style turkey with all the fixings and I've decided to bite the bullet and cook. I'm even going to invite my downstairs neighbors since there's way too much food for two. You remember them?"

"I sure do, loved their two well-behaved little boys too. You going to manage all right because you know they'll also bring the mother-in-law," Prudence remarked picturing the family who lived in Julie's condo complex.

"That was exactly the game plan because she'll help me do the cooking since she can't keep her nose out of things and that will make my meal far better than if I do it myself. You know I'm only a so-so chef and she is superb."

"You just make sure you stay in touch and keep me posted on your romance, okay?" Prudence said before replacing the unstylish telephone. One of her small triumphs was the shared tastes that now coincided within the remodeled framework of Gull House.

Pushing her plate aside, doing the same about the upcoming date with Nick, she began to work on the ad that would announce the opening of the newly named 'North Sky Books', chosen after weeks of debate. Somehow naming the businesses was more

187

difficult than actually running them and she remembered the difficulty picking the one for the St. Thomas store. A number of people had put in their two cents until they had finally settled on Yellow Bird Books for their visually beautiful location. Now there was a name! At least it had gotten everyone's attention. As did the reading nook, with a brightly painted rainbow, the special section designated for author presentations and story hour for the island children.

The reviewer, however, had panned most any attempt they had made to entice new readers away from the one and only other store carrying any type of books, a newsstand in actuality. The woman wasn't very bright *and* had no class! Julie had sworn that the reviewer must have been in bed with the owner of the rival store, because she had absolutely no other obvious talent. And fortunately, their strong reader base had agreed and shown their support by their continued attendance at Yellow Bird.

Prudence felt certain she would eventually come across more women like that, but it made her particularly happy that she and Vivian had fallen into their agreeable relationship, free from the shallowness of that certain type of female mind. Neither of them liked those who refused to be curious about the world and thought only of the small sphere surrounding them, a trait they hardly tolerated in anyone. And they both had difficulty with the vapid types who paid more attention to their possessions, their memberships or their connections than their friendships. Those with a 'shop-till-they-drop' mentality might put money in the store's coffers, but they would probably never be seated at their dinner tables. Both Prudence and Vivian had worked too hard to get to this point in their lives to be bowled over by people with high opinions.

Boy, did you go off on a tangential vacation, Prudence thought as she realized the time, still needing to contact Vivian about book arrivals. She had been assured by the suppliers that the books would be coming in any hour now and Herman would also have the wall shelving installed on time. The freestanding cases had already arrived, just in time to coordinate with the expected shipment.

Prudence had methodically established the bank account that would allow each partner to handle anything that came their way, as well as the credit card set-up. This required two phone lines instead of one; an expense they hadn't counted on. Phone service in Maine was turning out to be quite costly with long distance charges adding up from peninsula to peninsula even though a town might only be thirty minutes away. She and Vivian had not figured out how they would split their hours evenly in order to give them both enough time to accomplish things at home. Fortunately, Vivian also had some back-up revenue…a nice tidy sum called alimony that an aggressive lawyer had managed to pry away from her ex who had been hoping to lay low in the warm tax haven of Cayman Island.

And a week from now, she contemplated, she would be on the first *real* date she'd accepted since Jason had walked out on her. She supposed, as Julie had said, that it really was time, but why did it have to be Nick. She obviously wasn't sure about her feelings, making her all the more vulnerable, something she worked hard to keep to herself. But when he had called Friday morning to confirm, she again asserted her independence, insisting that they meet at the restaurant.

"You look wonderful," Nick stated as she reached the door to the pub. To her surprise, he'd been waiting outside to escort her in.

"You look pretty good yourself," she said in her altered universe…wondering what caused her to sound so bold. Her face, however, clearly showed her embarrassment.

Shirley—she'd forgotten about her—perked right up at the sight of them, waving enthusiastically and winking at Prudence from behind the bar. By tomorrow evening there would not be a soul left in the village that wouldn't know of this night's event. As Nick helped her off with her jacket, Prudence spotted a few of the regulars, particularly one of two couples in the back playing darts and waved. Mary, a strawberry blond who worked at the bank where they'd set up their business account, waved back. Her husband, Joe, was the local landscaper whom Prudence had met through Herman so she knew she'd be hearing from Mr. Jenkins in the very near future. This little date was going to be front and center on the gossip trail before long even though she'd always kept a low-key profile. A fisherman she recognized by sight only, dashed into a back room where the pool table activity was in full swing and she could practically see the rib-nudging as word was passed around that she was with a date. Prudence was certain there were rumors about her hermit-like behavior or even the possibility that she might be gay, which she neither affirmed nor denied. Especially to Shirley, a seasoned gossip. Prudence was positive she gave off vibes that declared a lack of interest anytime a man flirted with her. Everyone knew everything just like in the islands and what they didn't understand, they would probably make up. The interwoven connections were becoming uncannily similar and more often than not, she found that the threads of Village life would, just as in St. Thomas, lead back to a central location; in this case, the Dory.

"I don't believe they will have what you would consider fine Italian wine, but I'm sure Shirley can muster up an old bottle of Chianti from storage…you know the kind with the basketry around the base, the ones we used to put candles in that sat on checkered tablecloths," Prudence said warming to the conversation. "Or at least a big bottle of jug wine, Italian style." She was trying to put on a good date face in light of what she expected to be a whole new trail of gossip by morning, holding onto a smile until she spotted two rugged men walking through the door. They glanced her way as if they knew her.

"Sounds like you went to the same college; that's exactly what it looked like in the only Italian restaurant near the quad,"

Nick said with a twinkle in those black pools that reminded her of Moors who roamed across the Roman battlefields.

"Ours was a little pizza parlor on a side street not far from the dorm at Boston College and while the wine was pretty terrible, the pizza was the best anywhere."

"I went to Northwestern, studied finance...how about you?"

"I studied life; at least that's the way it seemed to my father. I dropped out after two years of boredom, wanting to experience it all, but he eventually understood. And, it saved him a lot of money at least for a while. Then he helped me out with our bookstore acquisition—my friend Julie and I started it together—and now I'm here trying it all over again."

Shirley had managed to find a bottle of red, though neither had ever heard of the name and somehow none of that mattered as they shared stories, the small, harmless get-acquainted type. The wine had given them the perfect topic to laugh over and break the ice. Then at Nick's insistence they ordered a full dinner, not just finger food that never satisfied. He wanted a real meal and who was she to argue...she knew she wouldn't be able to eat very much since she kept getting lost in his eyes. She tried watching the dart game every so often, but could tell when he was watching her. She was so nervous that she only picked at the standard baked-fish plate, having foregone the messy lobster that could have ended in disaster on her lap. When he wasn't looking, she surreptitiously watched him as he delved into the fried haddock in front of him like a man who'd chopped wood all day; had an appetite for everything life offered. It was only a ripple, not really a wave...the thought that crossed her mind of lusty maidens and scaled ramparts...scenes from an old 'naughty' novel found among some used books a long time ago that quite suddenly made her readjust her chair.

Nick found himself carrying the conversation, at least as soon as he'd realized that she had suddenly become very quiet. He couldn't tell if it had to do with his questions regarding her family or life on St. Thomas or the pendant she kept fingering, but she'd become pensive. All he could think of was that she might have been hurt and badly, never imagining the effect he'd had on her and since he didn't want to say goodnight, he ordered after-dinner drinks. The Dory was not what he would call romantic; he could think of many more places he would like to take her. But even in this poorly lit corner and with the surrounding noise from the bar crowd, Prudence gave off a lovely aura, especially in the lavender sweater that brought out her eyes...enough to make him yearn for more of her time.

He also noticed the attention she was garnering from the two men who had planted themselves on the bar stools nearest the woman called Shirley. If he was not mistaken, they were actually sizing him up as well. Something told him at least one of them could, given an opportunity, pose a potential problem and that made him unreasonably jealous.

"I'm glad you at least let me walk you back to your door," Nick said, having prolonged the stroll home as long as possible. It was a nice evening; cold but not unreasonably so and he would have used any excuse to put his arm around her. This of course, hadn't happened since she seemed not to be wincing with chill.

"Well it would have seemed rude to leave you back at the restaurant, especially with Shirley watching so closely. And you did after all, provide me with a lovely dinner and witty conversation."

"Thank you milady," he said grandly. "But you hardly ate, really."

Nick's playful graciousness amused her. A good sense of humor and intelligence were really far more sexy than great looks as far as she was concerned, which of course he had in abundance. She sensed there was a very kind heart beating beneath his well-fitting wool blazer. He'd surprised her with that little touch since most of the men in the Cove tended toward the leather look or flannel and field jackets, like the men who'd been staring at them. *Those were the cousins,* she suddenly realized, recalling the photographs that Shirley waved so blatantly about.

192

Shirley must have called the bachelor relatives the moment Prudence walked in with Nick. The woman had no shame! Of course, she hadn't mentioned any of this to him, but Nick would have noticed that they were on a scouting mission just by all their body language and of course, Shirley was not subtle.

Prudence started going up her walk when she noticed that Nick had stopped at the street.

"I'm afraid if I make it as far as the door, I'm going to try and kiss you and blow any chance I have of a second date. Interesting choice of colors, by the way," he said throwing a glance behind her. Gallantly bending his head, "So, let me bid you goodnight from here."

All she could do was laugh; he had spotted the unusual paint, probably as it referred to the part of his brain involved with real estate and had refrained from extensive banal commentary and that in itself, was a wonderful relief. As to the kiss, she had already built that 'mountain out of a molehill' as always contemplating what she would do 'when' and 'if' such and such a thing happened. She really was her own worst enemy. But here he was, being the perfect gentleman and of course, he knew now that she couldn't possibly say no to another date. What nerve! She had to admit, she found him totally fascinating and more to the point, she had wanted him to kiss her!

She walked into the house with an afterglow of satisfaction. She'd made it through a proper date with a very interesting man. As she entered the foyer, she placed her hand on the pretty table as she always did when coming home and felt a comforting sensation. There was no mistaking it, as far as she was concerned, Hannah's spirit was still in this house. *Great-gran, what are you trying to tell me?*

She had slept surprisingly well that night and in the coming days leading toward a Halloween opening, Vivian's birthday. Prudence still didn't know her actual age, seemingly as guarded as top military secrets. She also tried extremely hard not to anticipate Nick's call. He wasn't pushing her, which she appreciated, but then like a typical woman, she then wondered why she hadn't heard from him yet. Her feelings bounced back and forth like a ping pong ball and she still wasn't sure which side she was on.

In preparation for the big event, she had dropped the ad at the local newspaper office and then placed a few flyers in convenient spots around town, particularly the library. Everything was falling into place and the newly painted interiors had redeemed her reputation. Now when the sun streamed in through the front windows, all the walls became suffused in a soft soothing tone, one that could have been seen in Italy as Nick had inferred or even Mexico. The beautiful dusty rose and the faint tinkling of the water feature—an interesting pile of stones in actuality—were meant to be inviting.

They'd gone into Stonycroft one evening after cleaning up and ended up at a garden center where the little fountain was being removed for the winter only to be stored away. As they say in the movies, the new partners made the owner an offer he couldn't refuse. They had hefted it into the back of Vivian's boxy car and placed it into the corner of the store where they'd put the comfy wing chair and its newest partner, a used though still in great condition, brown leather chair with big rolled arms. It was almost an exact replica of one Ben had in his library and along with a new floor lamp, gave that part of the room the effect of a miniature den. And they had taken Julie's suggestions to heart and placed a small, lovely bamboo table that would hold the future tea fixings, near the wall just out of range of the lamp.

After stopping at the library, Prudence had met with the young woman they'd hired to cater the small event. She was a newcomer to the trade, but one who showed great promise and both she and Vivian had agreed it would be wonderful to jump-start Delores' career as well. She was the daughter of a friend of Beth's and had come highly recommended even without a long list of pre-existing clients. And their menu was to be simple with a plentiful if not wide-ranging assortment of canapés, which

194

would be served with champagne, priced moderately, and gotten at a discount by the case. Pru's money was beginning to run thin, but they planned on making a good first impression and what better way to kick off the pre-holiday season, especially since among the books were small gift items geared to young readers.

Through their ad they were encouraging the general public to attend the opening, but she still wanted to send a few special invitations and even included the seasonal bachelor next door to Gull House. He'd finally found himself a lady friend from a nearby town, though she couldn't remember exactly where, not that it mattered with everything else going on in her life at the moment. He'd talked the woman into going south for the winter and most likely they wouldn't come, but she dropped an invitation into his mailbox just the same. It was a constant amusement that after she'd renamed Hannah's cottage, Mr. Whitley had put a small wooden sign on his porch rail...#20 – Wren Cottage. Who knows, maybe she had already started a trend.

Hoping they would bring Aurora along, she had sent a personal invitation to Kitty and her husband, even though at the moment, he was working nights. Another invite went to Shirley who might very well turn up with one of the cousins and quite naturally the Beth and Herman. She toyed briefly with the idea of including Mrs. Bond, but found herself backing down at the last minute, still fearful of rebuke. Prudence hated the thought that Great-gran might be looking down on her with disappointment even if the widow Bond was the true culprit. Somehow she'd make it right, for Hannah's sake if nothing else, but not until after the party.

By the time she finished all the required stops and returned to the cottage, Prudence saw that the light was blinking on the new answering machine—a needy little red dot too annoying to ignore. Unfortunately, the unit was now a necessary item because she would be out of the house so often.

"This is your 'knight' calling to ask if you would care to join me for drinks on Wednesday. I have to be down there on business and thought maybe I'd bring a nice bottle of wine, a proper *Valpolicella Classico* to share on your great deck since the weather has been so mild, and then we could go over to the Dory for something to eat...that is if I'm not being too presumptuous. I realize you're very busy these days and the store looks great, by the way. I stopped in when I saw Vivian's car. I await your response...please say yes."

She caught her reflection in the hall mirror, a smile from ear to ear. He was having an effect on her no matter how much she protested. *Can't let anything distract me right now; the store is the priority and he is THE most distracting man ever.* Prudence had already surmised that Nick would hold nothing back if they physically connected, realizing as she did so, that Jason had been quite the opposite, something she'd failed to recognize at the time. She had only to call Nick back when she was certain he'd be out on business and politely request a 'rain check'. She knew full well that this was no way to handle it, but without a guidebook, it was the best she could come up with.

But Nick hadn't bothered calling back after her response or lack of. And while she made excuses that he too was busy, Prudence knew she had offended him in the less than subtle way she'd handled his invitation but it was too late to be worried about that now. The big opening night had finally arrived and after a blaze of creative energies, their special evening was actually coming true. Everything had been as considered and carefully crafted as possible, and planned out like a mosaic of a garden path, one which led directly to the hearts of readers everywhere. She and Vivian, wanting to add to the pattern of the evening, had also chosen to dress in autumn colors accentuated by newly done makeup...*the wall color even makes the complexion look wonderful...good choice!*

Both women were now flitting around the room with the speed and deftness that comes with a case of 'stage fright'.

Small, round borrowed tables that they would momentarily cover with oversized white linen napkins, a trick Delores had shown them to create elegance without expense, still needed to be put in position. She would arrive with the canapés by four o'clock and the invited guests and hoped-for patrons soon after. The ad stipulated an end time of six-thirty in order to restrict the consumption of alcohol and not run out of food. They didn't want the guests making dinner out of the simple though heavily laden trays; Prudence had witnessed that type of behavior first hand at island events and refused to cave on the subject.

"Are you nervous?" Vivian asked as she too paced around with pride of ownership in what they'd accomplished.

"Very, and I shouldn't be. But this is a very unclear market and we're not yet well known. I'm not sure that matters, but I'm still a little shaky. We have all the latest trends, at least all we could afford to carry for the moment and we'll be able to announce our first author reading during the party tonight. That should bring them back; it is after all, one of their very own cookbook writers and a popular one too. Within the pages of recipes, he's included short stories about the different Maine restaurants up and down the coast."

"There's Delores," Vivian said pointing toward the back door. "Let's give her a hand with the trays."

"Ooh, these look wonderful!" Prudence said lifting a corner of foil wrap. "Just put them down on this long table and we'll begin to spread them throughout the room; great idea for the napkins by the way. Is the champagne cold enough, Vivian?" She asked as Dolores began bringing in the glasses and napkins.

"Perfect, should we toast before the guests arrive? I rather feel like we deserve it."

Just as Vivian popped the cork on the first bottle, a huge basket of flowers came through the doorway. "Thought you ladies needed a celebratory offering on this very special night," Nick said, peering out from behind an elongated stem of yellow roses that were surrounded by many other varieties and abundant floral greenery. He had again worn a blazer and this time with a tie and button-down shirt. Even with chinos he looked elegant and she thought her quickening pulse could be seen across the room.

Prudence looked at Vivian, who shrugged her shoulders. She knew what Prudence was thinking, but the ad was certainly bold enough...why wouldn't he come? Pru's face grew warm but not from drink; she hadn't even had a sip yet. Looking at the gorgeous bouquet, she realized the error of not including the handsome landlord with a special invitation. How could she even assume that he wouldn't bother coming tonight?

"Where shall I put these?"

"I'm sorry, Nick, forgive my manners," Vivian said, jumping to the rescue on behalf of the now all but mute Prudence. "Let's set these on the stool near the desk where they'll look fabulous in front of this wall."

"Mind if I join you?" he asked, although he'd already sidled over next to Prudence, producing a large purposeful wink.

The gall, she thought but without rancor. She smiled, pretending to be completely at ease. "Why don't you give us a hand with those trays?"

She watched as he hefted them with ease while she and Vivian maneuvered a few of the little round tables into place near the new reading chairs, both secreting a 'coin' from the treats Vivian had provided. She had not wanted to leave to chance Delores' ability to duplicate the cheese logs. Prudence kept an eye on the time wanting everything just right and then satisfied, filled three flutes, pleased Delores hadn't provided plastic. They raised their glasses. 'Cheers' echoed in the room just as the first patrons stepped through the entrance giving Prudence the perfect opportunity to move away. The place where she stood had suddenly become terribly hot!

"What a wonderful evening," Prudence remarked as Vivian sold another book. "Everyone seems to be having a good time and I'm so glad we mentioned the signing next month...we already have ten customers promising to show up."

"Maybe you could take a moment to talk with Nick before Shirley gives him the third degree," Vivian said rolling her eyes in their direction. You really are a bit hard on him, don't you think?"

"Maybe, but this isn't the night to cause a flap...let her have some fun. By the way, what did you think of Marty? I kind of thought she'd drag the other cousin; this one doesn't seem the bookish type," Prudence indicated as she caught the large man's roving eye.

"You know she's been working her cause, trying to fix the guy up with any available female and right now, you're it. And in case you haven't noticed he's beginning to take the bait...see how he's watching the way Nick looks at you. Next thing you know, you'll have a boxing match on your hands."

"You've had too much champagne, there's no indication that any of that will happen."

Prudence had to admit, down deep she was flattered and even though she hadn't been actively looking it did feel rather nice to be paid so much attention. She instantly thought of Kate, feeling badly that she'd let so much time go by. With all that had been going on, they hadn't spoken in a couple of weeks. She would correct all of that tomorrow.

There was no way they could have predicted the welcoming response to their opening event. Vivian and Prudence worked side by side for the first week making sure the shelves were stocked and orders were filled promptly. What they didn't carry, they took requests for and broadened their inventory lists. By the second week, Prudence took the mornings to do the accounting work at home where she would be less distracted. Vivian was thriving as one of the new faces of North Sky Books, her vibrant personality matching her flame red hair had already become the asset Prudence had intuited early on. Vivian seemed to have found her niche.

And Julie, too, was feeling the pride, having been given the blow-by-blow accounting of their 'lift-off' by phone and a lush bouquet of flowers that would ultimately compete with one from Coop, both delivered to the 'Yellow Bird' store. He had been in hot pursuit ever since Julie had arrived back on St. Thomas, perhaps worried she may have forgotten him while away visiting Prudence.

The Halloween event held the day after the opening specifically for kids had proved hugely successful as well. The children along with their mommies had been creatively costumed, but it had been difficult to contain the kids as they squealed and squirmed while waiting for their special treats. Vivian had made pumpkin-shaped cookies spread with orange frosting and packaged in little cellophane bags tied with black and orange ribbons which they would receive once the costumes had been judged; all with an eye to making sure no child actually lost. Vivian was always looking for ways to push the bar higher and as Prudence noted, she got on especially well with children, much like the small creatures on her farm. It seemed to be the adult male variety drawn to her hair like moths to a flame, that she rarely took notice of.

Prudence often wished Vivian would remember that policy when trying to micro-manage her love life and worried as Thanksgiving loomed ahead, for Vivian had begun the plans for her annual party and of course, Prudence was invited. Vivian was known for rounding up 'strays' from all over the peninsula, men and women without families or reasons to cook a large meal and Prudence feared she might be stuck next to a dotty old bachelor or someone like her Thatcher Lane neighbor…'on the prowl'.

She had volunteered the extra hours in the store so that Vivian could work her magic in the kitchen and on her big trestle table, the one that she would lay with heirloom treasures. Prudence coveted that table, but knew even if she found one like

200

it, there was no practical place to put it in the cottage; the rooms were simply not configured to accept a piece like that.

Nick had given Prudence one more 'rain-check' since the bookstore party, but was beginning to give up hope of a meaningful relationship with a woman covered with the protective armor of a knight going to battle. He was certain she'd been hurt, but was baffled by his inability to break down that wall she'd built. She exuded the aura of a dreamer...could see it in her eyes when she talked about the Cove and since she'd at last opened up about her life spent on the different islands, the way she'd negotiated them alone, living on a minimum of funds. He saw it in her smile when he was being particularly charming, something he portrayed to her alone. She'd had a major effect on him and now he was totally bewildered. He knew she would be at Vivian's holiday dinner—'Red' was rooting for him but he doubted Prudence knew that he'd been invited.

The unseasonable warmth had fled, moving over for the looming days of winter with more wind and icy rain than was appreciated, not even by those who knew the good that water would do for the ground come spring. Even the easterly sun of an early morning that often left ribbons of colors behind as it broke through the start of the day, had fled ahead of these grim days. Prudence, unsteady about the snow, had paid extra attention to that diluted coloring as the days drew closer to her first major holiday in Maine.

On the day before Thanksgiving, the ominous sky—a puckered gray quilt that needed shaking out—had threatened to spill its contents on her tiny pale car. Then as heralded by the weathermen, the days of threatening ended and the first of November's flurries introduced Thanksgiving Day. As she approached Vivian's old Cape, the hard ground was sprinkled with a confectionary-like dusting that crunched under her boots and she wondered if the foreign auto might become a problem when the heavy stuff arrived. There was nothing to do but go in and talk with Zack soon and hope for the best.

As she entered Vivian's house, a hum of voices struck like well-tuned holiday notes and not for the first time, Prudence desperately missed having family. She had kept herself busy, especially with all the seasonal activities, so she wouldn't dwell on the thought of another major event passing without Ben in particular. And by now, it would have been presumed that she'd have a husband in tow and perhaps even a child being contemplated…all things that parents wished for their offspring.

"There you are," Vivian called from the kitchen, spotting Prudence standing there alone.

"Put your coat in the back hall and go mingle with my guests, you look like you could use cheering up."

"Thanks, I was just thinking about my folks. Can I help you with anything?"

"A little later, just go introduce yourself and catch some of their holiday cheer; it'll do you good."

Vivian's table was elegance personified. White tapers and fall colors bounced reflectively on the gleaming silverware and enhanced the place settings. There were little adornments without being overwhelming and Prudence was impressed but not surprised. Then she realized that because of her initial sense of sadness, she had forgotten to compliment Vivian on the new outfit when she first walked in. The ensemble had obviously been chosen to enhance the overall holiday theme, as that was Vivian's way. A large sparkly clip held her gleaming hair up and out of harm's way which was necessary as she prepared the many dishes. Prudence rarely saw it that way and should have commented on it when Vivian walked through the kitchen doorway to greet her. The messy, carefree effect was difficult to achieve on a woman like Vivian. Below the hairline was all sophistication, however…the soft brown, knee-length sweater wrap (just coming off because of the overheated kitchen) with a deeper chocolate-colored sleeveless shell over tweed slacks that broke perfectly over the top of low-heeled, brown suede boots. Her jewelry was amber, small cut pieces framed in silver that looked old and heavy. There was an apron on the counter waiting to be placed over Vivian's curvy hips and tied chef-like around her waist; nothing left to chance. The aroma of basted brown turkey wafted from that little doorway and biscuits were cooling on a nearby counter. It really did smell like her mother's kitchen during the holidays, even though Ben usually wound up doing much of the cooking by the time she'd had a couple of stiff drinks. Victoria had had a penchant for gravy-topped biscuits even if they did come from a mix which in the end, always made it easier for him to prepare.

Prudence saw only a few recognizable faces and shyly scanned the beautiful table setting buying a little time to herself in order to admire it. Christmas was just around the corner and these lovely items reminded her of Hannah's better china, pieces she'd been avoiding for fear of breakage. Perhaps she would at last take them out for a small gathering…maybe on the 24th…there were enough dishes and crystal stemware lying idle inside the built-in hutch off the parlor.

"Happy Thanksgiving, Prudence," Nick said, breaking her whimsy.

Startled, she looked up into smoky black pools that always surprised her with their depth. There was a highly inquisitive crinkling forming at their corners as he searched her face for the right response.

"Happy Thanksgiving Nick," she replied, a familiar heat rising in her body. "Lovely table, isn't it?" she offered, her words inadequate the moment they'd left her tongue. She could do better than that, certainly. "Have you been in the kitchen, it's remarkable the amount of food she's made and everything smells absolutely delicious?" *That's better; a little less impersonal at least.*

"Yes, I stopped there to hand over the wine I'd brought; the same brand I'd hoped to share with you before you shunned my efforts."

"Ow," she responded, now absolutely embarrassed. "I just got so busy, Nick, it wasn't personal, really." Even as she said the words she knew they were a lie. Of course, it was personal; she was terrified of falling in love with him.

"Maybe you'll make it up to me, then. How about Saturday night?" There's a new restaurant outside of Stonycroft that I'd like to try."

She was cornered...no way to say no without not only being rude, but probably cutting off the last chance to get to know this man. He wouldn't be rebuffed forever. "Thank you; I'd like that...pick me up at six?"

He nodded, actually a little surprised by her response. But before he could say more she excused herself to help Vivian in the kitchen.

"Wish you'd told me you had invited him," she whispered in Vivian's ear. "I have now been railroaded into a date!"

"Prudence, my dear friend, it was inevitable and I needed to round out the table...never liked uneven numbers. Try and enjoy yourself, please; it's the holidays for Christ's sake.

Vivian rarely swore, so Prudence knew enough not to cross her since she'd caught her mid-stir; the garlicky mashed potatoes were about to be plated.

"Here, let me help you; might as well be useful as well as a pain in the ass," she said, hoping to strike a balance in the emotional roller coaster she'd created.

Vivian's hospitality reasserted itself as she played hostess; reining them all in to help themselves to the magnificent buffet set up on the serving counter. She had outdone herself with the many pieces of china, some that had been in her family for years. The bowls were heaped with festive colors: shades of green represented by beans and peas and Brussel's sprouts; whipped orange sweet potatoes and vivid red cranberry sauce. They sat alongside gleaming platters of turkey with two kinds of stuffing laid out artistically. A large gravy tureen with ladle flanked one end and a huge basket of rolls sat at the other along with a leaf-shaped butter dish holding chilled pats made from a decorative mold.

The guests, now red-faced from the wine and heat from the large fireplace had formed an assembly line in order to get a little of everything. As they walked to the dining table, Prudence took note of the variegated mounds heaped upon each plate and she knew there would still be enough for leftovers.

Prudence had already been introduced to Shirley's employer at the lobster pound, but in a very few minutes of running into him here, she learned that he was divorced and in his early fifties, as though it might make a difference. But much to her surprise, he mentioned Shirley's harangue about the two young men, the ones she kept trying to pawn off on unsuspecting females. It seems that she had simply been trying to get rid of them; they were eating her out of house and home whenever they spent the weekends! And they apparently did that often since hers was the closest residence to their work.

Other attendees included an artist wearing a beret and a bright holiday sweater with reindeer on the chest and who happened to know someone who painted near the cottage. He was also divorced though very interesting and Prudence noticed that he kept circling the small group in order to end up next to her on more than one occasion. After that she had taken a sneak peek at the place cards only to find that she would be seated between a retired dentist and the postmistress from the Cove, both of whom in their brief conversations had already, to her way of thinking, become interested-in-the-world type of dinner companions. She also knew that other than Nick, she'd probably not remember any of the names by tomorrow, with the exception of Shirley's boss.

Everyone appeared to have upped their attire for the day or at least tweaked their average wardrobe choices to account for the season and just before the guests were in place, Nick, wearing a well-cut dark suit that enhanced his shoulder to waist ratio, had guided two diminutive women of indeterminate ages to their seats flanking either side of his. They were mirror images of each other with the exception of their boiled wool jackets…one wore burgundy, the other deep blue, but both with braiding along the lapels…and both were worn over dark skirts and black hose tucked into shoes that were probably sample sizes. It quickly became obvious that they were paying quality attention to Nick.

Vivian had already told her about the two spinster sisters, whom she'd met at the library five years ago and who had been at her Thanksgiving table each year since. His head now moved back and forth as though he were watching a tennis match, accommodating each woman in turn. Both were tiny enough to have to look up as he spoke and were obviously smitten with the handsome Mr. Pelletier. Though Prudence couldn't hear exactly what was being said, they were keeping up a steady stream of questions and small talk and she could tell he was having a good time. *He's so easy with people,* she thought as she admired the gracious way he listened; occasionally winking across to Prudence to let her know he was paying attention.

"I'd like to introduce my new friend, new business partner and newest guest to my table…Prudence Stone—whoops, sorry Nick—you too," Vivian said, interrupting the drone of conversation and raising her glass. "A toast to you, Prudence, and Happy Thanksgiving to you all," Nick immediately piped in to cover Vivian's embarrassment.

"Happy Thanksgiving," Prudence responded as everyone joined in and clinked glasses, not for the first time feeling the enveloping kindness of her new community. "I must confess that it's likely I won't remember all your names so please, when you see me out and about, remind me!"

Naturally, Sam, a name she would now remember and probably avoid when she visited with Shirley, offered to refresh

206

her memory, but Vivian caught that conversation in the bud and turned his attention to something else. The chatter continued as the various dishes were replenished. Vivian, the perfect hostess, brought a few of the large platters to the table to be passed around family style and when Prudence looked at her watch, nearly three hours had slipped by. Through this rich conviviality of gathered 'strays' she once again understood what a remarkable woman she had picked for this new adventure.

She stood, happy to move a little if only to perform a minor table clearing and at Vivian's instructions, just enough to make room for the three pies ready to adorn the center. As though on cue, the men quickly pushed their chairs back and stood up if only to help the food in their stomachs to process faster and the ladies attempted to lend a helping hand with the coffee cups, all except for the little Laramy sisters who acted as 'bookends' to Nick's broad shoulders. They appeared as refreshed and put together as when they first arrived.

Prudence didn't think she could attempt one more mouthful of the scrumptious offerings and yet, she somehow managed to tuck away a commendable piece of pumpkin pie—her favorite—topped with vanilla ice cream. She watched as Nick, now sans his suit jacket having been given the job of scooping the ice cream from their messy containers, clearly devoured a slice of banana cream while the diminutive ladies only picked at theirs. The only pie that didn't garner a lot of attention was the rhubarb with a mystery crumble on top that no one laid claim to having brought.

"What a spectacular dinner," she said as she helped Vivian clean up. The dishwasher was already running load two and another stack of cleared plates and glassware waited on the kitchen counter. Nick had been nearly the last to leave, escorting his new charges out to their car before saying his goodnights to Vivian and Prudence. But, not before reminding her that they had a date in a few days.

"You don't have to hang around. I'll tackle the rest in the morning. That is, unless you want to put your feet up and join me for a nightcap," Vivian said handing Prudence a decanter of brandy.

"I would, but since it will be a quiet workday tomorrow, I want to check on Aurora first thing in the morning, before I open up. She's in the hospital; seems she's picked up a bad cough and they're worried about pneumonia. Kitty called just before I left to come here."

"Get some rest then…really, I'm not going to do another thing tonight. I'm always just happy to rehash these events while I stare at the fire, grateful everyone has such a good time and that the food manages to come out hot and plentiful. Your Nick seemed to be enjoying the Laramy sisters, don't you think?"

"It was certainly obvious how much they liked his company…he really has a way with people…it's hard not to like him."

"My, my, now that's encouraging. Would there be hope for the dear boy yet?"

"Don't go all gushy on me, it's just an observation. We do have a date Saturday night, though, and I don't want to hear any more about this until it's a fete accompli…do you hear me? By the way, that's some bouquet of flowers over there…a secret admirer?"

"Maybe; we'll see after next week," Vivian said with such a clear implication that Prudence did a double take. What was the lovely Miss Sanford hiding?

Before she could say more, "Let me know about Aurora," Vivian said as she politely held the door.

Driving to the Medical Center the following morning, Prudence thought about Hannah's life along this coast and the many changes it had undergone. While the granite and the sea were timeless, development had encroached on much of the

208

shoreline. She admired the type of end results that certain renovations and additions had created, the ones that allowed better acute care facilities to expand and save lives. She didn't know whether or not Hannah had ever had to take advantage of that and then remembered Aurora's remark about an illness a long time ago. That was the type of question that would probably always go unanswered. Although the more she thought about it, she knew there was the slightest chance that a record existed somewhere. Perhaps a file detailing her child's injury or appendicitis or even related to the man who'd stolen Hannah's heart.

Kitty was sitting outside Aurora's room, watching through the glass as her pale-faced aunt struggled to breathe. She had been there through the night as Aurora had unexpectedly taken a turn for the worse. Even though it was too early for official visiting hours, Prudence knew Kitty had been expecting her. Prudence was worried; there was no color left in those now sunken cheeks...when did this all happen? It seemed like she had just had tea with her.

"She is nearly ninety-two and she's had a good life, dear," Kitty said gently, taking in Pru's expression.

"I know, and this must be even more difficult for you to watch. I guess I've adopted her to replace my great-grandmother and she's done a pretty good job of making me feel like family. I've lost so many loved ones, but it never gets easier."

"She's extremely fond of you too, you have to know that. And no matter what happens you'll always have that special bond to remember," Kitty said placing an arm around her shoulders kindly.

Prudence stuck around as long as she could and Kitty promised to call her if anything changed. *Please God, don't let anything happen to her,* Prudence silently prayed, needing more time with her sweet friend. Leaving the hospital with a heavy heart, she drove directly to the bookstore. It wasn't officially open today, but the catch-up type of work would help keep her mind off Aurora and the waiting that was so inherent in a situation like hers.

Vivian would open Saturday for a half day and by then anyone with any leftover time and leftover food would have put away their better dishes and thrown their stained tablecloths into the laundry and be just bored enough with housework and entertaining to search for a good read. Prudence kept checking the clock as she went through endless lists and Vivian's scribbles and then got out the vacuum to kill more time. If she wasn't thinking about Aurora, she thought of Nick. The upcoming date loomed large, perhaps more than an ordinarily sane person would allow. But then, Prudence never had thought of herself as ordinary. Just as she was about to call it quits, the phone rang.

"Yes, Kitty, sure. I can come back. I'm so glad she's out of the woods. See you shortly," Prudence said happy for this unexpected turn and that she hadn't driven all the way back home.

Kitty was inside Aurora's room when she arrived, beckoning her to join them. Aurora was still ghostly white, but she had a small smile on her lips that apparently had just been dabbed with a bit of pink. *This is so like her to want to look her best, even here.* Prudence could see Kitty's open purse on the chair, the telltale makeup peeking out. Unfortunately, they hadn't allowed the barrettes left in which probably upset her more than being sick.

"How're you feeling?" Prudence asked her as she bent over to kiss her cheek.

"I'm a little tired, but I've had the nicest dream. But I want to go home now; it's too noisy in here," Aurora whispered out slowly.

"You're right about that Auntie A," Kitty stated. "I never slept a wink when I had my appendix out—all those nurses in and out and bells and beeps everywhere."

"Well, see about getting me out of this place; it won't do me any good not to have my belongings around me," Aurora said before turning to Prudence. "You know, I think I dreamed about Hannah. Can't be exactly sure, but it seems like we were talking about you or maybe it was just my imagination. She had come to see me in my new apartment and she said she thought it looked like my house but would I please move the pictures. Why do you suppose she would want me to move the pictures…she knows how much I love those, especially Charlie's…he looks so handsome in that one, doesn't he?"

"Yes, Aurora, he really does, but it was only a dream; I'm sure she wouldn't want you to move them," Prudence said.

The nurse came in then to check Aurora's vitals and shooed them out of the room. "She's really much better, don't you think?" Prudence asked Kitty.

"Better than I'd hoped, but she can't go home just yet. It was pretty touch and go for a while, but she's tough, that one. I'd love to see her well enough to be up and around by Christmas."

"Do you think she'll really need to stay here all that long?"

"Well, it's her lungs and she began failing even before that. She's unexplainably losing weight and the cough has been getting very persistent. I asked the doctor why the weight loss and he said that she probably isn't absorbing the nutrients, perhaps anemia but they're running more tests at least."

"Is it okay if I come back on Sunday; that way she'll have had a chance for a bit more rest and we can have a good conversation?" Prudence asked.

"I know how much you two have begun to delve into the past and quite frankly, I'm glad. She's in that state of mind where she enjoys going back in time and without you around to question her, she would have no reason to talk about it. I never had much of an interest in the things that took place when they were all young; just been too caught up in my own problems and those of my kids, but she favors you and that makes me feel good. Come on Sunday whenever you can. I'm usually here in the early morning so that way she'll have more to look forward to that day," Kitty said giving Prudence a quick hug goodbye.

Leaving Aurora looking better gave Prudence the impetus to go back to the store and tackle that list of objectives needing to be accomplished before Christmas which was just around the corner. It would help keep her mind off the hospital for a little while and by the time she finished the housekeeping and a little of the bookkeeping, Vivian would probably pop in and maybe they'd go down the street to the corner café for a light meal, something to snap her out of the doldrums.

The hospital visit had zapped what little mental acuity she'd had earlier in the day, but when she switched the lights back on, the room filled with that soft dusty rose shade and she thought of Nick. She smiled to herself at the idea that this had reminded him of a faraway place meant for lovers.

She must have been daydreaming because the ringing phone startled her. "Vivian, it's Paul, can you hear me?" Paul, who was Paul and then Prudence thought of the mysterious flowers the day before, "Sorry, she's not in today; would you like to leave a message? Yes, I'll be sure to tell her."

"Someone named Paul called and said to let you know he'll be in town on Wednesday," Prudence said as soon as Vivian walked in later in the day. Prudence had just about tired of dusting and replacing books on the shelves.

"Thanks; apparently my home number had escaped him," Vivian replied to Pru's unspoken question, a flush of red indicating her embarrassment at being 'caught' somehow. I wish I could say more, but I promise I'll tell you on Monday; there's a lot I have to think about before then."

"Sure, whatever you want," Prudence responded, though something told her that she wasn't supposed to know about him. Could he have sent the flowers? Was Vivian having an affair? There wouldn't be a quick meal after all because the conversation would be awkward.

"How's Aurora doing by the way?" Vivian asked.

"It's still too early to tell, but I'll go over there again on Sunday for a visit and bring a book with me to read to her. The medications have made the dementia more of a problem and she'll likely fall asleep while I'm there, but I'd still like to talk with her more about my great-grandmother. She's the last of them...the widows, I mean...the ones I can only hope to emulate when I get that old," Prudence said and immediately thought she should cross Jean off that list. But since Vivian didn't know about her problems with Jean, it wouldn't matter. And now Prudence didn't know as much about Vivian either...tit for tat, or so Aurora might say. "But right now, I have to run home and figure out what to wear for my date tomorrow night...remember, Nick?"

"I had forgotten, sorry...have a great time," Vivian said but without much conviction, her thoughts already elsewhere. The last thing she had wanted to do was expose Prudence to a clandestine affair with a man she was still uncertain about. She was no goody two-shoes but she also didn't believe in adultery and she certainly didn't want to bust up his marriage. Actually, she was just weary of the cold and there were months of it ahead and maybe a short fling would take her mind off the winter blahs. And then the fool had gone and called the store! Now she would have to work this out and explain it to Prudence or there would be an awfully uncomfortable wedge between them.

Prudence wanted only to think about Nick and the preparations for her date, but the name Paul kept insinuating itself between the lines. Vivian's discomfort was so obvious and yet, it really wasn't any of her business. If she chose to have an affair, well then she would have an affair. There was nothing to be done as far as Prudence was concerned, not unless she asked for advice which wasn't very likely given Vivian's strong personality.

By the time the witching hour rolled around and Prudence had finished her scented bath and creamed the hydrating lotion all over her body, she had pushed all thoughts of her partner's issues out of her mind. Looking into the full-length mirror, the woman who gazed back had glowing skin peeking from the vneckline of her deep turquoise sweater that set off the color of her hair and picked up the smooth skin shadowed softly between her breasts, the place just below the nesting locket. Now that she'd let the blonde highlights grow out, she looked more like Ben and Hannah.

Nick might not even notice the rest: a black calf-length wool skirt worn with high leather boots and all of it topped with a faux fur jacket she'd found at the thrift shop. There were many such shops available for browsing, ones whose profits went to help good causes. They ran the length of the main thoroughfare and had been a heady bonus to living here. This little find was *tres chic* and very reasonable, and Vivian had tried it on and then despaired over its small size that struggled against her bosomy elegance. Prudence stared at her reflection, admiring the look that suggested she might again have fun.

When Nick arrived just a few minutes later, she was everything he'd hoped...an attractive, beautiful to be exact, woman waiting happily for her date to show up. This was more than he'd anticipated and as he helped her into his car, already warmed up against the evening chill, he almost crossed himself at his good fortune and then remembered he wasn't Catholic and simply smiled reassuringly instead.

The new restaurant did not tout glamorous furnishings and heavy atmosphere, but it regaled the palate with savory, sweet and seasonal dishes of all varieties. The feature tonight was homemade pasta topped with a lobster Alfredo and a simple grapefruit and olive salad on a bed of baby spinach.

"If we make it through this, I'll need to be carried to the car," Prudence remarked scooping up and winding the strands of fettuccine with her fork.

"I wouldn't mind that one bit...eat up!" Nick quipped comfortably. "By the way, don't look over your shoulder but the man in the corner is the food critic from the *New York Times*. Of course, then, to Nick's chagrin, she had to. A bespectacled gentleman with a few small dishes in front of him was making notes at the back table.

"Would you like more coffee?" the waitress asked as she cleared the dessert plates away. "Looks like we'll get a good review tonight," she said, glancing over her shoulder to indicate the reviewer.

"Well, you all deserve it," Nick replied, "And just brandy will be fine, thanks." He was swirling his drink and hadn't taken his eyes off his date. He wasn't particularly anxious to leave the restaurant, but he was dying to kiss her. Everything about the way she looked tonight made him want to touch her and breathe in that surprising fragrance she wore. And yet, it was impossible to know that if he chanced it, she might revert to the way she'd been in the store.

"What a great dinner, thank you," Prudence said as they drove through the inky night.

"I hope there will be more of them," Nick responded feeling hopeful for the first time since they'd met.

"I'd ask you in for a nightcap, but I'm going to have to get up early to go back to the hospital," she said when they finally reached the cottage, knowing full well she didn't have to be there until afternoon.

"I'd like to see you again," Nick said, leaning in to kiss her ever so gently on the lips.

"Only if we don't eat like we did tonight; way too much food," she said while trying to savor the feel of his lips. "I loved it all, but I'm not used to quite so much...how do the Italians do it?"

"I think they space it out better than the Americans, but I'm sure we can figure that out; how about next weekend?"

"Okay, call me."

Nick's footsteps were lighter as he walked away...she'd let him kiss her...he was making headway!

Prudence closed the door and peeked through the curtain hoping he wouldn't notice as he drove off. She hadn't wanted to seem over-anxious but almost wished she had brought him inside for a drink or something! Dating was again going to become problematic and for the first time since she'd arrived, she actually didn't resent that.

Sunday's drive was overcast and terribly cold, but Pru's condition could only be classified as rosy. Although she lacked sleep, hadn't been able to stop thinking of him and what might happen and when, she had managed to treat herself to a special breakfast of eggs benedict and strong Columbian coffee to jump start the day. Even the bleak, roiling sea that she'd stared at while she ate, hadn't been able to disturb or alter her good mood. Only Aurora's improved condition would make the day more perfect.

Kitty had left by the time Prudence walked into the hospital room but Aurora was awake and seemed alert, at least as much as could be expected.

"Look at you, your color's back!" Prudence exclaimed as she put a little pot of flowers on the stand. At closer look it was only a little of Kitty's blusher that had given Aurora's cheeks some life.

"I'm glad you're here Prudence; I need to tell you something."

"Oh this sounds important; another dream?"

"It's about Hannah; I think she's very upset with me. I didn't tell you everything about Jean."

"What didn't you tell me?"

"That's the trouble; I'm not sure, but I know there was a letter. Hannah had a letter, and that's what made her so sick."

"Did she show it to you?"

"No, I don't think so, but I can't really remember. I just know when she was out of her head, she said something about 'terrible words, spoiled everything', something like that and then she wouldn't let Jean visit her and wouldn't tell me why. Jean wouldn't either and we haven't spoken about it since. I think both of us forgot until you moved here."

"Don't tire yourself, I'll see if I can find it, but I imagine it was probably tossed out a long time ago," Prudence said never believing there would be one at this late date. Then she opened the book, a silly short story to occupy the time, and began to read to Aurora until she saw her eyelids flutter. A nurse came in to check on her; it seemed they did that frequently and Prudence whispered that she was leaving.

She had seen the frown on the nurse's face as she checked the machines and worried that she'd overstayed or had made Aurora more tired by talking. Then, just before leaving, she called Kitty from the nurse's station to let her know she'd just seen 'Auntie A'...how she loved that name. Then she drove home as quickly as the slick roads allowed.

By the time she arrived at the cottage, exhaustion had straightjacketed her entire body; she could barely move. There was no way she could hunt for a letter or do anything other than sit. All she wanted was to curl up in her favorite chair and think for a little while before even contemplating dinner. She was startled awake by the loud, insistent ringing. *Must have dozed off,* she realized checking her watch.

"Oh no, what's happened?"

Prudence listened as Kitty's strained voice told her that the doctor was worried. Aurora was slipping again. She'd gone back soon after Pru's departure; they'd both been so encouraged because Aurora seemed to have rallied earlier.

"Apparently she'd had another terrible bout of coughing so tonight Dan and I sat with her," Kitty said. "Just talking about his job and little mundane things so we wouldn't disturb her when suddenly she needed more oxygen. They've started pumping fluids into her but it's not looking good," Kitty continued nearly breaking down. Auntie A's heart keeps getting weaker and this is breaking mine."

"It's my fault, I shouldn't have tired her," Prudence said feeling guilty "I'll be there early, of course," she replied feeling her own heart breaking and then strangely uplifted by the fact that Kitty seemed to feel her important enough to Aurora to make the call.

Though dulled by sleep deprivation, Prudence put on a good face as she greeted Kitty who'd been sitting outside Aurora's room staring blankly through the glass. The monitors were hooked up and pulsing their signals to the desk. "Don't be silly, she was thrilled by your visit," Kitty said when Prudence apologized again. "She kept telling me over and over and then, well, we nearly lost her and I thought you'd want to know…I stuck around until they tossed me out, but this is nobody's fault. I knew you'd want me to call," Kitty said as she looked at Pru's crumpled face.

They had both shed their tears during the night, one for the woman who'd lived so long, and the other for those who hadn't.

"You look like you've been crying since I called," Kitty said kindly.

"Just dredged up a lot about my folks and all. I know I've placed a lot of importance on my relationship with your Aunt, but I couldn't help myself…I needed her spirit and longevity to hang onto, I guess. And now I'm worried it's been too much for her to handle."

"Don't be silly, she's a happy old woman who's lived a lot of years in that body and it's just worn out. She would never want you to blame yourself for anything. I certainly don't; you've been a godsend keeping her occupied with happier times of the past and if some weren't so pleasant, well, that's part of life too. I sensed from the way she talks sometimes, there has been some unfinished business about Hannah and the other one…Jean?" Kitty said questioningly.

"Yes, Jean Bond. Hannah and your aunt and Jean were, from what I'm told, like sisters in their day. I like the notion, but I guess I've discovered not all times were happy and because of my own inquisitive nature, I wanted to learn as much as possible. Your Auntie A has been very accommodating given the fact that

I'm a stranger, really," Prudence said using that lovable nickname.

"I've called her that ever since I can remember and it stuck even now into my midlife. Aurora sounds so formidable and yet she's a creampuff of soft sweetness," Kitty said as the nurse stood in the doorway motioning her to the room.

Prudence swiped at her nose. Between the cold air and threatening tears, it was already red and unsightly and she began digging through her purse for tissues as Kitty talked in the hushed tone that always reminded her of funerals. Then she went in while the nurse adjusted some new tubing and Prudence could see through the glass that Kitty was having a little trouble holding herself together even with her previously wise counsel. And then she kissed Aurora's face and lifted one of her small hands to her lips as well. By the time she walked out, Prudence knew what was coming.

"It won't be long and they won't use extra measures whatever happens now," Kitty said beside Pru's chair. "You need to be prepared and if you'd like, maybe go in now, but only if you're up to it."

She laced her fingers with Kitty's, "I honestly don't think I can…not one more goodbye like this…please understand."

"Of course I do, but stay with me for a while? Dan will be along shortly, and I don't want to be alone right now either."

Prudence got them some coffee and settled into the uncomfortable chair next to Kitty who seemed content to go in periodically and sit next to the bed though she received no recognition. Or with Prudence in the hall, both stuck in the cruel pastime of waiting. But this generous woman, the niece of the grand old lady connected to Hannah Ellison through a lifetime of joys and sorrows, was trying to make it easier for her. In their comfortable silence, nothing was expected of her and she almost wished there were. The only thing she had learned through the too young indoctrination into the realm of death and dying was to seek comfort rather than give it. Staying with Kitty, who expressed a need to have her present, to share in the grief, was for Prudence a step up on that ladder of maturity if nothing else. And so they sat, the silence broken only by the hush of whispered voices and a large-handed clock on the wall that grew louder as each took a turn at the coffee urn at the end of the corridor or just to have a stretch and a bathroom break. It was horrible waiting for someone to die.

Suddenly a loud beeping could be heard from the nurses' station and the duty nurse rushed through Aurora's door leaving another in her wake and then Prudence saw the white-coated intern come rushing around the corner and for a few moments, it was mild pandemonium.

Prudence felt for the locket as Kitty's gripping fingers stopped her from moving off her chair, but could not stop the default memories of the other times when nothing could be done to save a life. Ben had lasted only a day after the accident and long before that Victoria's overdose had left her in a coma and she'd never regained consciousness.

Everything would change for Prudence once again. The widows' story hadn't been entirely told; Aurora's death would be like putting a period at the end of an unfinished sentence leaving Hannah dangling like a bad participle. Then it registered harshly—loss upon loss—and she desperately tried to keep it together for Kitty's sake. But Kitty was letting go of her hand…the intern was signaling for her to go in and the exiting nurse was coming over.

"She's gone Mrs. Donnelly…go in and see her before the formalities."

"You can go in first," Kitty said kindly, "if you've changed your mind."

Prudence embraced Kitty and graciously declined, wanting to remember the feel of Aurora's soft round cheeks and the pink tint of her weakened smile; was that really only the day before?

"It's okay Prudence, really," consoled Kitty. "I'll call you as soon as I've made the arrangements and maybe you can help me pack up some of her things when it comes to that. Dan's shifts are not conducive and I'd like your company, if you don't mind."

"Oh Kitty, I'm honored," she said as they clung for just a moment in their shared emotions and then the only thing Prudence could do was turn and walk out of the hospital and absorb the pain of a short-lived and very unique friendship. As she did, she felt the tears, the ones she'd held back with difficulty…icy on her face where they encountered the cold, late November wind.

Chapter Ten

The usually joyful days before Christmas, the ones ordinarily filled with carols and gift-wrapping and scented candles, had taken a terribly sad turn after Aurora's death, and though not a family member, it had been particularly difficult for Prudence to accept. She had come to love their connection and the way it thread the past to the present and brought some of Hannah's personality back to life. Prudence had become used to the security of the elder woman's presence.

It had been Aurora's desire to be cremated and the family had decided on a small service for the sweet, cherubic woman, the second in their circle in the course of a year to depart this earth. It proved to be just right, heartrending in its simplicity and held in the little Methodist church on the hill, a stoic-looking building with darkening shingles and white trim in need of paint come spring. The pews were comfortable at least and were filled with people from the Lane and those from the Village, the ones left that is, who'd known her for many years. They had come to pay their last respects to one of their own, a darling woman who had years earlier according to Kitty, decided upon an urn that looked more like a flour canister. She had done this prior to losing her grip on reality which told Prudence more about Aurora's sense of humor than anything else could have. She knew the moment she saw it, that it would become the topic of conversation once they all gathered in the side hall. Refreshments—delicate cookies, finger sandwiches and coffee—were already laid out on the long tables with donated plates by the church committee. It was their way of remembering.

Prudence watched with leftover sadness and with a modicum of curiosity, at the outpouring of people, many of whom she didn't know at all and some whom she only recognized in passing during their daily activities in the Cove. She knew that the family would have a private burial of the ashes contained in the outrageous container, something that so declared Aurora's personality! After all, who was going to argue with her?

As soon as everyone was seated, the minister, a freckle-faced young man who looked about fourteen and most certainly new to the community, led the service. After the usual homilies he offered statements about Aurora's life that he must have gathered from others. She had obviously been an active parishioner before her mind had begun to fail and he noted the time that she'd given to many of the church-related activities.

Once the cleric closed his prayer book, Kitty, dressed in a plain dark blue wool coat and navy flats, walked carefully up to the lectern to say a few words on behalf of her family. She didn't get very far as she tried to describe her relationship with Aurora. Her voice began to break with an audible choking sound and surprisingly Herman, who'd been near the isle, jumped up to help her off the steps and lead her back to Dan.

"Well now, we can all see how difficult this is Kitty; and if you don't mind, maybe each of us could stand in place in our pews and share a story or memory we have of Aurora," he said as though public speaking were the most natural thing in the world.

"Most of you know that I was a much younger lad when Charlie Durn fell to his death," Herman began, his burliness out of place with his gentle words. "But as difficult and sad as that time was for Aurora, she always said that I must treasure each day, because we never know when we're going to do something so foolish. I never got over that and have tried to live up to her expectations ever since and I, for one, will miss her very much."

Prudence listened as a few more of the 'old-timers' that she didn't know—ones who had known Charlie well—took over after Herman and were then followed by Beth.

"I am embarrassed to say that I copied Aurora's lobster casserole recipe and have been pawning it off as my own all these years." Looking upward, Beth continued, "Aurora, please

224

forgive me because I've also been adding something new each time so you wouldn't know what I'd done."

A grateful, collective sigh went up and the expected sorrow turned to lightheartedness and stories continued in that manner for at least another forty minutes. Prudence had never attended a memorial held in this vein—a true celebration of life—and found it refreshing and much easier than sitting through the formal eulogies of her own family, experiences she'd be forced to remember for the rest of her life. And when it was her turn, she decided that the best thing she could tell these Oyster Cove folk was how much it meant to her to have known Hannah's dearest friend; how Aurora had taken her under her wing and given her the only real sense of her great-grandmother that she might ever have and something she would cherish forever.

While she'd been speaking, quite a few of Aurora's contemporaries had appeared to be nodding their approval and just before sitting down, she spotted Mr. Thayer who smiled at her and quietly exited obviously content with the way she'd handled herself. Perhaps all that she'd been doing to the cottage hadn't gone unnoticed either, especially by those who had truly cared about Hannah for there must have been many during all the years here. In good time, Prudence might find an opening opportunity to know them as well.

By standing Prudence had also been able to see all the way to the rear of the church and Mrs. Bond. She was seated on the left in a pew closest to the rear and on the aisle, able to escape easily if needed. She was straight-backed, dressed in a somber black coat with a small dark hat fitted to her upswept hair and the reason she'd stood out so to Prudence, a small peacock feather tucked into the little hat band. She had wanted to be seen. Prudence, on her way to the refreshments had disregarded her personal feelings toward the obstinate woman and cautiously approached her. Then she surprised them both by bending down and kissing Jean's hollowed cheek. She hadn't moved away but hadn't reciprocated either, nor had she said a word. This was what Prudence had to look forward to, the resolve leaving little compassion, but with what was left she would still do her best to be kind; it's the way she'd been brought up.

With Aurora's death, Prudence didn't have the emotional strength to fight her romantic demons nor the happiness factor that should have been associated with the impending date and a few days before had politely canceled on Nick. But he had surprised her by sliding in next to her at the service, even offering a handkerchief that looked brand new. And when she'd sat down, he'd taken her hand and patted it as if he'd been comforting her forever. He had bussed her cheek and slipped out before the refreshments. She was all out of struggle; life was just too fragile.

A week had passed in a desultory fashion when Prudence received an unexpected call from Kitty.

"Thank you for everything you did for Auntie A," she said. "I've already started packing up some of her belongings; got a little ahead of schedule that's why I hadn't called you, although I still need help with the boxed-up clothing and especially the kitchen tools and things. They weren't needed at all for the apartment, but she wouldn't let me leave them behind. Through the years she'd been given new gadgets, maybe stuff you can use at the cottage. But I also found something I think you would like to have now."

"You're most welcome, but I still feel she did much more for me. Shall I meet you tomorrow for coffee or something?"

"Let's. How about the deli since I have to see the realtor as to why her house hasn't had a nibble as yet…say nine-thirty?"

Prudence had wondered back in June how long it might take for property to move in this area. Funny, since she'd met Nick, she never thought to inquire. Ever since she had moved in, she'd heard people claiming it to be a timely seller's market. They must have been mistaken. Many of the older homes still had the little flagship real estate signs adorning their lawns. Aurora's house was old, no doubt, but not in nearly the rough shape as

Hannah's had been. It was probably a good thing, she thought, not to have simply turned it around for a quick re-sale expecting a nice profit. At least this way, she owns an old piece of history on a beautiful coastline and had made new life-long friends to boot.

By the time Kitty arrived, the coffee bar had just emptied out and Prudence was waiting on one of the wooden stools working on her second cup.

"Sorry to be a bit late; my husband needed a jump-start for his pick-up," Kitty said unbuttoning her coat and placing a small bag on the counter. "I found this book among my aunt's things and felt it might be important."

"This is very nice of you," Prudence said opening the bag. "I hope you didn't go out of your way with everything you still have to take care of, but I really appreciate your wanting me to have anything at all as a reminder." As she held up the small book, it was immediately recognizable. "It's another from the famous poet, like the one I keep next to my bed! I didn't know Aurora liked poetry."

"Well that's what's so interesting about it," Kitty stated as she poured herself a coffee from the self-serve counter. "Especially since I don't think I'd ever seen her with a book of poetry before seeing this one in the new apartment. When I asked about it she got all coquettish-like; said something about Charlie and that was it. But I never bothered about it before the other day. I was feeling all melancholy without her and wanted to see what had made her keep it; actually thinking it might even be a very overdue library copy given her state of mind and something I'd accidentally packed in with her belongings.

"But before you open it, you need to know there is a personal inscription written at the end. I know you and she had talked quite a lot about Hannah's acquaintance, Timothy; and I realize that while my theory may seem odd, perhaps this book was actually taken from your house…Hannah's house…after she died. Maybe Aurora went in when the cleaning woman was there

227

and took it as a keepsake; a reminder of her best friend. I'm sure if that's the case, it was a harmless gesture; I'd hate to call it stealing but you know how she'd gotten, wandering around on her own before we moved her and even before you came, she was failing. And by the time you arrived, she would have definitely forgotten all about doing something like that.

"Now I'm going to leave you on your own to sort it out. I wish I could say more but whatever happened, I know how much you loved her so I'm not worried that you'll harbor bad thoughts about the old gal. And I've got another appointment before I finish packing up the rest of her things. I'm just glad I found it. You know, I can almost see the twinkle in my aunt's eyes; perhaps the book will help put another piece of that love story in its proper place."

"Oh Kitty, I could never think badly of her and thank you for taking the time to return it," Prudence said, anxious to read it alone. She went out to her car and began flipping through it haphazardly wanting to savor it at home, to prolong the deliciousness of the gift, no matter how she'd obtained it. But then, on the end page just as Kitty had said, was the conspicuous inscription gifting the book to her great-grandmother.

Dearest Hannah,

You've taught me poetry and you've taught me love and what that truly means. This small token of my feelings will last the test of time and so will we.

Yours, Tim

His feelings so frugally stated, yet saying everything, would have disappeared into obscurity except for Kitty's curiosity. *That little minx!* Aurora could easily have taken it without a nod to its actual words; may never even have noticed the writing, especially if she had brought it home and put it on the shelf near

Charlie's photo. *Could she have thought it was from Charlie?* *She's been so confused.* It may never be clear, but what Prudence had hoped for was there on paper...Timothy hadn't left Hannah of his own accord.

"It is an incredible story and I'm honored that you decided to share it with me," Nick stated as they finished their dinner.

Prudence had been so thrilled with the discovery of the book that she'd succumbed to his desire to see her again and she apparently hadn't disappointed him. This was duly noted as she watched his responses to her animated version of a smattering of the circumstances regarding Aurora and the continuing saga that had bound them in their new friendship.

He had met the elder woman at the book party and remembered how sweet she'd been that night and could easily imagine how Prudence had fallen in love with her. He listened attentively through the various fits and starts that produced a tear or two and believed it would be obvious to anyone watching, that he was falling hard for this sensuous and sensitive young woman. Each time she stumbled in the telling, he would reach over and touch her forearm or hold her hand; that is, if she wasn't using it to express herself as appeared to be habit.

Prudence took in his beautiful eyes and the way they absorbed her words and tried not to watch his lips for fear she'd lose her train of thought. She had purposely neglected the mention of a coexisting spirit, a co-conspirator if she were right, and nearly epic melodrama she had created over the missing key, not while he was looking at her like this.

"I'm disappointed I hadn't ever met Hannah, even though I know some of your other neighbors through real estate dealings," he said thoughtfully. "I do know Mike and Kate, met them when they were first looking for a home, but never knew more than cursory information about the elder widows," he stated. "My office only came into play after Aurora's niece had taken over the legal matters in order to put her house on the market."

"You probably think me silly, but now I'm really determined to find out what happened to him," she remarked, tapping the inscription. Prudence had brought the book along purposely in order to make a point without ever once imagining his response.

"If there is a love like that left in this world, I want my share of it," Nick said. The candlelight flickered and held his gaze and his dark eyes bored into her very soul.

She had no answer, no more to query either. He had somehow managed to kindle a long dead flame, the type of anticipation that was nearly palpable. And yet, she knew she still wasn't ready to give in to the physicality of a relationship, not even with Nick, not yet.

"How long can you keep your guard up, Prudence? I think you want me as much as I want you, it shows in your eyes," he said once back in the car and with more gentleness than she expected.

"I'm sorry Nick. Maybe I'm not being fair; you deserve some answers and I might not be so appealing to you when you learn that I had been left at the altar on the day of my wedding."

"God, what kind of idiot would do such a thing?"

"The kind I obviously thought was pretty wonderful and truly loved me. I must have been the idiot and now I don't trust my own judgment."

"I'd like a chance to earn it, at least. What's that old adage, 'better to have loved and lost', or something like that?"

"I know that's the popular theory, but believe me, it isn't so easy losing either. And I can't promise how long it might take me, nor can you tell me how long you'd be willing to wait…that would be unfair."

"Why not let me be the judge of that, okay; a day at a time," Nick said as they pulled up in front of the cottage. "Christmas is around the corner and I can't think of anyone I'd rather spend it with than you."

"You really are a trooper or a glutton for punishment, I'm not sure which...but making it hard to refuse. I was hoping— before all of this happened with Aurora—to throw a small party to celebrate not only the new business, but also my new home."

"I just happen to be an excellent bartender; how about I give you a hand?"

"If you have any more talents up your sleeve, tell me now before I go any further...I'm not sure I can handle it!"

She could still hear his laughter as she walked away from the *Ranger*. *Where had this man come from?* As she entered the house, she wished she had a furry cat to hug...well almost. She couldn't help notice the sconce that she'd left on; the way it warmed the foyer. It was too late for a fire and besides, if she did that, she would yearn for his company. Better she just go to bed...like she wouldn't think about him there! She knew it! Now she was acting all 'girlie' and titillated, the last thing she had wanted to be. She was after all, a responsible, feet-on-the-ground businesswoman. *Oh get over yourself, you're falling in love you idiot!*

Vivian had offered to take over during the aftermath of Aurora's death since she hadn't really known the woman except through Prudence and was now glad to have her partner back in the shop. "You look pretty chipper this morning," Vivian shouted as Prudence entered briskly, stamping her feet from the new-fallen snow.

"My date with Nick was really nice, not as glamorous as the last one, but comfortable. I never believed for a minute that you would be so right about him. My apologies."

"God, you're positively gooey; look at you, a smile from ear to ear. This should make for an interesting day."

"Okay, I deserve that...what's on the agenda; how are sales?"

"Pretty darn good. Lots of Christmas shoppers. Thank goodness we've opened in the land of readers...must be these long winters."

Just then the bell tinkled and a young woman entered with a trailing leash, on the end of which was a most disagreeable-looking breed of dog, the type with an extended under-bite and mistrusting eyes.

"Is it all right if Henry comes in with me; it's awfully cold out there?"

"Of course," Vivian said, jumping up to take the leash and lead Henry behind the desk to sit at her feet.

Prudence understood her partner's love of animals, but she also saw a good merchant's ploy as well. *All the better to enable the mistress to shop,* she thought as she watched Vivian scratching old Henry's ears. She went out back to check some inventory, chuckling at the sound of cooing that didn't seem possible from such a cat lover and hoped the sales slip would be well worth it.

When they were alone, Prudence told Vivian about the projected party…just a small affair with a few friends like Beth and Herman, Nick, of course, and hopefully Kitty and Dan if they were up to it. Vivian immediately offered to help, but Prudence wouldn't hear of it; she had done enough in these past months. Vivian was to come solely as a guest and could also bring along a friend if she chose. There was a very brief and awkward silence because Vivian had finally expanded a bit on the situation with Paul and Prudence was now privy to an affair that made her uncomfortable. She was no prude, but a married man was outside her proscribed ideas…could only have a bad end as far as she was concerned. Out of respect for Vivian, she'd tried not to be too concerned over the fact that this pharmaceutical rep had made it a point to place this section of Route 1 on his list of professional visits.

"I won't be bringing him in case you're concerned. He'll be with his wife on a cruise with her family over the holidays anyway," Vivian stated defensively.

"I'm sorry and please, forgive what many would call an outdated attitude; I don't have the guts for something like that, is all."

"I probably wouldn't have said anything if he hadn't accidentally called here. I'm not particularly proud of this situation, but I can't say I mind the attention when he is around. It's far more than I ever got from my husband even though he wasn't cheating and I like the idea of getting out of town occasionally to do a little traveling, especially since he's hinted at an out-of-the-country conference. Even the thought of exotic hotels and ancient streets brings me to orgasm," Vivian said, obviously no longer shy about sharing.

"Too much information," Prudence yelped. "Can we talk about my menu, this has just become way too personal for me to handle right now."

"I get it, really. How about instead we figure out what you can concoct that won't be so difficult, either solely cocktails and finger food like our book event or better still, a nice roast that could be sliced up and put out with some great bread and platters of cheese and fruit," she offered easily, having regained some of her poise. "You could use that fabulous bakery just down the road from here; my waistline will tell you I've sampled a lot of their stock already," Vivian said making a little turn around to prove a point.

Prudence could see no difference whatsoever in her marvelously full-figured stature. A few pounds here and there on a woman like Vivian would disappear into her well-tailored clothing and no one would be the wiser. *Except Paul maybe.*

"And there's a great butcher the other side of Route 1 that I've used before," Vivian added. "If you choose a good cut of beef, the rest will be easy."

When she got back to the cottage that evening, Prudence threw her heavy coat on the peg that she'd placed for convenience and pulled off her clunky boots. She walked through the house in stocking fee until her toes thawed, too lazy to get her fuzzy slippers from her bedroom. She always kept an extra pair of thick socks for the boots so she could wear more fashionable tights or knee socks around the store, but even with those, she suffered from cold feet. Then, with thoughts of a holiday party becoming more real, she took the china and crystal pieces from the hutch and brought them to the kitchen to check for cracks and chips and make sure they were clean. She'd found that no matter how hard she had tried, once the oil heat had been turned on, a greasy dust found a way to float between the cracks. She supposed one day in the future, she would have to invest in a new system. At least she had gas for the stove, especially since she had finally ordered an efficient and somewhat attractive new range. She had to stay within the parameters set by the tone of the house; she couldn't afford an entire kitchen makeover, so she had stuck with off-white to go along with what was already there and she was more than ever enjoying the proprietary feel of the remodeled cottage.

At least Hannah had put in a dishwasher in recent years, though not high-end but fully functional and Prudence placed some of the pieces into it for the next run, finding that with cooking only for one, it took a bit longer to fill. That would change, she hoped once the stove arrived. She'd put in a priority order for a pre-Christmas delivery and was already imagining more entertaining, maybe even intimate dinners with Nick. Prudence had gone from the cold treatment to the nearly sizzling and that was definitely too fast but it was so typically her.

The next week flew by quickly. The store was doing well and she kept her evenings busy with the small party details and good to his word, Nick had not been pestering daily about seeing her, obviously respecting their choice to grow the relationship slowly. Even Beth had gotten in on the project, making the now 'infamous' casserole to include with the meat dish and had placed it in the freezer until needed.

Three days to go, Prudence realized as she stood in the kitchen going over last minute details before heading to work.

Suddenly the doorbell rang. *Who on earth could that be; it's only eight o'clock.* Nick stood at the open door, a box under his arm and a terrible expression etched on his face.

"What's wrong, you look awful."

"I guess I must; I'm still in shock. My sister was in an accident on her way to spend the holidays with my folks. She's in a coma. The whole family—aunts, uncles, everyone—are all gathered in Denver. It was meant to be their holiday reunion. I have to leave right away. I'm so sorry about leaving you like this but I have to be there."

"Of course you do; don't think anything more about my silly party; this is family."

"It's not wrapped, but I wanted you to have your present since I truly don't know when I'll get back."

"You didn't have to get me anything, Nick," she said slipping the lid off the package. "You got me ice skates, wow!"

"I thought it would be fun to take you out on the pond. It might be February before it's ready but I figured that if I got them for you, you couldn't refuse. So please get yourself some good warm socks while I'm gone, okay?"

Prudence was bowled over by the unusual gift, touched that he had taken the time to select something that had taken such thought. In light of his news, his presentation was even more meaningful. While he hadn't told her a lot about his family, what he had expressed indicated that they were quite a close-knit group, even if he didn't see them often enough for his liking. So in the past few years because of his business and difficulties with holiday travel, his parents had begun coming to Maine during the summers. But it had been years since he'd seen his big sister, Jillian. Prudence could tell he was already shoring himself up for the worst.

"Be safe," she said and kissed him goodbye, which at any other time, he might have actually noticed. *He'll come back won't he?* The unbidden thought had ridden in on the harsh wind that blasted through the foyer from the open door.

Prudence felt that she should cancel the party, but Vivian wouldn't hear of it; said that wouldn't be fair to the others. She knew, of course, that Vivian didn't want her stewing while he was away.

"There'll be plenty more parties, Prudence, you'll see," Vivian stated with the pronouncement of a wise sage when she arrived at the store.

"You're right and he has been terrific and patient about my sexual reticence, accepting it better than I'd imagined. What more could a woman ask for?" Prudence responded although without a lot of conviction.

"You're just a little down; after all, you've lost Aurora and you weren't doing all that well to begin with without your family; so you're in a slump right now. It'll do you a world of good to celebrate the season in your new home the way you had intended."

Prudence spent hours in a tense and gloomy mood, fueled solely by past experience. She had trouble concentrating even after the heartfelt pep-talk with Vivien. By evening she'd mellowed somewhat and then received an unexpected call from Nick.

"I came straight to the hospital; Jill's still in a coma," he said in a strained voice indicating he was distracted, killing time by calling her as he waited for answers.

"I wish I could do something, Nick; I can only imagine how you feel. How is your family holding up?"

But even as she said the words, knowing that the family would be praying for a miracle, just as she had once done, she doubted prayers would do any good.

"The doctors are skeptical and running a battery of tests. I can't bring myself to leave her side while that's happening."

"Please call anytime and know I'm thinking of you," she offered with a sinking feeling and a loss for further words.

He promised he would call again even if only to keep her updated. Then he wished her Merry Christmas without any real feeling and hung up and she was left with a horrible sense of emptiness.

As the moments grew closer to party time, she felt as though 'Christmas Eve' would be more like an uninvited guest than the planned-for merriment. She had sunk into a familiar memory, the one where she is constantly being left and even though it was unreasonable given Nick's particular situation, her body had been trained by others to react this way, to shut down before the pain can overwhelm. She had to force herself to think of what he must be going through and it only helped if she channeled everything into tidying the house and food preparation. She'd been on autopilot since his call and now with only an hour to go before the guests arrived, a pervasive unease threatened to spoil her party.

"The house looks wonderful, Prudence," Kitty said as she entered the foyer that evening. The candles lit throughout made a sparkling path to the kitchen where Herman and Beth had already set up camp. Herman wanted to help by filling in for Nick as bartender and Beth always happiest when able to be of service was beginning to unwrap the various platters.

"What can I get you folks?" Herman asked even before they reached the mock bar he'd set up on the countertop.

"How about two scotch and waters," Dan replied. He was a quiet man, but Kitty more than made up for it and it was their first real outing since Aurora's death. "It's brutally cold out there Prudence, but I have to say you've made a warm welcome with all of this," Dan indicated with a flourish of his hand.

"I second that, Prudence," Kitty added and the conversations began to flow as the others realized the Donnellys were going to be all right.

Herman and Beth had both come dressed in their best Christmas sweaters…striking colors with snowflakes and reindeers. Sewn-on bells that tinkled when she moved, were this year's add-ons Beth said as she was doling out some of the

237

casserole. Though out of sorts, Prudence appreciated all the effort the Jenkinses had put into her very first party.

While waiting for Vivian to arrive, Kitty and Dan both got into the storytelling mode, relating every tale they could of past Christmases with 'dear' Charlie and Auntie A and the many missteps over burnt dishes and fallen cheese soufflés. Prudence had tried to avoid the residual pall that might cloak the evening, but she had let slip why Nick wasn't there. Kitty had picked up on her feelings, not wanting their aunt's death to cloud the holiday either. By the time Vivian arrived, the party was in full swing and the mood had changed dramatically.

She came through the door in her very real looking fake fur with a man on her arm.

"Prudence, I'd like you to meet Howard, an old acquaintance," she said as she slowly removed her coat for the full affect it would have on anyone bothering to pay attention. She sure has rehearsed that move a few times, Prudence thought and then realized that while she'd not recognized the name his face was unmistakable. *Out of character without his golfing costume, but yep, it's one of the beefy guys who kept ignoring me.* He was apparently an often called-upon escort, a situation never once connected in conversations with her business partner about the Village environs.

"Here, let me take your coats," Prudence said to the man who had just kissed her cheek. He acted as though it were a very natural thing to do, even though he'd never once spoken to her.

"Howard is an old friend, Prudence, and I couldn't let him spend Christmas alone. He and Bernard have usually left by now, but they stuck around this year to have a white Christmas and Bernie is down with the flu."

Well, that explains it, thought Prudence as she hung up the coats. *And come next summer, will those two remember,* she wondered and showed them where the bar was and made the introductions. Of course, Herman immediately recognized Howard and nudged Beth, a motion only Prudence caught.

Amends, she could hear in his mind; they'll make amends and Prudence will feel better and she'll want to stay.

The doorbell rang again and out of the blue, her summer neighbor turned up with his new lady-friend. "This must be Lillian," Prudence said welcoming them. "I thought you couldn't make it Len; what happened?"

"Our flight was canceled due to a storm in Chicago; that's where we would have changed planes. No point in getting stuck in an airport for the holidays and we saw the cars from Lillian's place. You don't mind, do you?"

"On the contrary, I'm very happy you're here," she replied, pleased that he had found someone close to home as his new paramour. Now Prudence had a full house.

By the time she bothered to look at the clock; it was nearly midnight and Herman was just winding down. He turned out to be far more comfortable as a storyteller than she could have ever imagined…no one had seemed anxious to leave and she wondered if she had at last 'arrived'. Kitty made certain to mention how much Aurora would have loved the party and this was acknowledged with a toast from Herman as everyone raised a glass to the sky.

When the door closed on the last guest, Prudence was content that the neighborhood had become more inclusive in one well-orchestrated evening than she'd been led to believe possible. The snow was now falling in steady determination and becoming whipped into a fury by the wind which allowed only the intermittent thrum of snow tires to be heard grinding their way down the Lane. Even though missing Nick, she sensed a slight turn of the universe in her favor.

Vivian, standing outside packed into the fur against the wintry onslaught, was bidding everyone goodnight, taking charge of the farewells the way a secure forty-something woman can (her real age was still a mystery). It was probably a scene that bore a strong resemblance to many others in the years before Pru's arrival…a long ago Thatcher Lane snapshot.

Christmas morning thick white snow blanketed the Cove. The sky was pewter and it matched the water now subdued from the previous night's thrashing. It was ominous looking with short bristly waves that moved the rippling black shawl forward where it ended in layers of white fringe on the rocks. Rollers would have been prettier. Looking out through the second floor window managed to remind Prudence of Aurora's dear Charlie falling from the roof of his house many years ago. How nice it would have been if she could have wrapped up the leftovers and taken them down the Lane to visit that sweet cherub once more, but instead she shook herself from the melancholy and went downstairs to survey the damages still soaking in the kitchen sink. She could hear the plows traversing the streets as she sank her tired body into the window seat with her mug of coffee. It was that type of morning, easy to surrender to the atmospheric mood from such a cozy place, having weeks ago relinquished her granite platform because of the treacherous frost, the sheen that was continually replenished by the waves. These past months had not only yielded the harvest of new friends, but a surprising camaraderie with a neighborhood blend of individuals and a burgeoning business. And since no one would be out today, it gave her a chance to reflect and give thanks as she considered breakfast.

She had come to revere the lack of sound in the usual places and the winter cloak had forced her to pursue her books and music with more fervor than before, cherishing the strains of Vivaldi or Bach or like this morning, Strauss. Even to write more letters, especially to Kate and those islanders who'd slipped by the wayside in the busy months of renovating.

The kitchen has turned into a contemplative space, a place to watch the changing sky and sea. This room has given her a real sense of pride since she has achieved far more with a can of paint and a yard of fabric than ever thought possible. She had found a clever way to make the valances using a press-on fabric tape and had hung them from small bamboo rods found at a greenhouse.

Because of that, she'd discovered a wonderful use for the little metal screw-in cup holders that she'd almost thrown away when cleaning out Hannah's kitchen drawers. They are a wonderful innovation for hanging thin expansion rods as well, wherever she preferred not to use hammer and nail. Herman laughed but applauded her ingenuity.

Mulling should be a job category, she mused, slipping into it easily on a morning like this. After Julie's departure, she had begun to sink her teeth into the era of great-grandmother Hannah's generation piecemealed from the various records found in the attic. And Beth had put in her two cents about the inventiveness of the pioneer women, especially in her own family ranging from around 1602. Her generation had been schooled about honoring the past and she was comfortable sharing the struggles and hardships, the type that had bound the widows of Thatcher Lane so tightly.

So it had been no surprise to Prudence who had delved with great curiosity into Elisabeth's life, that like many women of Maine, Hannah's sister often had to make do with whatever was available. The small footnotes to the usual details of births, deaths and marriages had been brought to life by reading between the lines as to the hardships in extreme conditions. These remarkable women made their own clothes and sewed for others as a way of bringing in extra money, but also to save on the needs of fast growing children. Sewing had been replaced by knitting for the widows of Thatcher Lane, but each craft gave comfort where needed.

Elisabeth had been a survivor and Prudence, sitting in her modernly appointed kitchen, envisioned Elisabeth in her role as she managed the country house, toiling in the heat of summer and bitterness of winter without any of the luxuries that Hannah had begun to enjoy in her later years. The elder sister might have spent untold hours cleaning the farmhouse of its residue, the type that not only came from the fields, but also from the pain of having to stay there. Prudence pictured Elisabeth washing their clothes the old fashioned way and hanging them to dry on numerous lines strung behind the back door. Indoor images of a stew came to mind, one made from whatever she may have killed by her own rifle and cooked in the large cast iron pot that hung over the massive hearth. Could see her preparing suppers from the farm's bounty in the dreary khaki-colored kitchen.

To Pru's amazement, Elisabeth had been a keen hunter, so there was no way to tell what manner of protein would have been found on their dinner table. While digging through the old boxes, Prudence had found a photo of Hannah on a visit to the farm, perhaps when picking up Amanda, the clothing was right for the period. Hannah had a rifle in her hand; holding it awkwardly as a mock salute to her big sister who had been known for shooting deer right through the kitchen window if they entered her prized garden.

Assumptions had been made about the way of life on the homestead, but once the digging had begun, Prudence unearthed a wealth of information about strength of both body and soul. Women of that era in general had fortitude, especially within the framework of a farm. They sheared and spun wool and raised fruit and vegetables plentiful enough to allow the family to thrive through the winters on the harvested crops. Elisabeth like many, had become adept at canning and putting up the stores to sustain her family when all she'd really wanted was to help heal the sick. Back then, choices were often made for rather than by women no matter how they may have felt. Prudence was grateful Hannah had lived out her years without many of those hardships.

These discoveries helped Prudence to better understand her own needs and attitudes towards personal accomplishments. She had been self-sufficient for a long time, needed to be to survive living in the islands. Here in Maine, however, she had taken it a few steps farther; had tried her hand at a bit of wallpapering, though not very well and a great deal of wall painting. She'd always been good at that, but never on such a large scale. She had been good with a hammer, but now can add a saw and power drill to the list. Hunting and the use of guns have remained off the table no matter her ancestry.

The sense of familial pride predicated by the women of the past and discovered knowledge have been inserted into her psyche. She now finds it easier to walk taller and with the ease of being a descendent of such dedicated strength. Or in case Hannah is watching.

Through it all, the big surprise came when she found out about the photo in the valise, the woman shown with binoculars. She was not Tim's mother as first suspected, but was in fact a second cousin of Hannah's. Shockingly, she had been a lighthouse keeper, having taken over from her ailing father. It now seemed undeniable that lighthouses were to be part of the family legacy no matter what should happen from here on in. To think someone so delicate looking was capable of strength and courage when needed whether to maintain the light or for a rescue, was mind blowing!

But the men in Elisabeth's household had also come under fire, not literally from the hunting rifle, at least nothing that obvious, but for submitting to the ravages of alcohol. Apparently, both father Dalton and son-in-law Jared had been capable of raw anger and even long bouts of depression under the spell of dull, dreary, disheartening winter days and long frigid nights. The Dalton clan that Prudence traced went back a very long way, their beginnings somewhere in England and yet Prudence knew that firearms, alcohol and little money were definitely not the entire story. She also knew there would be time in the years to come to search more thoroughly, but for the moment, she had achieved all that she had wished for regarding her paternal roots.

Prudence had been in a deep reverie but suddenly realized she was very hungry. She walked to the stove with the images of those interesting women trailing along behind and pulled out the fixings for an omelet. The phone rang as she had the whisk mired in the yolks, stopping her hand mid-stir with a jolt. She quickly turned off the burner and as she rushed back to answer, her knee hit the edge of the window seat.

"Hi," Nick's voice crackled across the line. "Everything okay?"

"It's nothing, I just banged my knee. What are you doing up so early?"

"I never really went to bed. Jillian's taken a turn for the worse and we're told it's only a matter of time now. My parents are having an awful time dealing with the reality of what they have to do; the doctors need them to decide whether to donate or not before they remove the tubes. That's all that's keeping her going right now," Nick said choking back tears.

He went on to explain that his mother and father needed him now more than ever. His dad had cataracts and the strain on his mother to do all the driving only added to the necessity of his staying. She already knew that Jillian had remained single, something Nick had extolled with brotherly pride because she had opted for a career in the world of finance instead of giving in to his parents' desire for grandchildren…there was still time or so he'd thought. As he continued, she understood there really was no one else but Nick to take command. *He seems at such a loss; no wonder he's reaching out.*

"I'll be thinking of you," she offered with sincerity.

"I'm not sure what will happen next, Pru; I don't have any answers as to when I'll be back. I've turned the important details over to one of my leasing agents and have notified someone to check on my place periodically to make sure it's plowed regularly and for anything else that can go wrong. I caught the weather channel so I know it's been snowing heavily out there."

"Yes, and it's rather pretty even though it's been years since I've been exposed to a Christmas snow. My dad always enjoyed coming to the islands to get out of it," she responded as though reading a dull book. She never mentioned the party, what would be the point.

"You take care," he said without thought to anything else.

Prudence held onto the phone for seconds longer than required, afraid to lose the sound of his voice. He was so forlorn and she had been helpless to offer anything that would make it better. *What if he never comes back? There you go again; be patient, he's in crisis.*

Just then, as though being tapped on the shoulder, Prudence knew what she had to do. *Aurora would be happy about this,* she thought as she began packing up those leftovers to take down the road to Mrs. Bond. She pulled everything from the fridge that she thought that Jean might like, wrapped them in foil and put them into a canvas carrier she'd received from Beth and Herman for Christmas. Although she really had no idea what the cantankerous woman ate, she didn't think she'd go wrong with this stash. Then she hurriedly downed her eggs, finished her coffee, and rushed upstairs to dress for the chilling walk down the lane.

Even though the plow had made a couple of swipes, Thatcher Lane remained slippery underfoot. Prudence walked gingerly, her boots crunching against traffic-hardened ridges, trudging to stay upright against the infernal wind that had resumed around the time she was having her third cup of coffee. As much as she loved the sea, it was beginning to wreak havoc and the tossed-about spray stung her face. She bowed her head against it and with each difficult footstep, she thought of Nick being forced to walk through so much sadness.

She was all prepared to knock on the black painted door— that matched the shutters on the pristine white cottage—when she saw the curtain move in the window next to it. Perhaps Jean wouldn't be any happier to see her this time, but that didn't matter. She was doing the right thing; the neighborly thing and it made her feel good.

"I don't need charity, Miss Stone," the widow Bond said with eyes glinting like nail heads behind her glasses as she took in the near to overflowing bag. She had opened the door the moment she saw Prudence approach, startling her.

245

"This isn't charity Mrs. Bond, just Christmas leftovers that I wanted to share. I'm sure you'll enjoy them; there's even some of Beth Jenkins' casserole, you know the one she had confessed about at Aurora's service."

"Well I don't have anything for you, you know. Wasn't expecting any company and I don't buy gifts anymore."

"I'm not expecting a thing, really. Would you mind if I come in for a moment though, I'm freezing?"

Prudence was actually shocked that Mrs. Bond let her in and pounded her feet on the small mat releasing the slush she'd tracked in. "What a lovely room," she exclaimed truly surprised at the interior. From where she stood, she could see right into the living room that had a large window that looked out onto a garden or at least what will become one again in the spring. She recognized the wallpaper; it was the same as Hannah had used for her bedroom. *These women really were a sisterhood in so many ways.*

Jean had begun to rummage in the bag while Prudence tried not to be paying attention to the eager way which she groped the items. It wasn't that she didn't have food or even cook, because Prudence could smell the remains of breakfast coming from the kitchen. It was a childish mannerism that the unexpected package had brought out. Prudence felt her heart lurch with emotion to think how lonely she must be and convinced herself she had made the right decision.

"I hope you enjoy the roast beef," she said. "And especially the pie. My friend Vivian baked it and there was way too much for just me."

"I like pie all right," Mrs. Bond retorted. *Brace yourself; she's still a little huffy...defensiveness probably,* Prudence thought. "I'll have the beef for my lunch with my hash browns...be a nice change. Maybe you'd like to stay for a cup of tea Miss Stone," she added much to Pru's surprise.

"Please call me Prudence...Jean," she tried out tentatively, as if the personal exchange might alter the outcome. "I love tea,

246

just like my great-grandmother always did. I've heard so many wonderful stories about the three of you." Prudence knew she was pushing the envelope but there might not be another opportunity to make the connection. All she really wanted was the recognition that there had been one, from Jean's perspective at least.

"Wonderful, huh?" Jean stated brusquely. "Not so sure what you heard, but there was a time we were all the best of friends. It was years ago. I suppose that silly Aurora was filling your head with stories, however and maybe some I can't refute. Makes no difference though, they're gone now and my time will come soon enough."

"Aurora befriended me, yes," Prudence replied. "But there was nothing silly about it; at least not for me. They were stories meant to help me know Hannah in a way I'd never heard before and be comfortable in a house filled with her memories," Prudence said as Jean brought in the little teapot with its knitted cozy. "Did you make this?" she asked.

"Yes, we all made them. That's kind of how we became such good friends, over this type of 'busy work'. It allowed three strangers to talk with ease about matters that were at times difficult to discuss. Can't quite explain it, but something happens when you're working with your hands like that and you're focused on the task. It seems to help the words come out more easily. I know after I lost my husband, it was one of the few things that could settle me."

Prudence sensed they were entering uncharted territory and thought it might be a good time to take her leave. If she played her cards right, Jean would invite her back and maybe she could get at the heart of the matter regarding Tim. She didn't want to push her luck, but she did feel that perhaps her speaking up at the memorial service had been the ticket to get in the door this morning.

"Maybe you would show me how to make one of these sometime," Prudence said fondling the still warm cover, nearly holding her breath for Jean's response. "Sometime that is, when you're not busy and wouldn't mind my coming by."

"Don't know if I'm a good teacher, but I suppose that would be all right. Maybe you could come back after the holidays. Give me time to sort out my yarns and needles so you don't have to go buy any."

"That would be wonderful, Jean," Prudence said again, testing the sound of familiarity.

She didn't attempt to kiss the old woman goodbye like she automatically had done with Aurora; instead brought her own teacup to the sink, quickly assessing the tidy little kitchen with its quaint knick-knacks. She brushed her hand over the white enamel-topped table as she walked out, wondering if Hannah had sat here a long time ago discussing the day's concerns.

Jean had risen from the sofa and began shepherding her to the door. It took a moment for Prudence to put on her boots and she noticed that Jean was watching her with intent. Did she think that Prudence resembled Great-gran and if so, was that a good thing or not?

"I think we need to talk about that locket next time you come," Jean stated matter-of-factly.

"Okay, Mrs. Bond," she said as her hand flew to the pendant in defense.

"You can call me Jean; I won't bite." She sensed the young woman's trepidation; after all, she had done her best to avoid her. But how would this girl understand what she'd done? And when Prudence found out, she would definitely resent her...maybe even hate her. So much resentment through the years...it had eaten at her and now there was no one left to talk to. Jean watched as Prudence walked toward home...Hannah's home. She had been stupid to shut herself off, but what could she have said? How can she make amends after so many years?

Prudence had now lived on Thatcher Lane for the better part of six months and as she entered the house wondering what Jean had in mind for their next conversation, she sensed Hannah's

248

presence as though applauding a good deed accomplished. She knew it was just a case of patting herself on the back because she had made the effort to reach out to the elder woman, but in the end, it didn't matter. *Hannah knows.*

While it had been a gamble to take the food over to Jean's and she'd been pleasantly surprised, it was perhaps a false start, given how many times she'd sought that missing chapter in the long story of the widows. She had reached a point too, where lines had become blurred between what she required—for Hannah or herself—and if finding the answers would resolve her own mixed emotions regarding relationships. She had to consider at least, that in the end she might spend an inordinate amount of time trying to solve the unsolvable.

The weeks passed slowly with winter in full throttle. Nick's absence weighed heavily on Prudence and the only thing that helped lift her spirits was the available range of beauty, the changing scenery from her shoreline to Vivian's property…nature's vignettes in a landscape long forgotten. While the snow hadn't accumulated significantly around the cottage, it was magnificent in the way in which it glossed the ledges and frosted them with dollops of snow, a splatter effect that reflected the color of the sky.

She had her first glimpse of 'sea smoke' during this time. "That's what happens when the mix of water and air temps are just right," Herman said as she bombarded him with questions. "Beth calls it a shroud because of the way it gets lit by the sun, all pink and gold…she tells me it's an aura."

"I just can't believe how beautiful it is and the snow on the rocks make me feel like a kid again! All I see are sugary toppings that look like frosting and then it cracks and breaks apart, maybe because of the tidal changes or the sun, I don't know. But either way, it's like the icing on the black and white cookies of my childhood, the ones that came out of the oven too soon," Prudence said. The memory was of a time before her mother had sunk to that all time low; a time when she'd actually been a 'mom'.

Prudence rarely reflected on those long lost days; it was too painful but maybe this one could be taken out from the vault of stored memories occasionally; it might help her forgive some of the other things, savor a few sweet moments against the tartness of Jean's bitter ones.

"Wait till you see the farm after this last squall," Vivian challenged one Saturday. She had invited Prudence over to witness her private wonderland. "All of my trees, especially those giant spruce are weighed down with dense snow. It looks like it's been painted on," she exclaimed.

Vivian was absolutely right. The farm had been totally magical with its expansive fields of white, more snow than Prudence had witnessed in many years. As soon as they had finished brunch, Vivian had made her sit at the living room window and wait until tiny spots of red began dotting the otherwise colorless landscape. These were the princely cardinals going from branch to branch in search of their food, which she and Vivian had supplemented with seed kept handy in the mudroom so that the birds wouldn't disappear into the black and white diorama.

The new wall calendar said it was the twenty-fifth of January, a Sunday, and Prudence was in the kitchen with her cup of tea, a phase she'd been going through since the visit with Jean, when the phone rang. "I found some of my old knitting supplies, Prudence; they were buried in my blanket chest and I'd forgotten I'd put them there."

Without preamble, the old woman had invited Prudence into her closed off world once more, the slight rasping cough a reminder of Mrs. Bond's previous smoking habit.

"That's wonderful, Jean, why don't you tell me when it would be convenient to have me over," Prudence replied, hoping it would be soon.

"Why not this afternoon. Otherwise, it might not be till next weekend since you're working." Apparently, Jean knew much more about Pru's schedule than she'd anticipated since she hadn't divulged anything about the bookstore. Obviously, it was easy enough to learn someone's habits and routines just by going to the little village market, but Jean's consideration still surprised her.

"Great, I'll stop by around two if that's okay?"

"I'll put on the kettle," Jean said as though this were an everyday exchange.

Prudence hung up the phone, completely taken aback by the reversal of personality and realized that Jean had been longing far more than anyone could have anticipated, for the companionship of her old friends. Perhaps the great-granddaughter might be the next best thing, at least that's what she hoped from the bottom of her heart.

"Let's start with your basic knit/pearl stitches, Prudence," Jean said, handing her the needles and modeling the way they were to be held and how to loop the yarn.

She paid close attention; to be proficient might earn another visit. Prudence still feared a pulling back; no one could switch lanes so easily and yet, there seemed almost an urgency to Jean's actions.

"You're getting it dear."

Dear, had she heard correctly? "I'm getting a little mixed up on the 'pearl' but otherwise, I think I really like this," Prudence said.

"Do those last two rows and we'll have some tea," Jean stated as though they'd been doing this together forever. "Then I have something I want to show you."

She did as she was told. Jean was in the kitchen setting up the small table with the pot and cups, sugar and milk and even a small plate of biscuits. Prudence watched from the other room, wondering if she should go and help but worried she needed to be called first. She certainly wasn't comfortable just 'making herself at home', not in this house, not yet anyway.

"The tea's all ready, Prudence; we'll have it in here; it's brighter and warmer."

"This is very nice of you, really and thank you again for agreeing to show me how to stitch. Maybe when I get the hang of it, I'll be able to at least make a potholder."

"You'll do better than that; you're Hannah's great-granddaughter and she was a wonderful knitter."

"I've gone through the house pretty thoroughly, but I've never come across any of her work; crocheted things, but not knitted ones."

"She probably gave a lot of it away after she was ill. People had been very kind to her during that time and it may have been a way of thanking them. Or even to the church rummage sale so they could make some extra money for their new flooring. Everyone used to pitch in that way. Times are changing and I don't go there much anymore. Aurora's funeral was the first in many years."

"That's the second time I heard that Hannah had been very ill. Can you please tell me what happened?" Prudence asked, hoping against hope that Jean wouldn't suddenly clam up.

"It was after Timothy went missing," she said.

"Missing? I don't understand. Aurora just said that he died so I presumed he'd been ill as well."

"Well, it wasn't exactly like that. I owe you an apology, Prudence—not that it will help the past, because that wouldn't change things for you, but for things I've been keeping from you. And it wasn't that you had no business knowing, because you do, as Hannah's relative. Let me just say, it was my way of keeping the last of Timothy with me...not sharing him with anyone else...not after Hannah. I blamed her for a very long time and she had nothing to do with his falling in love with her. That couldn't be helped. She was beautiful, funny and always ready to lend a helping hand," Jean stated with more feeling than Prudence would have ever imagined.

"He moved away, as I'm sure you've been told, when Amanda came home. Things changed after that and I'll never know if he tried to tell Hannah that I went to see him at his rooming house near the docks. Shamed myself in doing so too; throwing myself at him when I knew he needed her and gaining nothing but one hour of physical attention. I was hurting…lonely and too immature to realize what consequences this might have. Try and understand if you can, when my husband was lost at sea, I thought it would be the end for me too because I was still young with nothing to look forward to.

"I won't bore you with all the ways that I had tried to get his attention away from Hannah, but when I found out from her that they'd been considering marriage, I lost my senses and told her what I'd done. I didn't think she really believed me, thought I was just being spiteful, but it was after that she got so sick. Nerves, the doctor said, but heartbreak is what it was. I had ruined something precious for her, and particularly our friendship.

"One day before she had fully recovered, he had been out on the *Dorcas-Anne*, working alongside his boss, Matt Kingsfield, when a call came in of a boat floundering on a shoal. It was all in the paper, and I'll always remember the jolt that shot through me when I read it. Anyway, later on I found out that by the time the *Dorcas-Anne* reached the small schooner, the captain was screaming for help. His arm was broken and his wife and child were already in the water after falling overboard while trying to get into the skiff. The seas were like usual out there past the Stonycroft light with a storm brewing—high—and Timothy heaved off his heavy slicker and boots and jumped in after them.

"Kingsfield said the next thing he knew, the woman had latched onto Tim and was putting up such a fuss out of fear, that she dragged him down with her. No one knows what happened after that, except that his body never came up—hers did—but he may have been caught underneath the schooner; we'll never know."

"My God, Jean, I don't know what to say."

"Not much to say. I'm not proud of holding onto that bit of guilt all these years; don't even think Aurora knew the real truth. Hannah wasn't the type to air her laundry in that way, not even with her. And I couldn't say anything…I was too ashamed. And the worst part is that Timothy may never have gotten the chance to apologize to her; he wanted to marry Hannah and I was just a meddlesome fool and he was lonely and I didn't have the guts to say anything."

"I'm shocked and please don't think me rude, but I can't feel as badly for you as Hannah at the moment, even though I'm grateful you've told me. The poor woman; how did she cope after that?"

"She put on her good Yankee face and continued working, raising Amanda till that got to be too tiresome. After she left, Hannah stayed close with Aurora, but as you can imagine, she and I didn't speak anymore…at least no more than was civilly required in public. And as you know, she never found anyone else. That locket you have remained around her neck for as long as I can remember. No matter what he'd done, she had loved him and missed him till her death last spring. That much I knew."

"That's why you looked at me so strangely that first time…you knew he'd given her this locket. Do you know if she had anything else that belonged to him?"

"Well, I did retrieve his jacket for her, the one left on the boat when he jumped in. I assumed it was still on the boat and I claimed it for Hannah. Don't ask me why, except maybe a small way of making peace with myself. I left it for her at the village Post Office with a message that only said it had come from Tim's employer, Matt. Hannah wouldn't have questioned that because Matt had given Timothy time off on her behalf to drive to the farm to fetch Amanda."

"This is a lot to digest; would you mind if I don't stay any longer. I really do appreciate the knitting lessons and I'm glad you came forward, but I need to go home and make a call," Prudence said, not knowing what else to say. It was way beyond the time for her to feel the anger and humiliation that Hannah must have, but she couldn't simply sit and listen as though it weren't a terrible ruination of her great-grandmother's dream. But, as Jean said, they had both been to blame for hurting Hannah and no one, of course, could have predicted the ill-fated accident.

Jean had one more surprise before letting Prudence go and brought out the faded newspaper clipping and as Prudence stood to leave, hugged her with sincerity and what was left of her guilt. This old woman whose soul had become as hardened as a winter landscape had carried her burden a long time and wanted it put to rest.

Prudence had used that as an excuse to leave, but as soon as she got home, she called Julie. And while she wept for all of them, Julie just let her keep talking till she ran out of gas.

"Thanks; I don't know where all that came from," Prudence said with a tissue to her nose.

"I do; you've stuffed so much down since Jason walked out; remember the 'wet slip'?" Julie asked.

"Oh God, you're right; I sound just like what you had to rescue me from. Do you think it's in my DNA to fall apart at the end of everyone's love story or heartbreak?'

"I hope not; I do not have *that* much patience, dear friend, but try and get a grip, okay?"

"I feel drained and like I've just finished the worst novel ever. Damn Jean and poor Hannah," Prudence responded. "And damn Tim!"

"See there you are reacting as if it were Jason all over again; do you get what you're doing?"

"I think I've seen the light!" Prudence exclaimed choking on a laugh that got caught with the tears, the type that make a person snort instead.

It had been good to hear Julie's perspective; there was no one here that knew her well enough to suss out that little tidbit. But she still slept badly that night, tossing in the sea, reaching for Timothy and when she woke in the early morning, she had a terrible headache. She had cried for herself in the wake of the news, another heartless man, she'd thought and now she couldn't breathe well either.

Vivian had to hear it all the next day...Prudence finally spilled everything out, telling her all that she had been holding back.

"I don't know what to say." And Prudence recalled those were her exact words too. "No wonder you always wear that locket and no wonder you sometimes seem distracted. I never liked to pry, but I always presumed it had something to do with a man, only I sometimes thought it was Nick."

"It hasn't been easy for me to talk about a lot of this stuff, but you've become a good friend and I need to get this off my chest if we're going to be around each other so much. Other than Julie, the only other person who knew any of this, is my friend Kate who's now in India. She used to have to cope with Jean too and she was the one who tried to help me find the missing key. But this might require a long letter to her; I don't know if I'm up to another crying jag with a long distance charge added on."

"Why don't you go home for the rest of the day; I can manage. Frankly, you look like hell."

"Thanks a lot! You're right though, I just checked my face in the bathroom mirror and I can hardly see through these slits after all those tears and I still feel like crying." She was aware that she was an 'ugly' crier, not the single tear running down a powdered cheek as in the movies, but the red nose, puffy-eyed type and only an ice pack will do any good.

"Go home, watch the waves from your window, have a drink or light a fire, or do both. Does Nick know any of this?"

"Just my being jilted and that I've been trying to find out about Tim for a while. But I'm not sure what's happening with Nick," she said confused about getting involved all over again, knowing what can happen when you lose your heart.

She took Vivian's advice and on the way home, stopped for a large baguette and two types of cheese. Hannah's situation deserved a little 'pity party'. *Maybe you'll let me share your sadness,* she thought even though it seemed selfish. The dramatic effect this discovery has had on her psyche completely surprised her and as soon as she got home, she lit a fire. *You're here, aren't you? You want me to know what really happened. Forget about Jason or even Nick, this is about what you lost.*

Once the room began to warm, she put some cold tea bags on her eyes to ameliorate some of the damage and then placed the simple fare onto a tray and brought it to the footstool in front of the fireplace. She had to rummage around for a decent pen and found one stored with her better stationery and finally began a very long letter to Kate. She had to stop periodically to blow her nose or talk to Hannah's spirit or just move around as she composed the words so they would also help her to understand. It mattered that she put the words into their proper context, to clarify as much for herself as to why these things happened. And by the time she was finished there were a few watermarks where the last of her tears had dripped. But Kate would understand.

Chapter Eleven

Nearly a month has gone by and Prudence hasn't as yet been back to Jean's house although they've spoken over the phone...and that was only once to inquire if the knitting supplies needed to be returned. It had not been easy to be polite to the woman who'd done so much emotional damage to a member of her family even if Prudence hadn't known her; it's called loyalty and she put a lot of store in that.

She tried putting it in perspective, because of Vivian, for she was on the verge of damaging someone else's dreams and while not the same, it was another nail in the coffin of infidelity. Prudence was becoming wiser by the minute, however, and discovering that life was definitely never black and white as some would like to believe.

The only way she knew to cope was to work harder. February is a tough month and she felt an unfamiliar ennui setting in. It seemed like just another test for her to master.

Sometimes driving helped, when the roads were good, anything to take her mind off the emotional conundrum that was all her own doing. Occasionally a change of pace or emotional tranquility could be found within little unexpected pockets of unencumbered beauty, the way nature had intended. Winter's white had expanded her time to think and reflect and on occasion, fall into an unfamiliar though mild depression. Then she is forced to shake this strange sensation away with a new habit like brewing imported tea in a Japanese pot that resembled an art form. A wonderful acquisition she'd found in a specialty shop in Portland. It is but a small ritual, but it brings a sense of solidarity to her household routines. In her worst state of mind, she lets the healing steam from the kettle flow across her face. When the mist clears, it also clears her mind and then she reverts to the other balm, the sea beyond and Hannah's time on this earth.

When even that doesn't work, she bundles up for a walk around the point, occasionally glimpsing something as innocuous as an ice-encrusted branch from a lilac tree that's been hit with the noonday sun and the world will seem bright again. Most of the cottage windows are tattered with frost and like her own, images from the trees and branches will be imprinted on the glass and from inside will look like feathery doilies and patterned webs. Small creatures keep her company, twittering and scurrying out of her way; everything was there if she opened her eyes, except for Nick. She hadn't heard from him in over two weeks.

Back at work it wasn't any easier even though she tried to keep busy.

"I hope you realize you're pacing," Vivian said as Prudence moved about in the storeroom.

"Can't help it; I'm a bag of nerves this morning."

"Nothing from Nick yet?"

"Not since the call filling me in on the latest repairs he was making to his parents' house. It seems, as he tried to explain, they've needed some work done to their bathrooms and the kitchen for quite a while and he feels he should be the one to do it rather than have them pay to have it all upgraded. Ever since Jillian died, they seem to be in limbo, at least that's what it sounds like to me. The only thing I could relate was how inadequate I felt around my father after mom died; but even that's not the same. I think he may even be harboring a bit of guilt for remaining so many miles away all these years. Who knows, Vivian, I'm no mind reader…just a woman who suddenly finds herself missing the man she never thought she would."

"What you need is a night out," Vivian suggested, hating to see her like this.

"Maybe you're right, but why don't you come stay the night; then you won't have to drive so far after we let our hair down."

"Great idea. I'll meet you there around six-thirty tomorrow after I've fed the cats, and secured everything for the night."

"Would you believe it?" Prudence said when they entered the bar. "There's Marty so the other one could be Tom," she said recognizing the man that had attended the book event. Shirley nearly dropped the beer mugs when she saw them walk through the big oak door. *She thinks she's struck gold,* Prudence thought as she pointed to the available bar stools which just happened to be near where the cousins sat in a nearby booth.

As they sat down, Marty got up to pick up his beer, saving Shirley the walk over which placed him on Pru's right-hand side. Tom quickly followed grabbing the space nearest the bar register to get Vivian's attention. Although casually dressed, at least for her, she still stood out with all that lovely hair reflected in the bar's mirror. *A moth to a flame* Prudence thought taking it all in.

Shirley set the stage for them with pieces of juicy local gossip and then turned to her other thirsty customers, leaving Marty gaping at Prudence with soulful eyes.

"Glad you came in tonight," he said with a hopeful stare.

"Well we needed a night out and this is always fun," she responded. He was really very good looking and as she peered more closely, she realized she'd paid no attention before simply because it was what Shirley wanted. This was not a man to be ignored she realized when the heat he was giving off began to envelop her.

He must be around six-three, and built like an Adonis, Prudence noticed. *Must be from hauling traps and all,* she presumed. His brown hair had grayed some since the time of the photo, something she hadn't picked up on in the bookshop lighting and he'd pulled the now longer hair back into a ponytail. *Not many men can get away with that!* He wore a solid red flannel shirt, snug jeans and suspenders which were obviously not needed, except possibly for slipping his thumb into as he held his beer mug.

"So how's the fishing when it's this cold?" Prudence asked naïve to the whereabouts of the lobsters in the frigid winter temperatures.

"Actually, I'm out on Monhegan in the winter, beginning with Trap Day, January first and stay through spring; that's the only place I can catch right now," he replied, obviously surprised she had taken an interest.

"Well, I don't know how any of you do it. It looks like backbreaking work and as I'm sure Shirley has mentioned, I've spent way too much time in the tropics to be truly delighted by these temperatures. Thank goodness it hasn't dropped below zero too often or they may have to remove me manually from wherever I've frozen to the ground."

"Not to worry, I'd be glad to assist any time you need me," Marty responded with a wink and then an unexpected, but very light shoulder hug with his only free hand. Neither of the men had let go of the mugs clutched as though frozen to their rather meaty fingers—another sign possibly of their type of work.

When Prudence looked at the clock, she realized that conversation with Marty had been easy, far more interesting than expected as he described life on Monhegan, especially since she had only spent the odd day here and there playing tourist. The population apparently dwindled down to around seventy or so fisherman; the lobster quotas and areas were guided by the Conservation Zone.

"It must be an awfully lonely life out there from the way you're describing the landscape. I would imagine a good blizzard would wreak havoc," Prudence said.

"Well, it does sort of look like everything has gone through a giant mix-master on the day after. The traps and gear take a beating for sure, not to mention the lack of power. The little stoves come in mighty handy, but it's a luxury to be on the mainland at Shirley's when I can. The cooking is good and the heat is plentiful," he added with such a boyish grin that Prudence actually grinned back and then caught sight of Vivian trying to get her attention.

"Did you see how flummoxed Tom got when he heard I had a black belt in karate?" Vivian asked as they stood in front of the ladies room mirror, shocking even Prudence.

"No, but then I didn't know either," she replied.

"Don't be silly; I wouldn't dream of doing that to my body; just wanted to put him off or at least throw him off the scent. He was like a dog in heat...Shirley should know better than to let him out at night."

"Maybe it's time to go, before he gets any further ideas," Prudence said as they went back to the bar to grab their coats. As they were headed out the door, she looked back thinking that Marty was the better built of the two and by far the more appealing.

As Vivian began sashaying around her kitchen, Prudence realized the time talking with Tom created another side to her friend, one she'd never seen before.

"Guess we both needed a change of pace," Prudence stated as Vivian opened up a bottle of red wine.

"The one at the pub was awful," Vivian answered. "I just nursed the one glass because I didn't want to be rude or bring down the wrath of Shirley who, bless her heart, had tried so hard to manage the outcome of the evening," she said with a giggle.

"Well, you know she's just trying to get the 'boys' off her hands, but I have an odd feeling I'm going to hear from Marty," Prudence said unexpectedly causing Vivian whiplash from where she stood rummaging in the refrigerator for something to nosh on.

"What are you talking about...did you actually encourage him after all you said previously?"

"All I'm saying is that he really isn't so bad after all and let's face it, how do I know Nick's not seeing someone out there...it's been a long time Vivian and no man, especially one like Nick, would be allowed to roam free without pursuit by those local maidens."

"I know you've been in a winter funk, but maybe, just maybe before you go and do something uncharacteristically foolish, you should call him. Surprise him with an 'I miss you more than you realize' kind of call; build his ego during his time of grief and solace or something to keep him interested at least."

"Maybe you're right; I'm just overreacting as usual. I don't seem to know how to handle these things anymore, if I ever did. I'm either playing cold fish or an overheated martyr, neither of which is attractive to anyone. Maybe I should look through a few of our 'how to' books and see if there is a new angle I can pursue."

"Pursue the best looking guy within fifty miles, if you ask me! Granted he is a long way off at the moment, but he will come back!"

It had been a raucous, eye-opening revelation to spend an evening out with Vivian, another dimension to her working persona. She was a woman who knew and spoke her mind, but she had a really soft side for those struggling and had at last tossed Paul aside as well. Prudence admitted that while Vivian had actually made her 'affair' seem harmless enough, she was happy it had ended before Vivian got hurt.

A few days later, she took Vivian's suggestion to call Nick out in Denver thinking if she didn't, she would regret that as well.

"Mrs. Pelletier?" Prudence asked, pretty certain they didn't have a live-in housekeeper. "May I speak to Nick; this is his friend calling from Maine,"

"Oh I'm afraid he's out right now; would you like to leave your number?" she responded graciously.

"Please accept my condolences," Prudence said with a heartfelt tone. And just tell him Prudence called; he has my number," she said still feeling hopeful.

264

"Thank you; it's been a rough time as you can imagine dear, but we're so grateful our Nick is here with us. I doubt if he'll be able to call back tonight, though," she said nearly as an afterthought. "He's at the Denver Ballet Theater and they usually let out late, but I'll be sure to give him your message."

She obviously has no idea of the significance of such information or she wouldn't be so forthcoming, she thought, realizing her instincts had been right. He must be seeing another woman; who else would he take to the ballet?

She sulked for days; Nick had not returned her call. "It was probably just his mother's absentmindedness; after all, the family has been through a lot. She probably simply forgot to give him the message," Vivian stated as she listened to Prudence expounding on her frustration.

How could she explain to Vivian or to anyone how insecure she suddenly feels? This situation with Nick has dredged up exactly the type of emotions she'd hoped to avoid. She carried around a guilty little secret…her feelings of inadequacy. She'd hidden them well with her travels, her zest for life; but underneath, she was scarred and unable to believe she was good enough to be loved. When Jason walked out, it was as though her mother's words had come back to haunt…the ones from her drunken rants…the ones that blamed Prudence for ruining everything she had wanted for herself and the ones that told Prudence she would never be good enough. Only Ben had made her feel secure.

When she'd met Jason she had managed to believe her mother had been wrong. When he left, she'd declared a moratorium on men; that is, until she met Nick, a man she hadn't wanted to date and who now occupied all her thoughts. Had she once again deluded herself into thinking that good things would come? With Ben gone, there was no one left to shore up the cracking façade, the one that had held her together rather precariously ever since.

She had gone through counseling soon after Victoria died and knew that her mother's jealousy had created this inability to find a middle ground on which to walk. It might not be playing fair, but Prudence decided she would go out with Marty if he called, at least someone wanted her.

There was only a nascent hue in the sky on an arctic Saturday morning when she pulled into the small clearing in front of a thickly frozen pond next to Marty's truck. He'd been listening to the radio and drinking his coffee, steaming up the windows as he sang along, his breath little puffs as though he were smoking. Her own car was no longer a concern, just as Zack had assured her. 'Little devils are built for everything', he'd pointed out at the time.

Marty rolled down the window and she heard the music blaring.

"Are you ready to have the experience of your life," he teased, hauling himself out of the truck with the laces bundled in his large 'paw'. His skates had a well-worn black boot and looked enormous hanging by the long strings and the blades looked just plain ominous as though they'd been honed to razor-sharp edges. She hesitated a moment before removing her small, brand new white ones and was suddenly terrified at what she'd gotten herself into.

"Maybe this wasn't such a great idea after all," Prudence said as Marty kneeled down in front of her. A tiny pang of guilt struck as she looked at Nick's Christmas gift and then she shoved it aside just as she felt he'd tossed her over.

"Here, let me help you," he said after she'd put on the extra pair of socks. She was seated on an old picnic bench next to the pond and as he helped with her laces, he could hardly believe his luck. He'd never expected her to say yes.

It was still early and they were alone on the ice. She clung to him as he pulled her to her feet as wobbly as a newborn foal. First he stood before her and led her in baby steps toward him as

266

she teetered and squealed. Then suddenly before she could object, he had her by the waist and was gliding her by the sheer strength of his body, onto the unmarred hoarfrost surface. He was as big as Herman but was obviously no stranger to such graceful movements and as she continued to screech in fear, he was actually holding her through a series of turns.

Marty never let go of her hand, nor did he allow her body to escape his protective closeness. If his hands weren't circling her waist, he was hovering in a way that it would be impossible for her to fall. She was quite a bit shorter and a lot clumsier than Marty, although his size would have disputed that, but he moved with her as though she were nothing more than a feather floating through the air.

"That was so much fun!" Prudence exclaimed after they'd rounded and crossed the span of ice for an hour until her toes numbed and her nose dripped unattractively and she claimed 'uncle'.

"You're a natural," Marty said.

"We both know you're lying, but thanks. It was my best and my first effort, so I suppose I shouldn't be too hard on myself. And as a thank you, I brought hot chocolate; it's in a thermos in the car. If we can get these blades off my frozen feet, I'll go get it and you can tell me how you learned to do all that."

She'd brought brownies too—from a box mix—but meant to say thank you.

"These are good," Marty said as he put one entire square in his mouth, none the wiser, chocolate was chocolate. "Before my folks moved, the family always came out to this pond. It's a nice little reservoir but doesn't really freeze over completely until about February. It's great for fishing in early summer. Dad liked catching the small-mouth bass whenever he could…a fun place for a kid to grow up. All the kids around here were taught to skate at a very young age…hockey's pretty popular so we all wanted to learn," he stated without affectation. "Even my parents would dance together as though they had a record playing in their heads and as a little kid, it was like watching a movie. I'd never seen them like that except on the ice."

"What a great memory; do they still skate?"

"Nah. Mom says her arthritis bothers her too much and dad is just too busy keeping his boat in running condition. It's been a tough couple of years for them financially and they don't seem to have the fun they used to. If you hadn't mentioned the skates, I might not have thought of this either. It's a shame too, because it's one of the prettiest spots around here."

Just then a carload of kids were emptied out with their parents trailing behind hollering for them to wait at the bench…a perfect cue that it was time to leave. She still found it hard to think of herself as a direct descendent of these hardy northerners the way she obviously detested the cold.

"Let's give this a try again the next time I'm back…this ice isn't going anywhere soon," he said walking her to the car wearing an ear-to-ear smile.

As she waved him off, Prudence sat in the little VW blasting the heater before taking off. Marty had left her with much to think about. She would have liked to savor the feel of his body-hugging warmth and the security of being held as though she were a glass ornament, but unfortunately guilt was rearing its ugly head. This was supposed to be Nick's moment, their time together. She returned to the cottage surprised by the physical effort carried out under what seemed like pounds of clothing and admittedly still chilled to the bone, only to find the answering machine light blinking in the darkened room. She was positive it would be Nick, which would serve her right, she thought as her throat constricted with enough guilt to choke the joy of the day right out of her.

She took off her outerwear and dumped the thermos in the sink, removed her cold socks, and put on her fuzzy slippers before playing the message. Then she breathed a huge sigh of relief…it was from Kate. Looking at the clock, she was immediately disappointed because of the time that meant she would have to wait until tomorrow to answer. *That was a close call,* she mused. *What if that had been Nick; then how would you feel?* Was she really so insensitive to his situation that she would continue to see Marty?

"How's my favorite American?" Kate asked through a hollow sounding tunnel. It had taken a few days for Prudence to finally reach her to see if the letter about Jean had arrived, the struggle to connect always hinging on the time, the system itself and even Kate's strange schedule as she suffered the woes of a misplaced person in a foreign country.

"Hasn't Michael gotten those phone lines sorted out yet; I can barely hear you."

"Don't even go there; the man is working round the clock and it's so hot that I began to miss the thought of ice and snow soon after touch-down. He is somehow in his glory, however, downing great British gin and loving the curried goat or whatever else they curry over here while I try and fraternize with the other ex-pats and find something to keep my brain occupied. He's 'happy as Larry' and I'm bored, Prudence, and I miss my dog so much," Kate wailed into the phone.

"That part I do understand, but when it comes to heated climes, I have to say it would be lovely to exchange locales with you at the moment. We're up to the sills at the store from where they've had to plow us out a few times and it isn't going anywhere for quite a while," Prudence responded while looking out the shop window.

"Are you doing okay Pru?" Kate asked knowing they could be disconnected very easily.

"Well there is so much to tell you, I don't know where to start. Everything seems to be a challenge these days and on one hand I really want to be disgusted with Jean and on the other, I feel sorry for the old bat."

"As you know, I have always disliked the way she's behaved, but not in my wildest imagination, would I have expected that," Kate responded.

"Me either, but since we have such a bad connection, I'm going to try again soon. It's too difficult to rehash this when we can hardly hear each other, and suffice it to say, there is more."

"I really hate it when you leave me hanging, but this connection won't do."

"I promise I'll write soon," Prudence confirmed even though she didn't know if she'd be able to explain the dating situation.

Two days later Vivian walked in on Prudence in tears.

"What's happened; did someone die?" she asked insensitively.

"He called and said things were still in limbo as to his return, AND his old friend DIANA has magically reappeared and apparently come to the rescue. She's been helping out with the everyday things for his mom and getting him through some of the residual sadness that I know never really goes away when a loved one dies.

"According to Nick, they've sort of picked up where they'd left off; happened quite by accident," Prudence quoted. "Trouble is, he hasn't said picked up from where!"

"We can't have you falling apart over a man Prudence Stone; I won't have it," Vivian stated like a schoolhouse matron in a bad movie.

"I can't help it; I feel dreadful, maybe I'm coming down with the flu."

"Look, even if I hadn't encouraged it before, if that were me I might have a closer look at your fisherman friend; he's easy on the eyes and what's good for the goose as they say…"

"Where do you come up with this stuff?"

"Maybe just years of listening to a tired out, mean-spirited husband, till I gave him the boot! Almost makes having an affair a little more palatable, right?"

"You make it sound so cold. We had a good time skating and even that one time we went out for a movie. He's not stupid, Vivian. I think he could tell my heart wasn't in it, but he has asked me out again."

"Here, you might need these," Vivian said taking two condoms out of her purse.

"Well, now isn't this just dandy!" Prudence said sarcastically.

"Better safe than sorry," Vivian retorted with a really bold wink. She wasn't going to let Prudence have any slack; the girl needed more gumption!

Prudence tucked the unexpected 'gift' into her bag, certain she would not be using them but to appease Vivian. But one part of her brain wanted to so that she could get even for what she believed Nick was doing. The other side wanted to be loyal to Nick even though they hadn't had sex either. Suddenly SEX was the only thing that made no sense. *Damned if you do and damned if you don't!* Then she couldn't decide if she should wear something sexy or plain so as not to entice. She simply didn't know what she wanted and for a woman like Prudence that could spell disaster.

Marty picked her up on time, opened the truck door for her and helped her in, all very gentlemanly. The heater was blasting. "Thought we might catch that sci-fi movie after dinner," he said easily.

She hated those but kept her mouth shut when she realized they'd be dining at the Dory. *Why here? That's all I need.*

"You're quiet tonight," Shirley said once she'd stopped talking and noticed Prudence staring off in space.

"I think I have a bad headache coming on; probably just the cold weather," she replied hoping that Marty would take the hint and order up some food before she really did get one.

"How about a couple of specials to go?" Marty offered. "We could take them back to your place so that you can relax, you've probably just been working too hard," he offered as if it were the simplest solution in the world.

"I do need to get some food in me, but are you sure you're ready to leave," she asked almost sorry she'd been impatient about staying. Now she would have to deal with him on her turf, but suddenly Shirley was ever so helpful. *She really does want him out of her hair and her kitchen!*

It seemed he couldn't get into her house and out of his coat fast enough. "Here, let me light the fire," Marty said, helpful as a boy scout as soon as he'd spotted the fireplace, shooing her off to plate the takeaways.

By the time they'd finished their dinner, the fire was roaring. He had built it up so much that she felt like taking her clothes off, which she realized is what he had been hoping. He'd already popped his boots off at the door and she could see his toes wriggling in his socks, crying for release from the oven he'd created in the room. He started to strip off his woolen sweater and as he began to lift it up, she saw the chest hairs peeking out of the tee and wondered what her fingers would feel like running through that small nest of curls. *What am I doing?* She wondered as she excused herself.

"I have to change into something lighter; I'm not used to such a big fire," she said, burning up. She had also gotten a whiff of pure male musk. *Oh brother, this is happening way faster than I imagined,* and reached into her closet for an old shirt. *Do you really want this?* In her confusion she hadn't heard him come up the stairs and yet there he was, his huge body filling the doorway. Before she could ask what he was doing, he took a long step toward her and wrapped her tightly with arms that would be hard to disengage from and kissed her full on the mouth, nearly crushing the breath out of her.

She pulled her head back, "Whoa, tiger! Isn't this moving a little too fast?"

"I thought maybe this is what you wanted," Marty said innocently enough. Somehow he'd managed to pull the puppy dog face again, and she just laughed out loud. *He's more like a comfortable pet,* she thought though not unkindly. He wants to be cuddled and held and paid attention to and here she was doing just that. "You're really pretty," he said as he stroked her hair and her face. *How did we get this far?* She wondered as his big paw started to undo the buttons on the blouse she'd awkwardly thrown on, noticing afterward that she'd not done them evenly. It was like she was in a dream sequence, not quite aware and yet recognizing the characters enough to participate. *It's like I'm drugged,* she thought as he continued without her. *The man's a genius at clothing,* she realized.

"So?" Vivian asked the next morning before she even had her coat off.

"Well, I hope you're happy; we screwed, and I'm screwed and when I face him, I'm sure I'll fold like a bad poker player," she fumed. "That is if Nick ever comes back," Prudence shouted. "Maybe if I hadn't held him at bay, I wouldn't be in this predicament."

"Easy girl; what if you had gone that far and he still got tangled in the mysterious Diana's web; wouldn't that just make you feel wonderful." Vivian shouted back. "Why shouldn't you have some fun without any commitment; no harm in that, right?"

"The jury is still out on that, Vivian!"

Maybe their mutual guilt was being telepathically communicated, because as if by magic, two days later, a letter arrived from Nick.

Dear Pru,

I hate writing letters but I couldn't bring myself to hear the reproach in your voice. I truly never meant for you to be hurt and even as I write, I know this sounds like a lie, because I did hurt you.

I've known Diana since high school; Jillian even dated her brother for a while. It never really went anywhere, just typical teenage feelings and then I saw her when she came home from college and we dated some and then the more adult feelings kicked in and we had a pretty steamy relationship for a while. I'm only giving you this detail because I say 'had' and it never really ended badly, so it was natural at least to me that she would show up after my sister died. And that's when it got complicated.

She knew exactly what I was going through and began to help all of us through a pretty rough patch and I liked having her around. She made me smile again, something that wasn't easy at first. I loved Jillian with all my heart; she was my rock when I needed her and even though my parents are devastated over losing their daughter, they have each other and I felt I had no one...until Diana showed up. I swear it didn't mean anything! When you told me you had taken a skating lesson from Shirley's cousin Marty; something I suppose you could have omitted or lied about in some way, I wanted to punch the wall, which if you think about it, says quite a lot. I obviously have strong feelings for you or I wouldn't have reacted like that. We haven't even had our chance yet and we're already heading down the wrong path. I'm sorry I've had to be away so long and I know I can't ask you to wait, but I have told Diana about you and that I will be going back to Maine very soon even if for only a little while as I may have to come back here periodically to check on things.

You scared me; I'm not ready to give up on us. Please try and wait for me.

Nick

She didn't need to run her response by Vivian and tucked the note card into its envelope, a 'yes' written in pretty script on the embossed stationery, and sent it off immediately. *Looks like we both tarnished this hopeful relationship.* It was amazing to her that he had even written such a lengthy and heartfelt letter; she'd not even ever had a card from Jason when he was away on business for the university.

After fourteen long days with each crossed off in red on the store calendar, Nick's large frame blocked the doorway, the wind buffeting the space as he stood there grinning from ear to ear. She ran to him and jumped into his outstretched arms grateful she was alone. It was both comical and touching, the way he picked her up and swung her around, smothering her face with small kisses, obviously happy to see her too. Then he put her down and kissed her with all his pent up passion and grief combined, neither of them aware of the frigid air.

"I don't think I realized how much I missed you until just this moment," Nick said. He tenderly swept her hair back and away from her face, even the wispy fringe on her forehead and studied her as if for the first time. He didn't seem to want to let go.

"Me too," she replied praying that she could get past her own guilt. "But I really have to close this door before the books blow off the shelf," she said suddenly feeling the cold air circling her legs. "Grab yourself some hot coffee from the storeroom; I can't close for another hour so we'll have to catch up right here."

"There was so much I had planned to tell you, rehearsed it all on the way here and now that I'm standing in front of you, all I want to do is kiss you again."

"Me too. I thought I would want a detailed report of your activities with Diana; but in truth, I don't really care…you came back. That has to mean something, right?" *We're not going down that path or I'll also have to fess up.*

"I meant what I said in my letter. I don't want to lose you Prudence; especially since we've really not even become a 'couple' if you know what I mean."

"Are you going to take my skates away if I don't agree?" Prudence said in the saucy way she'd once talked to him.

"No, but I may demand they never leave the house without me alongside...how does that sound?" Nick asked, hopeful that he wasn't too late. In truth they both needed to be careful and maybe that was all that needed saying.

"Perfect. How about Saturday? If you're extra nice out there, I might even make you dinner afterward. My new stove came in and I've become rather domestic since you've been away."

"All kidding aside, Prudence, I meant what I said. I want to make this work if there is any chance at all that it can survive my going back and forth for a while. My folks are doing much better but I would be remiss if I didn't see them through this next few months, at least until they feel up to coming here the way they used to. At the moment, they're not ready to travel, but I think it would do them a lot of good to be back in Maine even if only for a few weeks. I'm anxious to get them out on the *Mystic*; my sister would have wanted that. You've never seen my little boat, have you?"

"No, you left before you could take me over to the marina where she's stored. But I can't think of anything nicer than getting out on the water with you. Thank God you hadn't named her 'Diana'," Prudence said play punching him in the side.

"You really know where to aim, don't you?" Nick responded, once again pulling Prudence off her feet and kissing the words away.

"Take the next few days off," Vivian said when Prudence called her that evening. "Enjoy your beau without thoughts of Marty or Diana...mum's the word from me." She was good at keeping secrets, but hated what that had felt like with regard to

Paul. As it turned out, he was just as selfish as the unmarried men she had dumped. She had hated lying to Prudence who was such an open book. Vivian recognized something in Nick she hadn't as yet experienced and she envied her partner.

Prudence happily allowed Nick to court her. He was making up for lost time and trying to impress upon her that he had meant what he said. After immediately taking care of business that needed his hands on approach and making certain his own home was in good order, he made good on the first promise to go skating. Instead of trying to compare her time with Marty, she did her best to prove in a quiet, benign way, that skating was something she and Nick would only do together. She did not show off her new skills or play coy when Nick explained where or how she might improve. She just followed his lead and tucked herself in his protective arms and counted her blessings.

As soon as they left the frozen pond, Nick drove straight to his cottage. It was at the end of a lengthy drive and sat in the midst of a wide snow-covered field with a mere peek of river evident through dense pine trees. It looked to Prudence like a recently unwrapped present waiting for the recipient. "I banked the fire before I left," he said as she pointed to the smoke billowing from the stone chimney.

"What a wonderful surprise," she said as she scanned the room. Before leaving, he'd set out mugs for hot chocolate, extra wood to build the heat back up and a couple of woolen blankets ready on the couch before the hearth.

"This is really lovely," she said, never expecting his 'bachelor pad' to be so charming.

"It pays to have your finger on the pulse of the real estate market." he said. Then he kissed her nose affectionately and watched as she removed her down jacket, fleece vest, wool hat and two pair of mittens. She obviously disliked the cold. "I'm glad you like it."

Prudence was very taken by what she saw, though it might have been because it was his. It was easy to picture spending time within these rooms. That is, if things went well, beginning with today. As if he could read her mind, he brought her to the fireplace, set the steaming mugs of cocoa on the table and wrapped her in one of the woolen throws. And while she was snuggled cocoon-style, unable to move, he kissed her and she foolishly found tears forming in response. Wriggling out of the wool, she put an arm around his neck and with her free hand, began stroking his cold cheek already showing a telltale darkening where a second shave might be required. He would have been considered swarthy by some, but to Prudence, he was simply all man. "I've missed you." Until that moment, she hadn't realized just how much. His skin was bronzed even though it was winter. Colorado sunshine, he'd told her. It gave him a rugged woodsman look or that of a professional skier and it made her heart swell when she thought about a possible future together. She wanted so much to believe this possible.

"You can have the guided tour later," he said as he slid her down onto the large, plaid-printed sofa. He flung the extraneous pillows to the floor to make room. Then with all the gentleness he knew how, slipped his hands underneath the extra heavy sweater and stroked her soft skin.

Her breath quickened, the cold chill no longer a concern. "Come here you," she said, throwing off the blanket and pulling him in closer so that they were squeezed side by side on the couch. He was tall and had selected the furniture to suit his stature. Its length gave them ample room to stretch out together.

Nick looked at her intently and lifted the locket away from her skin. "I don't think I've ever seen you without this," he commented.

"I rarely take it off," she replied and kissed the enveloping fingers. It was not the right time to explain everything, especially Tim's drowning. That would come later. Sensing her mood, he let it go and stroked her hair instead and caressed her until she began to loosen up again.

His strength was almost overwhelming and yet he cradled her passionately, careful not to destroy the long-awaited moment in any way. They began to move in their quiet dance, lulled by both the soft music and the now roaring fire. "You certainly were prepared," she teased as she shifted her body. "The wood, the cocoa, the right songs, everything," she said mimicking his strokes until in the limited space they were in sync, their foreignness with each other gone completely. *No reason to be shy anymore,* she thought, wanting to wipe away any and all thoughts of Diana and Marty.

Then, something they'd both sensed from the beginning, that their movements would be fluid and rhythmic, until the only thing heard besides the murmurs of content was the crackle and hiss of blazing logs.

Prudence must have dozed for she awoke alone and then heard the water running. "Didn't want to wake you," he said as he walked in on her trying to stoke the fire. She gave him the long-handled tool and picked up their mugs to refill from the pot on the gas burner, dragging the oversized blanket along for cover. If this room was any indication, the rest of the house was freezing.

"Sorry about the heat," Nick said. "There didn't seem to be any point in cranking it up for the few hours a day I might be here. And since I can't stay very long this trip, I sort of imagined or at least hoped, I'd be spending most of my time at your place...especially since you offered to cook."

"As soon as I'm dressed I'm going to take a quick look around if you don't mind. These Maine cottages really fascinate me and by summer, I may be spending just as much time here; you never know," Prudence said with a wink.

"You have no idea how good that sounds...like you've actually been thinking about 'us'."

"Well, at least that far," she said, never skipping a beat.

The cold rooms were pretty much what she had expected. They were furnished with showroom pieces that probably came out of either a store in Stonycroft or Portland. Everything was simple, sturdy and masculine. There were two bathrooms, one up and one down and both were again plain, clean and unfettered by feminine touches. *You might be able to fix that* she thought taking it all in stride. Every room was painted in simple decorator white; a couple of the walls were the old horsehair stucco types and doing most anything to them would be a bitch, his word when describing the ancient house. Drapery had been excluded in favor of roll-up shades, something else she thought needed sprucing up, all in good time. But she was freezing and could hear Nick straightening up downstairs and putting things away, making sure the fire was out before they left for Thatcher Lane. As she headed back down, she felt that her guilt had been assuaged. His loving attitude was enough to scale the imaginary barriers that cheating had instilled.

They had stopped to pick up a pizza on the way to Thatcher Lane and then cozied up to another fire, this one in her inviting living room. Hopefully, there would be many similar days to share. Finally, exhausted from both outdoor and indoor activity (they had repeated their earlier union in front of her fireplace), they fell into the sleigh bed in the room at the top of the stairs. She slept soundly for the first time in weeks; no one invaded with night terrors and when she woke, she felt refreshed and renewed.

"See you later," she said, hugging him to her as he stood at the sink in charge of the breakfast dishes.

"Is this my plight now that I've been allowed in your bed, milady?"

How she loved his novel way of handling something as mundane as a kitchen chore and as she headed out the door, she heard him humming the tune from *Camelot. Vivian will get an earful this morning.*

"So?" Vivian queried the moment she walked into the store.

"I don't know where to start, but it was fabulous. Suffice it to say, we did the deed and we are now 'official', but I reserve the right to dole out what I want when I want; just enough to satisfy that lusty curiosity of yours."

"Some friend you turned out to be," Vivian shot back with a knowing grin plastered ear to ear.

Nick spent most of his time at Pru's cottage as they'd predicted. The roads were more treacherous near the farmhouse and once they had established a nice routine and especially the enjoyment of cooking together—he always cleaned up—it seemed foolish to do otherwise. It was also a joy to have him all to herself, snuggled in the big sleigh bed, as she imagined the sighs of the former occupants, still cognizant of Hannah and Tim's presumed presence in this same space.

"It's gone so fast," she said. The week was coming to an end and a mild depression threatened her happiness. "It's been a wonderful week," she whispered as she poured his coffee, so afraid to jinx her joy by shouting at the top of her lungs.

"There are only a few more details I have to finalize before I head back," Nick said, picking up her mood. "I've loved every hour we've had and I promise, I'll be back before you know it…you have my word," he said as he kissed her tenderly and shooed her playfully out the door.

Once in the privacy of the little 'bug', Prudence allowed the flow of tears she'd been holding back. She was suddenly overwhelmed by the lack of time they had left, the precious hours before he'd be on the plane to Denver.

"You look a little glum this morning," Vivian said before Prudence had even closed the door.

"I need to do something to distract me, anything to take my mind off his departure," she replied. "And I'm way behind as you may have noticed," she added. "Nick is spending the day taking care of general office matters and handling something for one of his clients regarding a recently purchased plot of land. He said it paid to keep his hand on the pulse or something like that…maybe it was eye on the ball," she stated, not really caring.

"And then he'll be gone again," Prudence said with more difficulty than she thought possible.

Vivian walked over and embraced her. "It'll be all right this time, you'll see."

"But Diana is still there; what if he changes his mind?"

"There you go again, getting way ahead of yourself. You've been together constantly since he's been back; it'll be fine!"

Vivian tried to jolly Prudence out of the glum mood, but by the time she and Nick got together that evening, she was no better.

"I'm actually going to miss your cooking," he said after dinner.

"Well if that's all you're going to miss, I'll just package up the food and you can take it with you," she said haughtily, taking his comment the wrong way.

"Now don't get all huffy…I meant to say that I'm going to miss everything about you, including your cooking."

"That's better," she said, pouring him a glass of wine as they sat in front of the fireplace in her now updated parlor. He had commented on the brightness the moment he'd seen it, which actually surprised her. She didn't think men paid much attention to that stuff. But then, remembering some previous thoughtfulness, re-sized her opinions. He wasn't what she would call 'average' by any means.

While he had been in Denver, she and Beth had stripped wallpaper. Then Prudence and Vivian had painted the room together on the weekends and had taken Hannah's chair in the back of Vivian's car to the upholsterer she'd recommended. The same one who had made all the slipcovers for the odd collection of furnishings Vivian treasured. The only thing left for Prudence to accomplish with regard to the furniture, was to redo the sofa in good time. She was still very conscientious about money and even with the business doing well, she staggered her expenditures as best she could.

Beth had also helped her rearrange the kitchen with some of the items retrieved from Aurora's storage cartons. With Beth's guidance, Prudence had learned to make a few of the dishes she now prepared for Nick, except for the infamous casserole. Said she couldn't part with that recipe for anyone since she was still fine- tuning it. The new gas range had already proved to be fun to cook on and Prudence found that she was better at it than expected and obviously now Nick thought so too.

"I want you to have something," he said walking over to the coat rack.

She watched as he pulled something from his jacket pocket. *He's already given me my Christmas present* she thought as he handed her a small box.

"Oh Nick, this is stunning," she cried as she lifted a heart-shaped silver pin from its white satin pad.

"I wanted you to have something to put on other than the skates; something to keep you thinking of me while I'm away. And I think you now know you're in my heart, don't you?"

She kissed him again, this time an affirmation. "Of course I do." But even as she said it, the little nudge came back *what about Diana* and of course, she also realized that he hadn't as yet told her that he loved her. Maybe it was just way too early for that sentiment. She knew she was falling in love, but was reticent to say it first. Maybe he was just following her lead and now he was leaving for Denver in the morning.

But even as she palmed the pretty pin, thoughts of Diana infiltrated her brain. *God, don't go there, not tonight. Leave it alone; Vivian will kill you if you spoil this evening.* She had tried really hard to be in the moment, could almost hear Vivian scolding her about jumping to conclusions and as she pinned it to her sweater, she focused on his words instead.

"Let's get this over with," Nick said as he helped her clear the kitchen. He disliked facing a chore like that on his last morning. "I have better things in mind for us."

Even as he rushed through the small chores, she knew he was trying to console her because of the imminent departure. "What could you possibly have in mind?" She flirted as he led her up the stairs. Logically, she shouldn't have been so concerned. He'd already hinted about *their* future, had been talking about making some changes to his cottage with her in mind. He'd mentioned the possibility of a leisurely trip through Tuscany when the time was right and had laid out the day trips he wanted to share with her in the *Mystic* in the coming summer. It all sounded so full of promise and hope, but even as they made love, the doubts came back and once he fell asleep beside her, they roamed her brain without constraint. She had hardly closed her eyes all night.

"You were awfully restless last night; everything ok?" Nick asked the next morning over coffee. He hadn't wanted any fuss about breakfast claiming he'd grab something at the airport.

"Probably just the wine," Prudence lied. She felt adrift without their ritual food preparation. It was a cold way to leave it, but the necessity for conversation seemed to have been packed in his suitcase.

Nick knew she wasn't handling his leaving very well. She'd been on the verge of tears since last night. "I'll call as soon as I arrive, and I plan to tell Diana about us," he said confidently. "Please don't worry; I'll be back in three weeks." He had decided on the timetable before leaving Denver and had worked out a calendar with his parents, hoping they would agree to a spring trip to Maine.

Putting his arms around her one last time, he kissed her goodbye at the door, leaving her in her chenille robe and funny fuzzy slippers that he always chided her on, to wave him off. It was gray and humorless outside, the sky reflecting her resistance to parting. No matter how hard she tried, the demons of jealousy had already scored their mark. Leave-taking brought back too many bad memories and even though she knew his folks were counting on him, her old 'what ifs' had already come home to roost.

Now what? She wondered as she drove to work without any desire to be there. *This won't do at all...you can't let any man keep you from your new goal.* But she had fallen in love, against all the odds and was now left to fend for herself until and if, he returned. Exactly the feelings she had hoped to avoid.

"You look absolutely dreadful," Vivian offered along with a hot cup of coffee as soon as Prudence had removed her coat.

"Thanks."

"No, I mean it; you didn't even put lipstick on."

"I forgot because I had other things on my mind. Remember my telling you I didn't want to go through this stuff again? Well, here I am, playing the waiting game and expecting my heart to be broken—as always—because I don't seem to know better."

"Prudence, Prudence, please don't go all melodramatic on me this morning. I was up with a sick cat last night, and I'm not so perky myself."

"Sorry, which one?" Prudence replied guiltily. "I just get so unnerved when I think of that 'predator' waiting in Colorado."

"Thanks for asking...Tulip, but she's better this morning," Vivian said knowing Prudence could care less about a cat. "Have a little faith, okay?"

"I'll try, really, starting now. What's on the agenda for today?" she asked, refilling her cup and pulling up a chair at the desk. Vivian would cut her just so much slack and then she'd tell Prudence to 'suck it up'.

"That's better; how about we go over the books for the coming quarter?"

With their noses in the ledgers, the hours passed with little thought of Nick or Diana or anything troubling. Then she went home to an empty house. Turning on the lights as she headed to the kitchen, she thought of all the candles and the party he'd missed at Christmas. His absence was again palpable and she looked about for any vestige of his presence...the smell of his cologne in the air, a forgotten toothbrush or toiletries, anything, even the soap that always smelled like fresh air that might still reside on the pillowcase still rumpled from morning. *This is pathetic; look what you've become?*

Then, and probably because she was already on the second floor, she did something she hadn't in a long time, at least not since the cold weather had set in. She went up to the attic to commiserate with the departed. Perhaps it was a silly thing, but having learned of Tim's fate, it felt appropriate to say her final goodbyes in that room. As she entered the black space, she groped for the little toggle switch and the overhead fixture cast an eerie glow across the old oil slicker. The room was in good order though she hadn't begun to make all the changes that she planned to tackle in the spring. But it was neat and clean and she had brought one of the wicker chairs from the guest room after Julie's visit so that she wouldn't have to sit on the floor anymore.

She had pushed Timothy's disappearance aside as though the last door had been closed, but seeing the jacket in the odd light she desired to put it on, to feel the weight of it; the room was so cold. And while it was not her place to do so, she felt she had to forgive him as she had chosen to do with Jean. Prudence could no longer remain lofty about infidelities; she'd learned a lot about herself in these past months. And besides Hannah must have or she wouldn't have worn the locket for so long.

She reached for the jacket, intending to put it around her shoulders while she searched for one of Hannah's books. *Not again,* she thought as she felt the resurgence of warmth through the metal on her chest. *Why now?*

She turned off the light and shut the door in haste and carried the jacket back down. On the way, she picked up the clipping she'd taken from Jean's house and went to the kitchen since she hadn't built up a fire as yet. She re-read the article and replayed that fateful conversation from beginning to end. Naturally, Jean hadn't taken umbrage over Pru's inability to continue the knitting lessons. She'd obviously anticipated the reaction. And while Prudence knew they would never have a warm and fuzzy relationship, she was cautiously optimistic they would be respectably pleasant. She would never be able to confide in Jean the way she used to with the widow Durn and that was understandable but whatever small gesture she could extend, might assuage some of Jean's guilt and therefore, ease their co-existence on Thatcher Lane.

Maybe it's a good time to call her; keep my mind off Nick, she thought heading for the phone in her room.

"Nice of you to call, Prudence," Jean said affably enough.

"Jean, do you really think Timothy intended to marry Hannah, or did you just say that to make me feel better," Prudence blurted without preamble.

"You might think that Prudence, after all this time of silence between you and me, but I knew the moment I walked away from his room, seeing the remorse written all over his face, it was what he still intended to do," Jean said with sincerity.

"Aurora was too protective of Hannah's feelings to tell me anything more that might help you. Besides, she thought she was protecting Hannah from my jealousy and not from what actually happened between Timothy and me. As I told you before, I don't think Hannah ever knew what I'd done because then Tim disappeared. But then, I could be wrong too and believe me after she recovered from her illness, it was never the same between us. So perhaps she had found out some way. All I do know is that I'm sorry I didn't make amends with them both. I'm old Prudence and it's hard to think of dying with all that baggage weighing me down. I took a cheap shot in my own pain and sorrow and I've paid plenty. Hannah was my dearest friend and I can't ever have that back," she said before hanging up.

Prudence replaced the receiver and plucked the jacket off the chair, almost sorry she'd forced that pain to resurface. It was obvious in Jean's tone how much that one hour had cost their friendship. Prudence was suddenly aware of how cold she was and instead of putting it around her shoulders, carried the jacket into the front room and put it over the back of the newly upholstered chair while she got the fire going. The slicker looked so natural there, hugging the frame as Tim might have once hugged Hannah. And as the room began to warm, Prudence snuggled into the substantial white on white jacquard weave now casually wrapped in the yellow trim, and tucked her legs comfortably beneath her body.

Hannah's house, the Ellison house, Gull House, she thought of the transformations as she stared into the flickering flames…no matter how long she remained, it would always be Great-gran's house and that would always seem right. Prudence had already begun to surmise that her identification wouldn't be formed by where she lived, but by how. And as the fire continued to mesmerize, she was convinced deep in her bones that she had been meant to discover this imposing love story. *Oh Hannah, what have you done?* Would she suffer true love the way Great-gran had? *God, I hope not,* she thought, turning on both lamps as the room suddenly seemed overshadowed by that old doubt. Nick might not return; would she be strong too?

Why not take a few measurements before you fall into a melodramatic funk, she thought as there wasn't much else to do for the rest of the evening. She circled the room looking for the tape measure, knowing she'd left it behind the last time she considered additional reupholstering. It was always a toss-up as to whether it was more prohibitive than purchasing new and she'd left the sofa for last because of the expense. Pondering the same question, she took in the furniture from various angles and spotted the tape on the windowsill. *It must have been left there when we wallpapered.*

The only other chair in the room and off to one corner was a black-painted Windsor which she hadn't as yet decided whether to repaint. She knew better than to simply discard it or she'd have Herman's wrath to deal with. Admittedly, it had its appeal though, especially with the intended white sofa, and it was not really like any of the other furniture in the house. She had never bothered to look at these pieces as a coordinated set, always happy to sit in Hannah's favorite spot and each time just pushed the idea of another expenditure out of her head.

When Julie was here, they more often than not ended up on the floor in front of the fire. Or Julie might sprawl out on the sofa and watch the flames saying how much they helped her relax and that it was comfortable enough, a good place to read. But then Julie had cushioned wicker furniture in her St. Thomas apartment, not a perfect comparison and the last thing on their minds had been the furniture.

Prudence took a really hard look at the room and its contents and then did something rare and sat on the sofa, testing the cushions as if they'd speak for themselves. She favored Hannah's chair so much, that these were usually relegated for the rumps of her occasional guests although she and Nick had enjoyed snugging up there during his recent visit. But she certainly wasn't attached to it like she was the chair. Running her hands around the piping and skirting, she was hoping for a decorative idea to spark, something that might make her like it more so she wouldn't have to go shopping. She still had to be practical and it was in decent condition. *There must be a few decorating magazines lying around somewhere.* Maybe this was the perfect evening to begin a project that would take her mind off everything else. As she jotted down the measurements, she began to feel a tiny thrill of anticipation, the excitement of remodeling that she'd had over the little powder room. *This might just be the ticket to occupy the empty hours while he's away.*

Like a silly kid, she bounced on an end cushion, testing her weight and the springs. *Oops, what was that?* She heard a rustle of paper as though she'd dislodged something and quickly got up and tossed the cushion to the floor. Seeing the edge of something plastic peeking from beneath the middle one, she stacked the remaining two on top of the first. *What on earth?* Prudence looked aghast at the collection. The sounds had come from the assortment of newspaper clippings that were rubbing against some bizarre plastic rain caps. There was also a large manila envelope sealed by only a clip and a small 'exercise' book with rows of figures listed inside, some type of accounting.

In her early thirties, Prudence had no way of knowing whether this type of habit was part of the aging process, but she apparently had stumbled onto a small unexpected trove, as accessible as a desk if there had been one. Opening the little book first, she realized it was a budget of sorts but the entries seemed years old. She brought the clippings to the lamplight as the print was small and creased. Two were obituaries of women she assumed must have been friends of Hannah's, but the third, was identical to the one Jean had given her relating the loss of Timothy Parker during an attempted rescue at sea. As her anticipation rose, she carefully pulled papers from the large yellow envelope and there, between a few important receipts— tax payments and one for the dishwasher along with an outdated warranty—was a much-handled, white, letter-size envelope. Folded within was a single piece of paper. Prudence drew in her breath…but no, these were not the words of an anguished lover caught with his pants down, literally, and hoping for forgiveness. This was an expected note from one longing for his lover.

Hannah my love, how I miss you! It has been a long two weeks with only one letter, but I understand, really. Amanda is a full-time job and I can tell from your past letter that you are worried about her behavior since we brought her back to the coast. I wish I could help, but we both know my presence would only make matters worse.

Fishing is not as good as we'd hoped, so Matt says we'll begin to set our traps further out in colder water; longer days mean more profit but only if we're hauling full traps. The weather hasn't been cooperating either, 'portending' a storm as he likes to say. I hope you will come and meet me here when the

290

week is over and my pockets are rich with my portion of the catch and I can show you how I care.

Yours Tim

Prudence put it back and reread the clipping: '**Timothy Parker, 37,** died during the rescue of passengers on the *Mariah*, a 36' schooner that went aground near Stonycroft. He was a stern man on the *MV Dorcas-Anne*, a fishing boat owned by Matthew Kingsfield of Trescott Mills. Due to the circumstances, there will be no burial service.'

Disregarding anything but her gut feeling that while there was nothing left in plain sight, she was extremely close to the truth. Not knowing what else to do, she plunged her fingers into the space of the cushion-free sofa, wedging them between the tight crease of seat and arm as far as she could reach. As she wiggled them, she felt a smattering of stray crumbs and the odd coin that always managed to get into such crevices but continued to work her hand back and forth until her nail snagged the edge of something not normally found. She was careful not to rip it as she slipped it from its hiding place because the paper had been made small enough to be lost to anyone other than the person who knew it had been placed there. Prudence laid it out and smoothed the many folds. *It's from Tim*, she thought holding her breath, struck once more by Hannah's fortitude. While humiliated and hurt to the point of illness, her great-grandmother had still desperately needed to have these items where she could put her hands on them. And from the condition of this one, Prudence knew it had been handled often.

This is the most painful letter I've ever had to write and the torn paper around my feet is evidence that I've tried many ways to say the one thing I never thought possible. I have betrayed you, the person who means more to me than life itself. I won't pretend it wasn't my fault, because I let it happen. And I'm sorry to have to accuse Jean of her betrayal of your friendship, but I need to tell you what happened and in order to do that, she has to claim some responsibility but in fact, I'm certain she will only claim victory.

She came to the boarding house to see me and I will spare you the tawdry details, but by the time she insinuated that you might have another suitor and having brought along a bottle of whiskey to share, let's just say the deed was done. By the time I came to my senses and realized she was up to her old tricks, just like the picnic baskets she would haul to your place when you weren't there, it was too late. Please, Hannah, somehow forgive me.

Whatever else was written at the bottom had been torn away. He may have pleaded; said more to convince her or just merely signed it with an extraordinary heartfelt flourish. Prudence would never know. Perhaps Hannah couldn't bear the imagined proposal, the one that would more than likely have been offered in other circumstances. Maybe that's what she had waited for and why her grief at this horrible truth nearly killed her. Jean had not paid quite enough, Prudence thought, and yet, what could be enough to right such an offense?

She put the letters back in the larger envelope along with the clipping and threw the rest away, even the funny plastic head coverings with the ribbon endings…the type that women used to wear as they escaped the beauty parlors on rainy days. Now she was too pent up to do anything constructive so she paced like she sometimes did at the store; it helped to think. So much had been resolved and she still felt a sense of emptiness…a longing for completion. Maybe it was her own story that needed completing, she contemplated, not her great-grandmother's. Poor Hannah—the cruelty of fate, after all. Maybe in time she would have forgiven him had he not been stolen from her by the swollen, raging sea. *But we'll never know now, will we?*

To try and settle her nerves, Prudence sat and wrote a lengthy letter to Kate…this tale was way too long for those overseas charges and it was actually easier to chronicle such an extraordinary find on paper. After that and because she had forgotten to eat, she fixed a sandwich and a cup of cocoa and took it to her room where she decided to read through the small tome of collected poems, if for Hannah's sake only. She still hadn't come to grips with poetry as a whole, but that didn't matter right now.

Tucked under the covers she reread the sonnet first heard in Mr. Thayer's office and at last it made sense…the death at sea of the man she'd dared to love. It wasn't terribly late so she called Julie; it couldn't wait till tomorrow.

"He didn't! Julie squealed into the phone. "How could she?" She yelped again with each blow-by-blow account.

"I know; do you believe what guts it took for Jean to even do that?" Prudence said without waiting for an answer. "This reminds me of an old movie but since its Hannah's story, I'm not so inclined to enjoy it."

"Are you going to call Nick and tell him what you've found or is that not of interest to the debonair Mr. Pelletier?" Julie asked.

"Don't be such a wise-ass; of course it would interest him, anything about me does, don't you know that by now?" Prudence replied, mimicking Julie's tone. But it's a little late even on his time for this type of dialog."

"But it's a love story and by the way, speaking of that, Coop is flying down here to meet my folks since I've finally broken the news that things are heating up. And, I can't leave to fly back to Nebraska again; it's too busy."

"Wow, that's a breakthrough; congratulations!"

"Well, I won't say I'm not anxious about that meeting, but they are kind people and when they see how well we get along,

I think—I hope—it's all going to go well. In the end, it's still my choice, but it's always nice when things go smoothly."

"Maybe there'll be a summer wedding, huh?"

"Don't get ahead of yourself, please…but I have actually thought about it and are you sitting down…in Oyster Cove!"

"Oh, Jules, please, please, please."

"Okay, enough begging already! We're not quite there yet. I'll be in touch soon. Get a good rest, and please don't start planning the festivities just yet; I know you."

"Goodnight—sweet dreams."

Wow, getting married here…do we have any bridal magazines at the store? Prudence wondered, immediately turning the mental gristmill much against her friend's advice. Somewhere between the end of the sonnet and the beginning of imagined scenarios for Julie's nuptials, Prudence had fallen asleep and a ringing phone woke her. Looking at the bedside clock she wondered who would be calling at midnight.

"Hi," said the distant voice.

"Nick, is that you?"

"Who else would be calling you at this hour…have you been seeing another man?"

"Wouldn't you like to know?" She teased brushing sleep from her eyes. "I just fell into a deep sleep while reading and it startled me."

"I know it's a little late, but I really wanted to hear your voice. It's been a long day and the folks are out and I'm sitting here by myself thinking about my girl…you haven't changed your mind, right?"

She thought she heard a note of doubt in his voice. "Yes, I'm still your girl."

"Good, so what have you been reading; nothing too juicy I hope."

"All right, enough…so much has happened that I don't know where to begin. First off, I found out what happened to Tim,"

Pru said, hurriedly and then told him at length all the details from start to finish.

"Wow, she must have been quite the 'hottie', don't you think?" He quipped trying to imagine the very old widow Bond in a love triangle. "And by the way, your instincts were spot on; you knew something big had happened."

"Well, I do have my moments of clarity," she huffed. "By the time you get back…you are coming back soon, right?" She asked before completing her thought. "Because the best news is that Julie is thinking of getting married in Maine this summer, here in Oyster Cove."

"I didn't know she was engaged?"

"Well, she's not actually, but my bet is on it happening very soon and I know I'm jumping the gun, but wouldn't it be great if I could do something fantastic for her here? Maybe you could help me think about that."

"What did you have in mind?"

"I don't know, maybe a day trip on the boat to acclimate them to the Cove or even a reception out on the field at your house under a tent for the wedding party or whomever, since I don't know any of these details. I'm pretty sure she'll want some sort of church ceremony, but I think that should also be really unusual, a quaint chapel maybe. You must know of a few around here."

"I'll be back in a week and if I know you even a little, you will have everything mapped out for me when I get there. I miss you."

"Miss you too; sleep well."

Why bother to sleep at all she thought as she looked at the clock again. She might as well stay up all night and feel just as tired in the morning. But of course, waking at six, she realized that idea had had no merit whatsoever. And, since she'd fallen asleep before finishing the sandwich, she was starving. She bustled about with a new fervor just thinking of a wedding and while she prepared a really big breakfast, she turned on her favorite classical music station that began broadcasting early morning. Her mood had changed considerably. *A wedding!*

"Hey Prudence, look at you…beaming like a cat with a canary. What's up?" Vivian asked the moment she strolled through the door.

"Nick called; what else? He's coming back in a week *and* I talked with Jules and she just may be getting engaged soon. Isn't that terrific?"

"So that's why you have the bridal magazines in front of you?" Vivian asked as she came around the desk.

"I'm jumping the gun as always, but these are so yummy," she said as she flipped through pages of billowing dresses with toile layers and petite beading that in themselves looked like resplendent cakes, not at all what she'd chosen for her big day on St. Thomas. "I never cared for anything like these before, but I can really see Jules in one."

"Does she know you're picking out her wedding gown?"

"No, and I'm not *picking* it, just checking them out."

"Okay, but I have a favor to ask. Would you mind filling in for me for the next three days. My latest beau has invited me to join him in New York and I'm dying to see a play."

"Sure, I can do that—really," she emphasized since she saw Vivian's concern.

"I know what you're thinking, but Jim is single, someone I used to date," she offered easily. "I'm giving him a second chance but only because I have cabin fever."

"Things probably won't pick up till late March, so go and have fun; you've covered for me plenty," Prudence said happy for her partner and grateful she was back into the singles dating again.

Without Vivian around the next few days flew by quietly. The weather had been ponderous as it switched from icy cold to spring-like teases as the sun began to change angles. "April could bring a whopping nor'easter," Beth, the pseudo-weatherman had said ominously.

Prudence never did know how much of what she heard around Oyster Cove was simply hyperbole and not fact, but by now she didn't really care. The weather here would always be a constant source of dialog!

She took the opportunity of Vivian's brief absence to do some extra cleaning and polishing, rearranging the shelves and bringing in a couple of new plants as a surprise for Vivien, a show of appreciation. Prudence took particular pains not to allow Hannah's long ago plight to consume her thoughts...*busy work Aurora would call it, many little things to take your mind off heavier matters.*

And when she thought she could stand it no longer, had cleaned all she could, both at home and the store; had filled the freezer with enough chicken and beef to feed at least three people for a week, Vivian returned. Prudence had even itemized the needs of a future wedding if and when Julie gave her the go-ahead and all that was left was to focus on Nick's return.

Prudence stood before the terminal window as the metal giant inched forward. So much had happened since she'd last been here, she thought waiting for the gate door to open. Layer upon layer played out before her...those whom she's come to know, lives that were built upon the solidness of coastline ledges. Thatcher Lane was now her neighborhood and not just an unknown entity that would keep her from her beloved islands.

"Wow, this is a wonderful greeting," Nick said ignoring the jostling passengers as he let himself be embraced by his lover.

Prudence had flung herself at him, nearly knocking him over. He looked like good health personified as he always did when he came back from Colorado. The mountain air and continual sunshine gave him a perpetual tan and he'd walked in wearing a suede jacket and his cowboy boots amidst a throng of parkas and woolen coats. She caught the appreciative looks from more than one envious woman in the crowd. They unabashedly eyed him and she put her arm in his and eyed them back, enjoying the little buzz of excitement at their expense.

"Thought you'd enjoy being chauffeured home this time," she said as she took in the earthy scent of his skin, that clean fragrance of his cologne, the one she could never describe because it was so unique.

"Does that mean I can stay with you too?"

"What do you think," she said with a kiss.

"Anything new since we talked," Nick asked.

"Not really. Vivian's been away for a few days and Julie says that I have to stop pestering her; that there is no ring on her finger yet."

"How about the Cove…all well there?"

"I haven't spoken with Jean, don't want to really, not yet. And otherwise, it's been pretty quiet, especially with the hunkering down type of weather we've had. We should have the place more or less to ourselves I guess."

"That's not a bad thing. I have a little work to do and after that, I'm all yours," he said as they walked hand in hand to the car.

Is he really mine? She pondered as they drove home. Because of the gear shift, he couldn't hold her hand, but instead placed his lightly on her thigh, just enough to send tingles of anticipation all over her body. They never made it through dinner that evening, just curled up together like lovers in a Gustave Klimt painting and she wanted for nothing more. By the time they were sated enough to require conversation, it came in the nature of the preposterousness of Jean's so-called tryst discussed over what remained of their earlier meal.

One night over dinner, Prudence mentioned that Vivian was dating again and decided it would be a good time to share the little tidbit about her earlier affair. Prudence thought it was most prudent to let him know just where she stood on infidelity, in case he might still have thoughts of Diana.

298

"I hope you're not implying that I might be doing the same when I'm in Colorado, because nothing could be further from the truth," Nick said looking her straight in the eye.

All she could do was kiss him and believe him and take a chance, finally. So each evening while they stirred pots and mashed vegetables and fried fish, they became a closer unit...and they also danced...a lot...and to all kinds of tempos. She would put on some of her Latin music taken out of storage and to her delight, he really could dance and well. Even a salsa, though once he attempted a rather clumsy tango and they'd ended up on the floor in a tangled mess of legs. She soon found out how quickly he could become aroused by the mere thought of dancing!

Nick was always there when she came home from work, waiting with whatever wine choice he thought appropriate, sometimes he even had a simple dinner simmering on the stove. They would talk for hours in front of the fireplace, sharing things they'd never had time to explore before and once or twice drove out to his place to check on it, relishing the plans for the upcoming summer. Then before he was scheduled to leave and when she was finally ready to share him and their precious time together, they made it a special occasion to have dinner at the Jenkins home as Beth insisted on preparing her lobster casserole.

Nick quickly surmised that this made her dear friends happier than she could have explained without him bearing witness. It was pretty obvious they had a lot to catch up on and as Beth explained, what with the weather and some of their other commitments, there just hadn't been time. Nick could tell by the end of the shared evening and the way Beth and Herman looked at each other, their mental wheels were cranking away as they watched the beginning of a love story.

At the end of the week, Prudence closed the store early stating with a small sign on the door that there was no heat due to a boiler problem—a small lie she wasn't a bit guilty telling. Nick had planned a short jaunt to Portland for an evening out…dinner and a plush hotel room to sink into afterward. It was such an unexpected and thoughtful gift from the man who'd pursued her even when she hadn't been willing. Though incredibly cold and disregarding all good sense, they wandered through the Old Port, their bodies pressed together as they walked arm in arm. Pru's frosted breath blew into her twined wool scarf and her teeth chattered and just when she thought she couldn't take another minute in the wind, Nick steered them into an alley and stopped directly in front of a categorically chic and highly advertised establishment where they would dine.

Nick knew his restaurants and he knew how to have a good time and he even seemed to know a few of the staff as well as the proprietors, telling Prudence he had met clients here on occasion who had come from out of state looking for property up the coast.

After an absurdly rich three-course meal at the chef's recommendation, and a brutal walk back in the unabated wind, they were finally ensconced in the luxury of the well-appointed room with no thoughts of leaving until absolutely necessary. With the king-size bed and tapestry drapes that shut out the rest of the world, Prudence knew instinctively that she was in for a night to dream upon long after he had gone.

Nick insisted on the small wall sconces rather than turning on the bedside lamps. He knew what he wanted and that was the caress of soft lighting to enhance her supple body, one that he felt was cause for celebration.

Prudence couldn't believe the way the room's trappings exuded a sense of opulence. Anyone occupying it would feel special. There were many unexpected touches in the use of materials, the type she often associated with privilege. It secretly delighted her that she'd been fantasizing about their night, things that would happen that hadn't happened in Hannah's bed. She realized it was trite and harkened back to something her late mother had said after she and Ben returned from whatever trip they'd taken; that is, before he could no longer stand the drinking. 'Wicked', Victoria had teased before realizing Prudence had been within earshot and they'd both blushed profusely and scooted her out of the room. Now she understood what that must have meant, because something about being in a hotel room was very freeing, though not quite what she would call wicked, but a whole lot more adventuresome and playful.

Prudence had reason to be profoundly touched by everything that night, all the loving gestures that allowed her to take pride not only in her appearance but in the way she was meant to love a man, something she'd never known possible, not even with Jason. She gave herself over completely and joyously took all that he offered.

"You're beautiful," he said while exploring her body in the light of morning.

They'd slept in, luxuriating in the room service tray and each other once again. Fluffy robes had come with the mini-suite and they drank champagne sans strawberries since Nick was allergic (a good thing to find out before the season and homemade shortcake). They were curled up in the thick robes on top of the covers after a tingling bubble bath.

"I hate to leave," she said unselfconsciously as her hair dripped onto the robe, her skin tinged with pink from the hot tub water.

They had very little time left before she would take him to the airport. "Come here you," he said laughing into her wet locks of hair, undoing her robe and sinking her back into the covers. "Let's not waste time."

And then, it was over…and he'd left her at the terminal gate where she'd met him only a week before. The time had disappeared with a blink of an eye. Every minute of the overnight hours had been filled to perfection and she was left to drive home alone with his scent still clinging like the aftermath of a summer shower.

Chapter Twelve

There was an emptiness, a bottomless chasm when Nick left. It was the unimaginable place she'd tried to avoid for so long, that neediness of a woman in love, no matter how independent of spirit she might be. She found herself daydreaming as she willed her way through work, often checking the clocks until she realized she was simply wiling away the time, replaying the little touches and important words they had exchanged over and over again like a broken record. Time couldn't go fast enough.

Then a wonderful letter from Kate arrived amidst her doldrums, heralding words that lifted Pru's flagging spirit. She and Michael would definitely be coming back, probably around the end of June...*perhaps in time for that summer wedding*, she contemplated, her thoughts quickly escalating. In truth there were no reasons left to keep her from savoring how bright her world had finally become, except she hadn't as yet resolved the lingering and unsettled tension of the locket. The previously spoken words—unfinished business—kept popping into her brain.

Then one day she picked up on Vivian's mood, embarrassed that she hadn't noticed that something was bothering her.

"I hope you're not going to say 'I told you so'," Vivian said when spilling the beans about the junket to New York. "It was so not what I'd planned and I've learned my lesson, believe me; you can never go back."

"I'm sorry," was all she could think to say. "Why don't we make some changes around here; spruce things up before summer?"

Vivian rarely talked about what happened to end her relationships and Prudence didn't pry. When the time was right, Vivian would tell her why the men in her life seemed to fall from grace, but in the meantime they could keep busy. That would do them both good. It was easy to make small changes in the décor to prepare for a new season and they even managed to line up two more book-signings…one for a volume written about the Maine woods and another cookbook illustrated by the author, which proved a nice touch.

"So Julie got her ring?" Vivian asked. "The squealing was pretty obvious," she said after Prudence hung up the phone in the back.

"Yes, *and* she wants to be married here as I'd hoped. Now we just have to figure out the venue, and see if we can't coordinate it with Kate's arrival…this is just too perfect!"

"It'll be great to see her, but it's only April and you and Nick will be busy when he fully opens his place up again and you said he also wants to get his sailboat back in the water."

"That's why I have to start now. This region will be booked solid by early summer from everything I've been told."

"Must be all this happiness," she quipped. "I've lost track of how quickly things move once the season starts. But all kidding aside, I'm so over men and even though I like not having to answer to anyone, I'm happy for Julie. I on the other hand, have realized how much I like being in business this way instead of working as some clerk or even catering baked goods. Who knows, if you and Nick really get serious, maybe I'll buy you out."

"Wow, that's a shocker! Not that you wouldn't be great by yourself, but I hadn't given anything like that even a consideration…and I'm a little superstitious to think of Nick and I in that way just yet," she responded. In truth, she already projected time away with him, going places that he'd been to and those they would discover together. Her imagination had already had them traipsing the Tuscan hills and Roman ruins, not to mention Paris. She certainly couldn't do any of that if she had to remain at work. When she began this new journey and had once again plunged into a new business with all her energy, it had never occurred to her that she might be willing to give it up this quickly, but she was certainly getting ahead of herself and she still needed to earn her keep.

The next day Prudence called Beth about Julie's good news and some of her thoughts about planning and Beth had put her two cents in as expected. "Better get 'crackin' young lady and let me know if there's anything I can do to help; you'll be next, you'll see," she'd stated with certainty.

"I haven't thought that far, believe me," she fibbed. "But thanks for the vote of confidence. And by the way, Nick called and said he's coming back sooner than expected, so I don't want to hear you've said anything to him about marriage, you hear?"

"Fine, fine; just let me know what we can do for Julie; this will be very special."

The next days were consumed with thoughts of a summer wedding and getting out on the boat as soon as Nick arrived.

"She's a beauty," Prudence said as she surveyed the wooden-hulled *Mystic*. Nick had called the yard ahead as soon as he realized he'd be coming back and now the sailboat sat dockside to be cleaned up. She was thrilled that he had enlisted her help, immediately acknowledging how much she had missed this activity. For the next week, they'd be getting both boat and house ready in preparation for his parent's arrival the first week in May. "What is she?"

"A forty-one Concordia yawl," Nick said with pride.

"I don't remember ever seeing one like this in the islands." The boat was truly a dream. Her mahogany planks gleamed and there was far less chrome than the types she had sailed on. It had the look of a highly sophisticated lady and not a plaything.

"I bought her from a widow in Massachusetts whose husband loved to race. She couldn't bear to look at it after he died, so she made me a sweet deal," Nick said as he glanced over her lines and then back to Prudence.

At that point she couldn't tell who he might one day love more.

"We have just enough time to get her ship-shape before they get here," he said without realizing the silent question he'd posed, and handed her a can of polish and a rag to touch up the bronze and buff the lacquered wood.

The project suddenly took on the excitement of Christmas as they unwrapped the yacht from its storage mode. They worked quickly but in unison. Nick sensed as he watched her changing expressions, that she still had doubts about Diana; he knew her qualms about meeting his folks. "They're not going to compare you to her if that's what's hidden in the back of your thoughts," he said reassuringly.

She knew he could now practically read her mind when Diana's name or any reference to Colorado came up. He'd been saving a note that Diana had left at the Pelletier house for just this purpose and after she digested it, there was only one line that she insisted on rereading. *'Wishing you well with this wonderful sounding woman. Give her your full attention, please, and do not screw it up!'*

"I won't, I promise," he'd said to Prudence immediately after showing it to her.

"By the way, you make a really good first mate; I've never seen anyone apply polish with so much enthusiasm!"

"Lots of training. Those sixty-footers have a lot of chrome."

"Sixty! Are you sure this one isn't too far beneath you?" Nick teased. "After all, I might not get my big yacht for at least another ten years."

"You won't be too old by then; I might stick around."

Then he threw a rag at her and captured her in his arms and kissed her until she yelled at him to stop...all eyes inside the marina office were focused on them.

The weather had turned warmer than expected after the mind-boggling nor'easter earlier in the month—the likes of which she had never seen—the exact type Beth had cannily predicted. Now the hints of spring were everywhere; its evidence had come in like a benevolent god to melt the snow away.

Unfortunately, it also left behind a lot of unattractive brown slush and what seemed tons of dirt from the sanding trucks, but the air smelled like hope.

Then in what seemed the blink of an eye, Mother Nature was lifting her skirts revealing the green shoots and the earth began coming to life from its long slumber. There were robins chasing each other around, building up nests and tugging at worms. And along the shore, the earth still felt cold to Pru's touch, but the ledges absorbed the sun that heated the rocky surface with a tantalizing warmth, a place once again to sit and ponder and sometimes even share with Nick as they marveled over the ever-changing sea. On April 28th they launched Nick's boat, just days before his parents would arrive. He'd made plans for them to stay at his cottage, which had been cleaned by the women he hired for his rentals, and it had been made guest-friendly by Prudence since he would be staying with her. The Pelletier family was now ready for their privacy.

"What a glorious day!" Prudence exclaimed shielding her eyes from the glare as the sails filled voluptuously. The air was still too cold for her total pleasure, but the sun made up for it. She was bundled with a heavy sweatshirt, windbreaker and jeans while Nick moved about easily in shorts, woolen sweater and Topsiders. He was too macho to bother about the fact that little raised 'goose bumps' had appeared on his bare legs.

"This is what it's all about, slogging through winter to get to this moment; at least for me," he said as he pulled her next to him in the cockpit.

"I never thought I'd say it or even still be here; but I really love this place," Prudence said as she took it all in.

"And I love you," Nick said for the very first time.

She shyly said it back, but it got muffled into his neck when he'd pulled her close to kiss her. Could she be any happier? This moment was everything. And by the time, they had the yawl tidied up and snugged to the dock with the big white fenders, they were practically flaunting their need for each other and totally starving for food.

"That was fabulous!" she exclaimed. "I'd nearly forgotten how much I missed sailing. My face is burning, and I feel whipped from all the wind and I loved every minute of it!"

"Me too; it's been a long time since I've had her out, but now I'm hungry!" he said as they drove through the village.

As soon as they got back to Thatcher Lane, Nick immediately took charge of the grill she'd bought at his direction while he'd been away, because as everyone knew, **men loved to grill!** And he was no different. Each time she brought something out to him, he'd stop and kiss her and tell her he loved her and each time, she couldn't believe her ears.

"Great salad," he said, peering intently over his beer glass.

"Good steak too," she replied, lifting hers.

They stayed outside talking until dusk, trying to come up with ideas to toss at Julie, things that might make things easier to plan a wedding long distance. He generously offered to lend whatever the couple might need...perhaps even his cottage prior to or right after the ceremony if they wouldn't be escaping immediately to a honeymoon spot.

"Kate and Michael will be back by then too," she declared to the warm-hearted man before her. "I can't wait for you to get to know them better."

"Sounds to me like you're making big plans."

"You are very savvy Mr. Pelletier!" she said, knowing as always, she was WAY ahead of herself. *Jules, Kate and me, here in Oyster Cove...the three of us; has a nice ring don't you think, Hannah?*

"Where does Vivian fit in?" he asked, already understanding that she probably didn't. He thought she must be at least ten years older and with an agenda unlike any of Pru's friends.

"You know perfectly well she is not susceptible to the charms of men like you, so I guess she doesn't!" she said with a poke at his ribs.

308

"Help, woman on the loose," he yelped until they ended up laughing and necking as though they were sitting in the back of a car like a couple of teenagers.

She was clearing away the debris of dinner plates and silverware and empty bottles, readying trash for Nick to dispose of and washing up a few of the grilling tools when she found herself ruminating more seriously about their conversations. Her mind wandered off to that place where she could practically see what it might mean because of Kate and Jules, to be able to share a similar 'sisterhood' even if not exactly on the same beautiful lane where it had all begun for Hannah.

Then he was there—in the middle of her thoughts—he'd come up behind her. He turned her around and she quivered at his touch. She wasn't cold, not really…just anticipating what she now understood would follow. They'd been flirtatiously skirting this moment the entire day. But now that he'd declared his love, she was experiencing first-time jitters, as though sexual intimacy had never happened. She was suddenly quite shy. He took her hand, drying it with the towel before leading her up the stairs.

The sleigh bed beckoned and still they took their time, standing by the window that looked over a swath of dark water that had quietly settled for the night as well. The day had been one long blissful event, the motion still felt in her muscles—the slight rocking natural after being on a boat for hours. The room, exquisitely peaceful in its simplicity could have been a suite at the Ritz for the way it held them rapt, but really it was the sea and both knew it. They would have many hours together to share in the vast ocean beyond this window no matter the size of the boat.

Then he began to slowly undress her as he propelled her closer to the bed hardly aware of her moving feet. He too was acting as though it was a new beginning, that this night was perhaps more special than any before it and laid her near-naked body onto the bed with characteristic gentleness. The remembered way he'd done in the hotel room, as though she were a breakable doll. His face was darkly shadowed with the stubble to come by morning, the bristles that would scrape her cheek when he kissed her awake. Just the nearness of him made hers burn with anticipation and she never was able to hide this fact from him.

"We have all the time in the world," he whispered as he softly stroked her skin.

Her body in response had already begun to convulse ever so slightly, each tingle headed to its desired target. The necklace had fallen to one side and though it was always a comforting piece, she didn't want it to get in the way of their lovemaking. She began to undo it with a very small movement, trying not to break the spell.

"Shh," he whispered as she started to apologize. His soft lips did the rest as they enveloped her slightly parted ones and breathed the warmth of new promises and she melted. She wasn't certain if she was imagining it, but then his tongue became his voice and he soundlessly moved his hands over her. She gulped and closed her eyes, no longer embarrassed at what they were intimating...*where had he learned this little gift?* By now she was nearly swooning over the light wisp of his expert touch. He continued until she thought she would pass out from the intensity of feelings it created and began to wish more than anything for final completion. Just when she thought she could bear no more, there he was, not like someone who'd held back or been denied pleasure because of the intrusive distance between them, but with the same searing tenderness that felt like a spring thaw as it flowed through her body. He had brought her to the edge, their bodies in unison with the same perfect mating as sailboat and sea gliding and cresting the long swells earlier in the day, replete with joy.

Breathless and complete at last, he slowly rolled away in order to see her entire body.

"You look happy; are you?" he asked as if she might have changed her mind.

"More than you know; I really do love you."

He put his arm under her and pulled her closer, already giving in to his heavily lidded eyes. The salt spray from earlier in the day still lingered lightly on their warm skin, a familiar scent for all time she hoped.

Hannah was on a rising wave, unable to control the direction of her body as it floated on the sickly green water when she heard a cry of joy. Timothy was waving, reaching out through the high swells and she was smiling back with an expression of love and relief. The locket tethered by a cord around her neck, floated out in front of her and rose and fell with her breasts as the water surged around her body. Prudence watched from a distance the long-awaited embrace as they slowly disappeared beneath the surface.

Nick was shaking her awake. "You were crying out; bad dream?"

"Quite the contrary; it was beautiful, but they're gone, Nick," she said. "Hannah and Tim, they've really gone."

"Of course they're gone; it was only a dream."

"But this was different, I saw them…they were together…that's why everything has seemed so unsettled, why I have felt her presence; this was the unfinished business!"

"If that's what you believe, who am I to dispute it. After all, you're the beautiful—though often very complicated—woman I'm going to marry," he said. "That is, if you'll have me." He'd caught her off guard, her expression said it all. He had completely shocked her.

A movie reel of imagined activities, weddings and shared friendships, travel locations and a cottage by the sea raced across her brain instigated by that proposal. The people of importance in her life, past and present marched alongside with silent scripts and happy endings floated on an imaginary screen.

She rolled to her side and reached for the locket on the nightstand letting him wait for her reply. It felt as it should, just cool metal…though no one else would be the wiser. *Thank you Hannah.*

Before she said yes to this wonderful man, she said a silent goodbye to them, the lost ones, the loved ones and no matter what he'd said about a dream or its import, she was certain Hannah and Tim were at last united. And because of them and this longed-for trusting love with Nick, she too would come to know what that felt like.

About the Author

CHERYL BLAYDON is the author of the novels, *The Memory Keepers* and *Island Odyssey.* She lives in East Boothbay, Maine. www.mainelyseascapes.com.

CPSIA information can be obtained
at www.ICGtesting.com
Printed in the USA
FFOW03n2114220515
13565FF